OZY AND MILLIE

PERFECTLY NORMAL

Also by Dana Simpson

Ozy and Millie

***Phoebe and Her Unicorn* Collections**

Phoebe and Her Unicorn

Unicorn on a Roll

Unicorn vs. Goblins

Razzle Dazzle Unicorn

Unicorn Crossing

Phoebe and Her Unicorn in the Magic Storm

Unicorn of Many Hats

Phoebe and Her Unicorn in Unicorn Theater

Unicorn Bowling

The Unicorn Whisperer

Camping with Unicorns

Virtual Unicorn Experience

Activity Books

Rainy Day Unicorn Fun

For Young Children

Today I'll Be a Unicorn

OZY AND MILLIE

PERFECTLY NORMAL

Dana Simpson

Andrews McMeel
PUBLISHING®

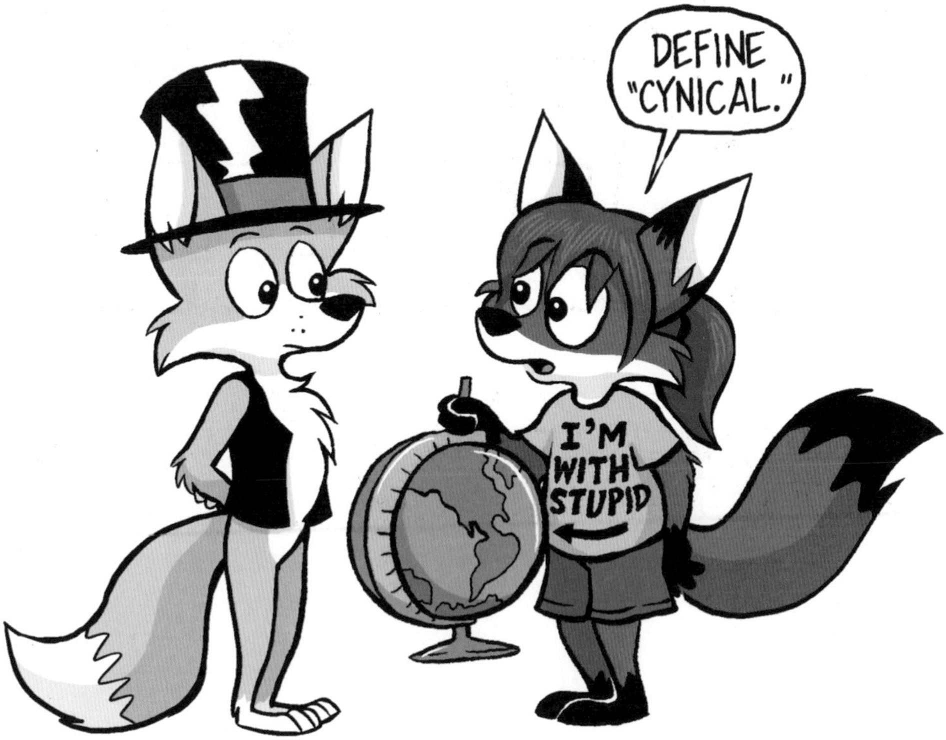
DEFINE "CYNICAL."
I'M WITH STUPID

INTRODUCTION

I'll be quick, because this is the second *Ozy and Millie* collection that Andrews McMeel has published (thanks, guys!), and I wrote a longer introduction for that first book.

For those of you who didn't read that book, and who haven't met Ozy and Millie and the other residents of their world before, Ozy and Millie are kids and they're foxes. Ozy's dad is a weird but gentle dragon. Their friend Avery is a status-obsessed raccoon, who is very annoyed by his cheerful younger brother, Timulty. (Tim wasn't in the first collection, but he's in this one.) And there are various other characters you'll meet if you keep reading.

That's not really what the comic is about, though—it's just the setup.

Ozy and Millie was the comic I wrote and illustrated before I made *Phoebe and Her Unicorn*. I drew it for ten years and loved drawing every line. I'm very happy people still enjoy it. And I hope you enjoy these!

On with the show.

Dana Simpson
September 2020

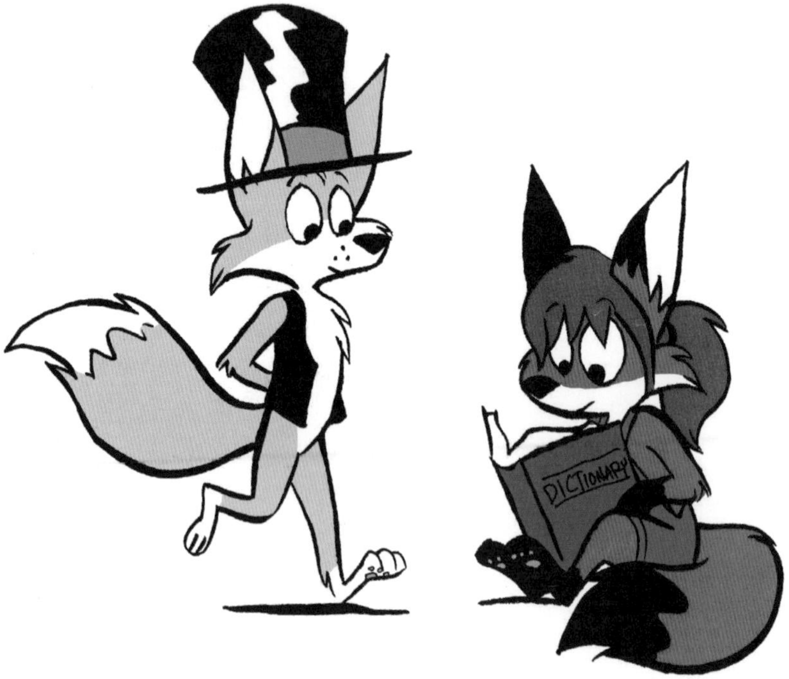
DICTIONARY

Hey, kids!

Check out the glossary starting on page 171
if you come across words you don't know.

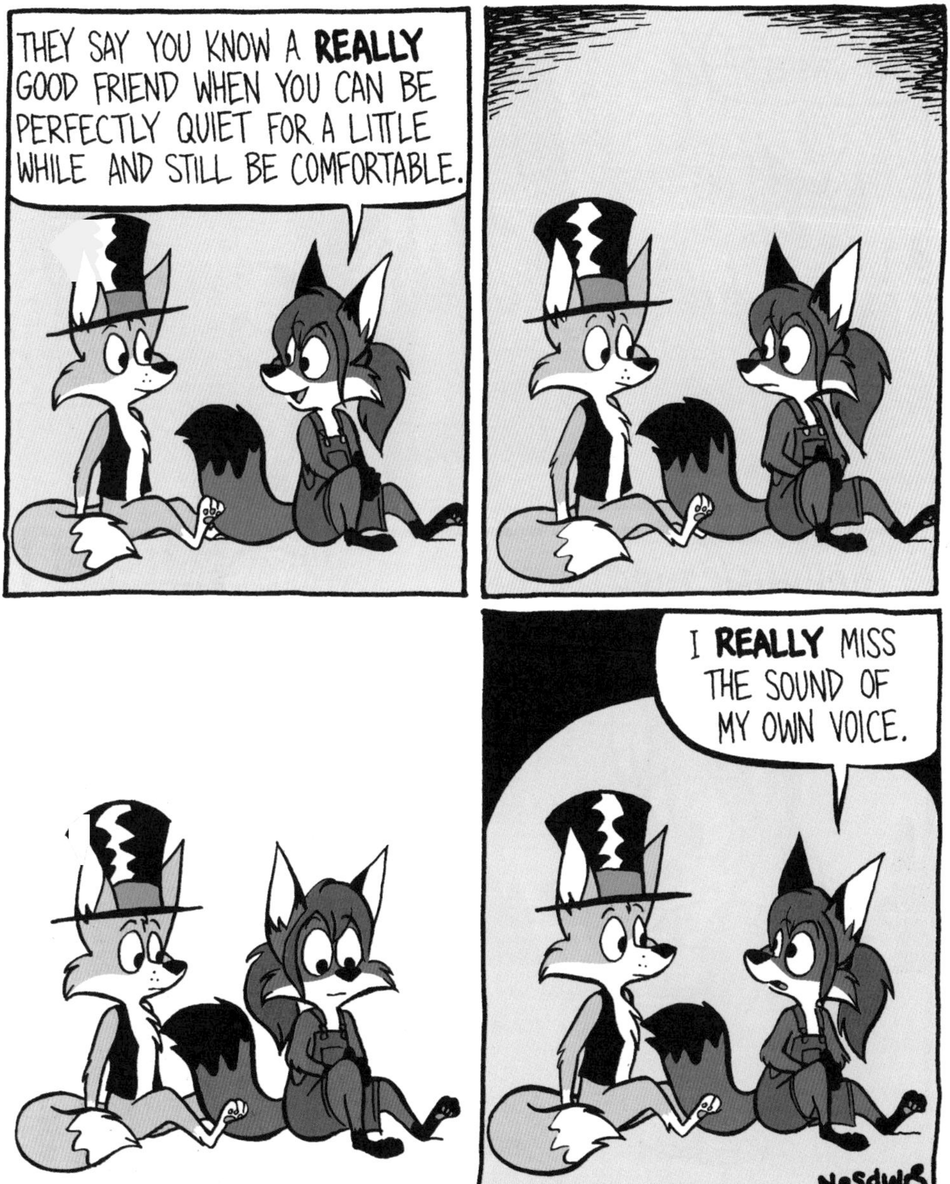
THEY SAY YOU KNOW A **REALLY** GOOD FRIEND WHEN YOU CAN BE PERFECTLY QUIET FOR A LITTLE WHILE AND STILL BE COMFORTABLE.
I **REALLY** MISS THE SOUND OF MY OWN VOICE.
NOSDWRS

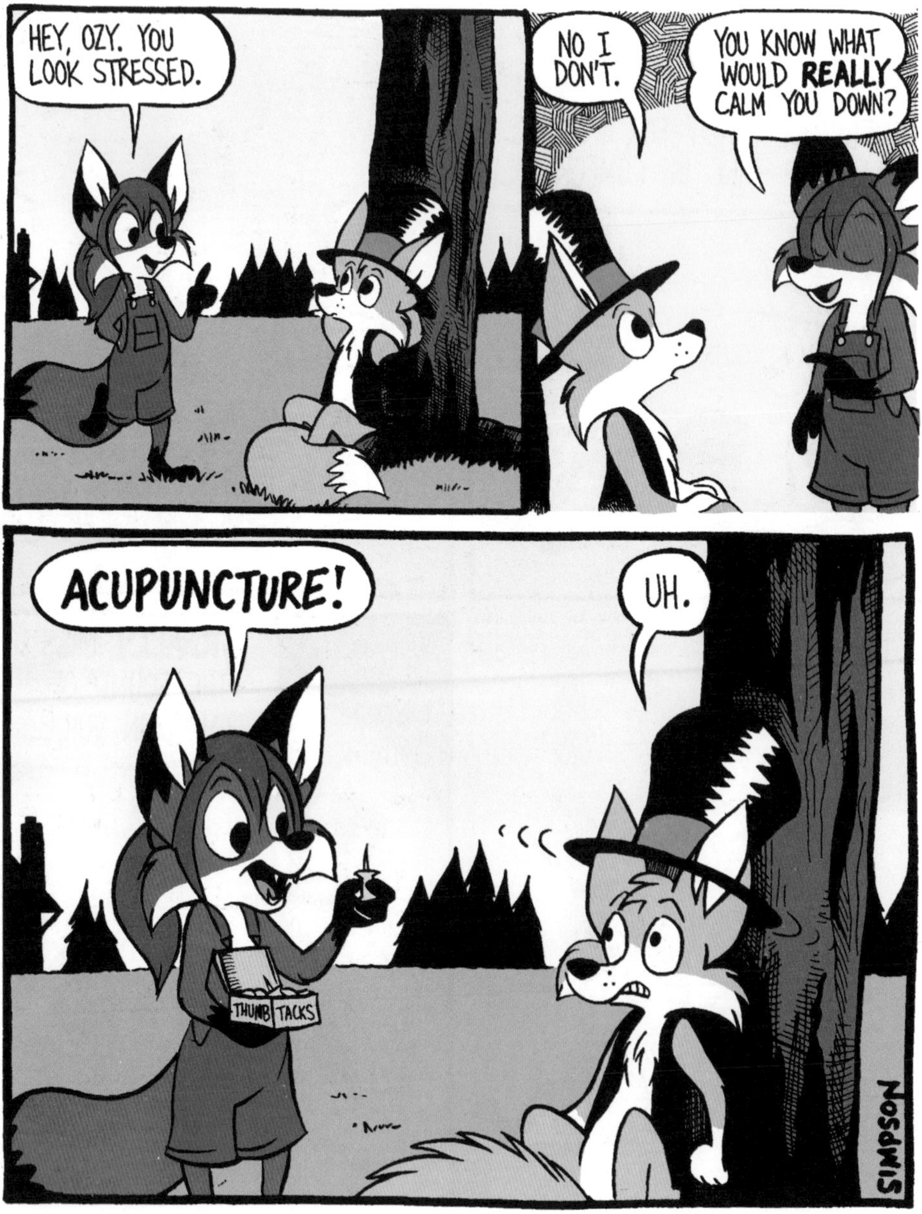
HEY, OZY. YOU LOOK STRESSED.
NO I DON'T.
YOU KNOW WHAT WOULD **REALLY** CALM YOU DOWN?
ACUPUNCTURE!
UH.
THUMB TACKS
SIMPSON

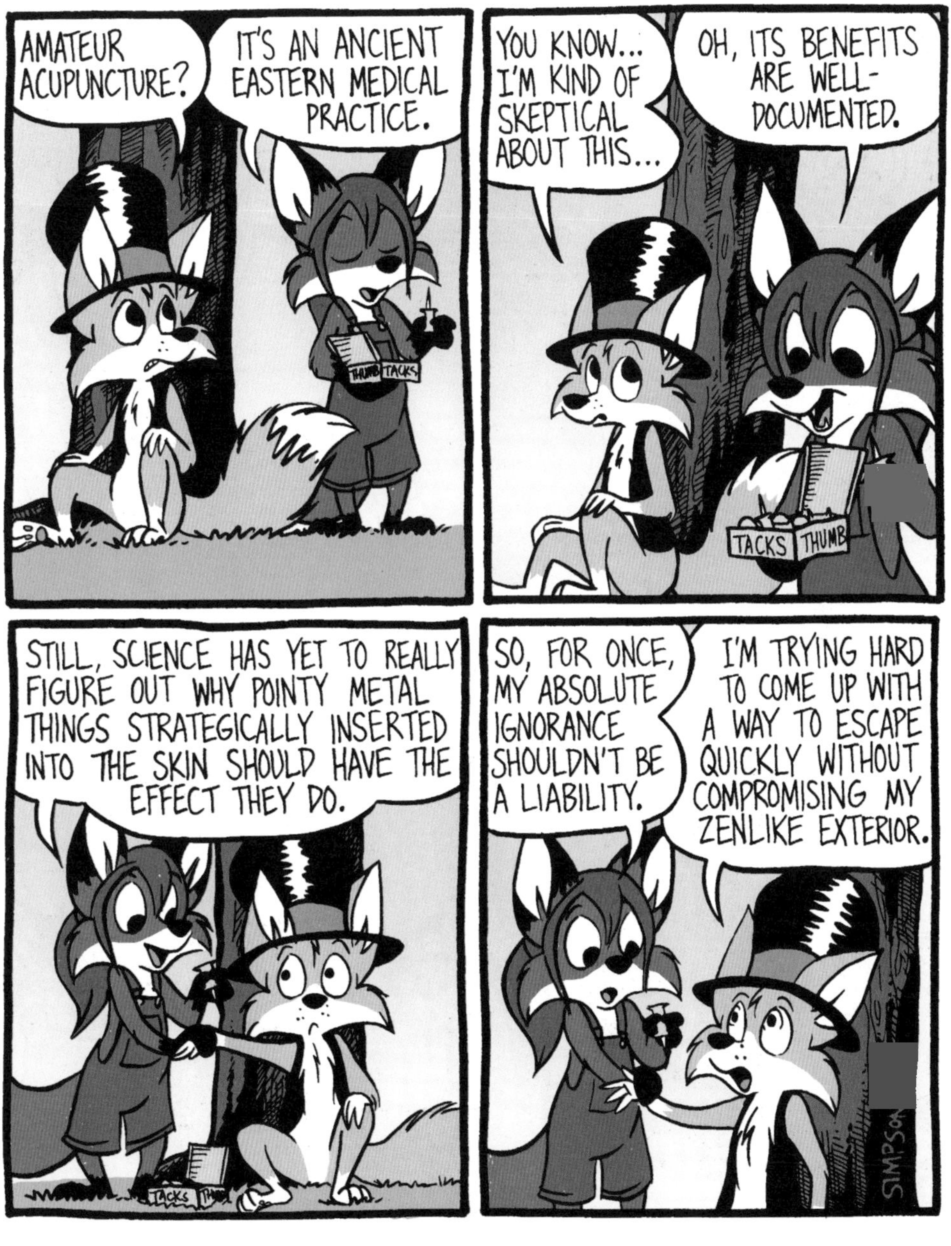
AMATEUR ACUPUNCTURE?
IT'S AN ANCIENT EASTERN MEDICAL PRACTICE.
THUMB TACKS
YOU KNOW... I'M KIND OF SKEPTICAL ABOUT THIS...
OH, ITS BENEFITS ARE WELL-DOCUMENTED.
TACKS THUMB
STILL, SCIENCE HAS YET TO REALLY FIGURE OUT WHY POINTY METAL THINGS STRATEGICALLY INSERTED INTO THE SKIN SHOULD HAVE THE EFFECT THEY DO.
SO, FOR ONCE, MY ABSOLUTE IGNORANCE SHOULDN'T BE A LIABILITY.
I'M TRYING HARD TO COME UP WITH A WAY TO ESCAPE QUICKLY WITHOUT COMPROMISING MY ZENLIKE EXTERIOR.
SIMPSON

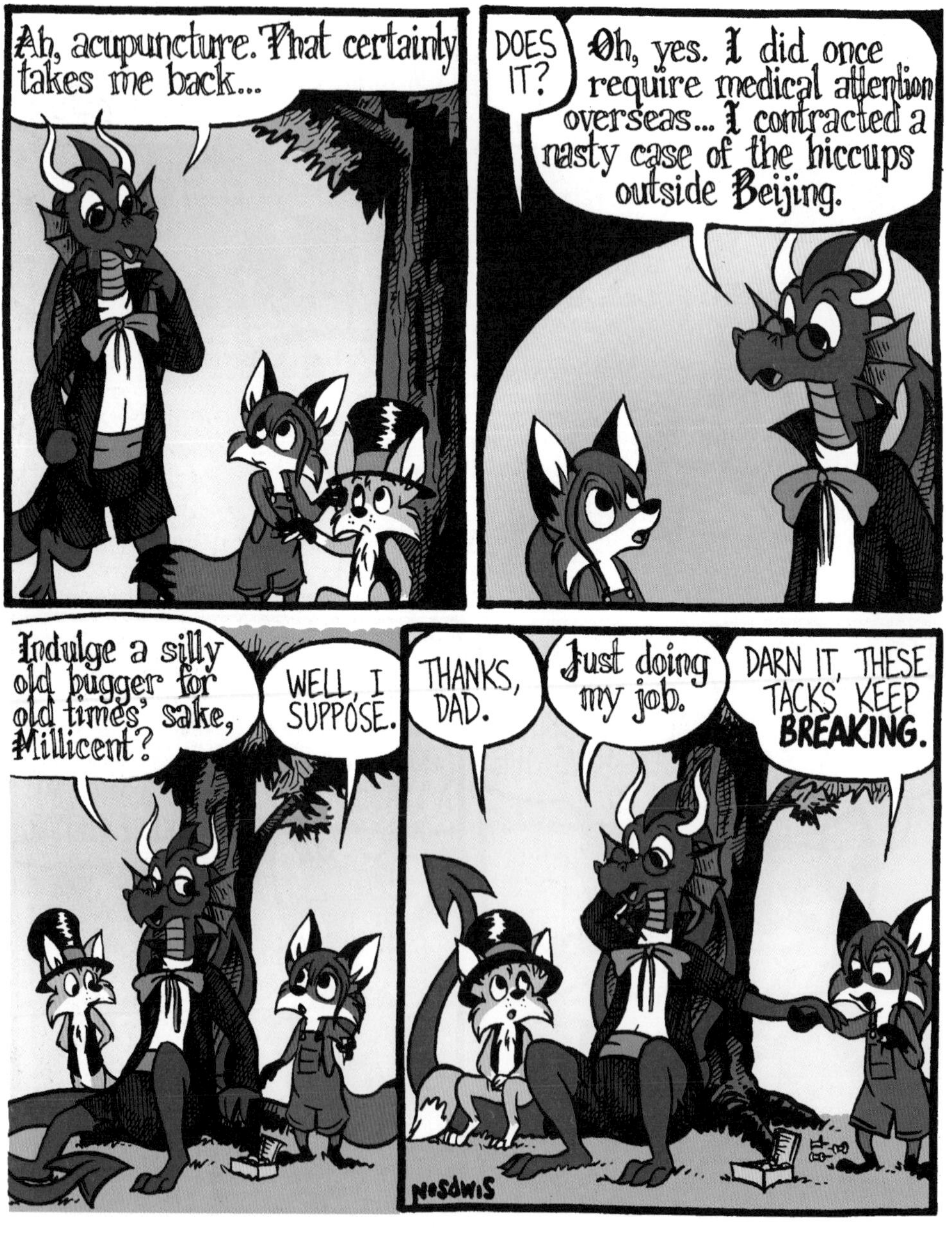
Ah, acupuncture. That certainly takes me back...
DOES IT?
Oh, yes. I did once require medical attention overseas... I contracted a nasty case of the hiccups outside Beijing.
Indulge a silly old bugger for old times' sake, Millicent?
WELL, I SUPPOSE.
THANKS, DAD.
Just doing my job.
DARN IT, THESE TACKS KEEP **BREAKING**.
NOSAWIS

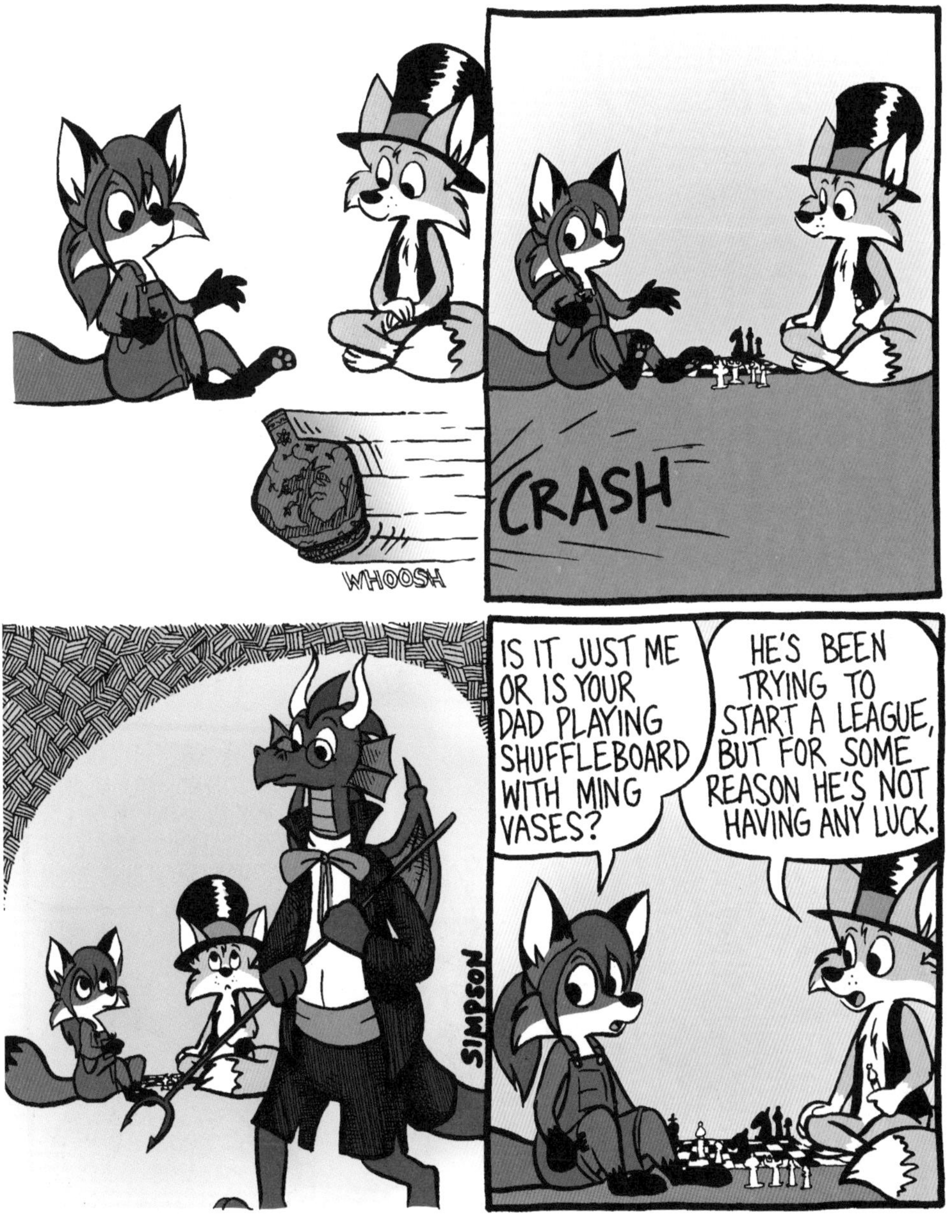
WHOOSH
CRASH
SIMPSON
IS IT JUST ME OR IS YOUR DAD PLAYING SHUFFLEBOARD WITH MING VASES?
HE'S BEEN TRYING TO START A LEAGUE, BUT FOR SOME REASON HE'S NOT HAVING ANY LUCK.

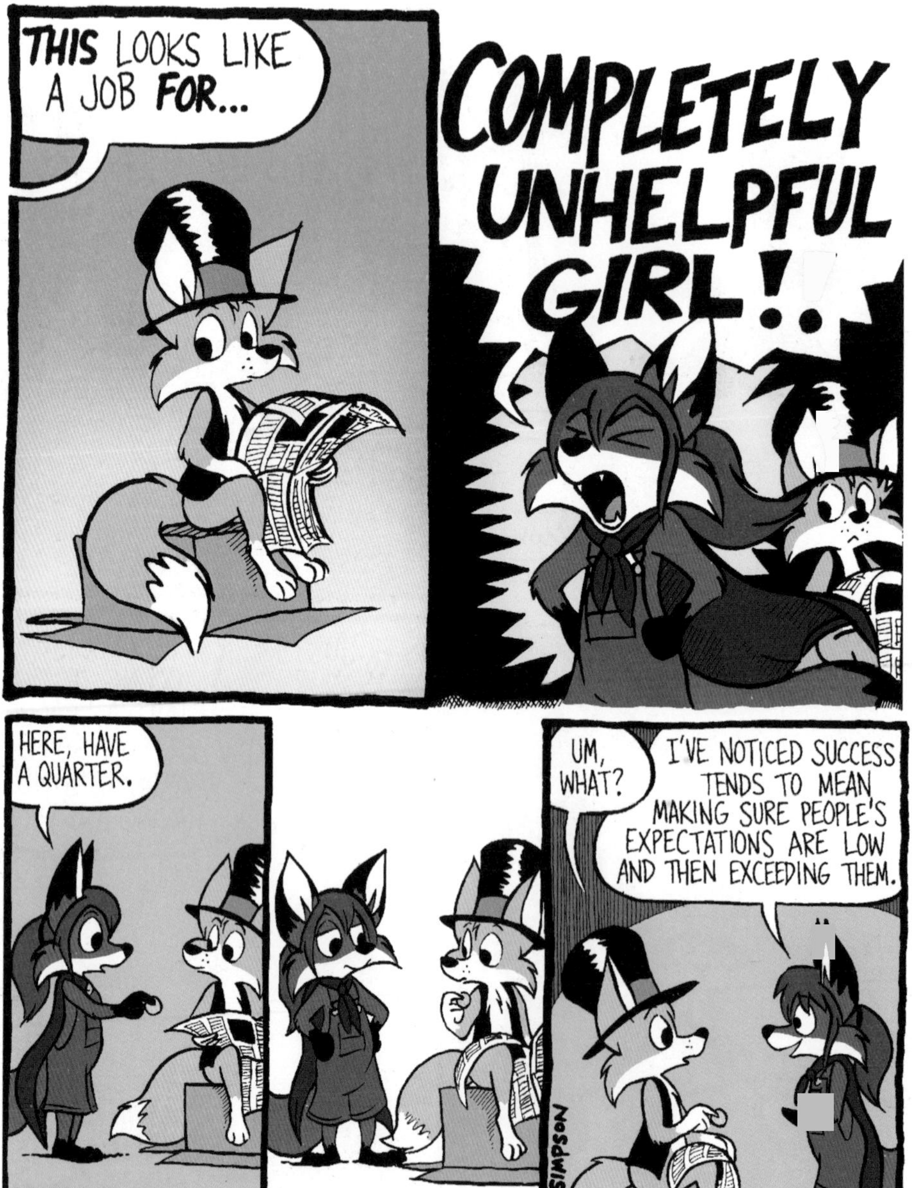
THIS LOOKS LIKE A JOB FOR...
COMPLETELY UNHELPFUL GIRL!!
HERE, HAVE A QUARTER.
UM, WHAT?
I'VE NOTICED SUCCESS TENDS TO MEAN MAKING SURE PEOPLE'S EXPECTATIONS ARE LOW AND THEN EXCEEDING THEM.
SIMPSON

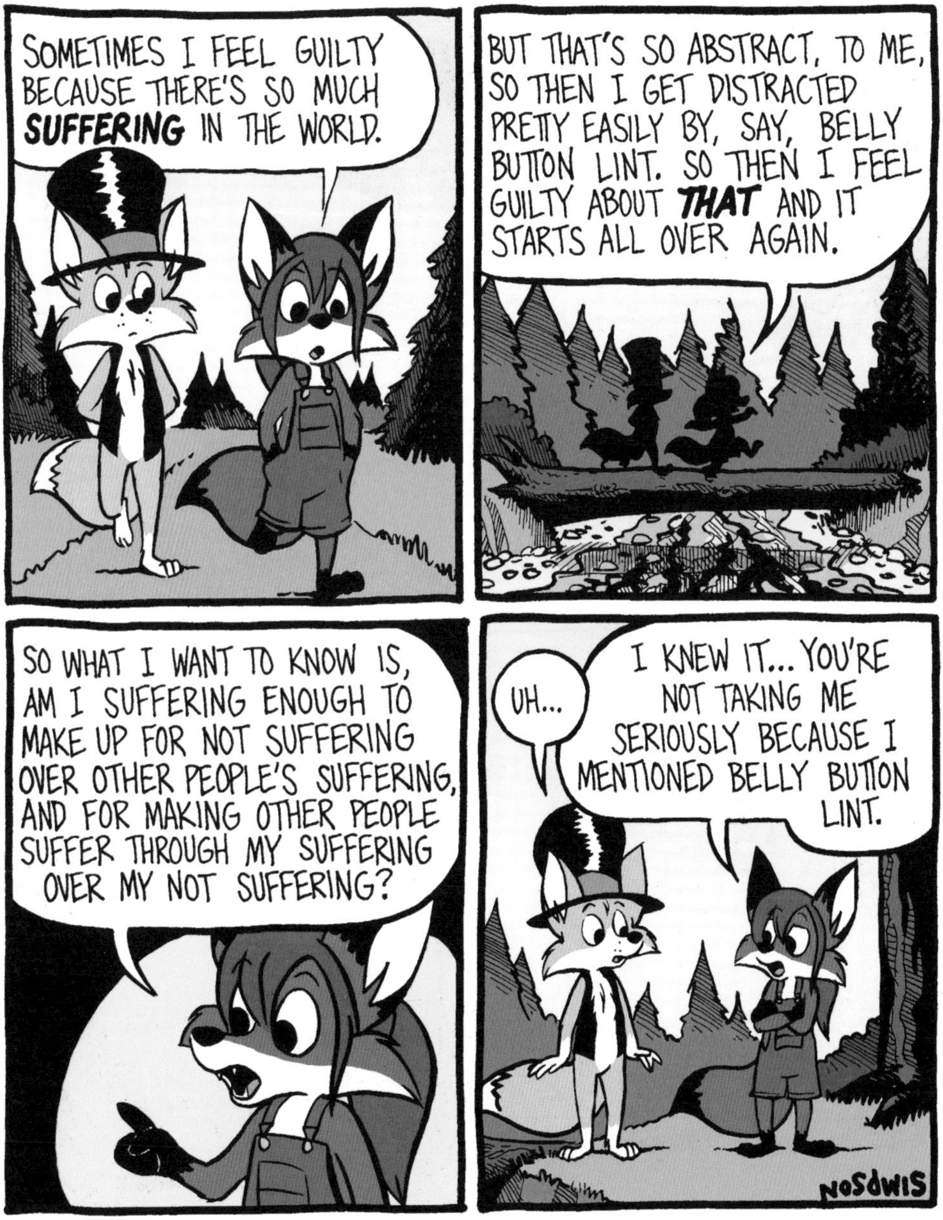
SOMETIMES I FEEL GUILTY BECAUSE THERE'S SO MUCH **SUFFERING** IN THE WORLD.
BUT THAT'S SO ABSTRACT, TO ME, SO THEN I GET DISTRACTED PRETTY EASILY BY, SAY, BELLY BUTTON LINT. SO THEN I FEEL GUILTY ABOUT **THAT** AND IT STARTS ALL OVER AGAIN.
SO WHAT I WANT TO KNOW IS, AM I SUFFERING ENOUGH TO MAKE UP FOR NOT SUFFERING OVER OTHER PEOPLE'S SUFFERING, AND FOR MAKING OTHER PEOPLE SUFFER THROUGH MY SUFFERING OVER MY NOT SUFFERING?
UH...
I KNEW IT... YOU'RE NOT TAKING ME SERIOUSLY BECAUSE I MENTIONED BELLY BUTTON LINT.
NOSDWIS

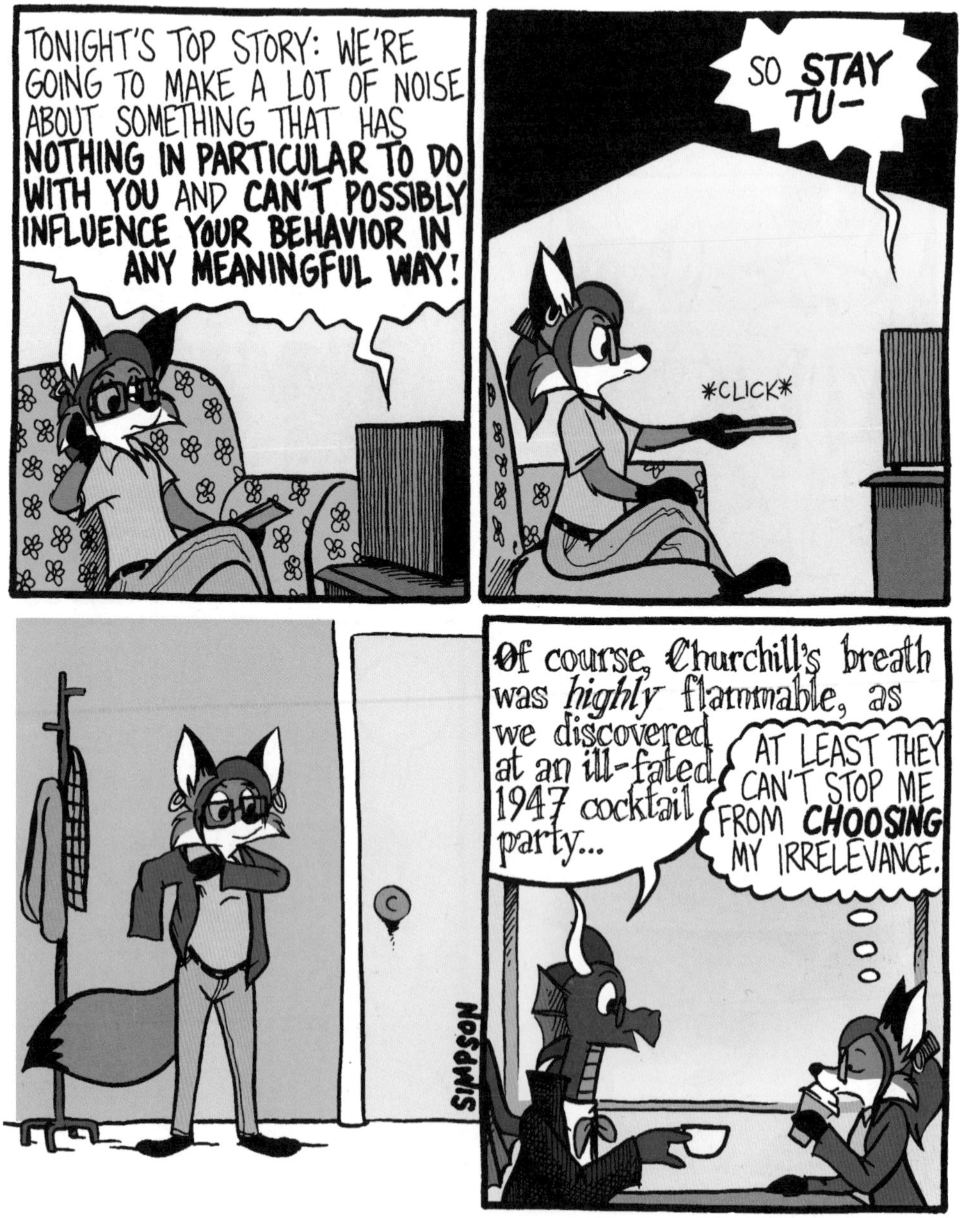
TONIGHT'S TOP STORY: WE'RE GOING TO MAKE A LOT OF NOISE ABOUT SOMETHING THAT HAS NOTHING IN PARTICULAR TO DO WITH YOU AND CAN'T POSSIBLY INFLUENCE YOUR BEHAVIOR IN ANY MEANINGFUL WAY!
SO STAY TU-
CLICK
SIMPSON
Of course, Churchill's breath was highly flammable, as we discovered at an ill-fated 1947 cocktail party...
AT LEAST THEY CAN'T STOP ME FROM CHOOSING MY IRRELEVANCE.

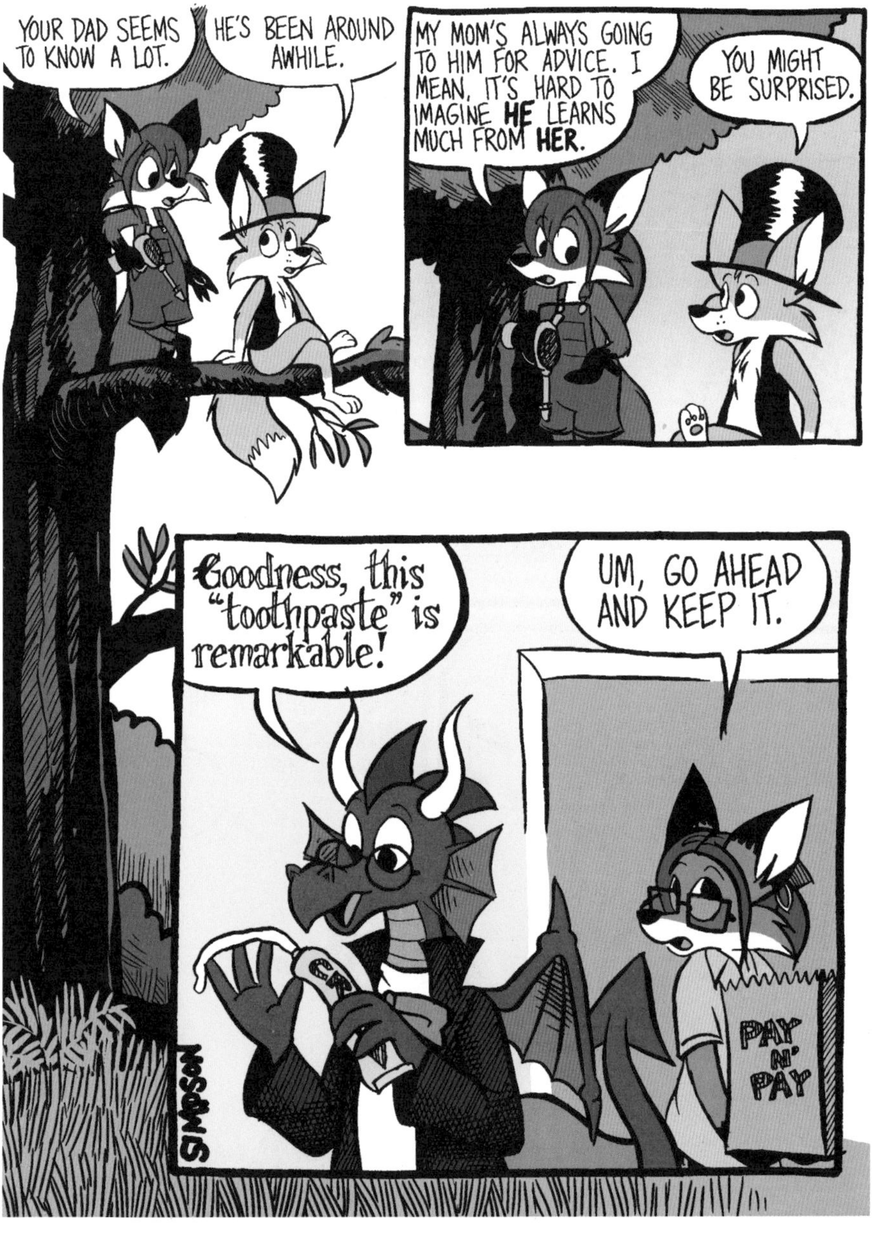
YOUR DAD SEEMS TO KNOW A LOT.
HE'S BEEN AROUND AWHILE.
MY MOM'S ALWAYS GOING TO HIM FOR ADVICE. I MEAN, IT'S HARD TO IMAGINE **HE** LEARNS MUCH FROM **HER**.
YOU MIGHT BE SURPRISED.
Goodness, this "toothpaste" is remarkable!
UM, GO AHEAD AND KEEP IT.
PAY N' PAY
SIMPSON

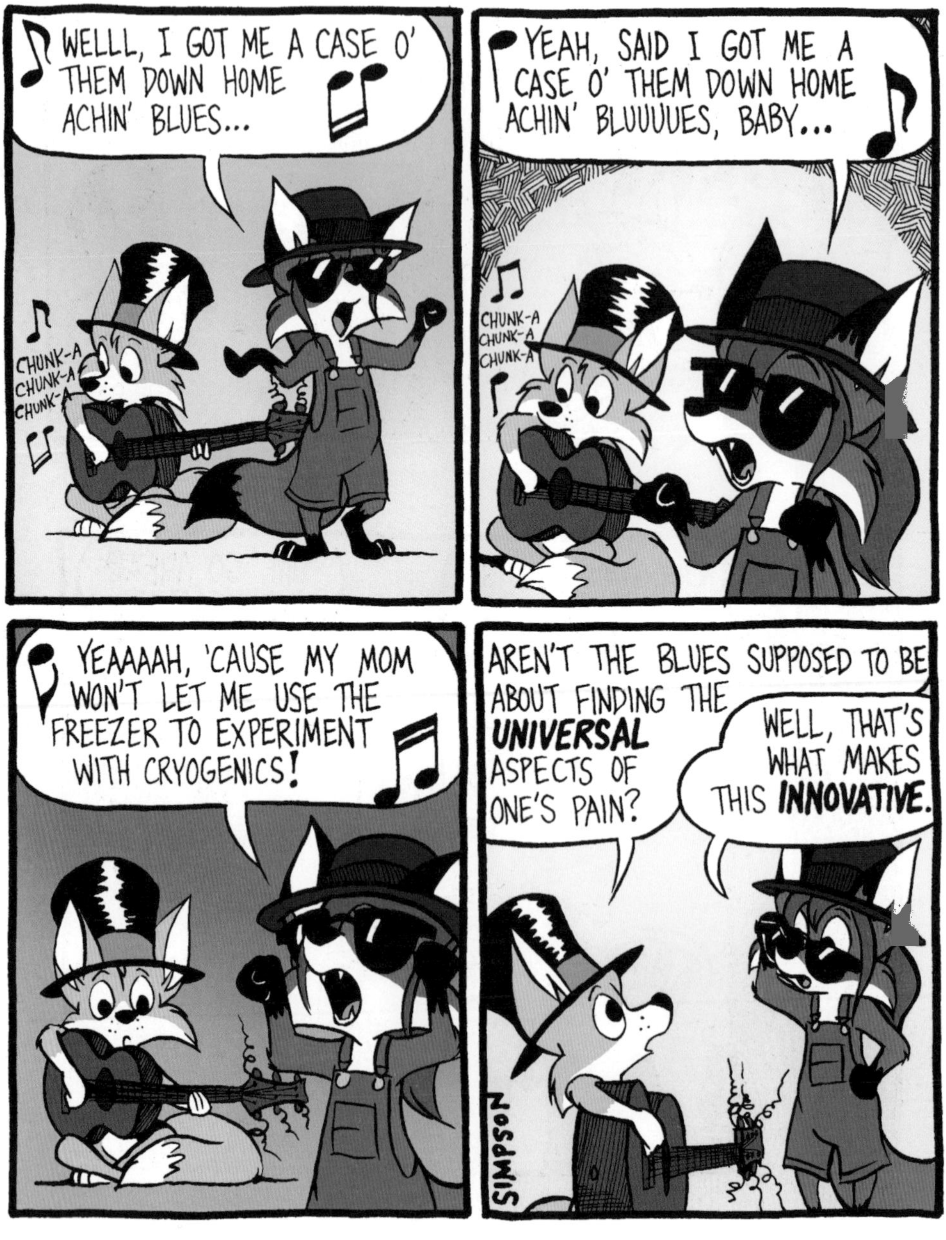
WELLL, I GOT ME A CASE O' THEM DOWN HOME ACHIN' BLUES...
CHUNK-A CHUNK-A CHUNK-A
YEAH, SAID I GOT ME A CASE O' THEM DOWN HOME ACHIN' BLUUUUES, BABY...
CHUNK-A CHUNK-A CHUNK-A
YEAAAAH, 'CAUSE MY MOM WON'T LET ME USE THE FREEZER TO EXPERIMENT WITH CRYOGENICS!
AREN'T THE BLUES SUPPOSED TO BE ABOUT FINDING THE **UNIVERSAL** ASPECTS OF ONE'S PAIN?
WELL, THAT'S WHAT MAKES THIS **INNOVATIVE.**
SIMPSON

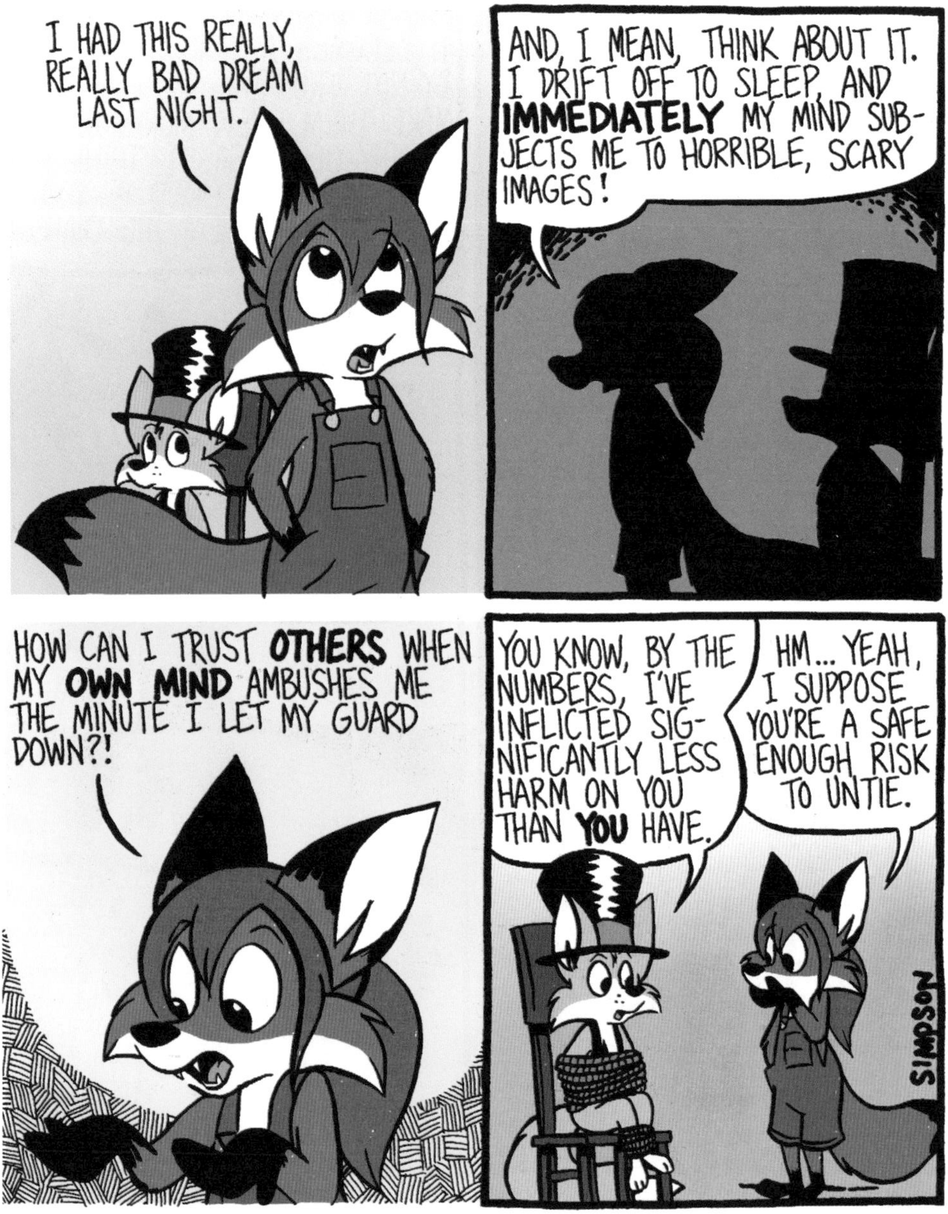
I HAD THIS REALLY, REALLY BAD DREAM LAST NIGHT.
AND, I MEAN, THINK ABOUT IT. I DRIFT OFF TO SLEEP, AND **IMMEDIATELY** MY MIND SUBJECTS ME TO HORRIBLE, SCARY IMAGES!
HOW CAN I TRUST **OTHERS** WHEN MY **OWN MIND** AMBUSHES ME THE MINUTE I LET MY GUARD DOWN?!
YOU KNOW, BY THE NUMBERS, I'VE INFLICTED SIGNIFICANTLY LESS HARM ON YOU THAN **YOU** HAVE.
HM... YEAH, I SUPPOSE YOU'RE A SAFE ENOUGH RISK TO UNTIE.
SIMPSON

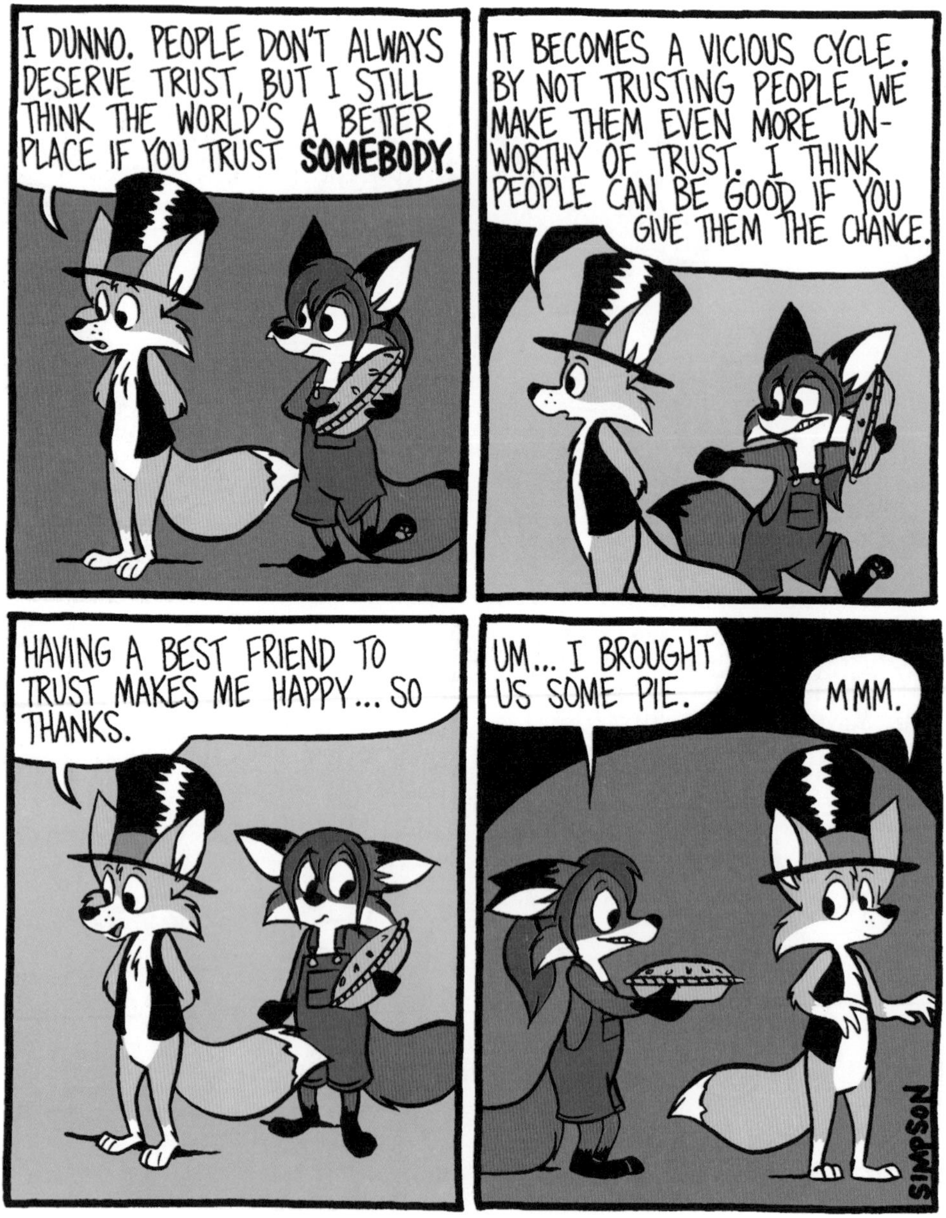
I DUNNO. PEOPLE DON'T ALWAYS DESERVE TRUST, BUT I STILL THINK THE WORLD'S A BETTER PLACE IF YOU TRUST **SOMEBODY.**
IT BECOMES A VICIOUS CYCLE. BY NOT TRUSTING PEOPLE, WE MAKE THEM EVEN MORE UN-WORTHY OF TRUST. I THINK PEOPLE CAN BE GOOD IF YOU GIVE THEM THE CHANCE.
HAVING A BEST FRIEND TO TRUST MAKES ME HAPPY... SO THANKS.
UM... I BROUGHT US SOME PIE.
MMM.
SIMPSON

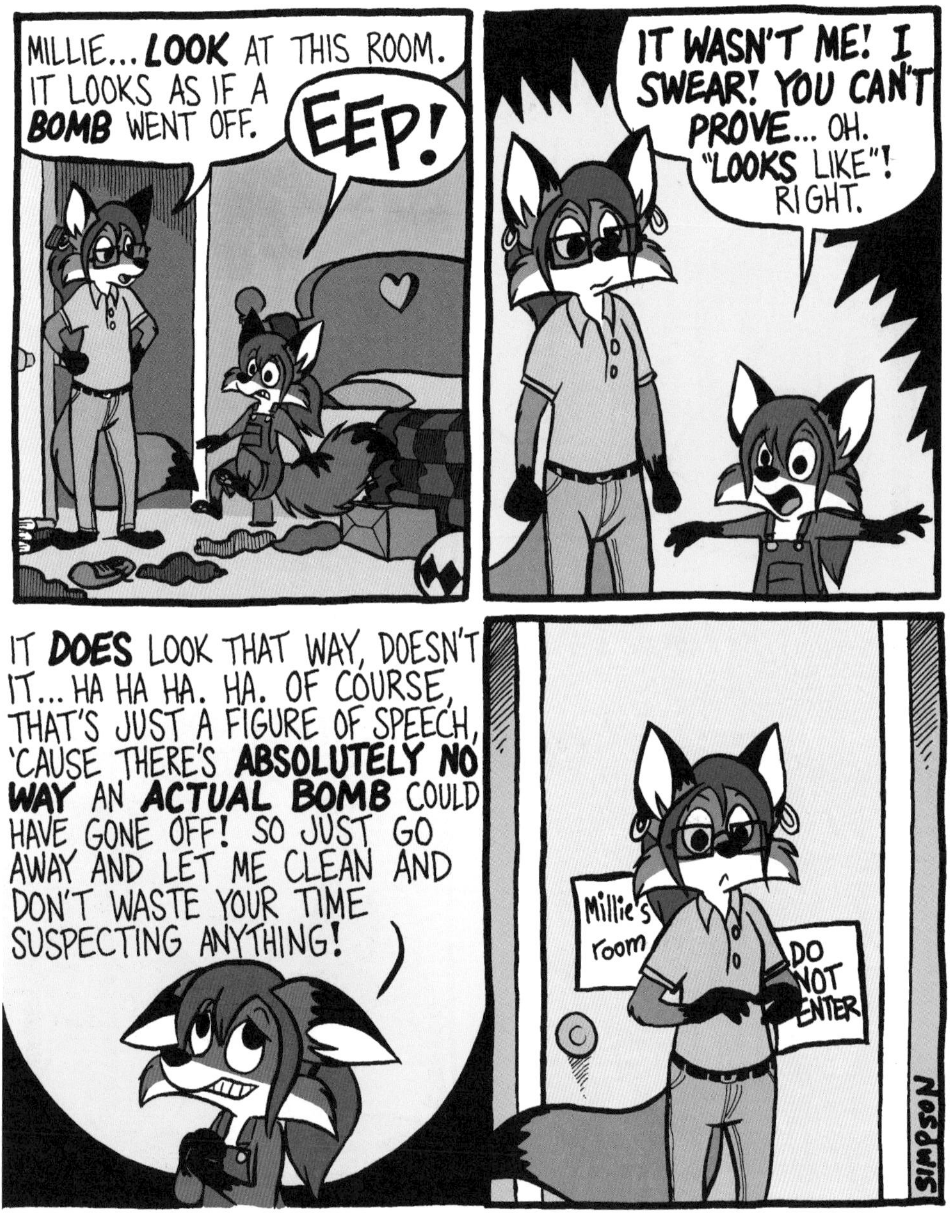
MILLIE... **LOOK** AT THIS ROOM. IT LOOKS AS IF A **BOMB** WENT OFF.
EEP!
IT WASN'T ME! I SWEAR! YOU CAN'T PROVE... OH. "LOOKS LIKE"! RIGHT.
IT **DOES** LOOK THAT WAY, DOESN'T IT... HA HA HA. HA. OF COURSE, THAT'S JUST A FIGURE OF SPEECH, 'CAUSE THERE'S **ABSOLUTELY NO WAY** AN **ACTUAL BOMB** COULD HAVE GONE OFF! SO JUST GO AWAY AND LET ME CLEAN AND DON'T WASTE YOUR TIME SUSPECTING ANYTHING!
Millie's room
DO NOT ENTER
SIMPSON

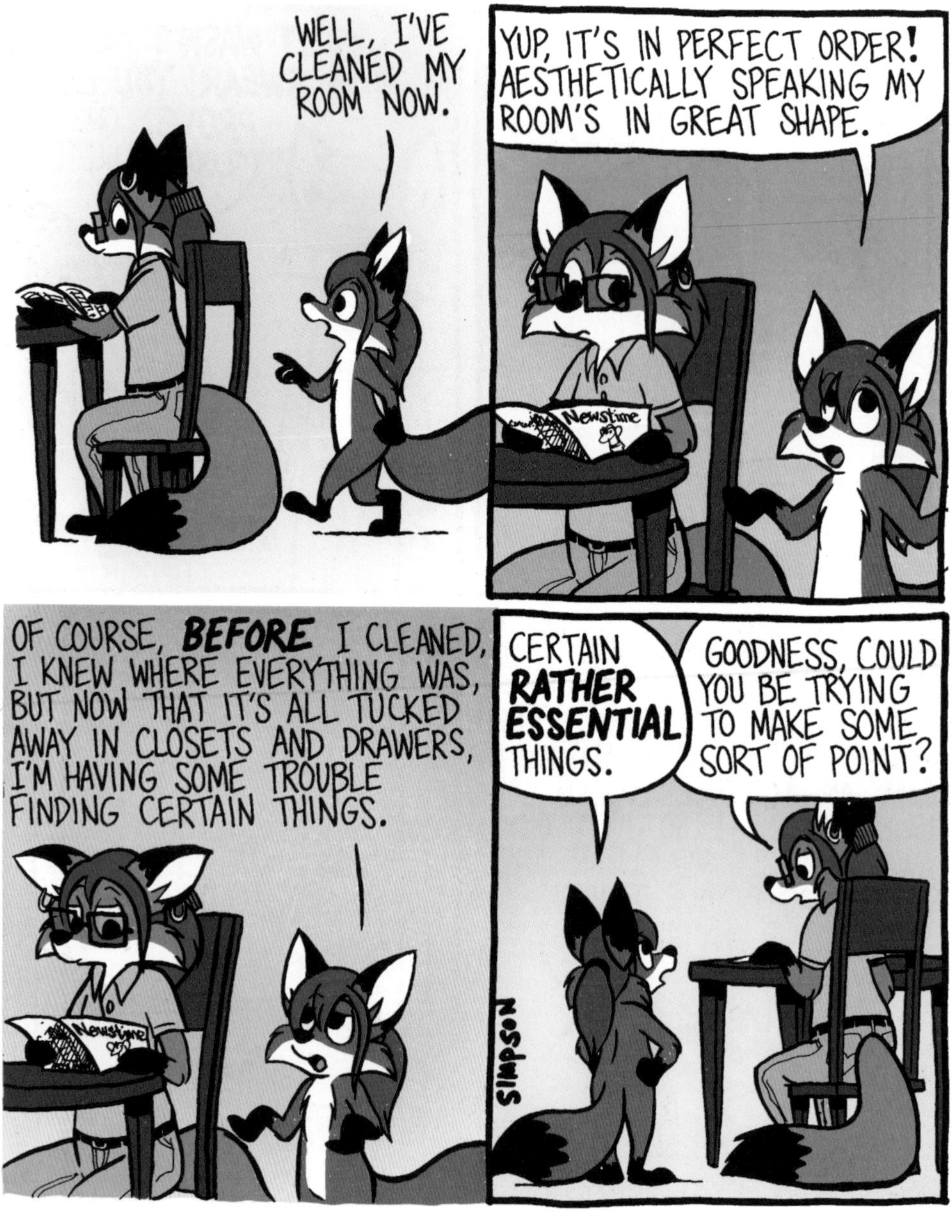
WELL, I'VE CLEANED MY ROOM NOW.
YUP, IT'S IN PERFECT ORDER! AESTHETICALLY SPEAKING MY ROOM'S IN GREAT SHAPE.
Newstime
OF COURSE, **BEFORE** I CLEANED, I KNEW WHERE EVERYTHING WAS, BUT NOW THAT IT'S ALL TUCKED AWAY IN CLOSETS AND DRAWERS, I'M HAVING SOME TROUBLE FINDING CERTAIN THINGS.
CERTAIN **RATHER ESSENTIAL** THINGS.
GOODNESS, COULD YOU BE TRYING TO MAKE SOME SORT OF POINT?
SIMPSON

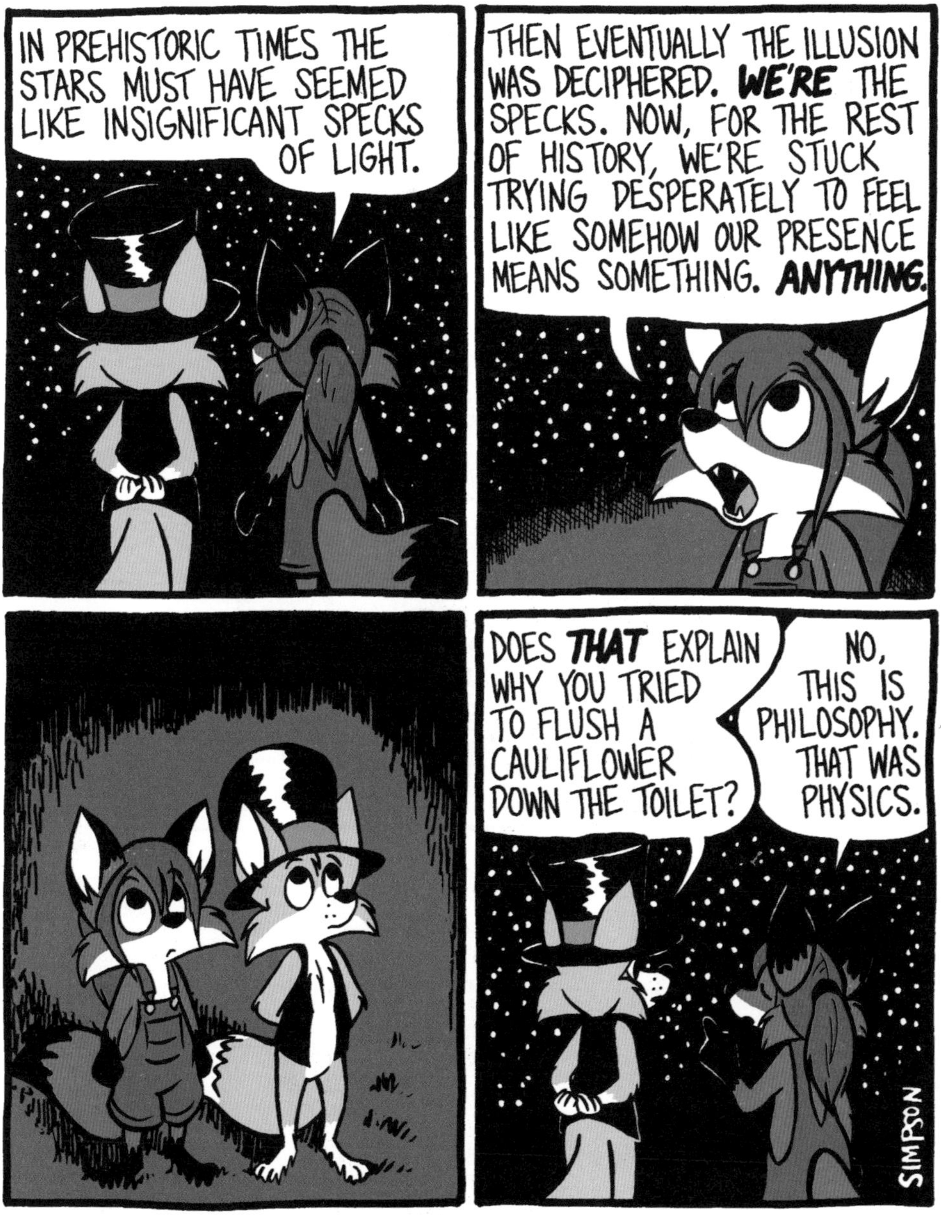
IN PREHISTORIC TIMES THE STARS MUST HAVE SEEMED LIKE INSIGNIFICANT SPECKS OF LIGHT.
THEN EVENTUALLY THE ILLUSION WAS DECIPHERED. **WE'RE** THE SPECKS. NOW, FOR THE REST OF HISTORY, WE'RE STUCK TRYING DESPERATELY TO FEEL LIKE SOMEHOW OUR PRESENCE MEANS SOMETHING. **ANYTHING.**
DOES **THAT** EXPLAIN WHY YOU TRIED TO FLUSH A CAULIFLOWER DOWN THE TOILET?
NO, THIS IS PHILOSOPHY. THAT WAS PHYSICS.
SIMPSON

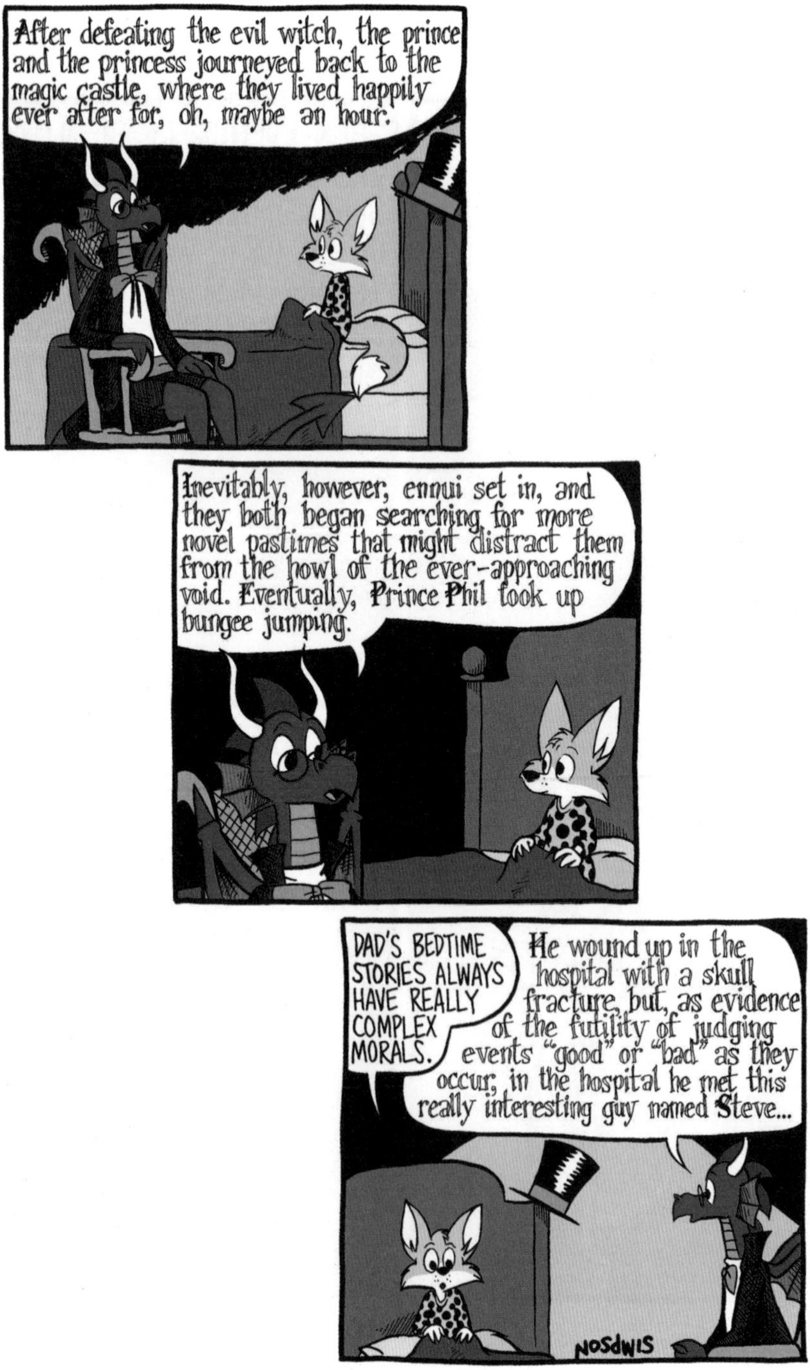
After defeating the evil witch, the prince and the princess journeyed back to the magic castle, where they lived happily ever after for, oh, maybe an hour.
Inevitably, however, ennui set in, and they both began searching for more novel pastimes that might distract them from the howl of the ever-approaching void. Eventually, Prince Phil took up bungee jumping.
DAD'S BEDTIME STORIES ALWAYS HAVE REALLY COMPLEX MORALS.
He wound up in the hospital with a skull fracture, but, as evidence of the futility of judging events "good" or "bad" as they occur, in the hospital he met this really interesting guy named Steve...
NOSdWIS

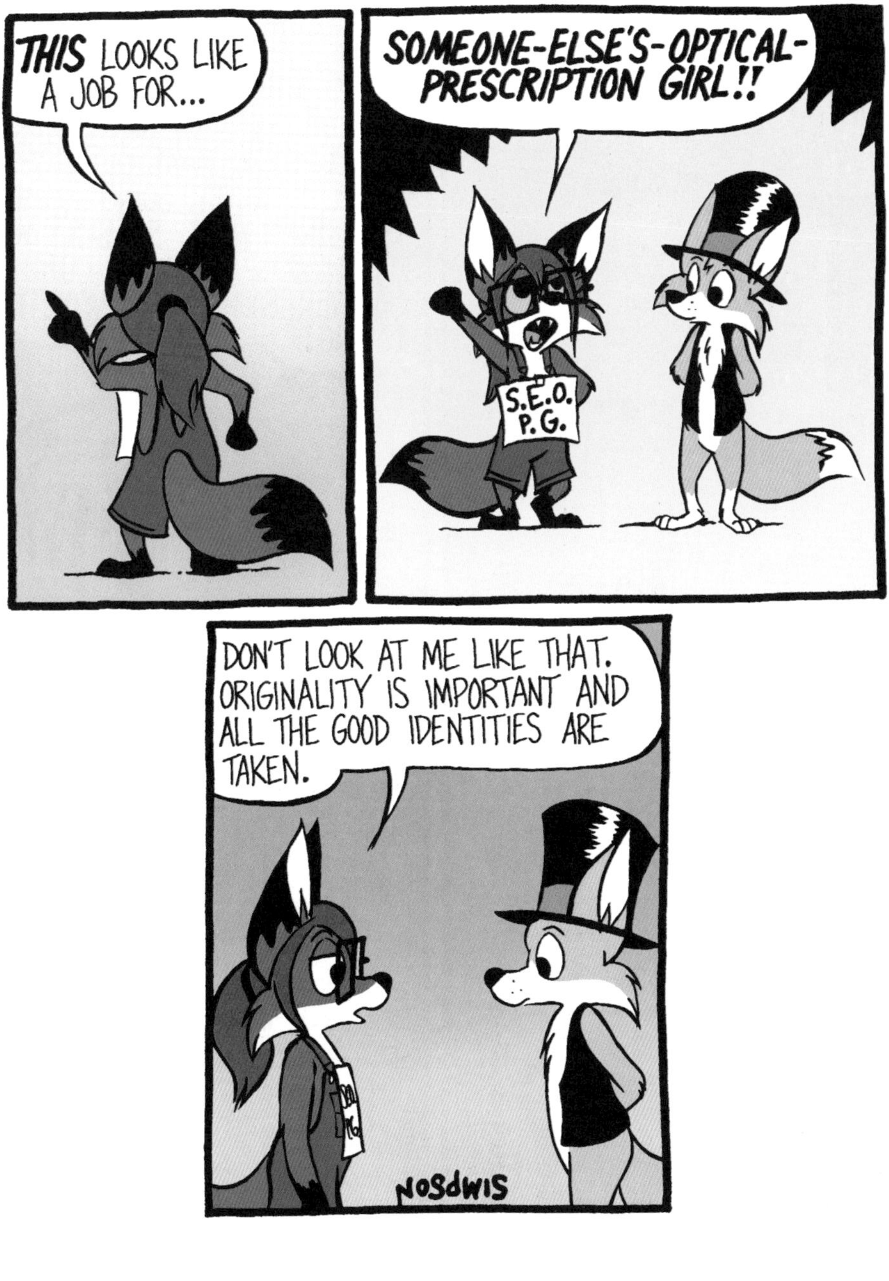
THIS LOOKS LIKE A JOB FOR...
SOMEONE-ELSE'S-OPTICAL-PRESCRIPTION GIRL!!
S.E.O. P.G.
DON'T LOOK AT ME LIKE THAT. ORIGINALITY IS IMPORTANT AND ALL THE GOOD IDENTITIES ARE TAKEN.
SIMPSON

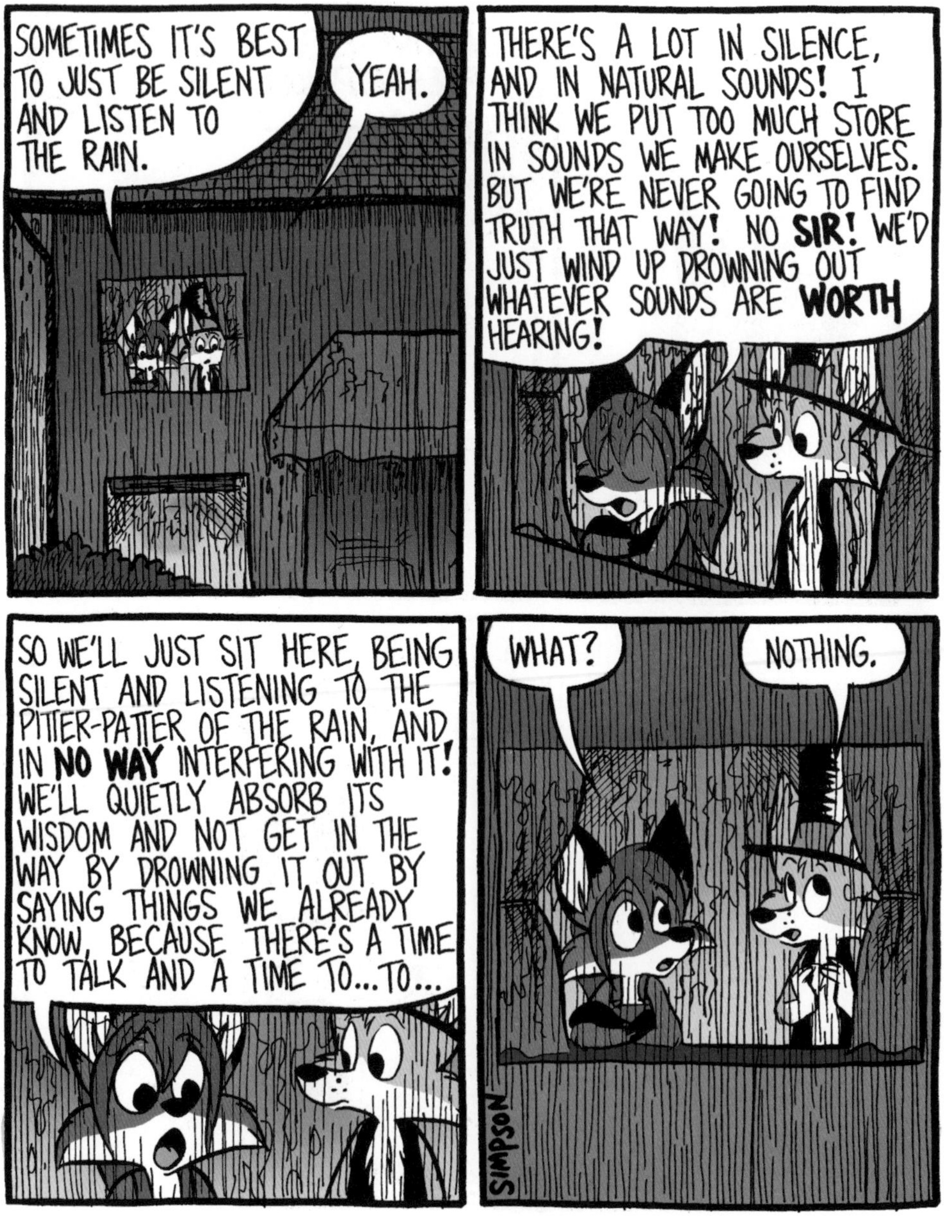
SOMETIMES IT'S BEST TO JUST BE SILENT AND LISTEN TO THE RAIN.
YEAH.
THERE'S A LOT IN SILENCE, AND IN NATURAL SOUNDS! I THINK WE PUT TOO MUCH STORE IN SOUNDS WE MAKE OURSELVES. BUT WE'RE NEVER GOING TO FIND TRUTH THAT WAY! NO SIR! WE'D JUST WIND UP DROWNING OUT WHATEVER SOUNDS ARE WORTH HEARING!
SO WE'LL JUST SIT HERE, BEING SILENT AND LISTENING TO THE PITTER-PATTER OF THE RAIN, AND IN NO WAY INTERFERING WITH IT! WE'LL QUIETLY ABSORB ITS WISDOM AND NOT GET IN THE WAY BY DROWNING IT OUT BY SAYING THINGS WE ALREADY KNOW, BECAUSE THERE'S A TIME TO TALK AND A TIME TO...TO...
WHAT?
NOTHING.
SIMPSON

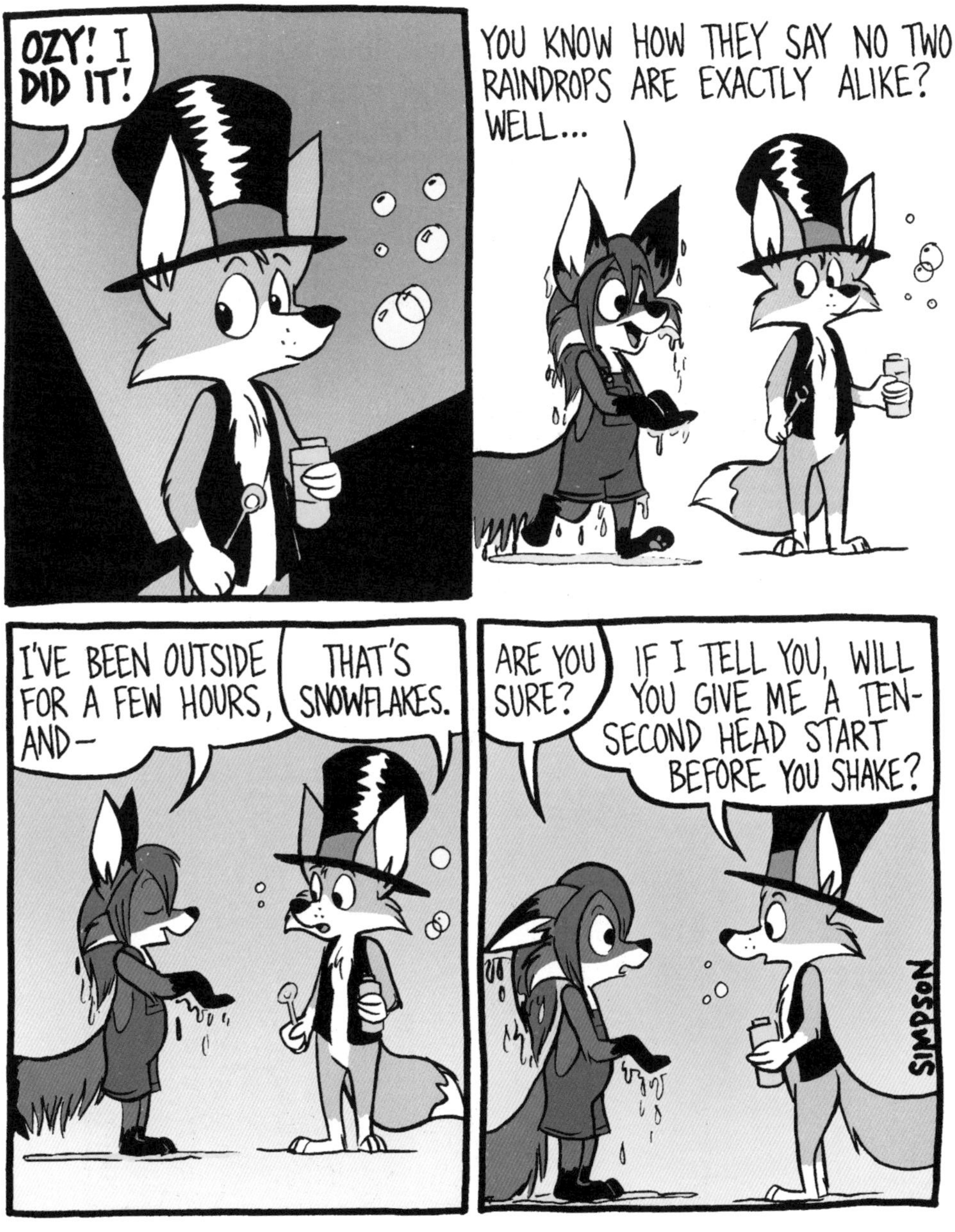
OZY! I DID IT!
YOU KNOW HOW THEY SAY NO TWO RAINDROPS ARE EXACTLY ALIKE? WELL...
I'VE BEEN OUTSIDE FOR A FEW HOURS, AND–
THAT'S SNOWFLAKES.
ARE YOU SURE?
IF I TELL YOU, WILL YOU GIVE ME A TEN-SECOND HEAD START BEFORE YOU SHAKE?
SIMPSON

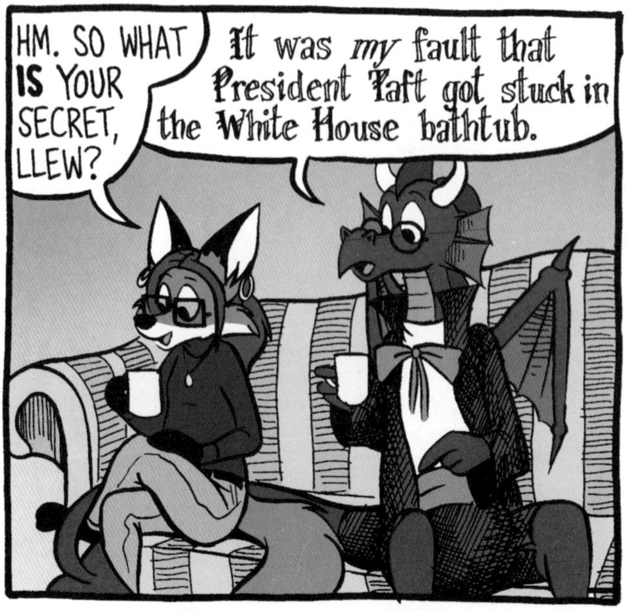
HM. SO WHAT **IS** YOUR SECRET, LLEW?
It was *my* fault that President Taft got stuck in the White House bathtub.

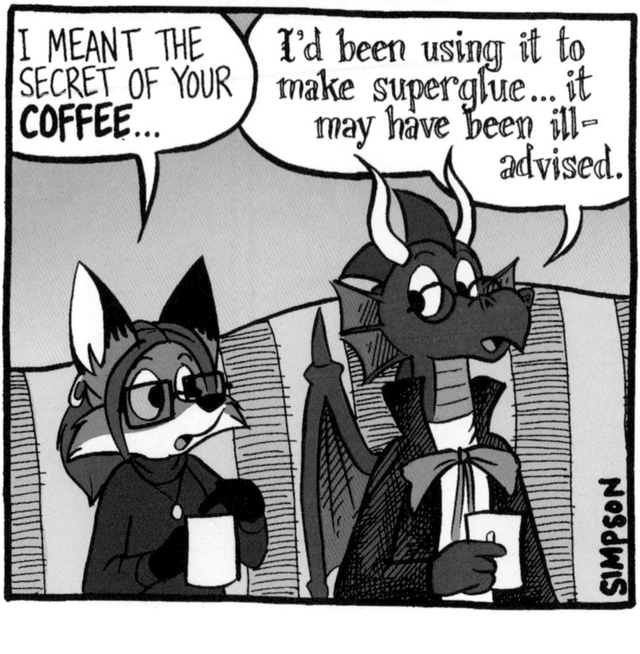
I MEANT THE SECRET OF YOUR **COFFEE**...
I'd been using it to make superglue... it may have been ill-advised.
SIMPSON

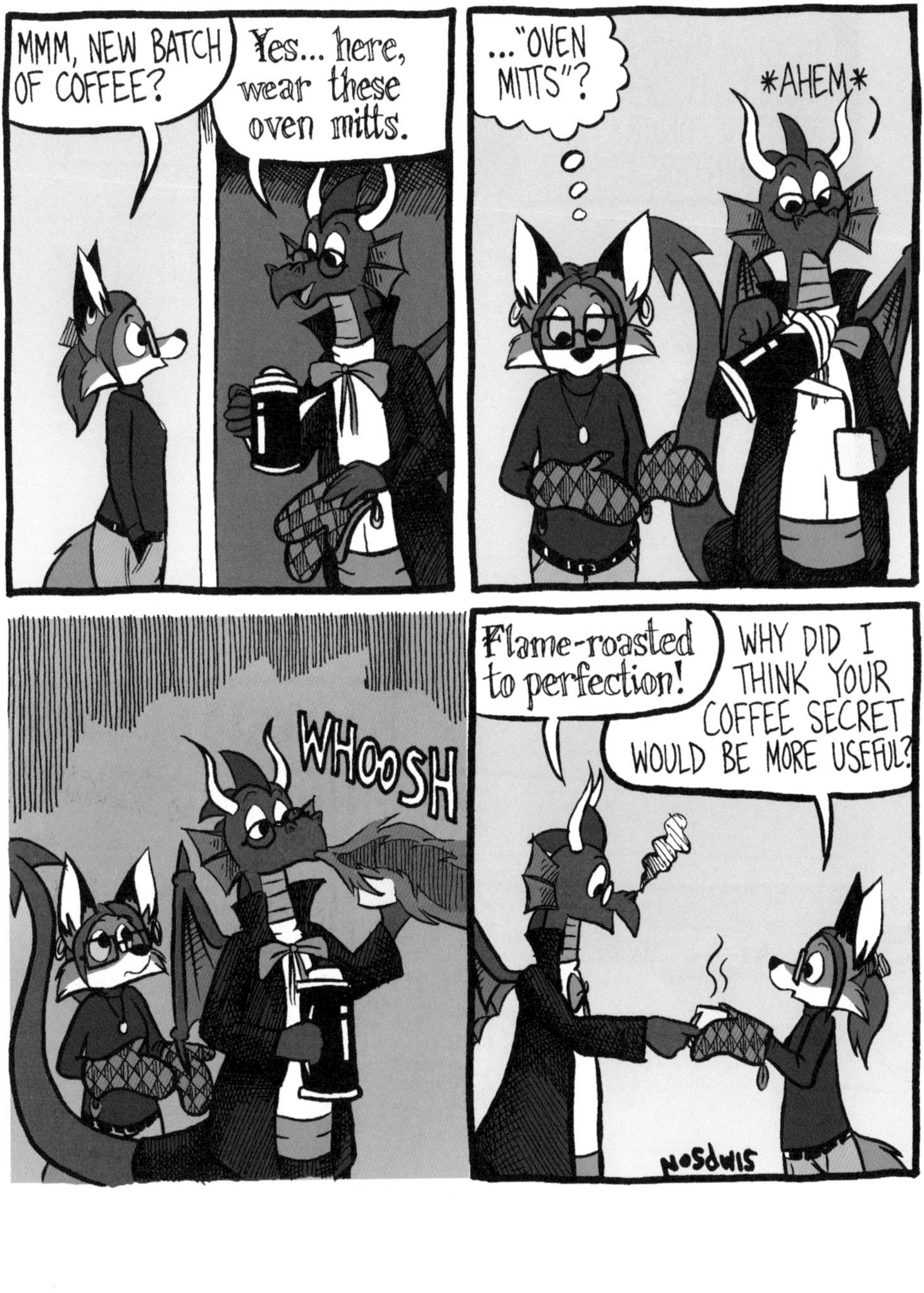
MMM, NEW BATCH OF COFFEE?
Yes... here, wear these oven mitts.
..."OVEN MITTS"?
AHEM
WHOOSH
Flame-roasted to perfection!
WHY DID I THINK YOUR COFFEE SECRET WOULD BE MORE USEFUL?
SIMPSON

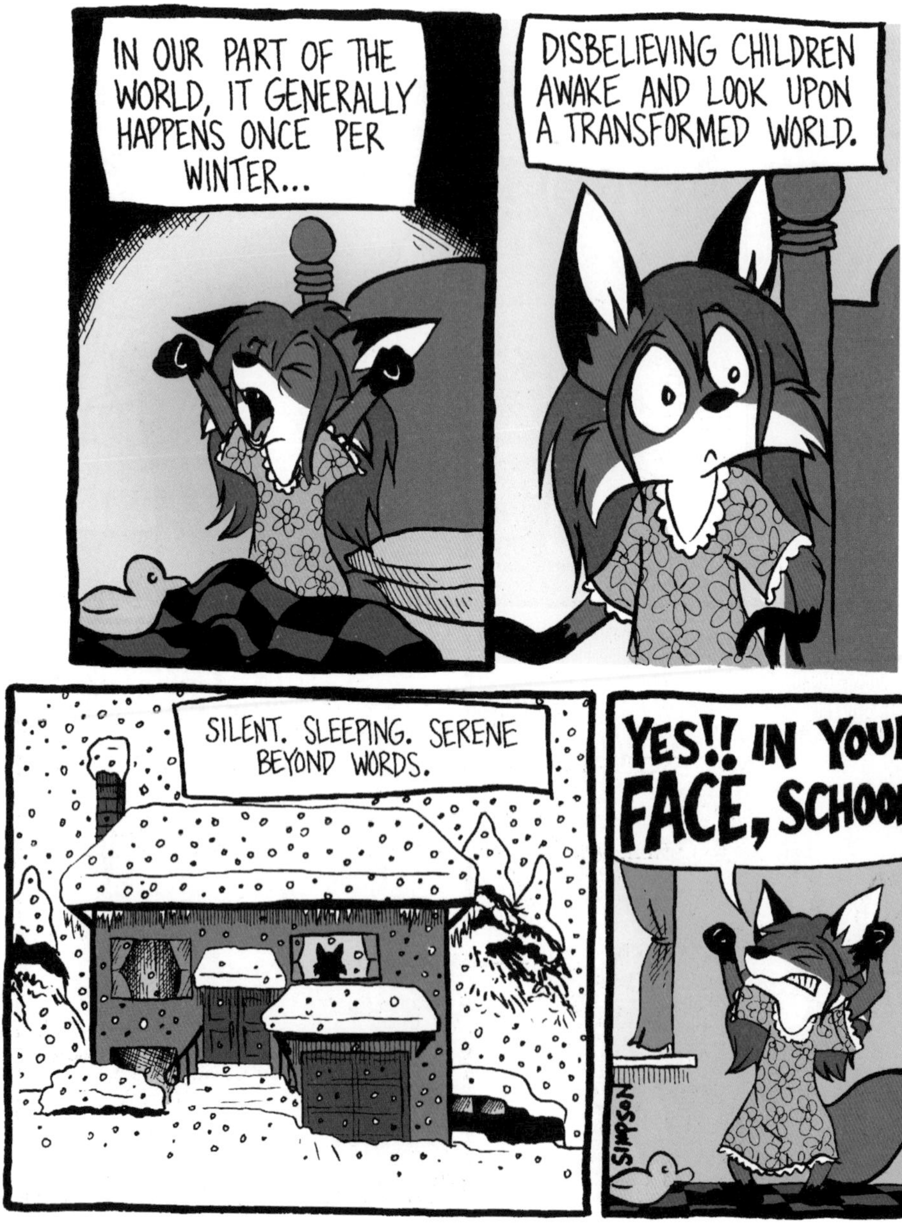
IN OUR PART OF THE WORLD, IT GENERALLY HAPPENS ONCE PER WINTER...
DISBELIEVING CHILDREN AWAKE AND LOOK UPON A TRANSFORMED WORLD.
SILENT. SLEEPING. SERENE BEYOND WORDS.
YES!! IN YOUR FACE, SCHOOL!
SIMPSON

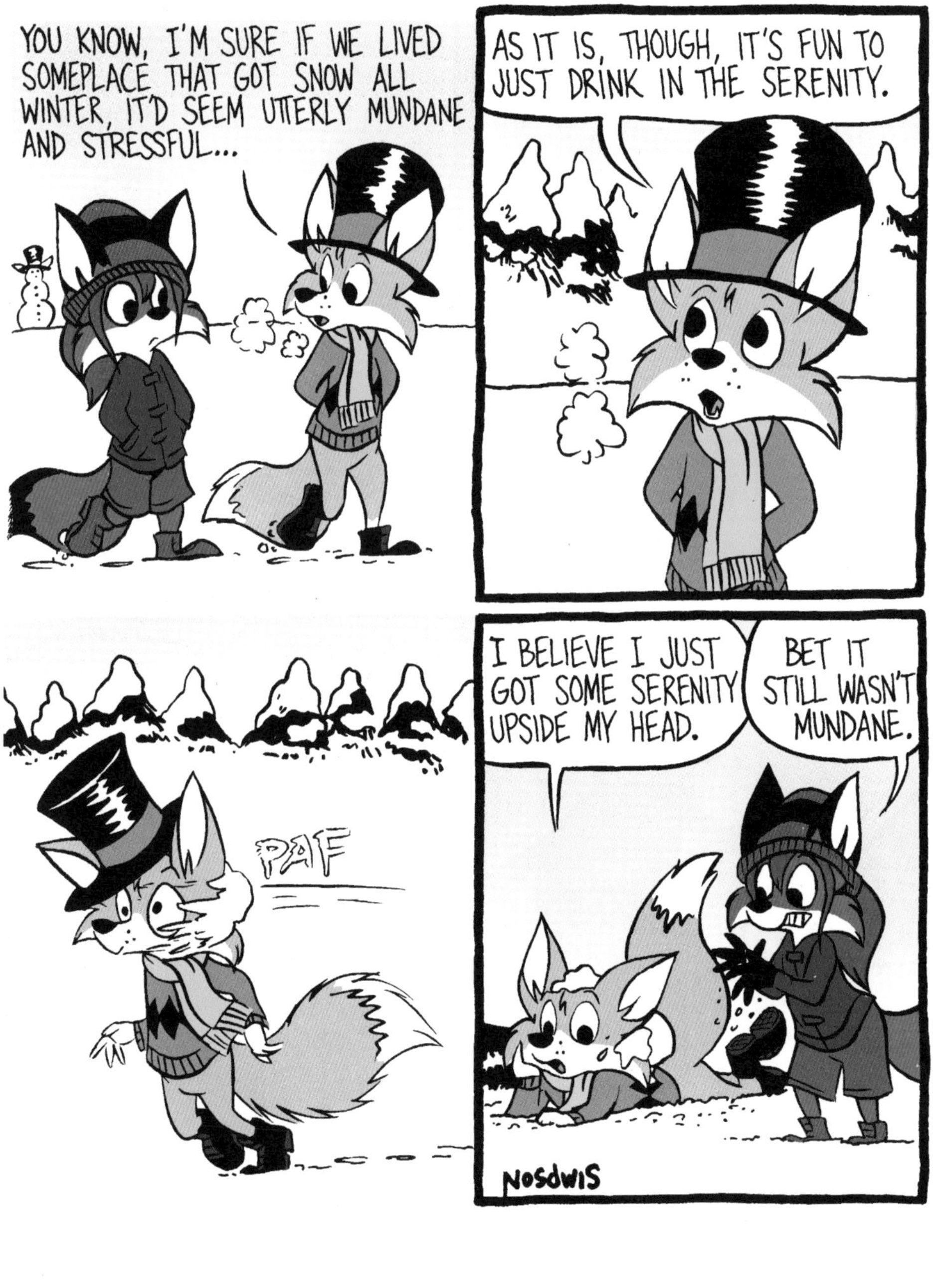
YOU KNOW, I'M SURE IF WE LIVED SOMEPLACE THAT GOT SNOW ALL WINTER, IT'D SEEM UTTERLY MUNDANE AND STRESSFUL...
AS IT IS, THOUGH, IT'S FUN TO JUST DRINK IN THE SERENITY.
PAF
I BELIEVE I JUST GOT SOME SERENITY UPSIDE MY HEAD.
BET IT STILL WASN'T MUNDANE.
NOSDWIS

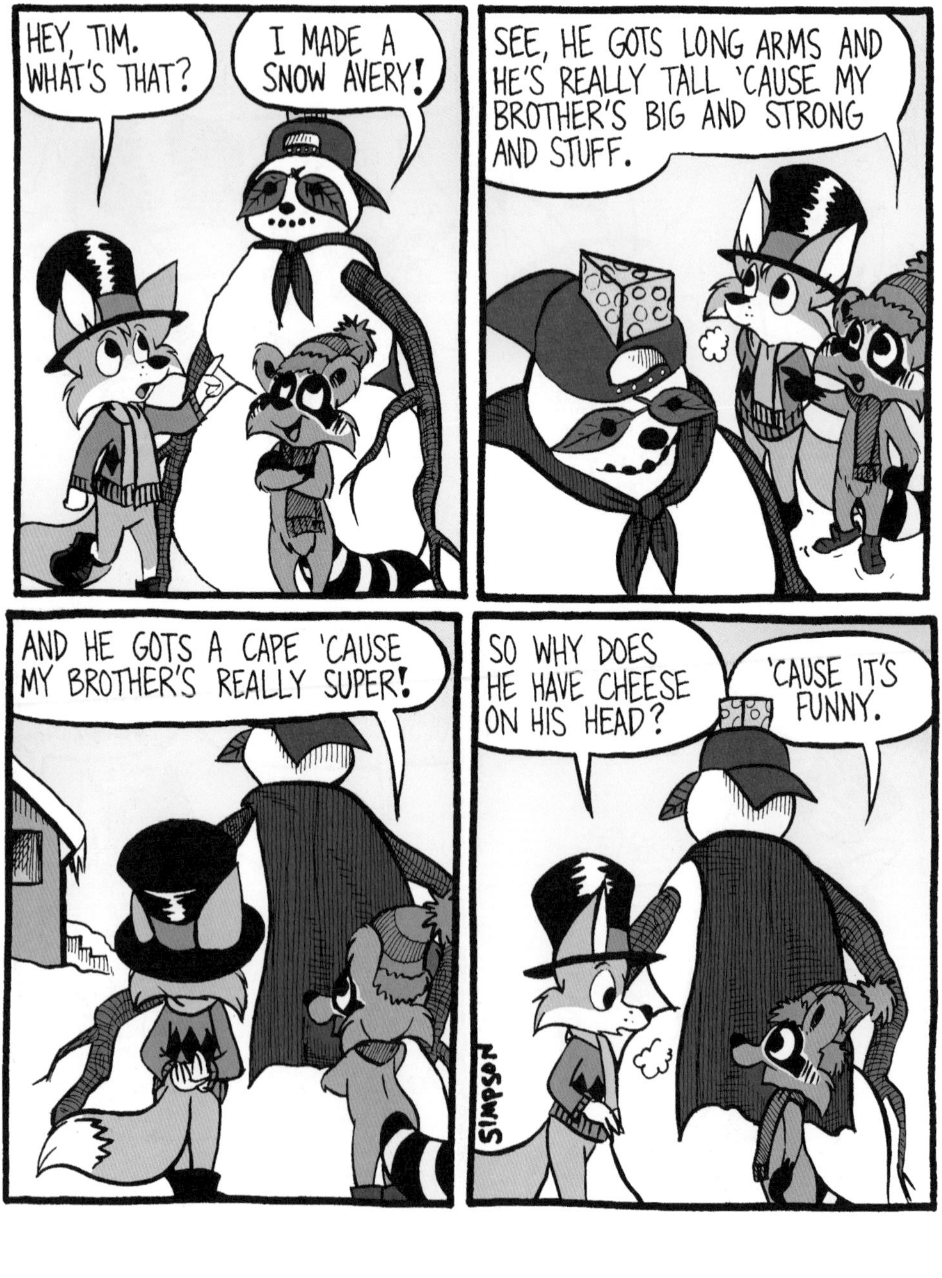
HEY, TIM. WHAT'S THAT?
I MADE A SNOW AVERY!
SEE, HE GOTS LONG ARMS AND HE'S REALLY TALL 'CAUSE MY BROTHER'S BIG AND STRONG AND STUFF.
AND HE GOTS A CAPE 'CAUSE MY BROTHER'S REALLY SUPER!
SO WHY DOES HE HAVE CHEESE ON HIS HEAD?
'CAUSE IT'S FUNNY.
SIMPSON

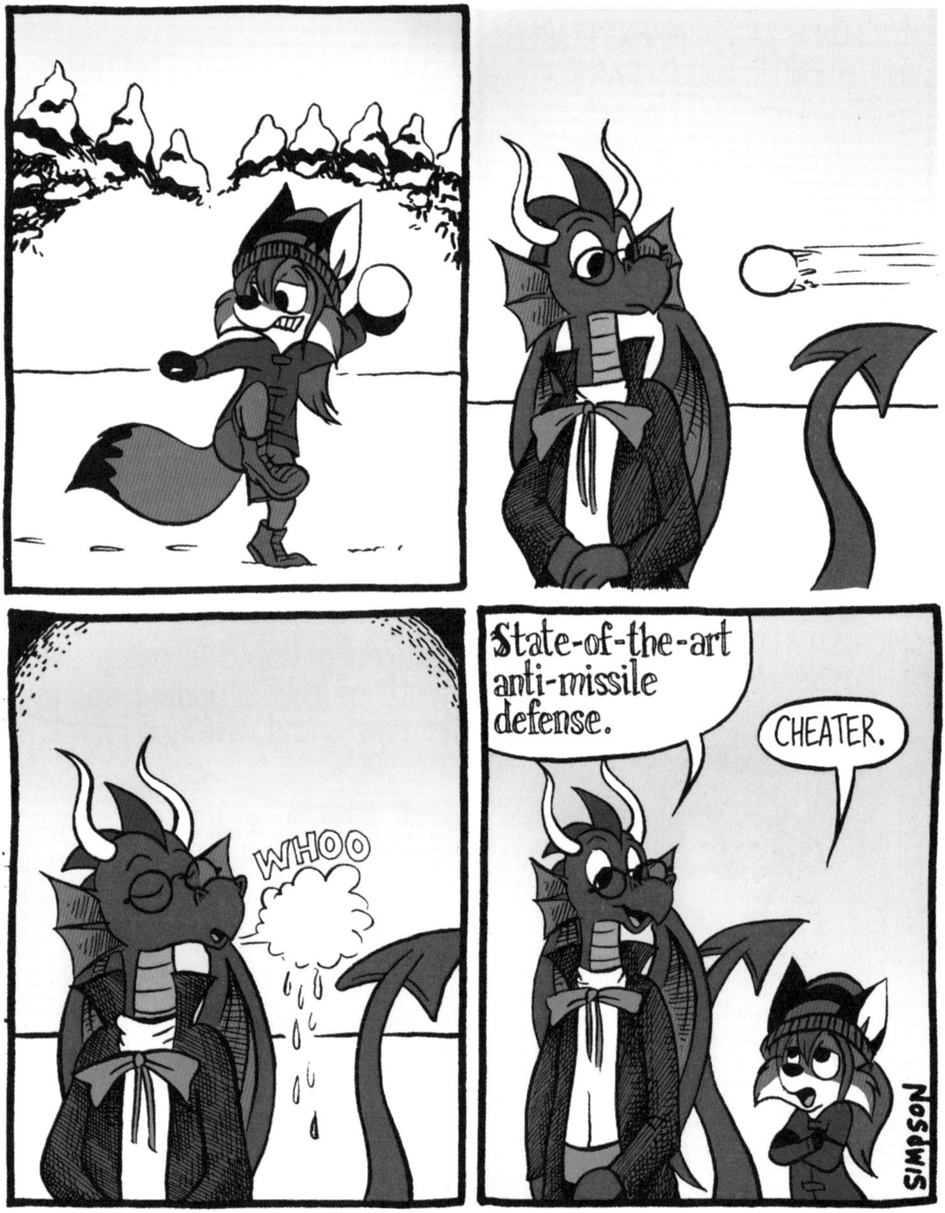
WHOO
State-of-the-art anti-missile defense.
CHEATER.
SIMPSON

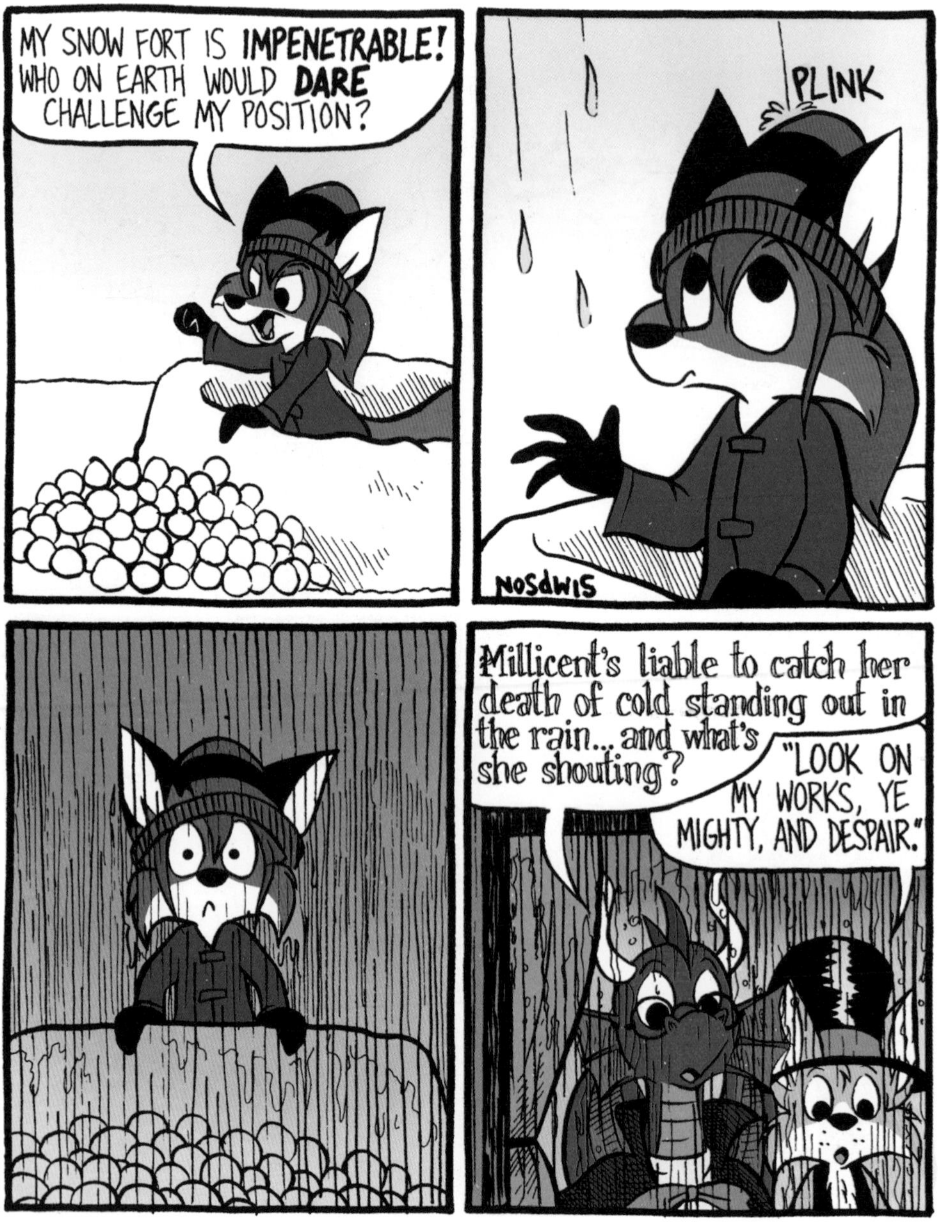
MY SNOW FORT IS IMPENETRABLE! WHO ON EARTH WOULD DARE CHALLENGE MY POSITION?
PLINK
NOSdWIS
Millicent's liable to catch her death of cold standing out in the rain... and what's she shouting?
"LOOK ON MY WORKS, YE MIGHTY, AND DESPAIR."

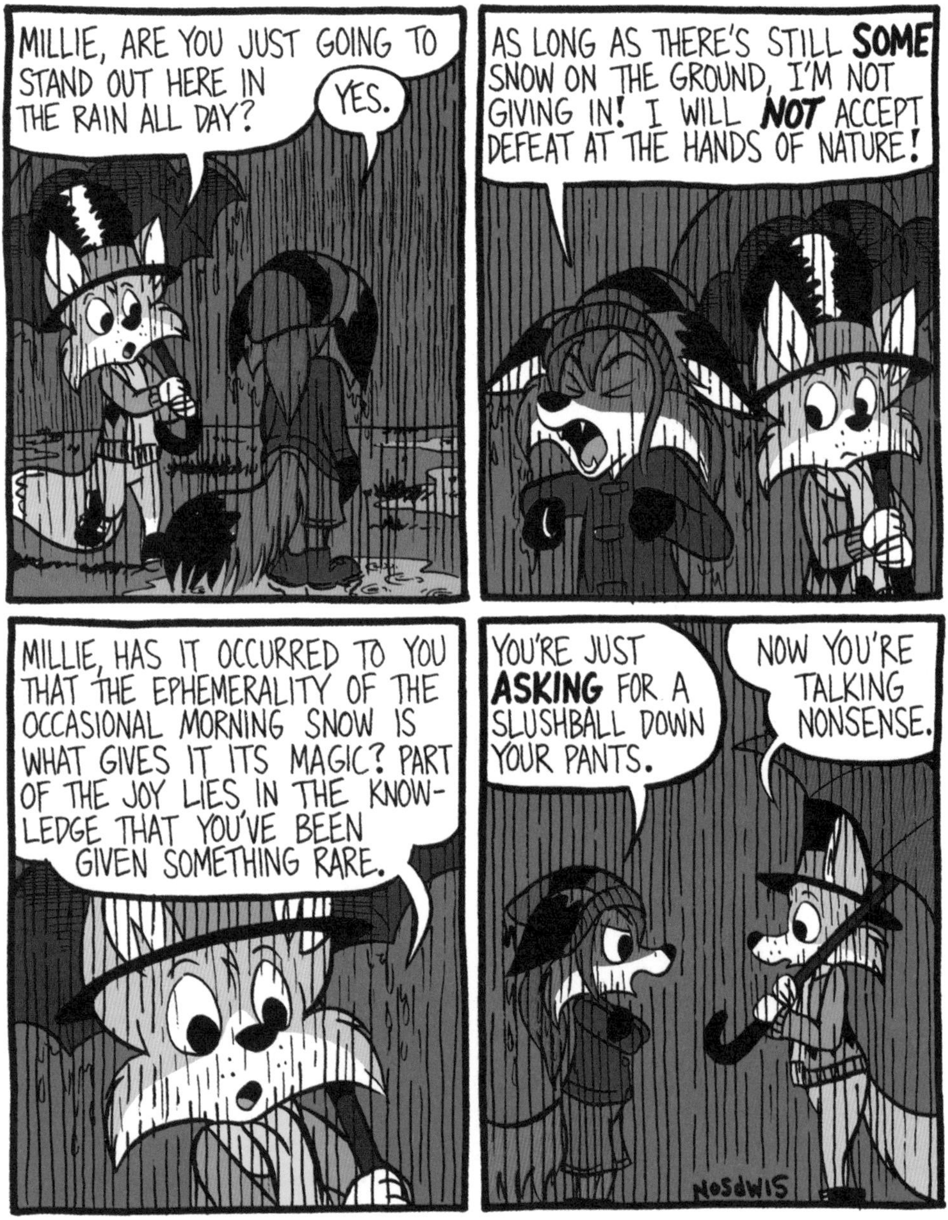
MILLIE, ARE YOU JUST GOING TO STAND OUT HERE IN THE RAIN ALL DAY?
YES.
AS LONG AS THERE'S STILL **SOME** SNOW ON THE GROUND, I'M NOT GIVING IN! I WILL ***NOT*** ACCEPT DEFEAT AT THE HANDS OF NATURE!
MILLIE, HAS IT OCCURRED TO YOU THAT THE EPHEMERALITY OF THE OCCASIONAL MORNING SNOW IS WHAT GIVES IT ITS MAGIC? PART OF THE JOY LIES IN THE KNOWLEDGE THAT YOU'VE BEEN GIVEN SOMETHING RARE.
YOU'RE JUST **ASKING** FOR A SLUSHBALL DOWN YOUR PANTS.
NOW YOU'RE TALKING NONSENSE.
SIMPSON

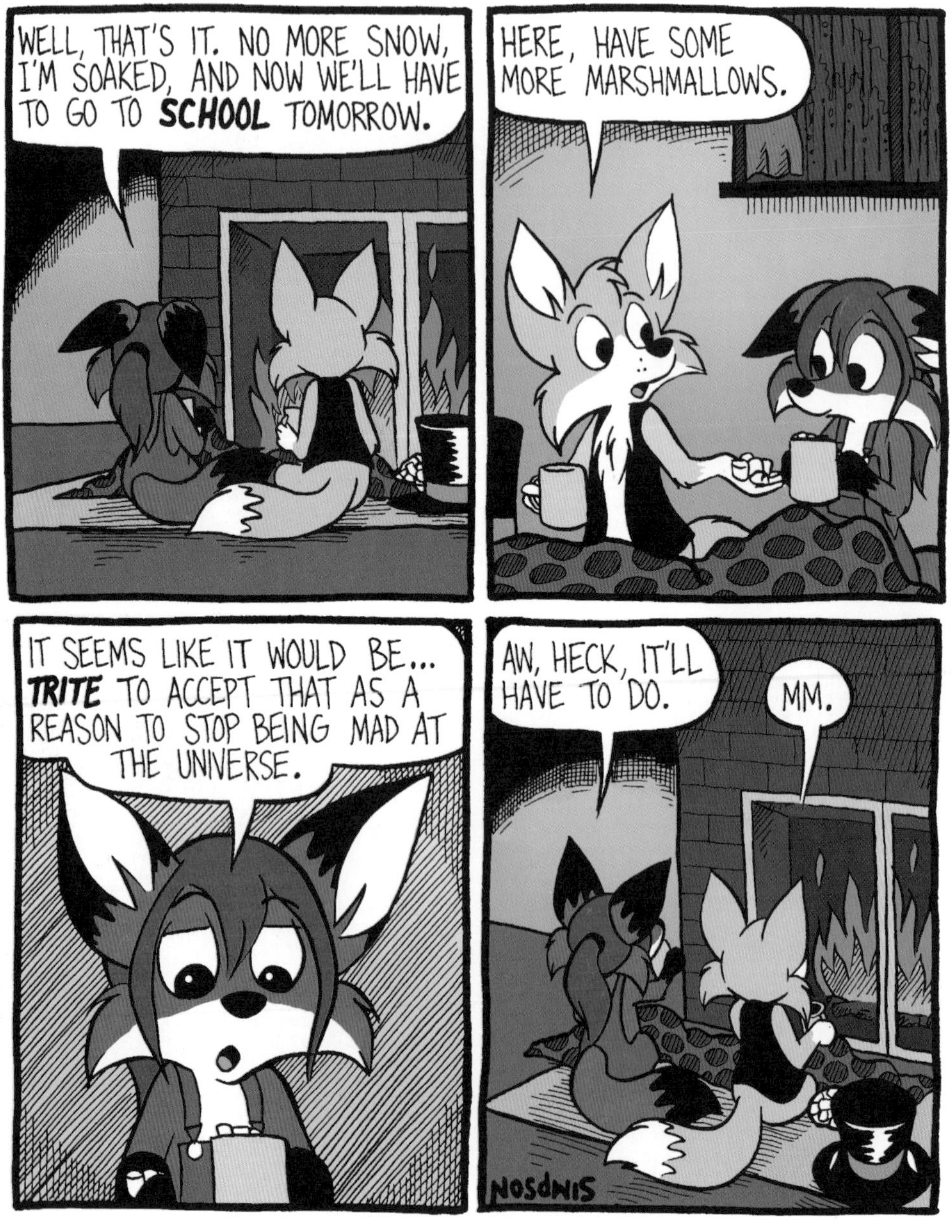
WELL, THAT'S IT. NO MORE SNOW, I'M SOAKED, AND NOW WE'LL HAVE TO GO TO **SCHOOL** TOMORROW.
HERE, HAVE SOME MORE MARSHMALLOWS.
IT SEEMS LIKE IT WOULD BE... ***TRITE*** TO ACCEPT THAT AS A REASON TO STOP BEING MAD AT THE UNIVERSE.
AW, HECK, IT'LL HAVE TO DO.
MM.
NOSDNIS

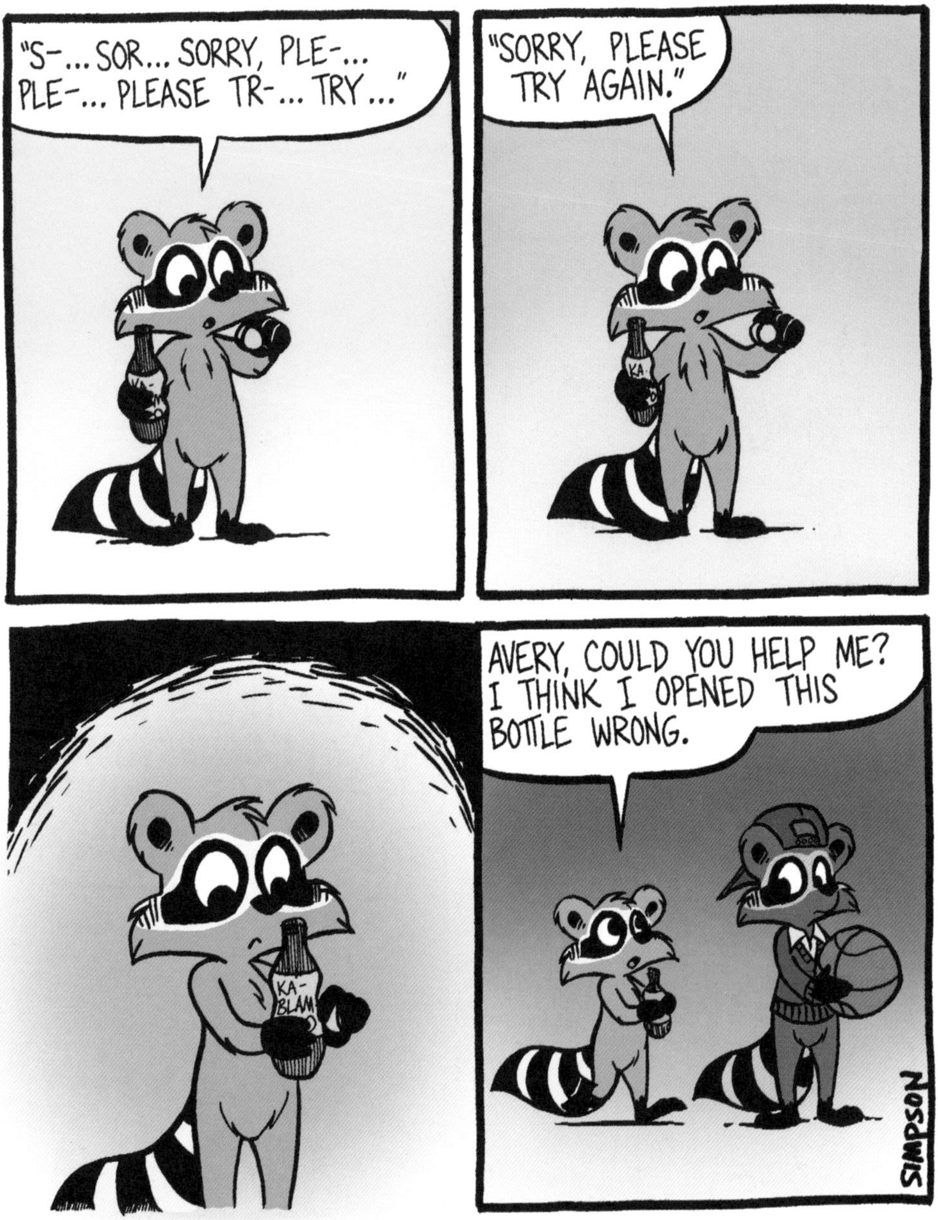
"S-... SOR... SORRY, PLE-... PLE-... PLEASE TR-... TRY..."
"SORRY, PLEASE TRY AGAIN."
KA-
KA-BLAM
AVERY, COULD YOU HELP ME? I THINK I OPENED THIS BOTTLE WRONG.
SIMPSON

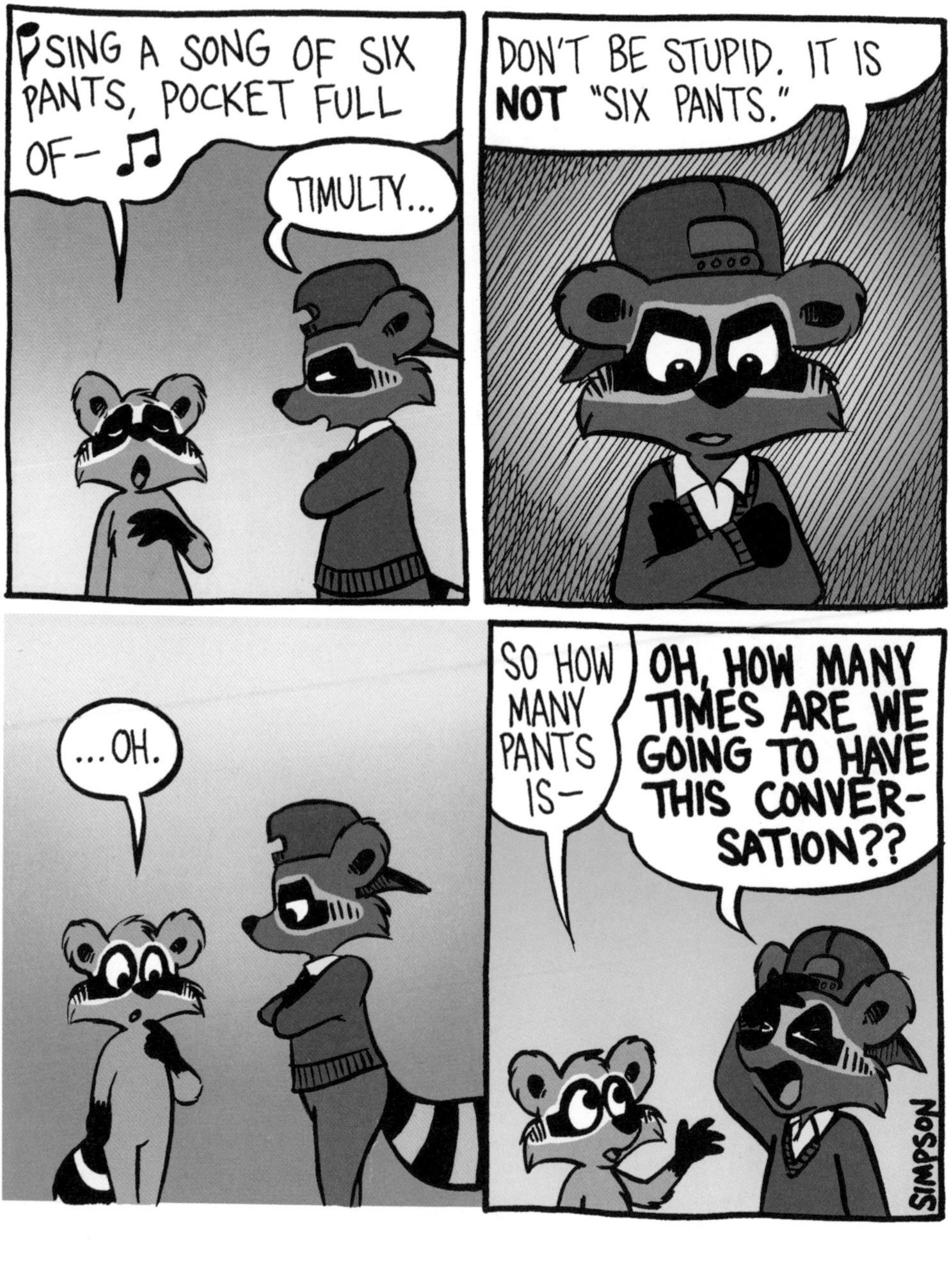
SING A SONG OF SIX PANTS, POCKET FULL OF–
TIMULTY...
DON'T BE STUPID. IT IS **NOT** "SIX PANTS."
...OH.
SO HOW MANY PANTS IS–
OH, HOW MANY TIMES ARE WE GOING TO HAVE THIS CONVERSATION??
SIMPSON

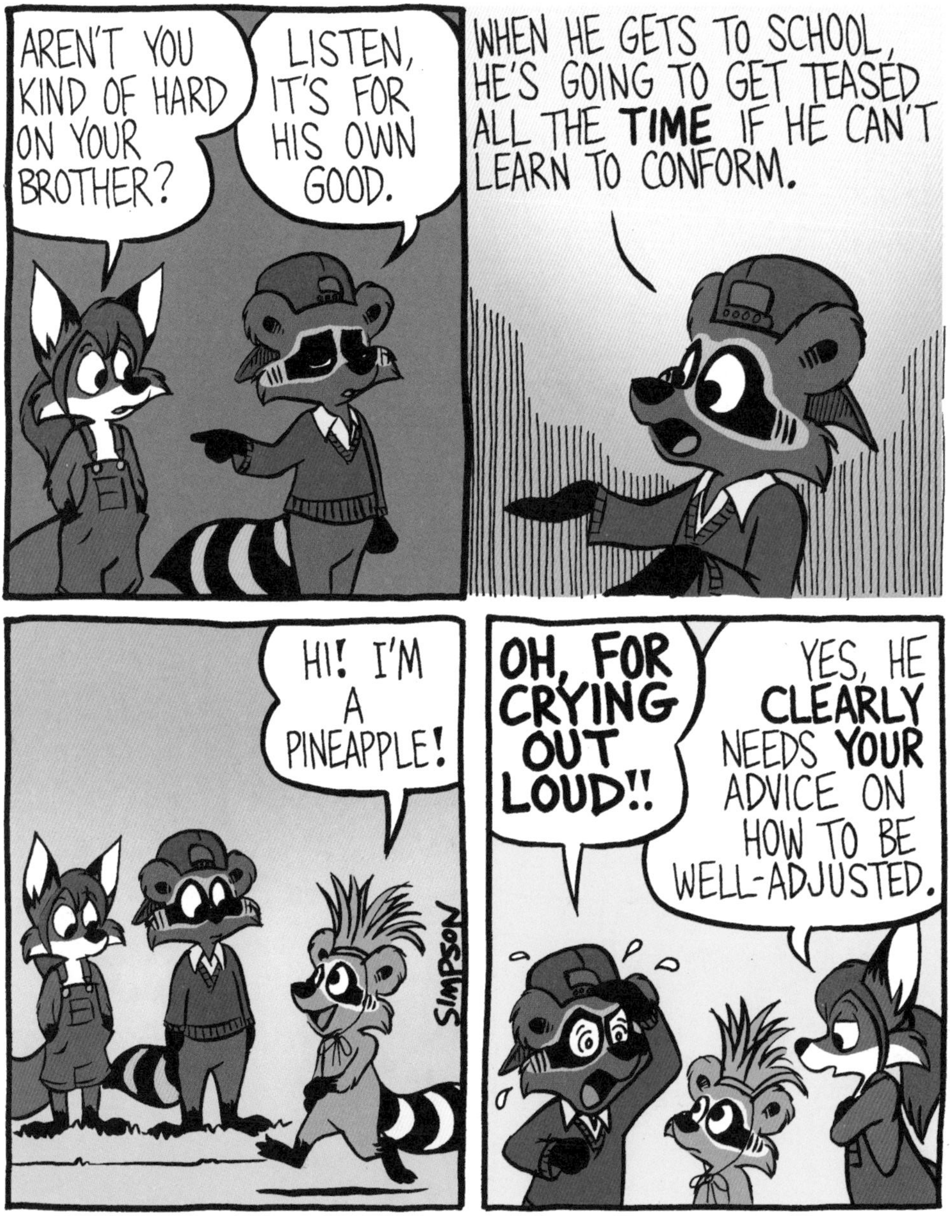
AREN'T YOU KIND OF HARD ON YOUR BROTHER?
LISTEN, IT'S FOR HIS OWN GOOD.
WHEN HE GETS TO SCHOOL, HE'S GOING TO GET TEASED ALL THE **TIME** IF HE CAN'T LEARN TO CONFORM.
HI! I'M A PINEAPPLE!
SIMPSON
OH, FOR CRYING OUT LOUD!!
YES, HE **CLEARLY** NEEDS **YOUR** ADVICE ON HOW TO BE WELL-ADJUSTED.

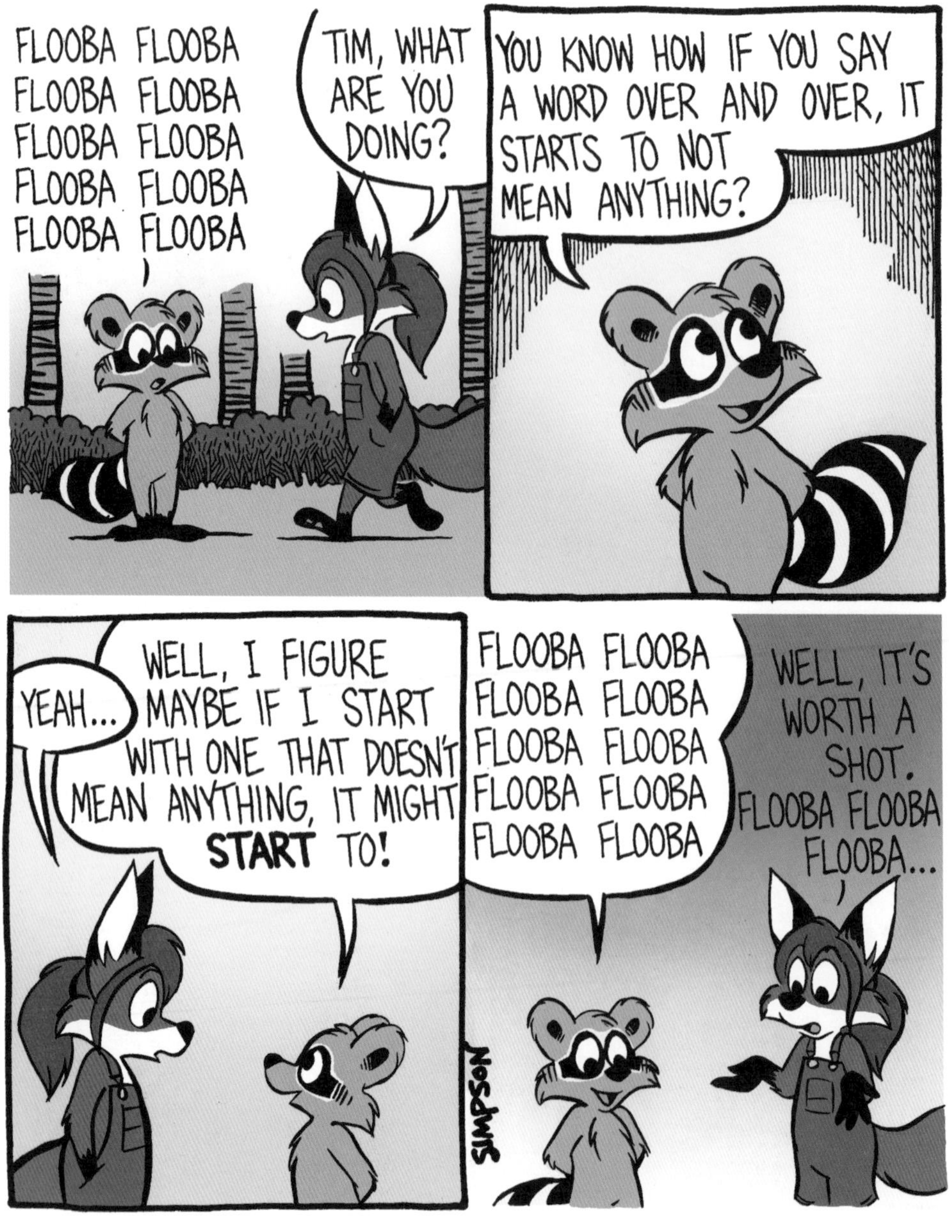
FLOOBA FLOOBA FLOOBA FLOOBA FLOOBA FLOOBA FLOOBA FLOOBA FLOOBA FLOOBA
TIM, WHAT ARE YOU DOING?
YOU KNOW HOW IF YOU SAY A WORD OVER AND OVER, IT STARTS TO NOT MEAN ANYTHING?
YEAH...
WELL, I FIGURE MAYBE IF I START WITH ONE THAT DOESN'T MEAN ANYTHING, IT MIGHT **START** TO!
FLOOBA FLOOBA FLOOBA FLOOBA FLOOBA FLOOBA FLOOBA FLOOBA FLOOBA FLOOBA
WELL, IT'S WORTH A SHOT. FLOOBA FLOOBA FLOOBA...
SIMPSON

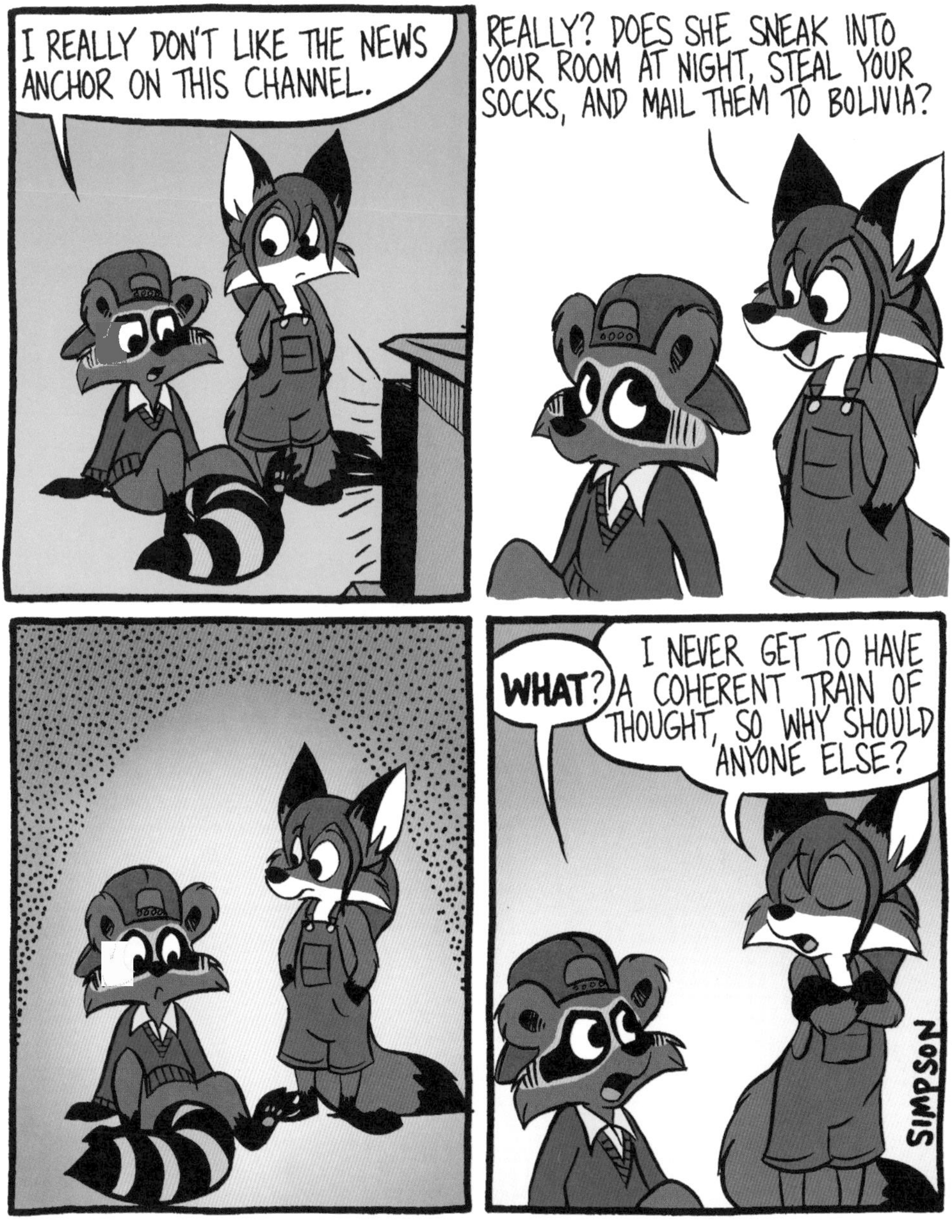

I REALLY DON'T LIKE THE NEWS ANCHOR ON THIS CHANNEL.
REALLY? DOES SHE SNEAK INTO YOUR ROOM AT NIGHT, STEAL YOUR SOCKS, AND MAIL THEM TO BOLIVIA?
WHAT?
I NEVER GET TO HAVE A COHERENT TRAIN OF THOUGHT, SO WHY SHOULD ANYONE ELSE?
SIMPSON

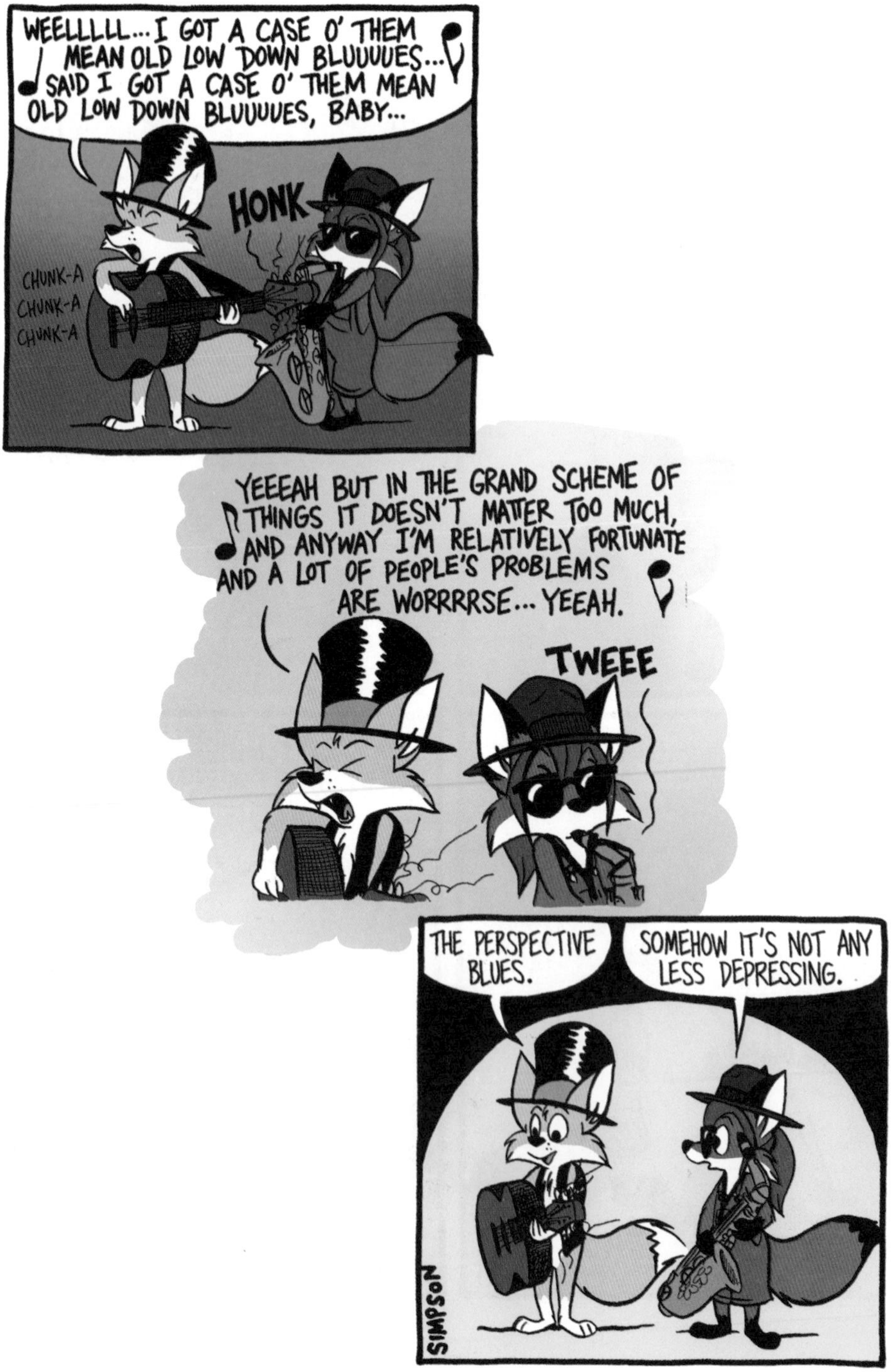
WEELLLLL... I GOT A CASE O' THEM MEAN OLD LOW DOWN BLUUUUES... SAID I GOT A CASE O' THEM MEAN OLD LOW DOWN BLUUUUES, BABY...
HONK
CHUNK-A
CHUNK-A
CHUNK-A
YEEEAH BUT IN THE GRAND SCHEME OF THINGS IT DOESN'T MATTER TOO MUCH, AND ANYWAY I'M RELATIVELY FORTUNATE AND A LOT OF PEOPLE'S PROBLEMS ARE WORRRRSE... YEEAH.
TWEEE
THE PERSPECTIVE BLUES.
SOMEHOW IT'S NOT ANY LESS DEPRESSING.
SIMPSON

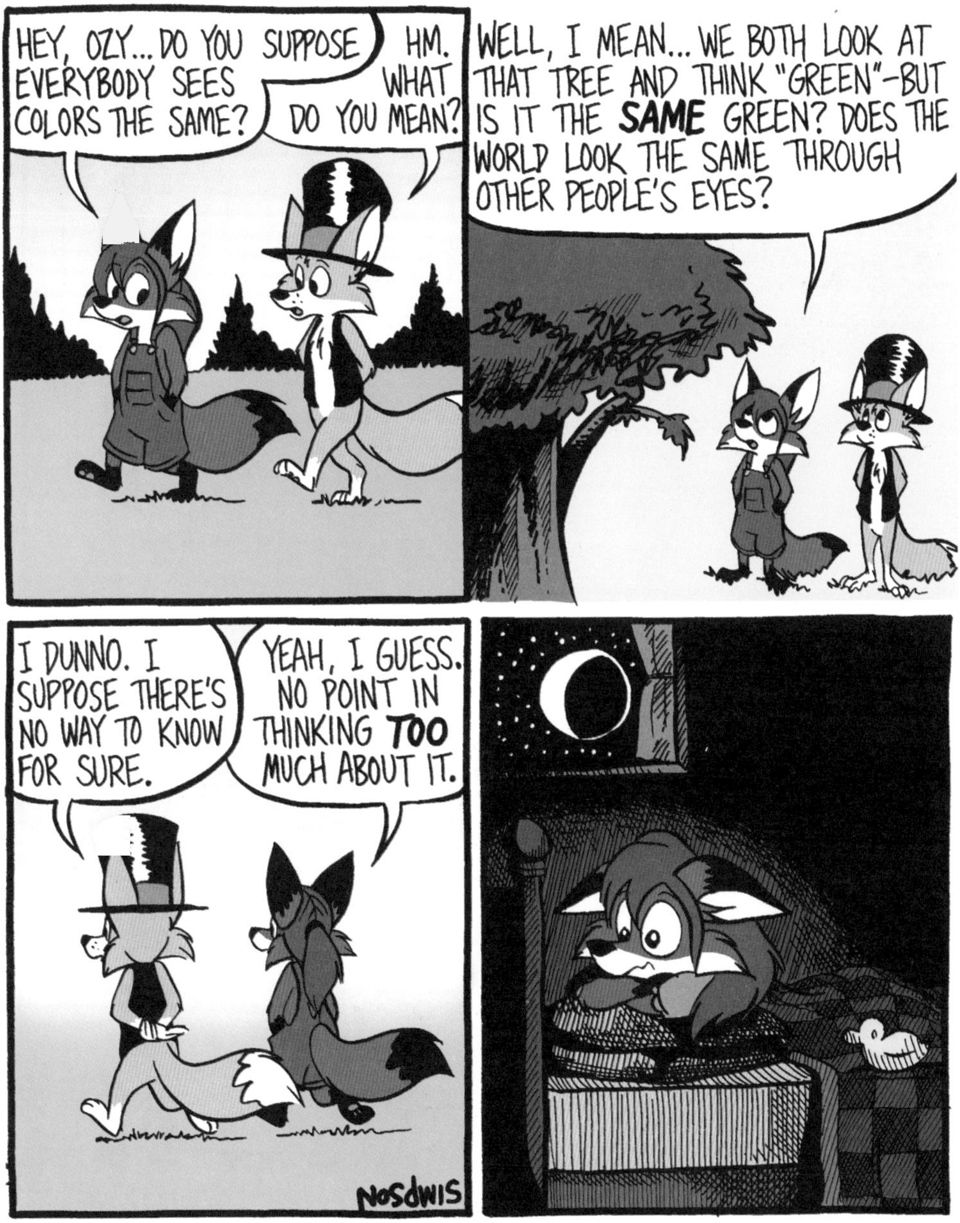
HEY, OZY... DO YOU SUPPOSE EVERYBODY SEES COLORS THE SAME?
HM. WHAT DO YOU MEAN?
WELL, I MEAN... WE BOTH LOOK AT THAT TREE AND THINK "GREEN"–BUT IS IT THE **SAME** GREEN? DOES THE WORLD LOOK THE SAME THROUGH OTHER PEOPLE'S EYES?
I DUNNO. I SUPPOSE THERE'S NO WAY TO KNOW FOR SURE.
YEAH, I GUESS. NO POINT IN THINKING **TOO** MUCH ABOUT IT.
SIMPSON

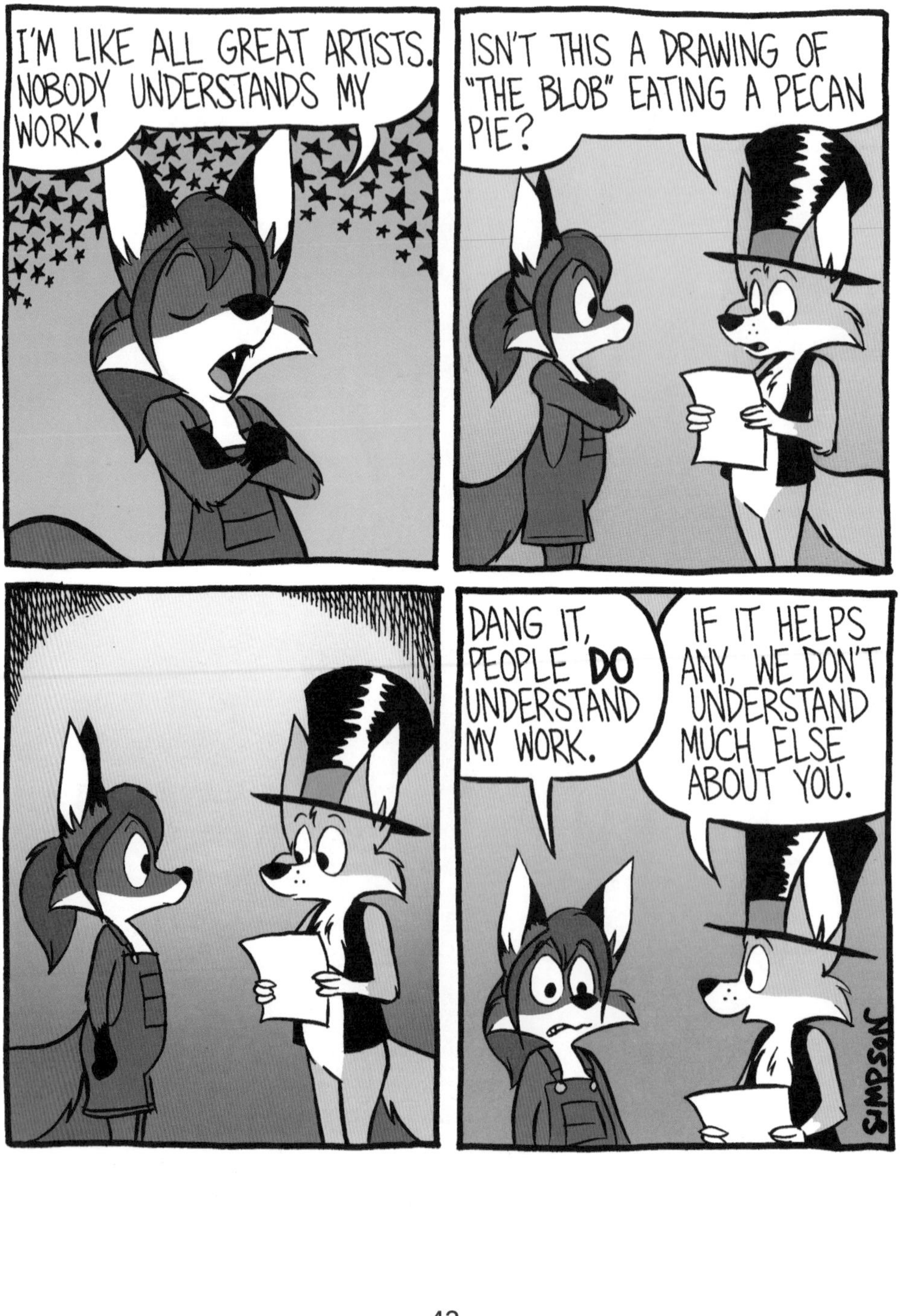
I'M LIKE ALL GREAT ARTISTS. NOBODY UNDERSTANDS MY WORK!
ISN'T THIS A DRAWING OF "THE BLOB" EATING A PECAN PIE?
DANG IT, PEOPLE **DO** UNDERSTAND MY WORK.
IF IT HELPS ANY, WE DON'T UNDERSTAND MUCH ELSE ABOUT YOU.
SIMPSON

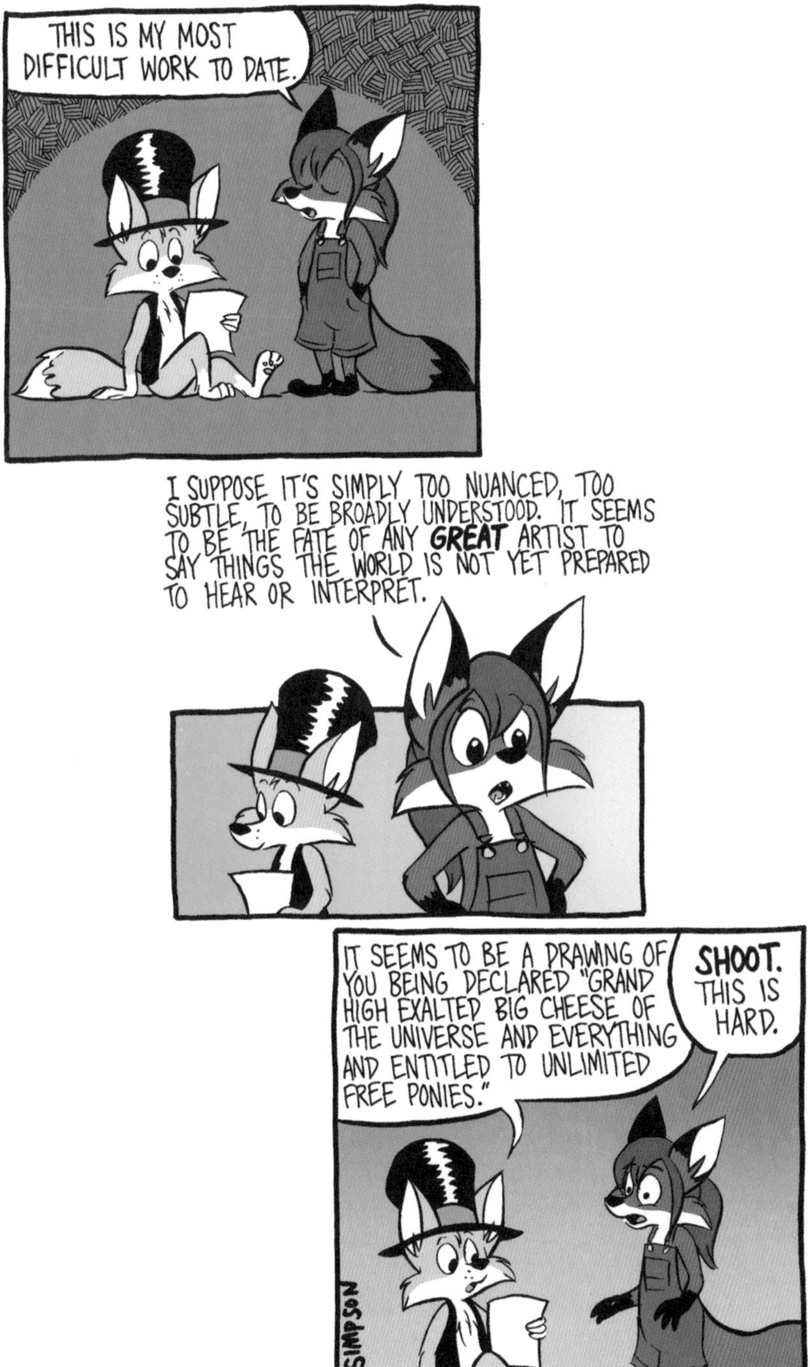
THIS IS MY MOST DIFFICULT WORK TO DATE.
I SUPPOSE IT'S SIMPLY TOO NUANCED, TOO SUBTLE, TO BE BROADLY UNDERSTOOD. IT SEEMS TO BE THE FATE OF ANY **GREAT** ARTIST TO SAY THINGS THE WORLD IS NOT YET PREPARED TO HEAR OR INTERPRET.
IT SEEMS TO BE A DRAWING OF YOU BEING DECLARED "GRAND HIGH EXALTED BIG CHEESE OF THE UNIVERSE AND EVERYTHING AND ENTITLED TO UNLIMITED FREE PONIES."
SHOOT. THIS IS HARD.
SIMPSON

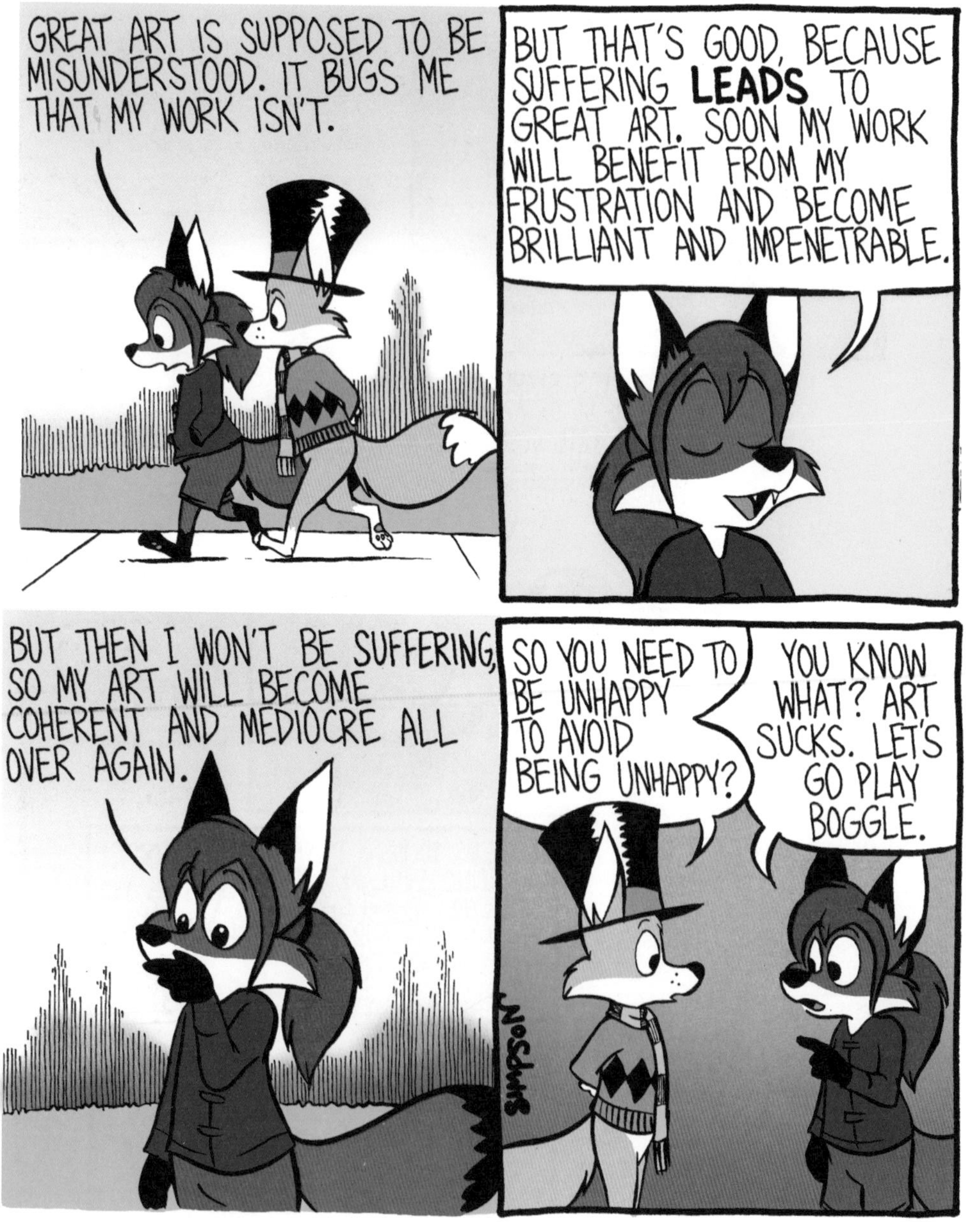
GREAT ART IS SUPPOSED TO BE MISUNDERSTOOD. IT BUGS ME THAT MY WORK ISN'T.
BUT THAT'S GOOD, BECAUSE SUFFERING **LEADS** TO GREAT ART. SOON MY WORK WILL BENEFIT FROM MY FRUSTRATION AND BECOME BRILLIANT AND IMPENETRABLE.
BUT THEN I WON'T BE SUFFERING, SO MY ART WILL BECOME COHERENT AND MEDIOCRE ALL OVER AGAIN.
SO YOU NEED TO BE UNHAPPY TO AVOID BEING UNHAPPY?
YOU KNOW WHAT? ART SUCKS. LET'S GO PLAY BOGGLE.
SIMPSON

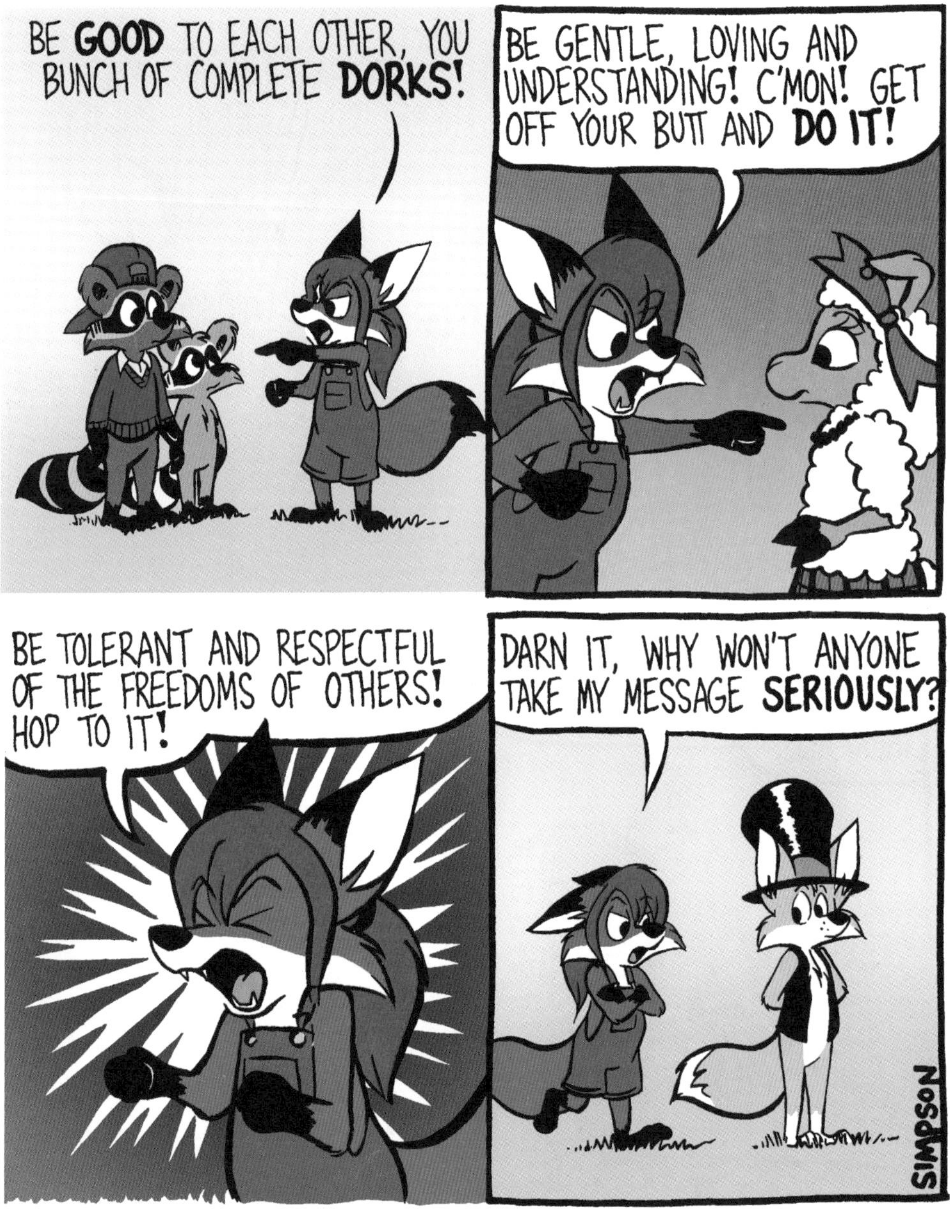
BE GOOD TO EACH OTHER, YOU BUNCH OF COMPLETE DORKS!
BE GENTLE, LOVING AND UNDERSTANDING! C'MON! GET OFF YOUR BUTT AND DO IT!
BE TOLERANT AND RESPECTFUL OF THE FREEDOMS OF OTHERS! HOP TO IT!
DARN IT, WHY WON'T ANYONE TAKE MY MESSAGE SERIOUSLY?
SIMPSON

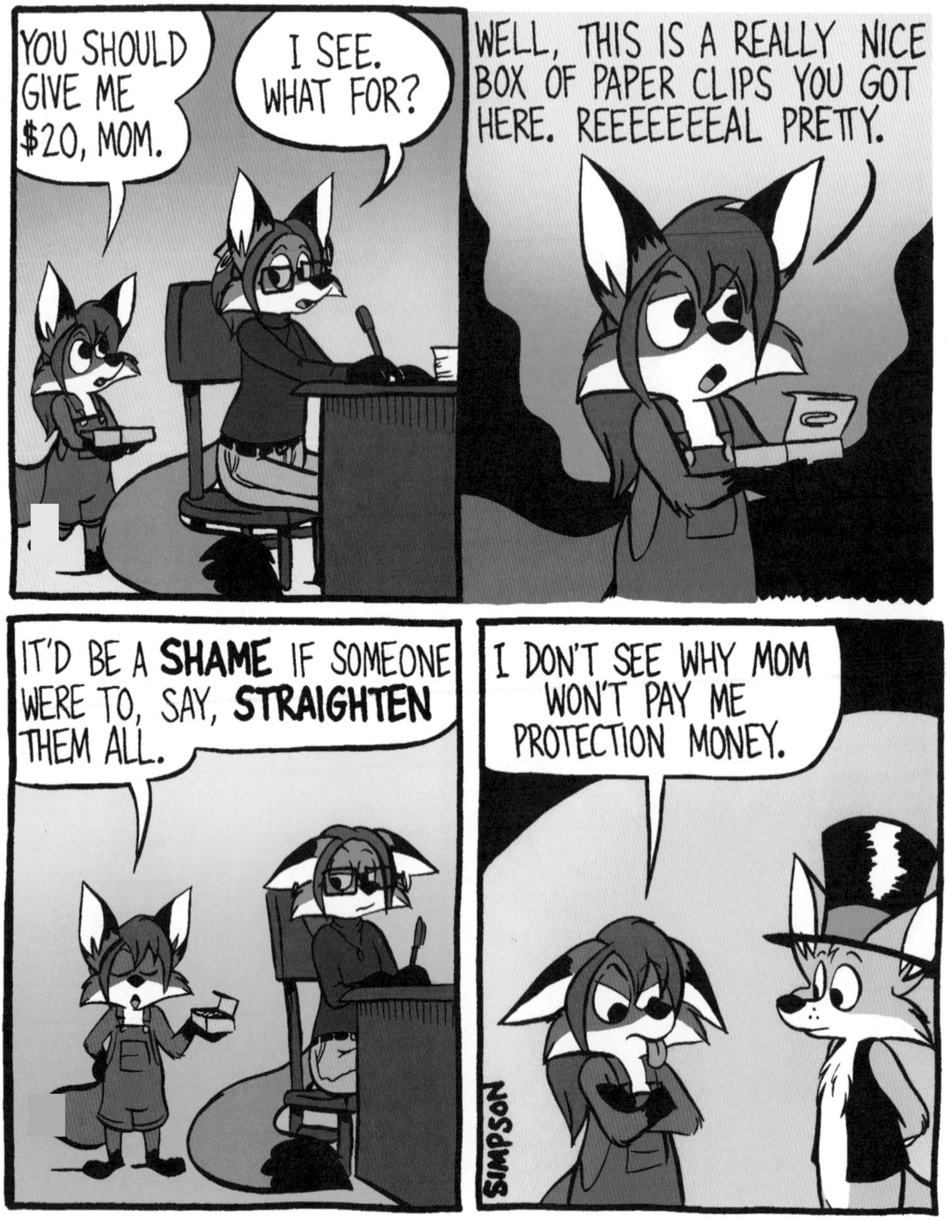
YOU SHOULD GIVE ME $20, MOM.
I SEE. WHAT FOR?
WELL, THIS IS A REALLY NICE BOX OF PAPER CLIPS YOU GOT HERE. REEEEEEEAL PRETTY.
IT'D BE A **SHAME** IF SOMEONE WERE TO, SAY, **STRAIGHTEN** THEM ALL.
I DON'T SEE WHY MOM WON'T PAY ME PROTECTION MONEY.
SIMPSON

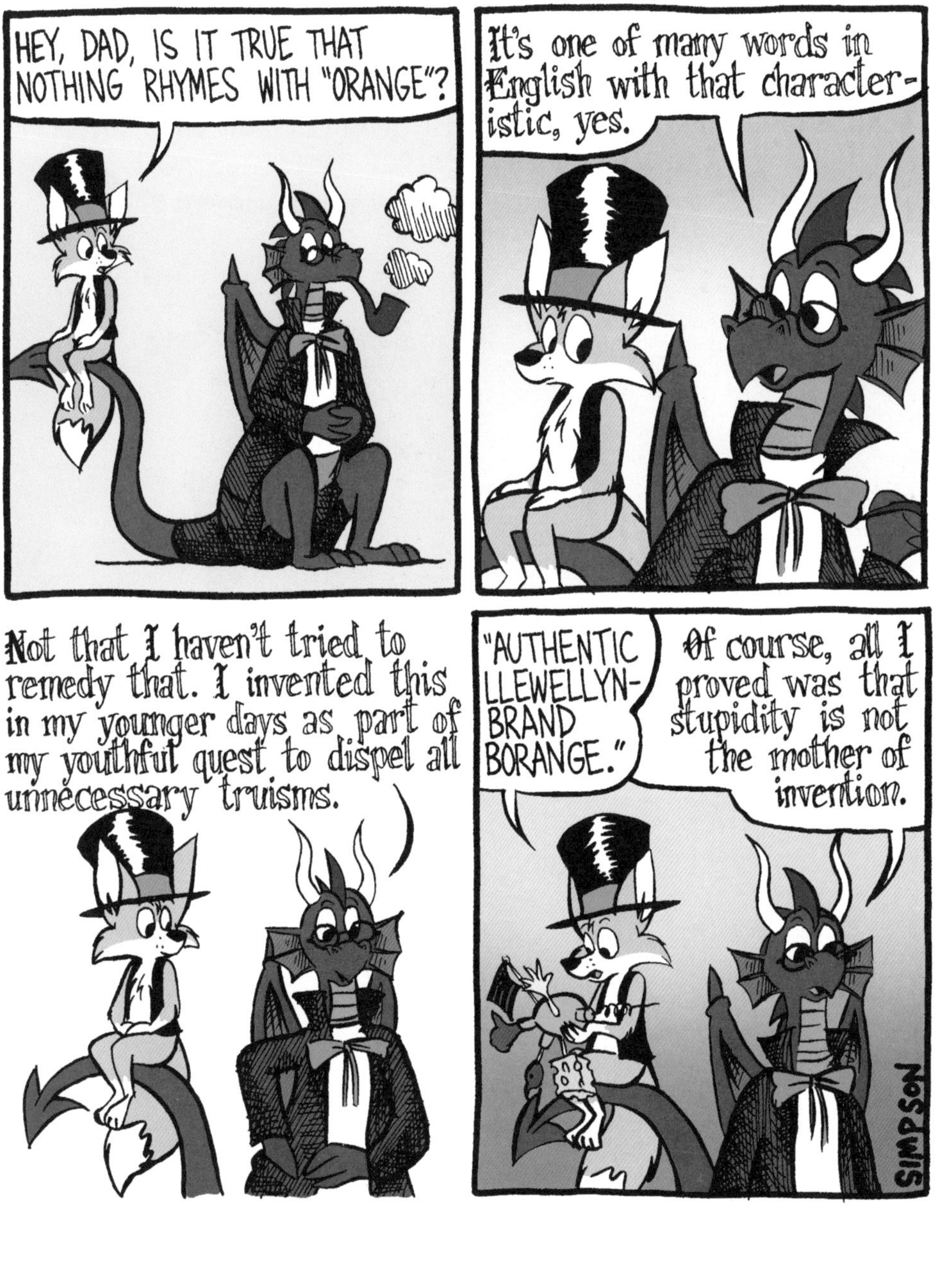
HEY, DAD, IS IT TRUE THAT NOTHING RHYMES WITH "ORANGE"?
It's one of many words in English with that character-istic, yes.
Not that I haven't tried to remedy that. I invented this in my younger days as part of my youthful quest to dispel all unnecessary truisms.
"AUTHENTIC LLEWELLYN-BRAND BORANGE."
Of course, all I proved was that stupidity is not the mother of invention.
SIMPSON

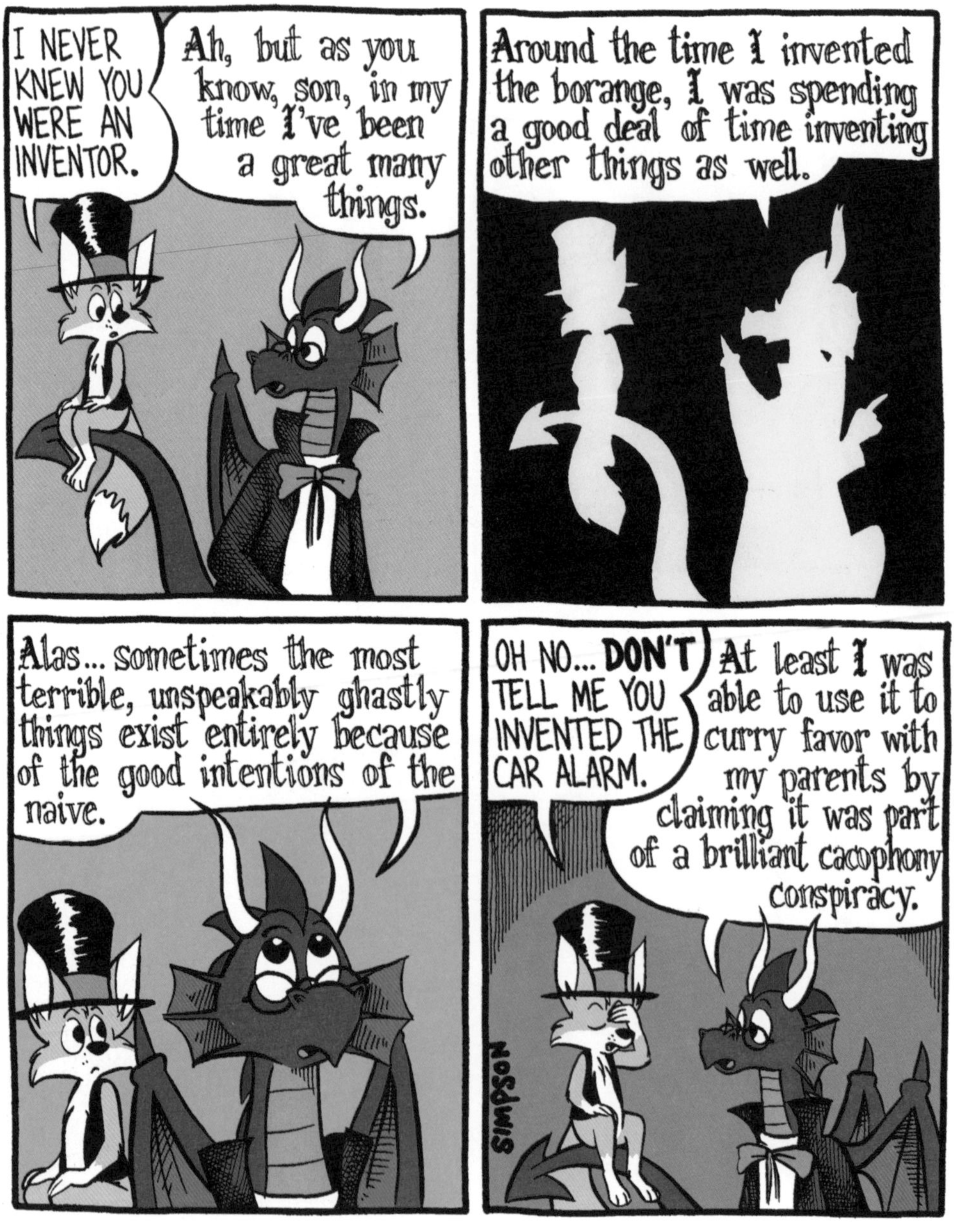
I NEVER KNEW YOU WERE AN INVENTOR.
Ah, but as you know, son, in my time I've been a great many things.
Around the time I invented the borange, I was spending a good deal of time inventing other things as well.
Alas... sometimes the most terrible, unspeakably ghastly things exist entirely because of the good intentions of the naive.
OH NO... DON'T TELL ME YOU INVENTED THE CAR ALARM.
At least I was able to use it to curry favor with my parents by claiming it was part of a brilliant cacophony conspiracy.
SIMPSON

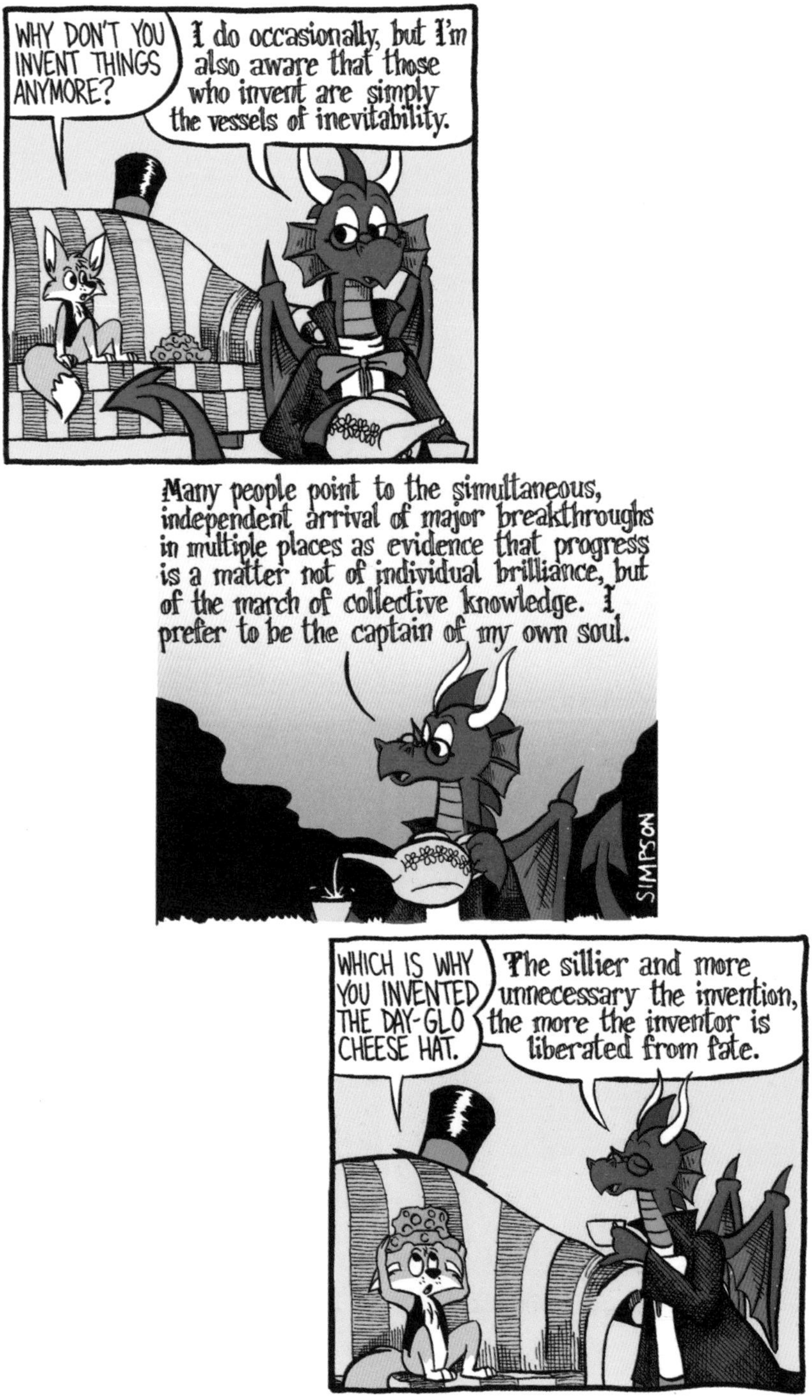
WHY DON'T YOU INVENT THINGS ANYMORE?
I do occasionally, but I'm also aware that those who invent are simply the vessels of inevitability.
Many people point to the simultaneous, independent arrival of major breakthroughs in multiple places as evidence that progress is a matter not of individual brilliance, but of the march of collective knowledge. I prefer to be the captain of my own soul.
SIMPSON
WHICH IS WHY YOU INVENTED THE DAY-GLO CHEESE HAT.
The sillier and more unnecessary the invention, the more the inventor is liberated from fate.

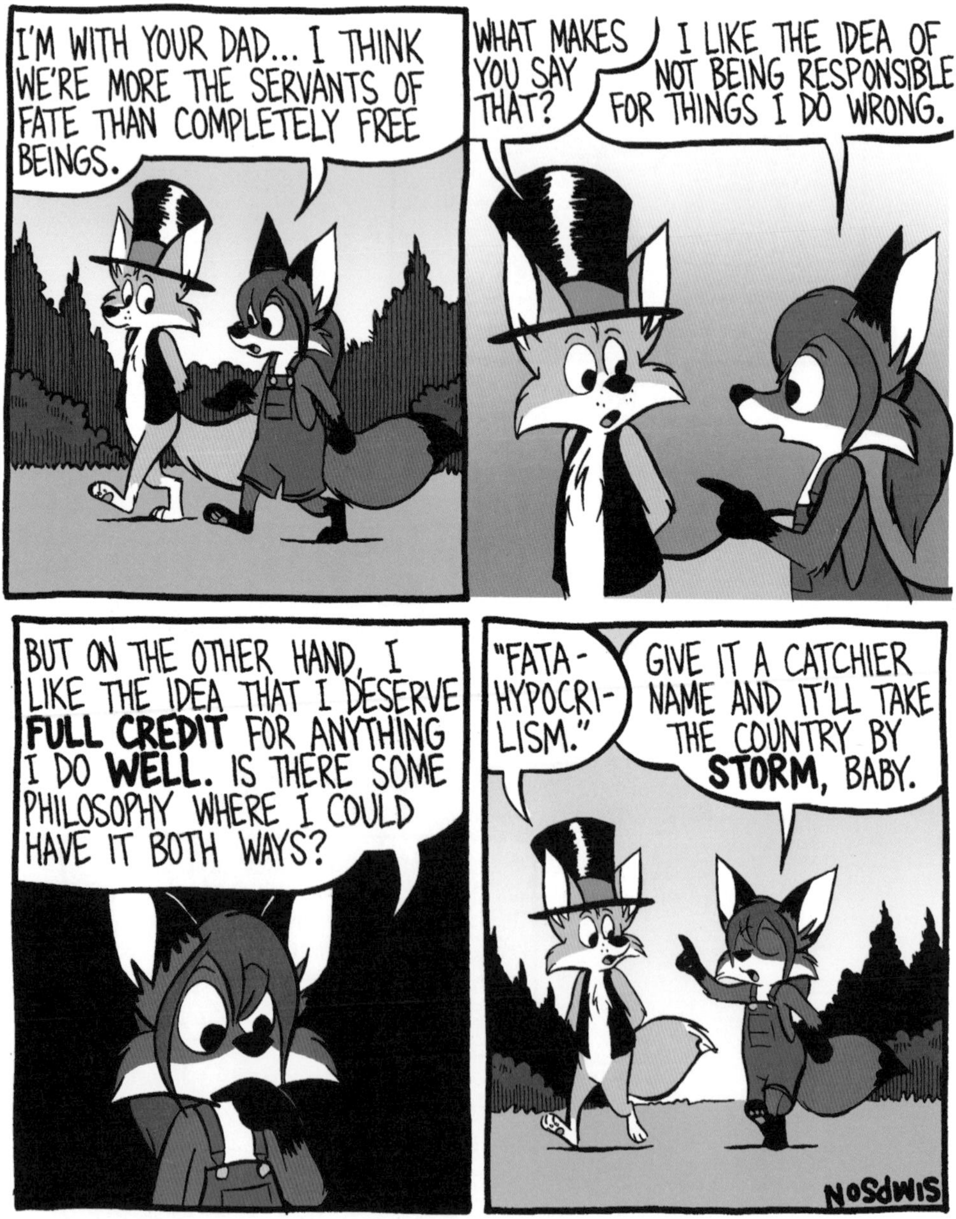

I'M WITH YOUR DAD... I THINK WE'RE MORE THE SERVANTS OF FATE THAN COMPLETELY FREE BEINGS.
WHAT MAKES YOU SAY THAT?
I LIKE THE IDEA OF NOT BEING RESPONSIBLE FOR THINGS I DO WRONG.
BUT ON THE OTHER HAND, I LIKE THE IDEA THAT I DESERVE **FULL CREDIT** FOR ANYTHING I DO **WELL.** IS THERE SOME PHILOSOPHY WHERE I COULD HAVE IT BOTH WAYS?
"FATA-HYPOCRI-LISM."
GIVE IT A CATCHIER NAME AND IT'LL TAKE THE COUNTRY BY **STORM**, BABY.
SIMPSON

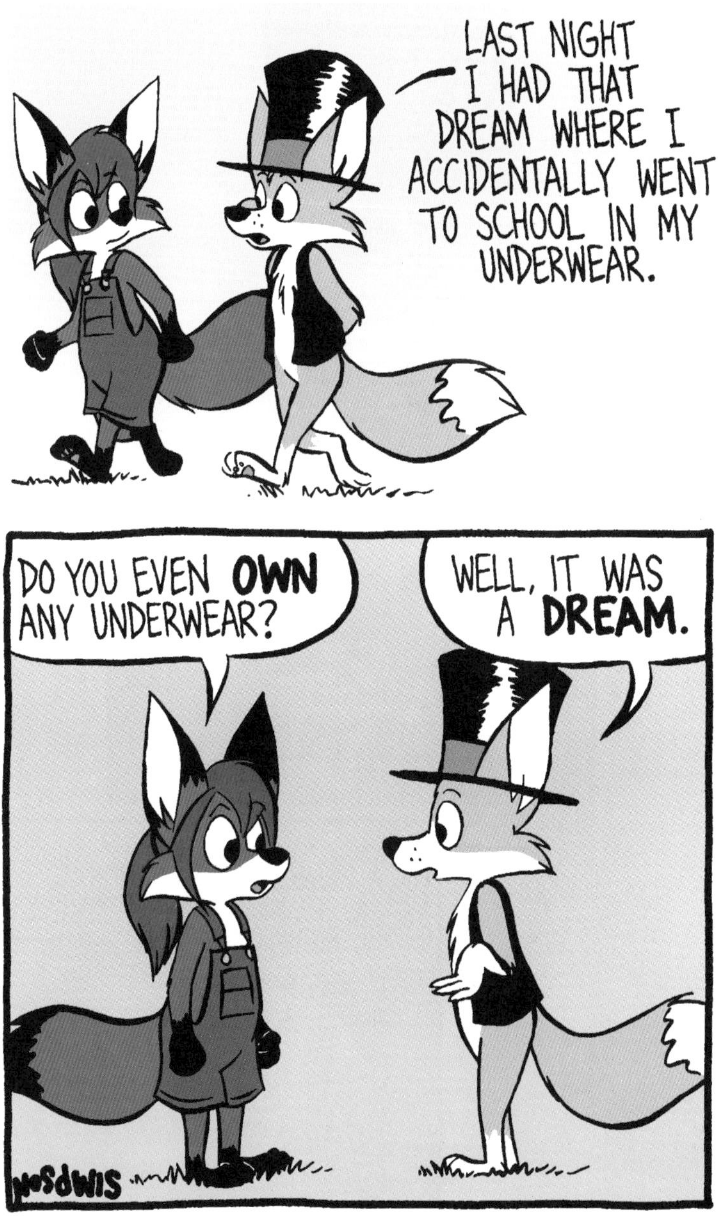
LAST NIGHT I HAD THAT DREAM WHERE I ACCIDENTALLY WENT TO SCHOOL IN MY UNDERWEAR.
DO YOU EVEN **OWN** ANY UNDERWEAR?
WELL, IT WAS A **DREAM.**
SIMPSON

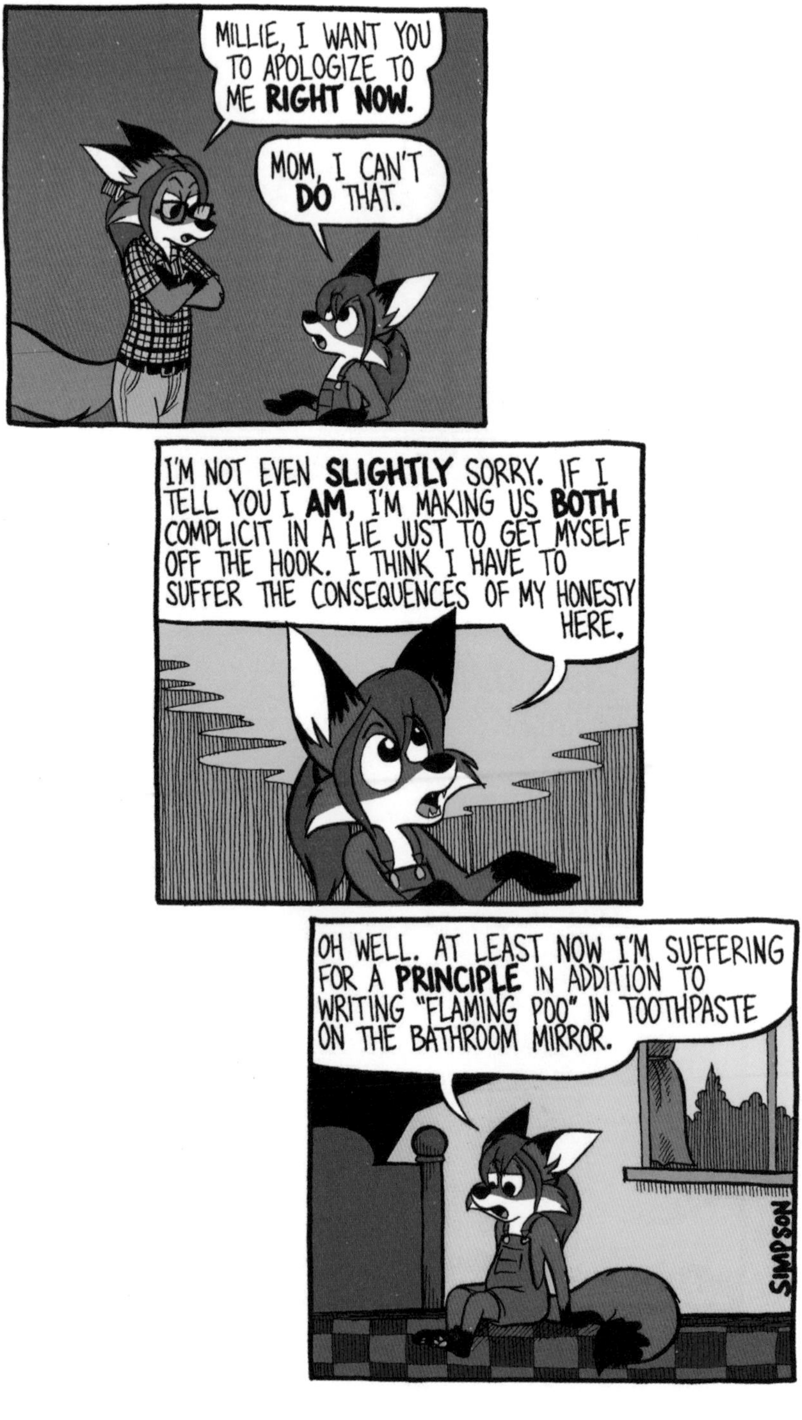
MILLIE, I WANT YOU TO APOLOGIZE TO ME **RIGHT NOW.**
MOM, I CAN'T **DO** THAT.
I'M NOT EVEN **SLIGHTLY** SORRY. IF I TELL YOU I **AM,** I'M MAKING US **BOTH** COMPLICIT IN A LIE JUST TO GET MYSELF OFF THE HOOK. I THINK I HAVE TO SUFFER THE CONSEQUENCES OF MY HONESTY HERE.
OH WELL. AT LEAST NOW I'M SUFFERING FOR A **PRINCIPLE** IN ADDITION TO WRITING "FLAMING POO" IN TOOTHPASTE ON THE BATHROOM MIRROR.
SIMPSON

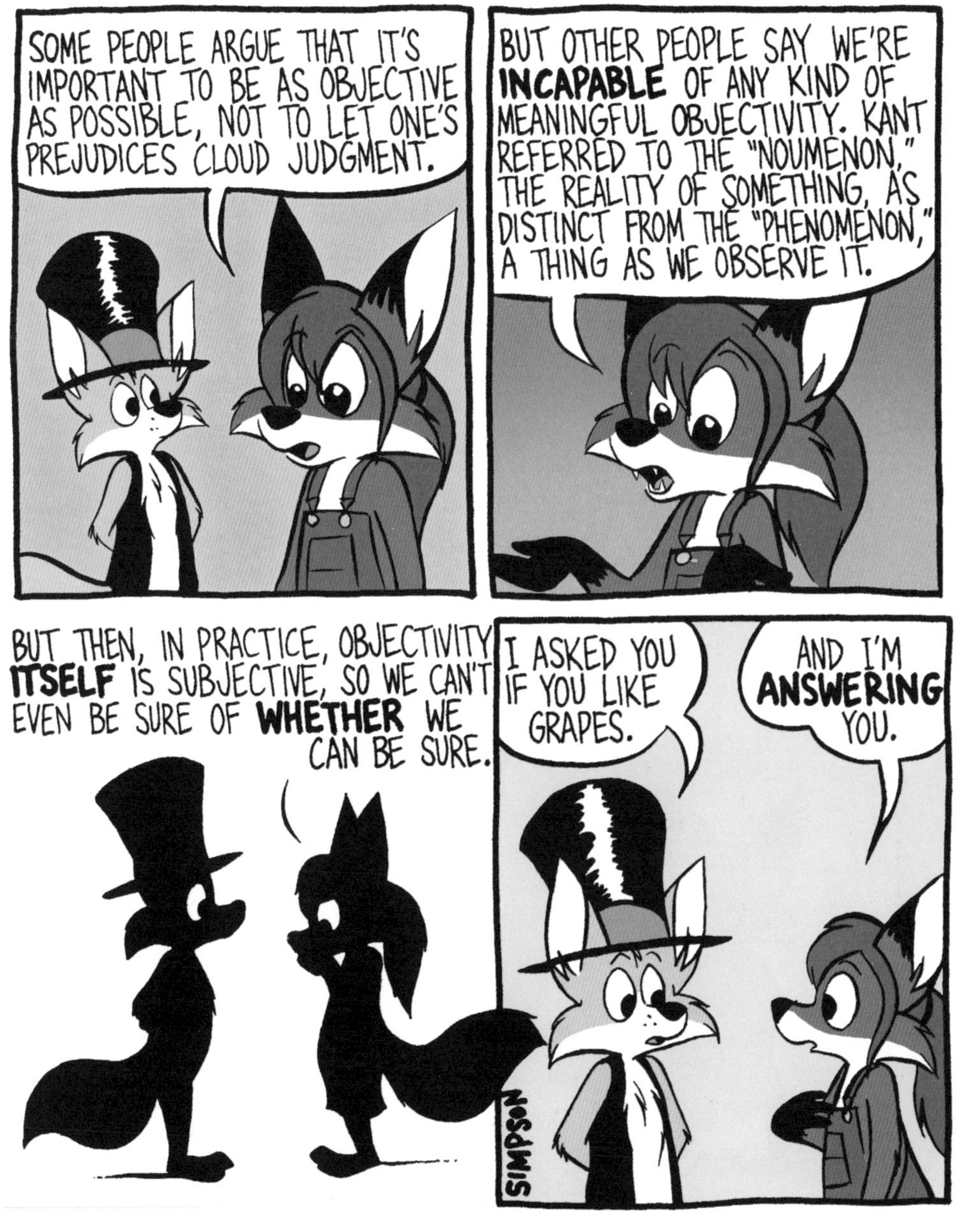
SOME PEOPLE ARGUE THAT IT'S IMPORTANT TO BE AS OBJECTIVE AS POSSIBLE, NOT TO LET ONE'S PREJUDICES CLOUD JUDGMENT.
BUT OTHER PEOPLE SAY WE'RE **INCAPABLE** OF ANY KIND OF MEANINGFUL OBJECTIVITY. KANT REFERRED TO THE "NOUMENON," THE REALITY OF SOMETHING, AS DISTINCT FROM THE "PHENOMENON," A THING AS WE OBSERVE IT.
BUT THEN, IN PRACTICE, OBJECTIVITY **ITSELF** IS SUBJECTIVE, SO WE CAN'T EVEN BE SURE OF **WHETHER** WE CAN BE SURE.
I ASKED YOU IF YOU LIKE GRAPES.
AND I'M **ANSWERING** YOU.
SIMPSON

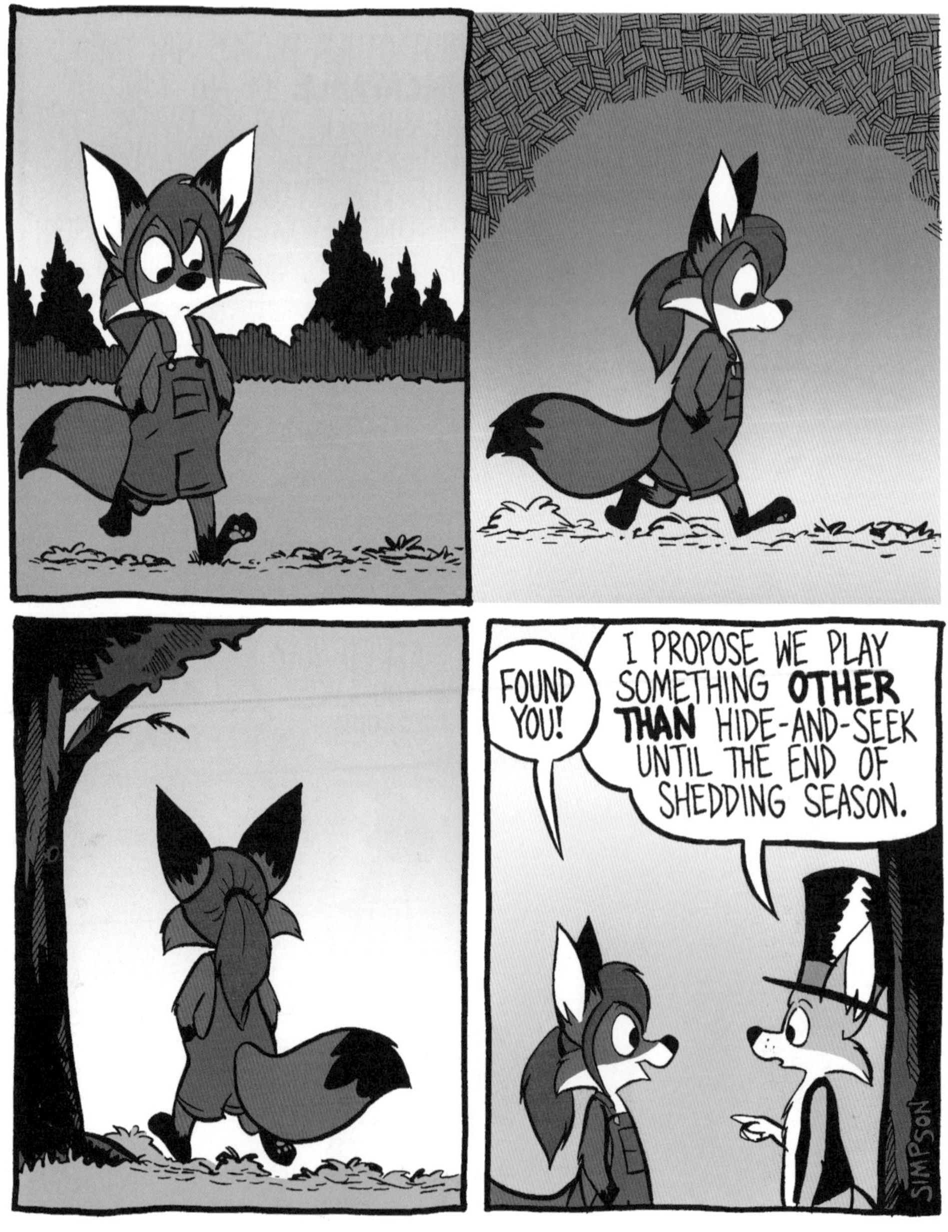
FOUND YOU!
I PROPOSE WE PLAY SOMETHING **OTHER THAN** HIDE-AND-SEEK UNTIL THE END OF SHEDDING SEASON.
SIMPSON

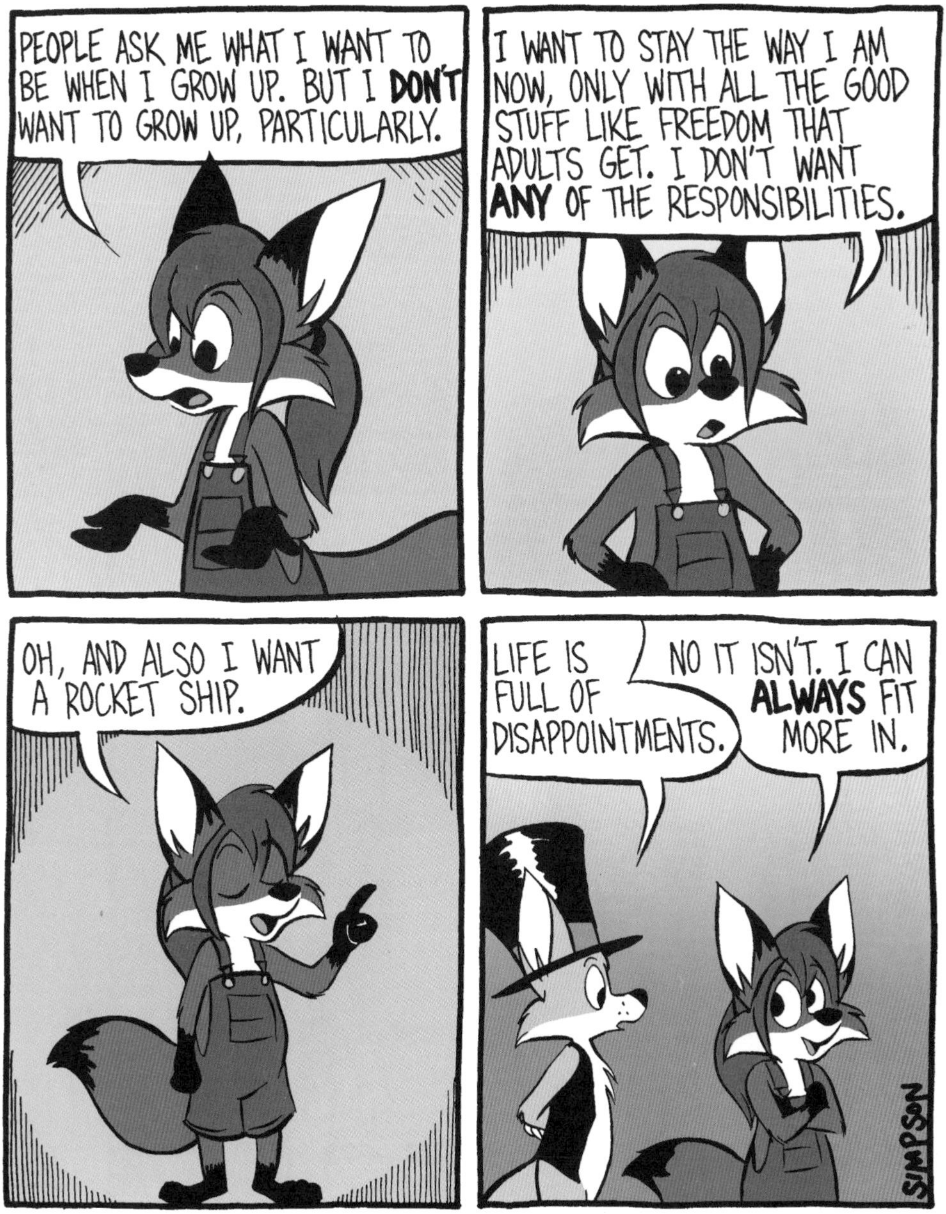
PEOPLE ASK ME WHAT I WANT TO BE WHEN I GROW UP. BUT I **DON'T** WANT TO GROW UP, PARTICULARLY.
I WANT TO STAY THE WAY I AM NOW, ONLY WITH ALL THE GOOD STUFF LIKE FREEDOM THAT ADULTS GET. I DON'T WANT **ANY** OF THE RESPONSIBILITIES.
OH, AND ALSO I WANT A ROCKET SHIP.
LIFE IS FULL OF DISAPPOINTMENTS.
NO IT ISN'T. I CAN **ALWAYS** FIT MORE IN.
SIMPSON

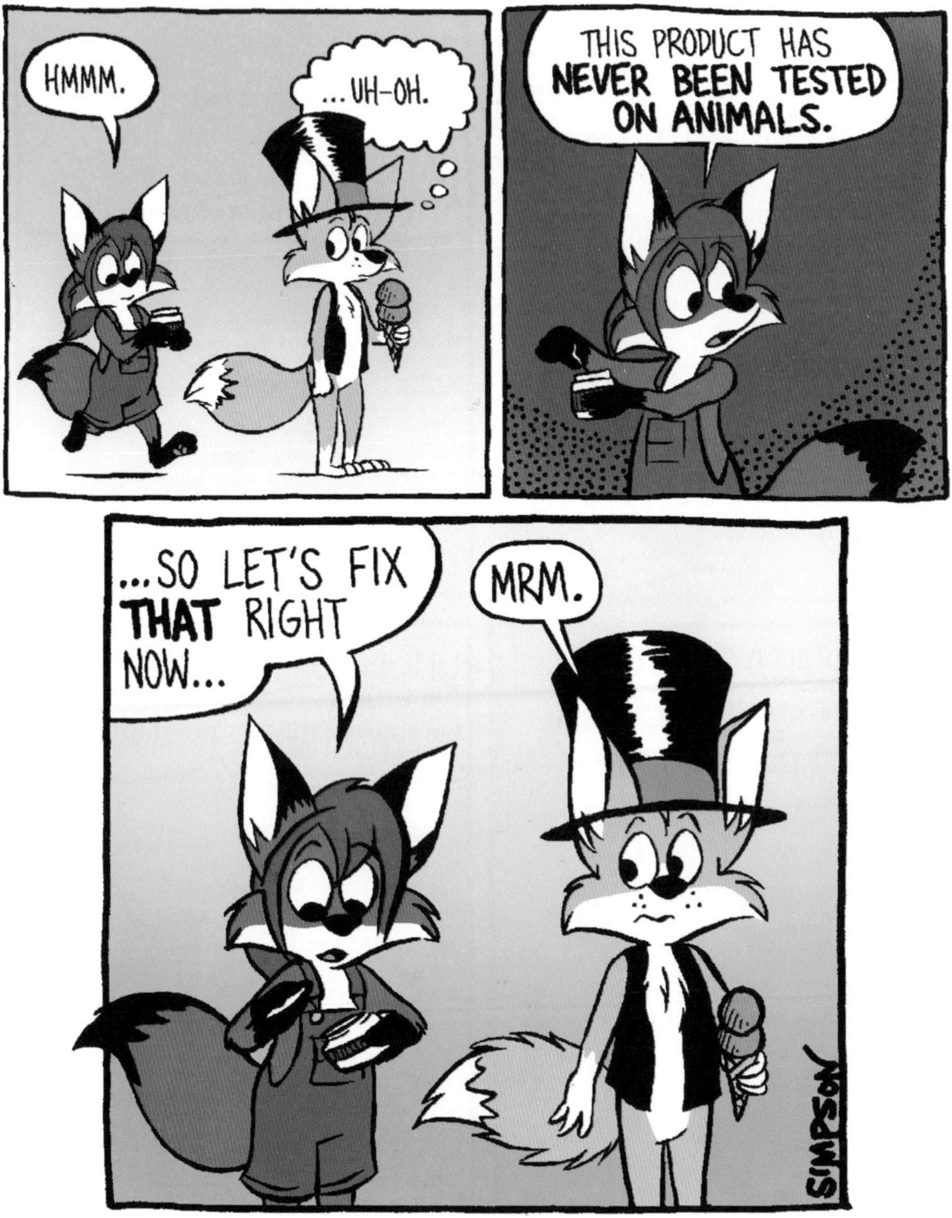
HMMM.
...UH-OH.
THIS PRODUCT HAS NEVER BEEN TESTED ON ANIMALS.
...SO LET'S FIX THAT RIGHT NOW...
MRM.
SIMPSON

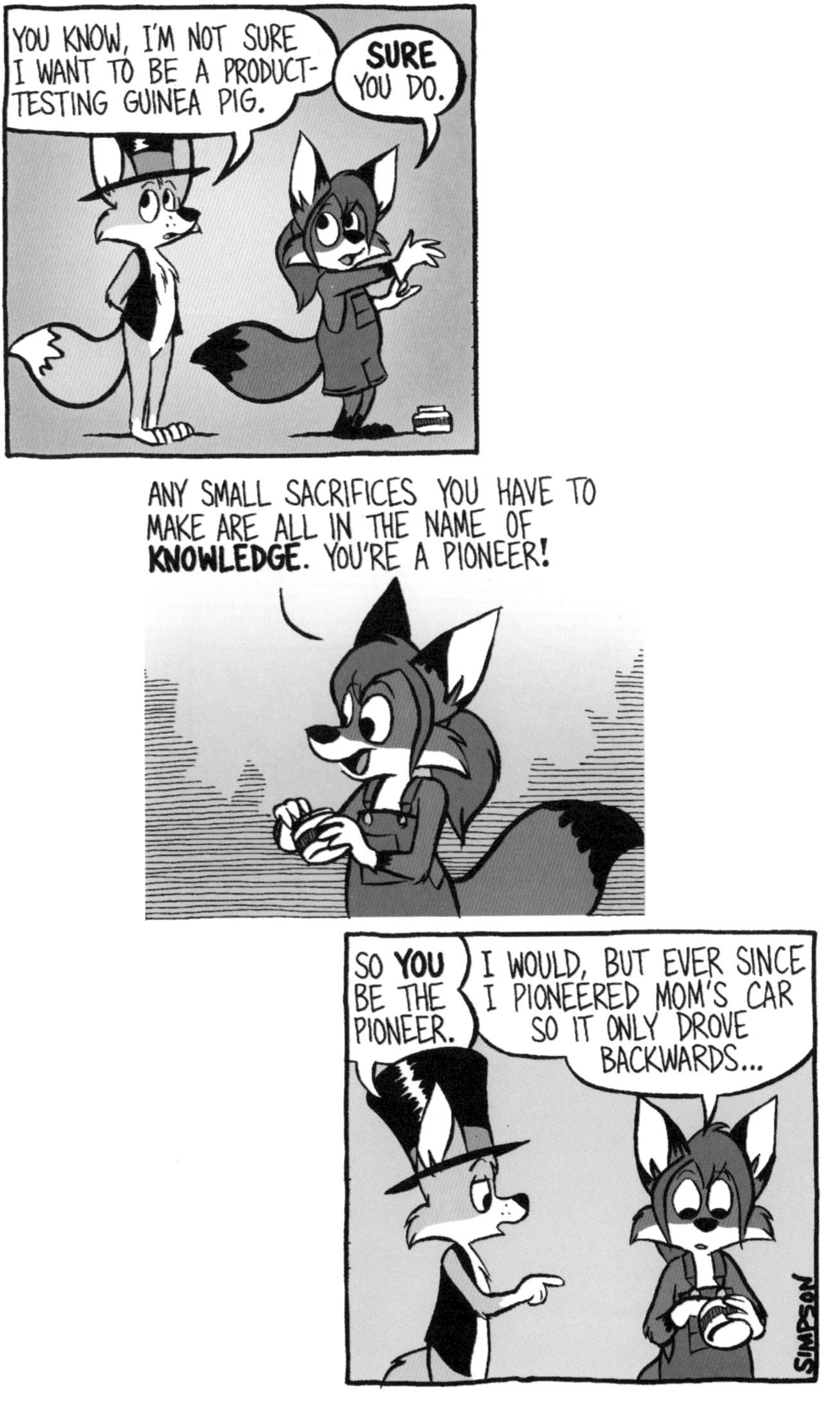
YOU KNOW, I'M NOT SURE I WANT TO BE A PRODUCT-TESTING GUINEA PIG.
SURE YOU DO.
ANY SMALL SACRIFICES YOU HAVE TO MAKE ARE ALL IN THE NAME OF KNOWLEDGE. YOU'RE A PIONEER!
SO YOU BE THE PIONEER.
I WOULD, BUT EVER SINCE I PIONEERED MOM'S CAR SO IT ONLY DROVE BACKWARDS...
SIMPSON

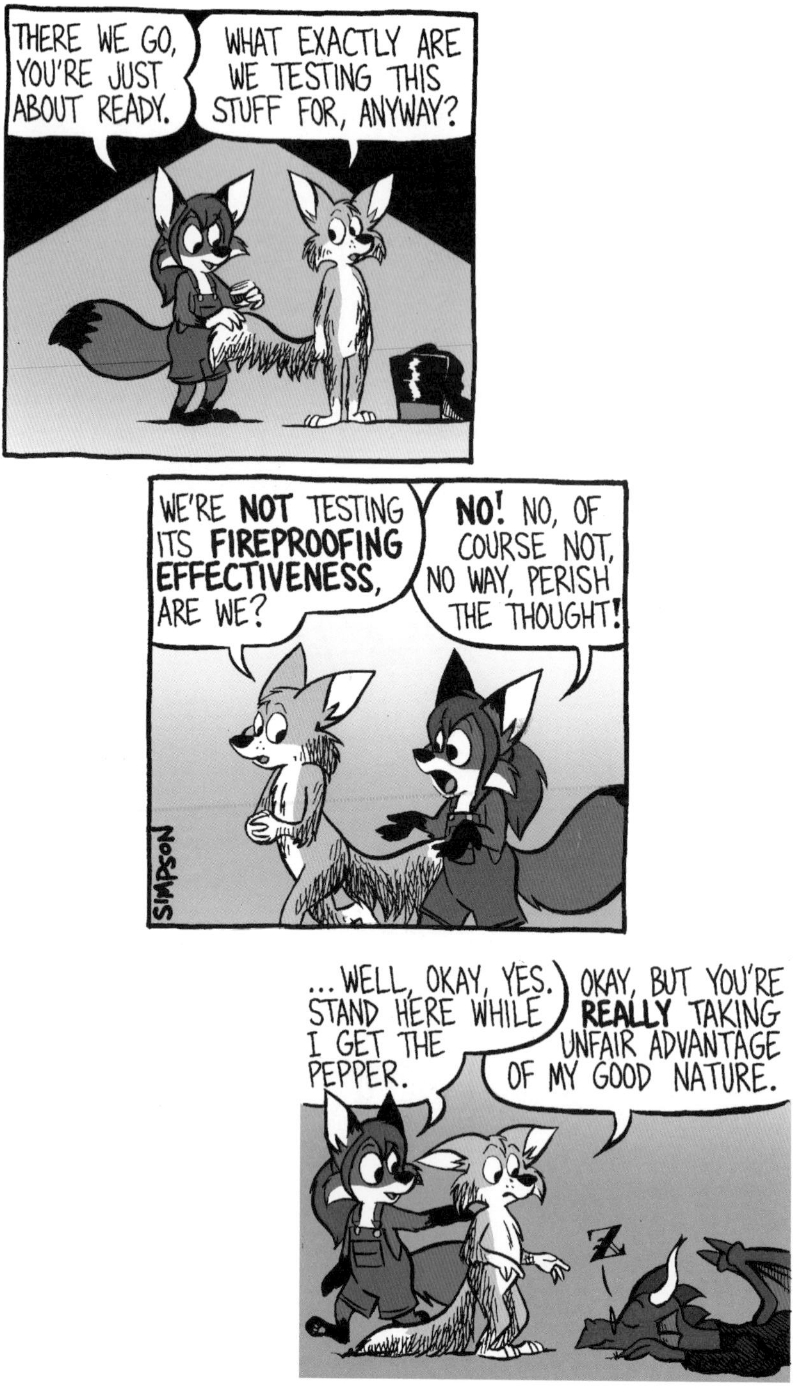
THERE WE GO, YOU'RE JUST ABOUT READY.
WHAT EXACTLY ARE WE TESTING THIS STUFF FOR, ANYWAY?
WE'RE **NOT** TESTING ITS **FIREPROOFING EFFECTIVENESS**, ARE WE?
NO! NO, OF COURSE NOT, NO WAY, PERISH THE THOUGHT!
SIMPSON
...WELL, OKAY, YES. STAND HERE WHILE I GET THE PEPPER.
OKAY, BUT YOU'RE **REALLY** TAKING UNFAIR ADVANTAGE OF MY GOOD NATURE.
Z

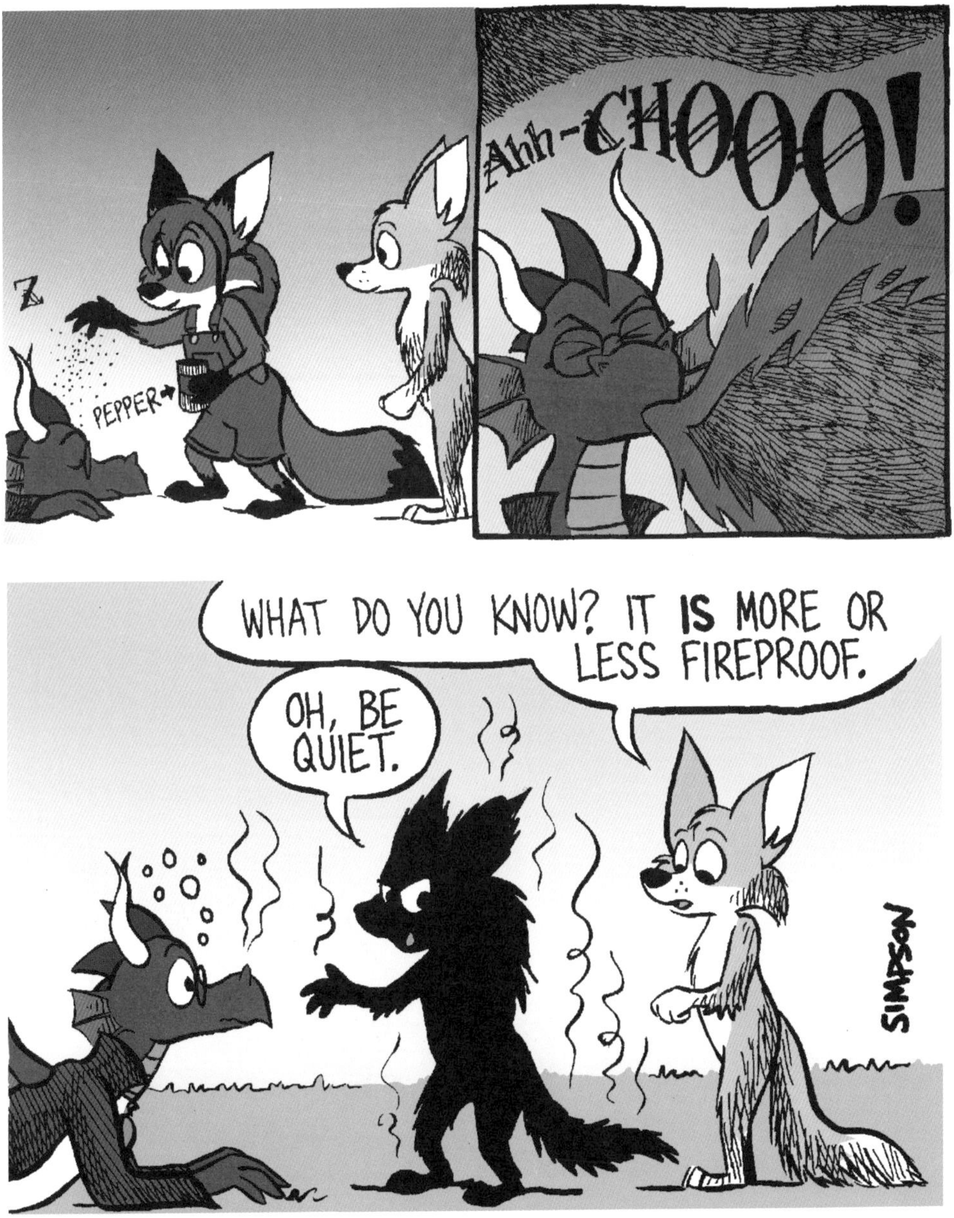
Z
PEPPER
Ahh-CHOOO!
WHAT DO YOU KNOW? IT **IS** MORE OR LESS FIREPROOF.
OH, BE QUIET.
SIMPSON

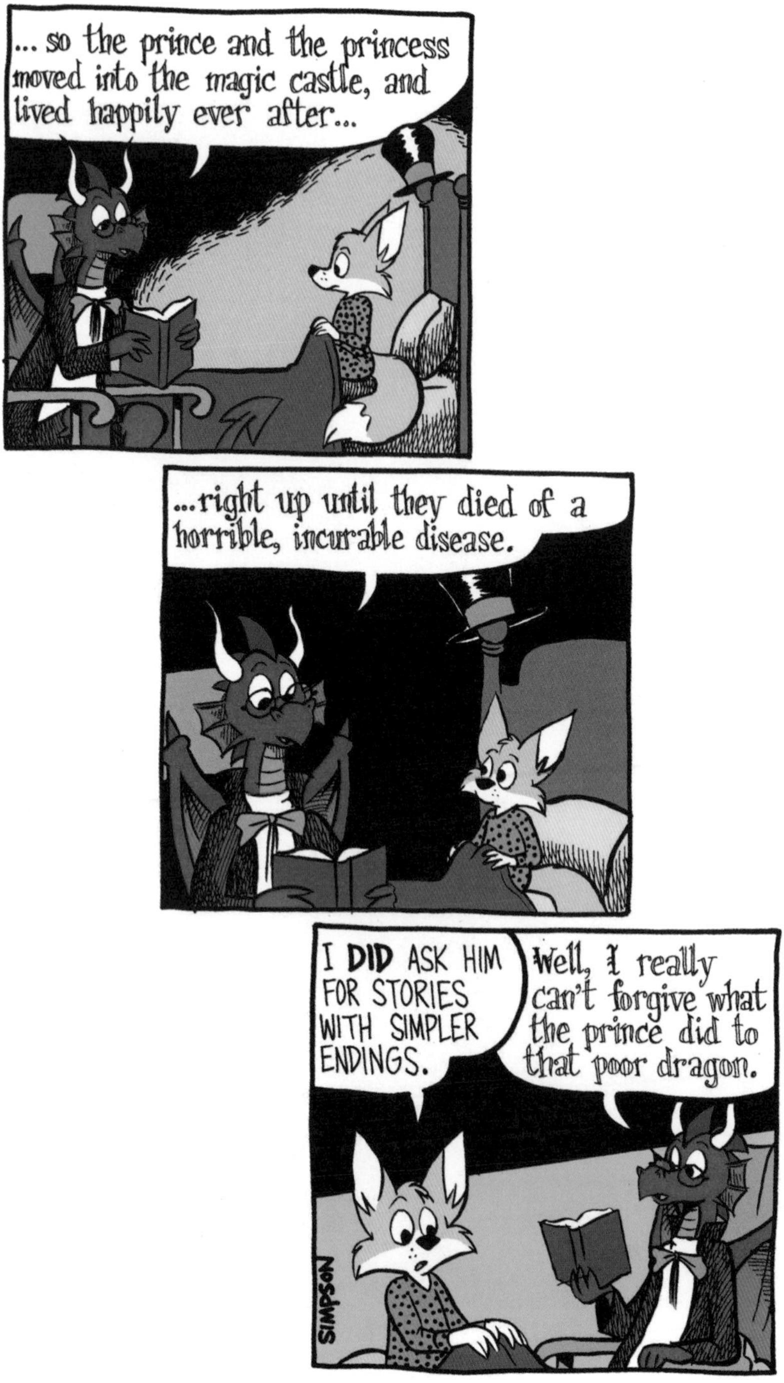

... so the prince and the princess moved into the magic castle, and lived happily ever after...
...right up until they died of a horrible, incurable disease.
I DID ASK HIM FOR STORIES WITH SIMPLER ENDINGS.
Well, I really can't forgive what the prince did to that poor dragon.
SIMPSON

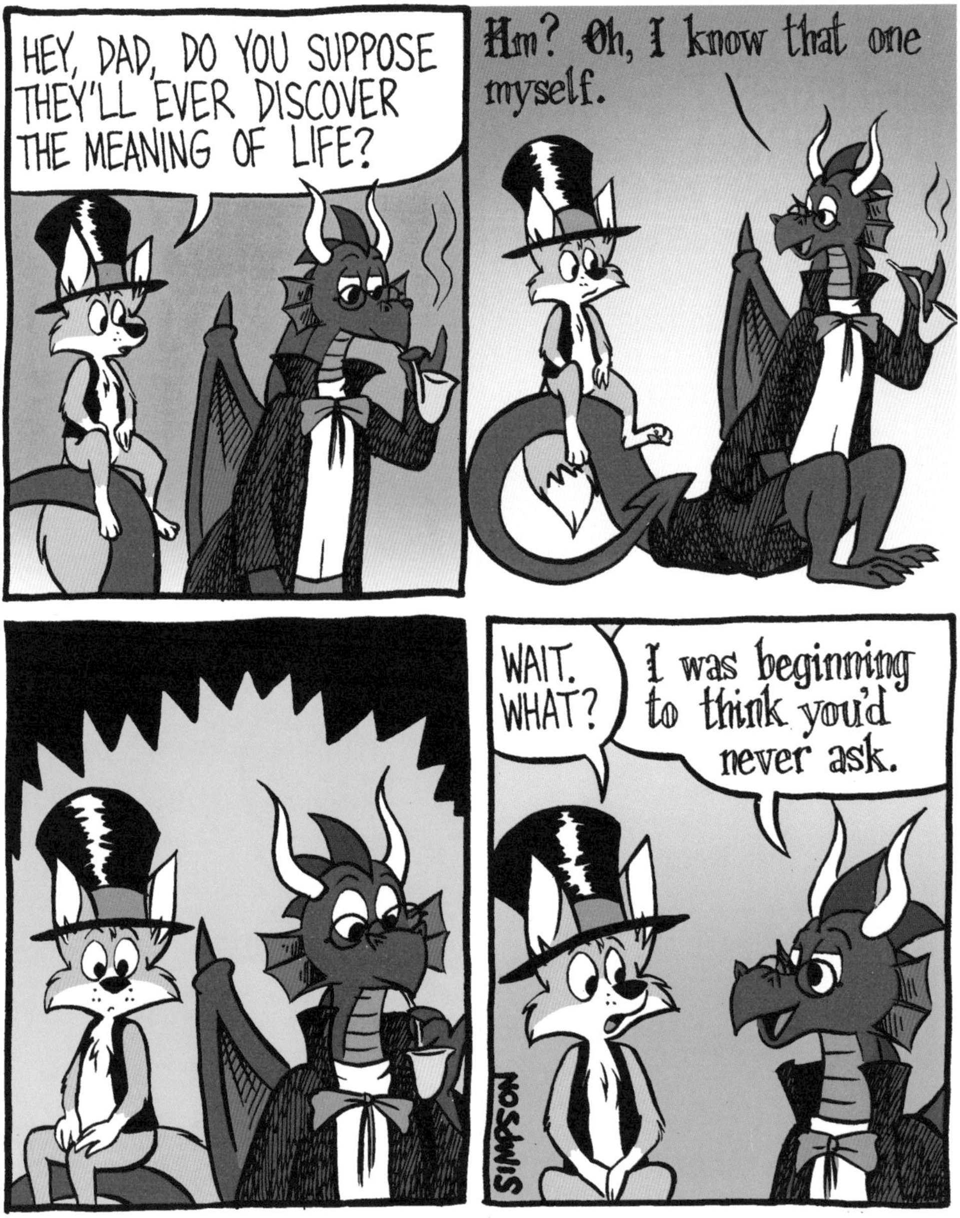
HEY, DAD, DO YOU SUPPOSE THEY'LL EVER DISCOVER THE MEANING OF LIFE?
Hm? Oh, I know that one myself.
WAIT. WHAT?
I was beginning to think you'd never ask.
SIMPSON

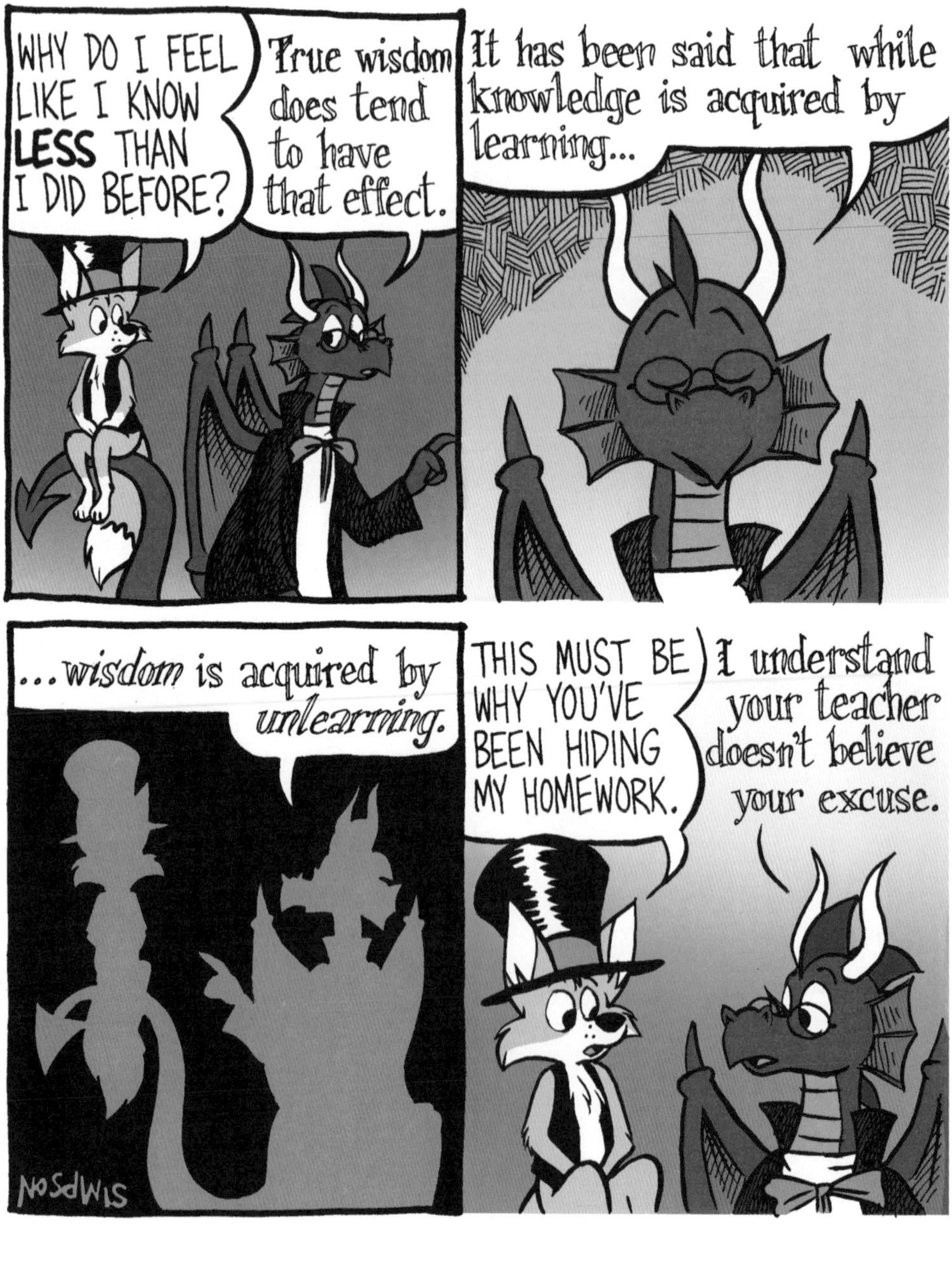
WHY DO I FEEL LIKE I KNOW **LESS** THAN I DID BEFORE?
True wisdom does tend to have that effect.
It has been said that while knowledge is acquired by learning...
...*wisdom* is acquired by *unlearning.*
THIS MUST BE WHY YOU'VE BEEN HIDING MY HOMEWORK.
I understand your teacher doesn't believe your excuse.
SIMPSON

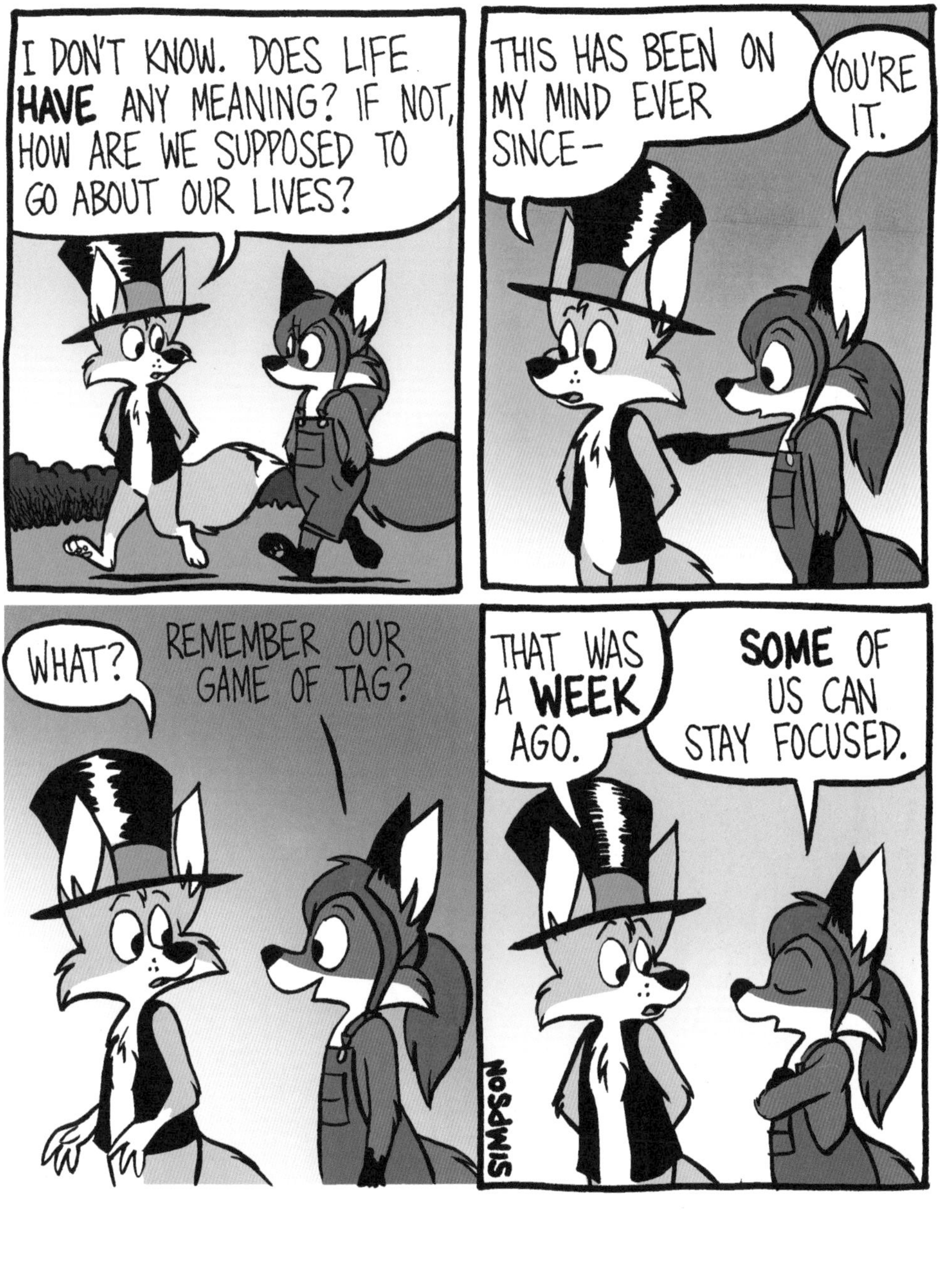
I DON'T KNOW. DOES LIFE **HAVE** ANY MEANING? IF NOT, HOW ARE WE SUPPOSED TO GO ABOUT OUR LIVES?
THIS HAS BEEN ON MY MIND EVER SINCE–
YOU'RE IT.
WHAT?
REMEMBER OUR GAME OF TAG?
THAT WAS A **WEEK** AGO.
SOME OF US CAN STAY FOCUSED.
SIMPSON

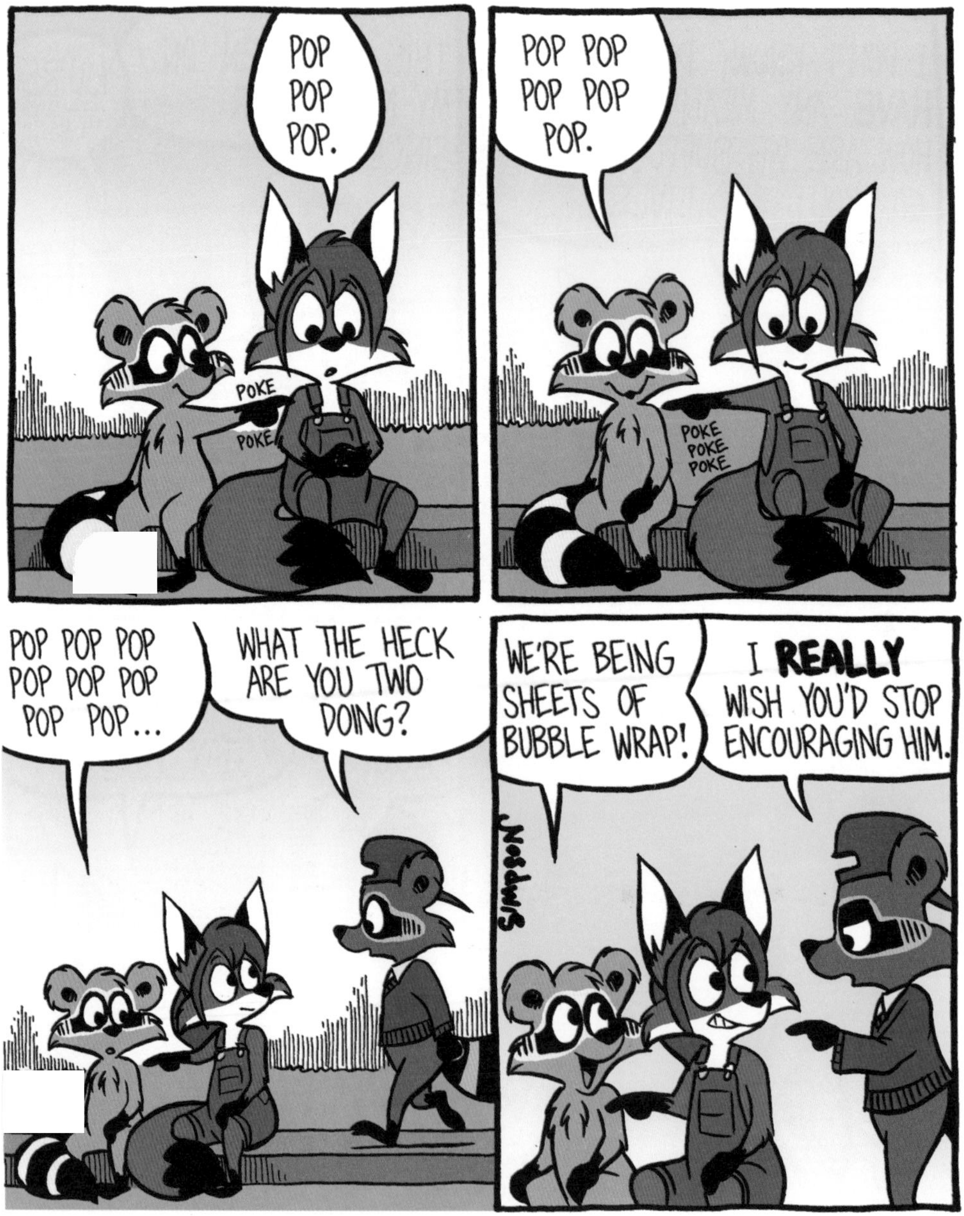
POP POP POP.
POKE
POKE
POP POP POP POP POP.
POKE POKE POKE
POP POP POP POP POP POP POP POP...
WHAT THE HECK ARE YOU TWO DOING?
WE'RE BEING SHEETS OF BUBBLE WRAP!
I **REALLY** WISH YOU'D STOP ENCOURAGING HIM.

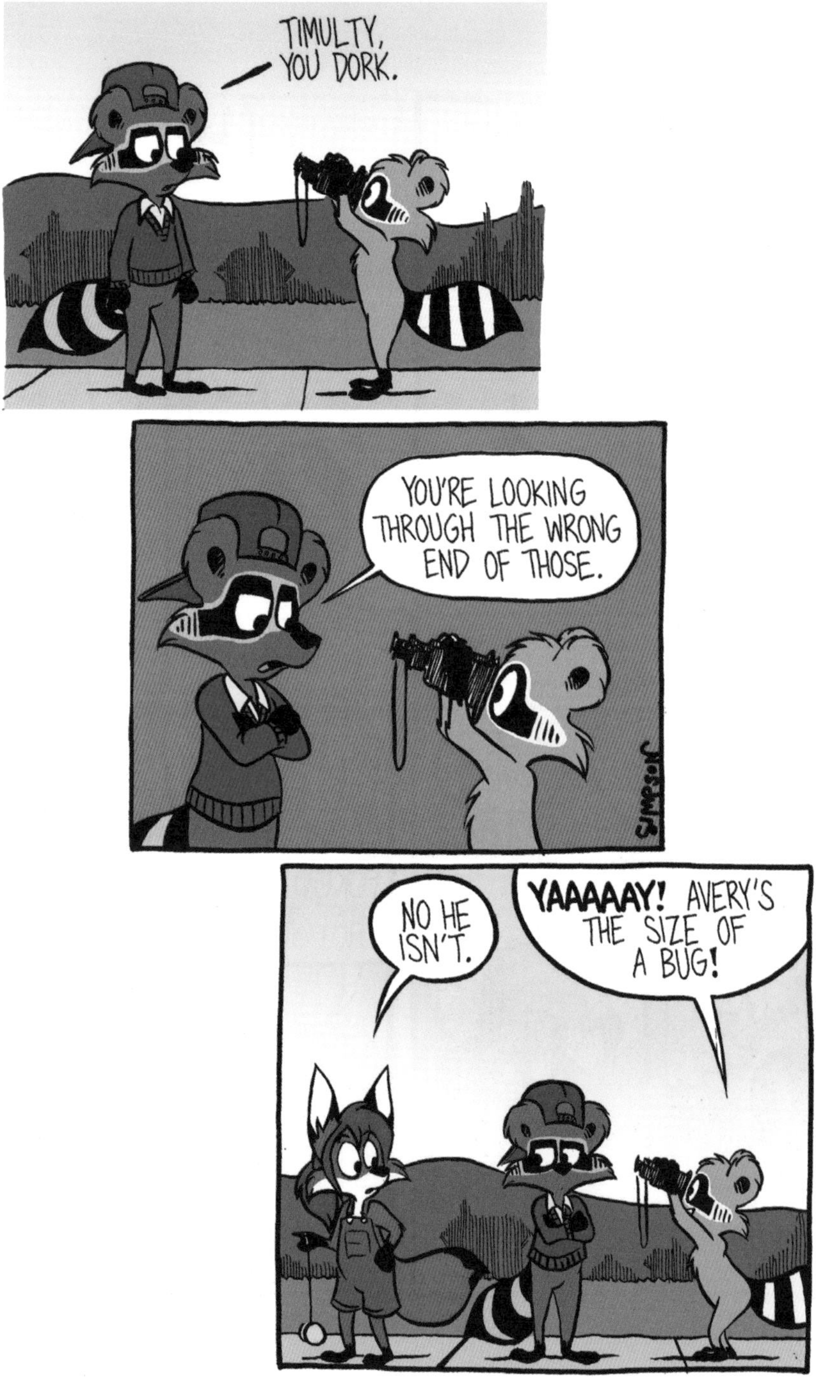
TIMULTY, YOU DORK.
YOU'RE LOOKING THROUGH THE WRONG END OF THOSE.
SIMPSON
YAAAAAY! AVERY'S THE SIZE OF A BUG!
NO HE ISN'T.

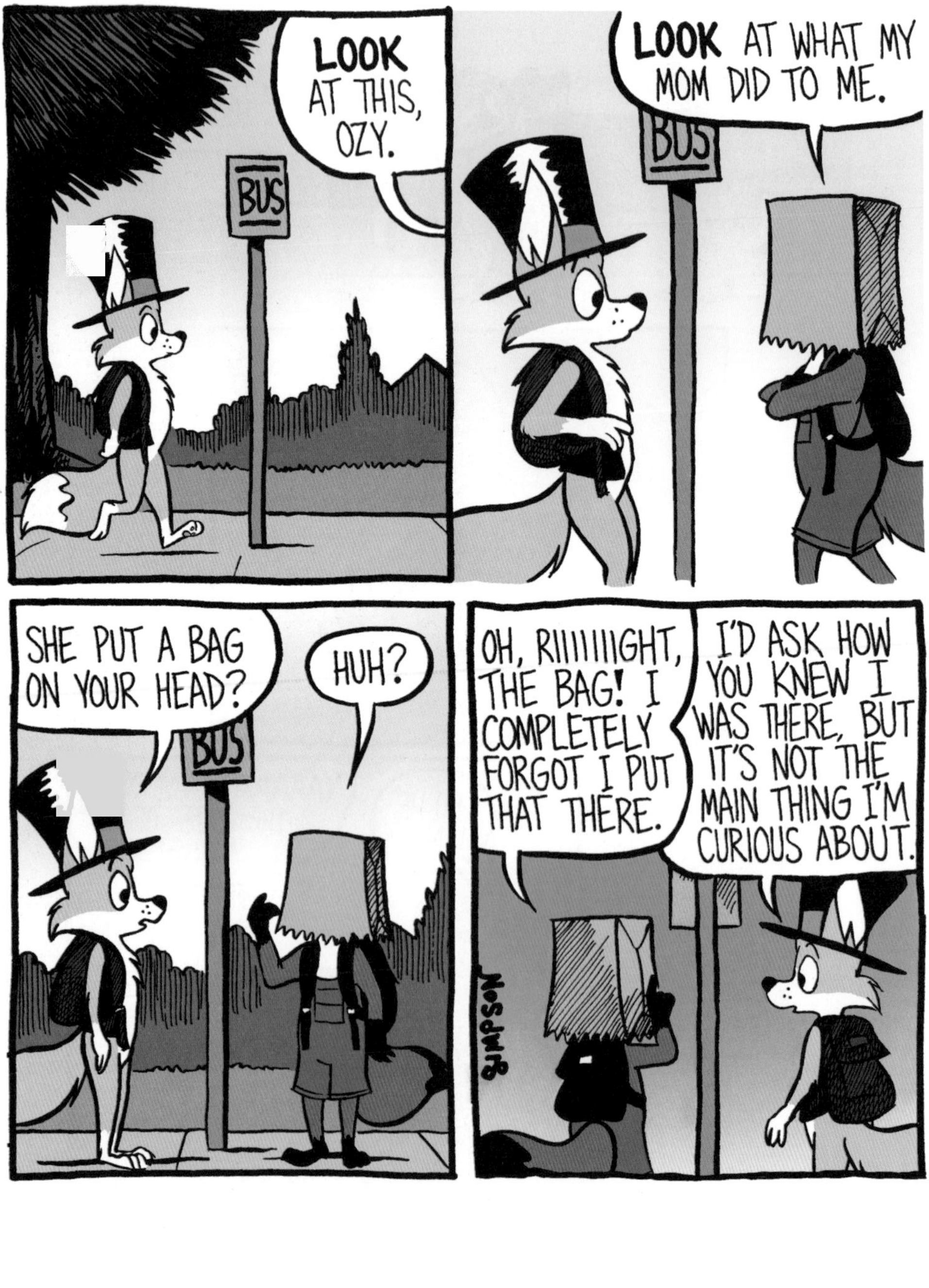
LOOK AT THIS, OZY.
BUS
LOOK AT WHAT MY MOM DID TO ME.
SHE PUT A BAG ON YOUR HEAD?
HUH?
OH, RIIIIIIIGHT, THE BAG! I COMPLETELY FORGOT I PUT THAT THERE.
I'D ASK HOW YOU KNEW I WAS THERE, BUT IT'S NOT THE MAIN THING I'M CURIOUS ABOUT.
SIMPSON

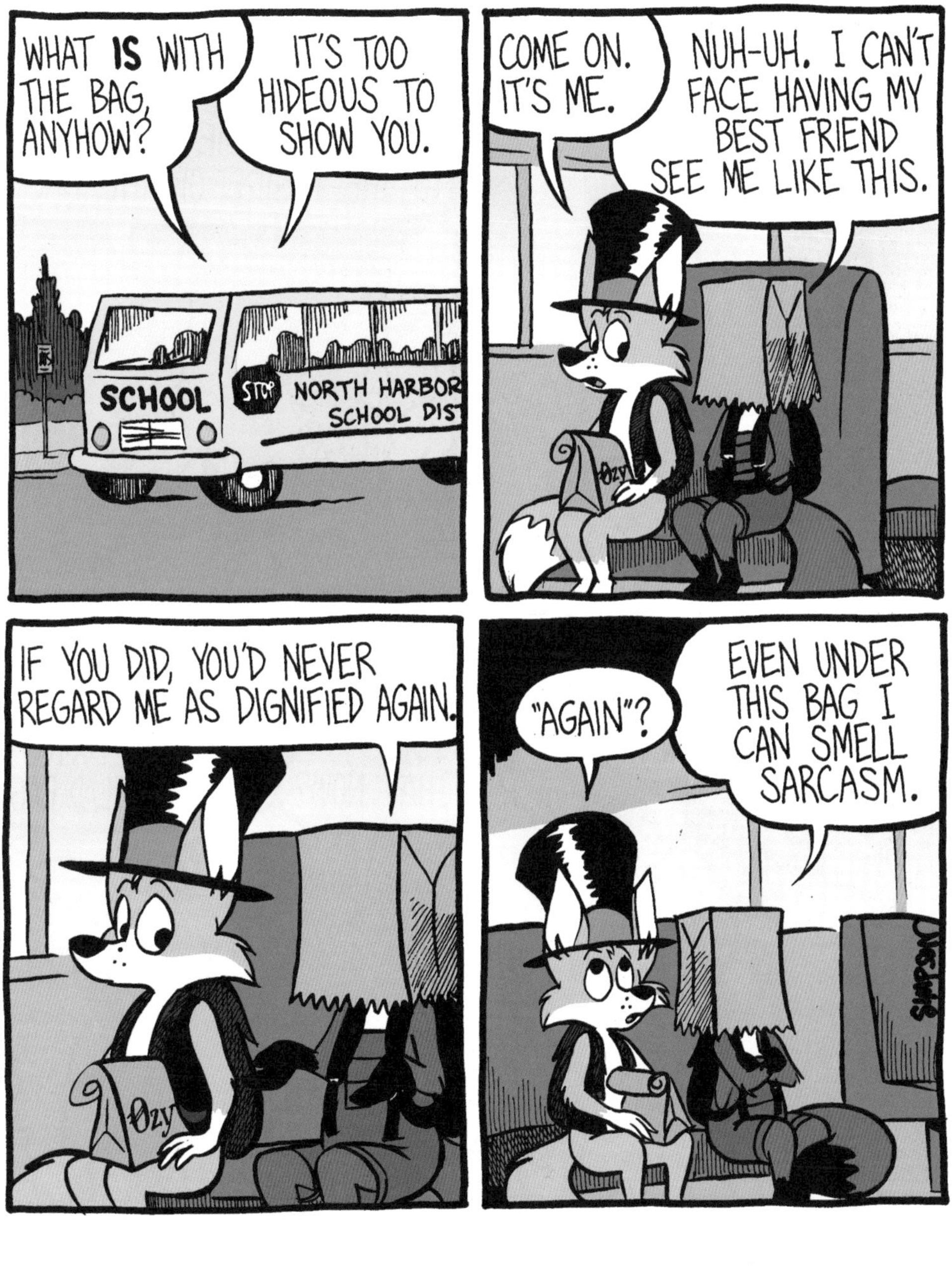
WHAT IS WITH THE BAG, ANYHOW?
IT'S TOO HIDEOUS TO SHOW YOU.
SCHOOL
STOP
NORTH HARBOR SCHOOL DIST
COME ON. IT'S ME.
NUH-UH. I CAN'T FACE HAVING MY BEST FRIEND SEE ME LIKE THIS.
IF YOU DID, YOU'D NEVER REGARD ME AS DIGNIFIED AGAIN.
"AGAIN"?
EVEN UNDER THIS BAG I CAN SMELL SARCASM.
SIMPSON

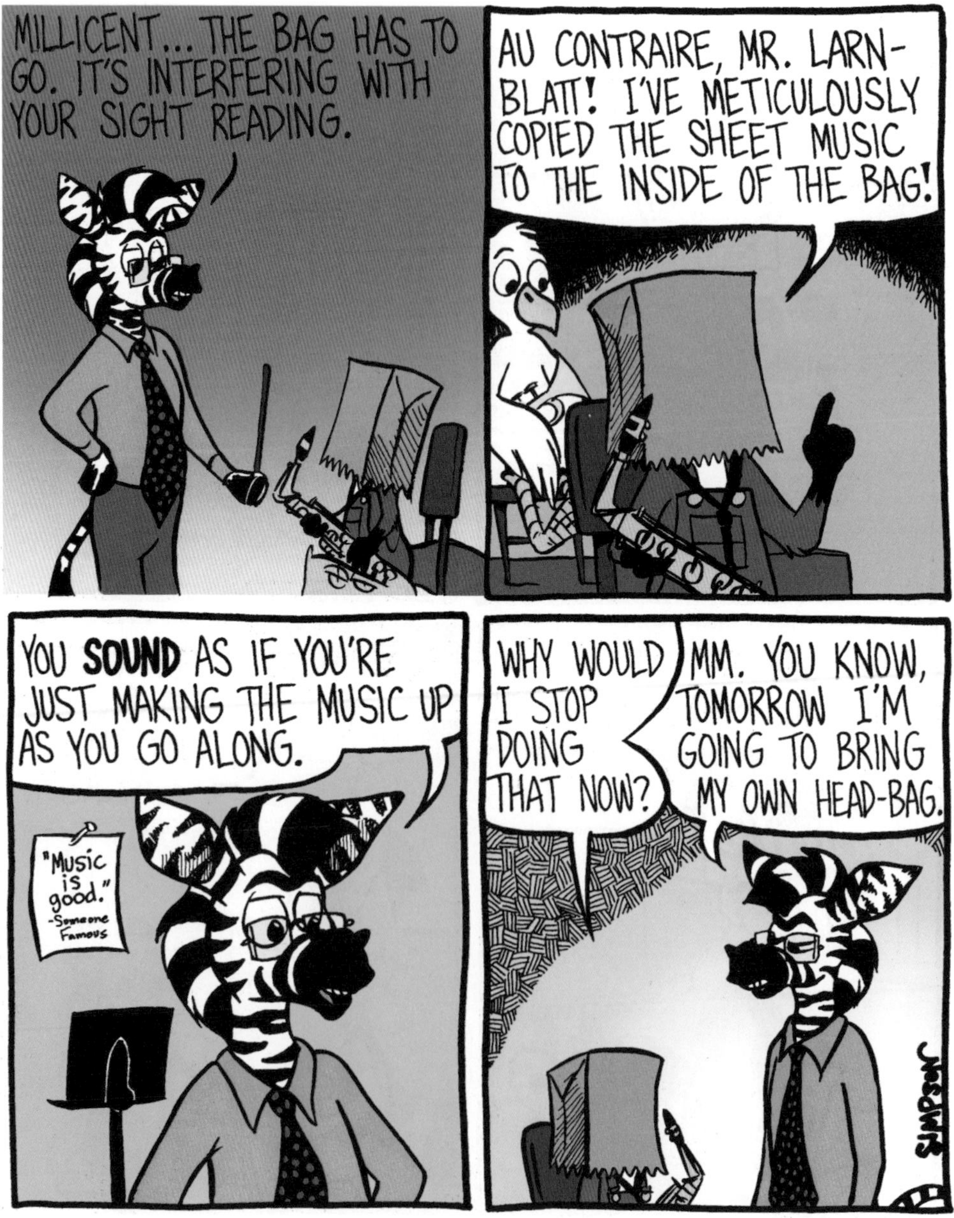
MILLICENT... THE BAG HAS TO GO. IT'S INTERFERING WITH YOUR SIGHT READING.
AU CONTRAIRE, MR. LARN-BLATT! I'VE METICULOUSLY COPIED THE SHEET MUSIC TO THE INSIDE OF THE BAG!
YOU **SOUND** AS IF YOU'RE JUST MAKING THE MUSIC UP AS YOU GO ALONG.
"Music is good." -Someone Famous
WHY WOULD I STOP DOING THAT NOW?
MM. YOU KNOW, TOMORROW I'M GOING TO BRING MY OWN HEAD-BAG.
SIMPSON

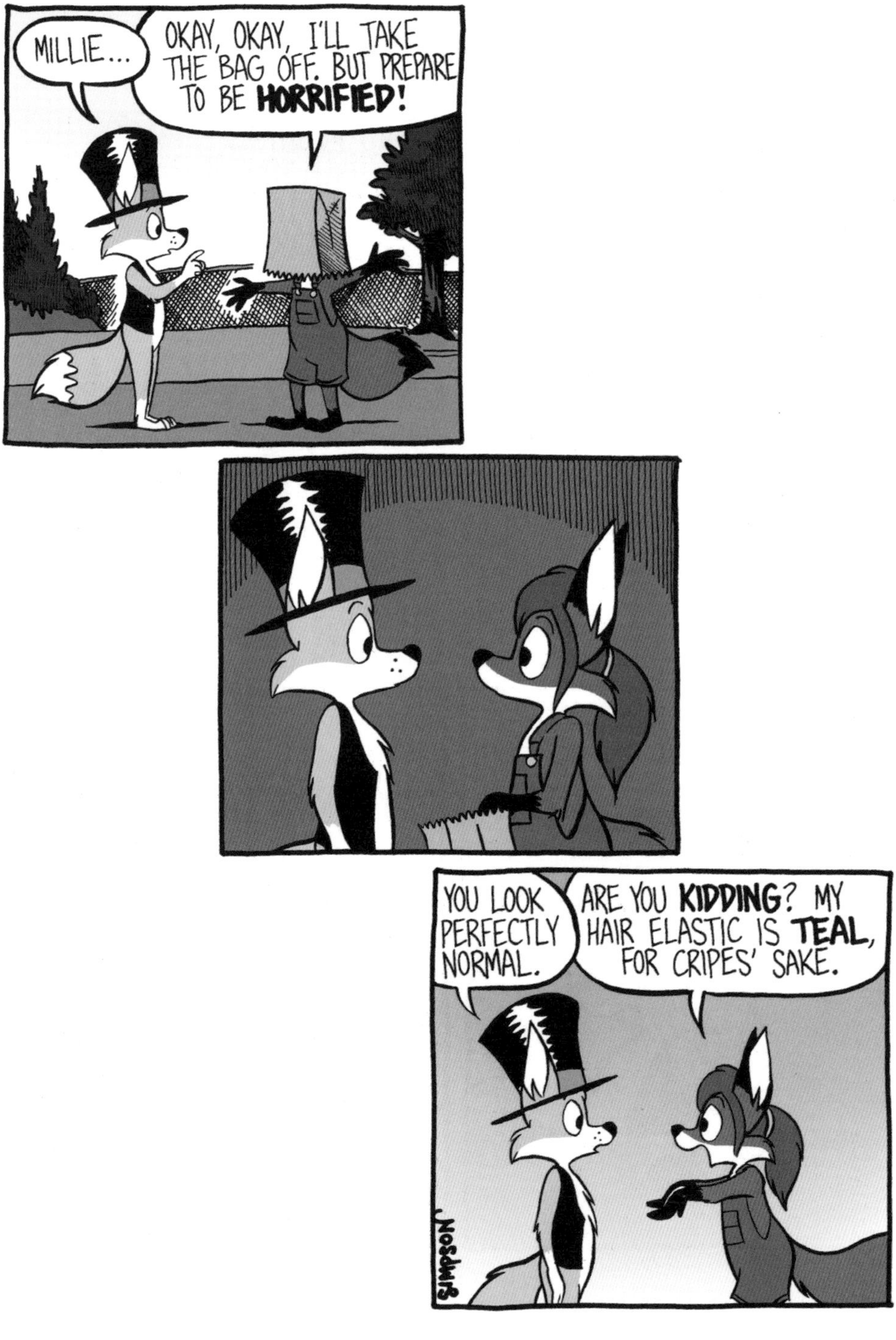
MILLIE...
OKAY, OKAY, I'LL TAKE THE BAG OFF. BUT PREPARE TO BE **HORRIFIED**!
YOU LOOK PERFECTLY NORMAL.
ARE YOU **KIDDING**? MY HAIR ELASTIC IS **TEAL**, FOR CRIPES' SAKE.

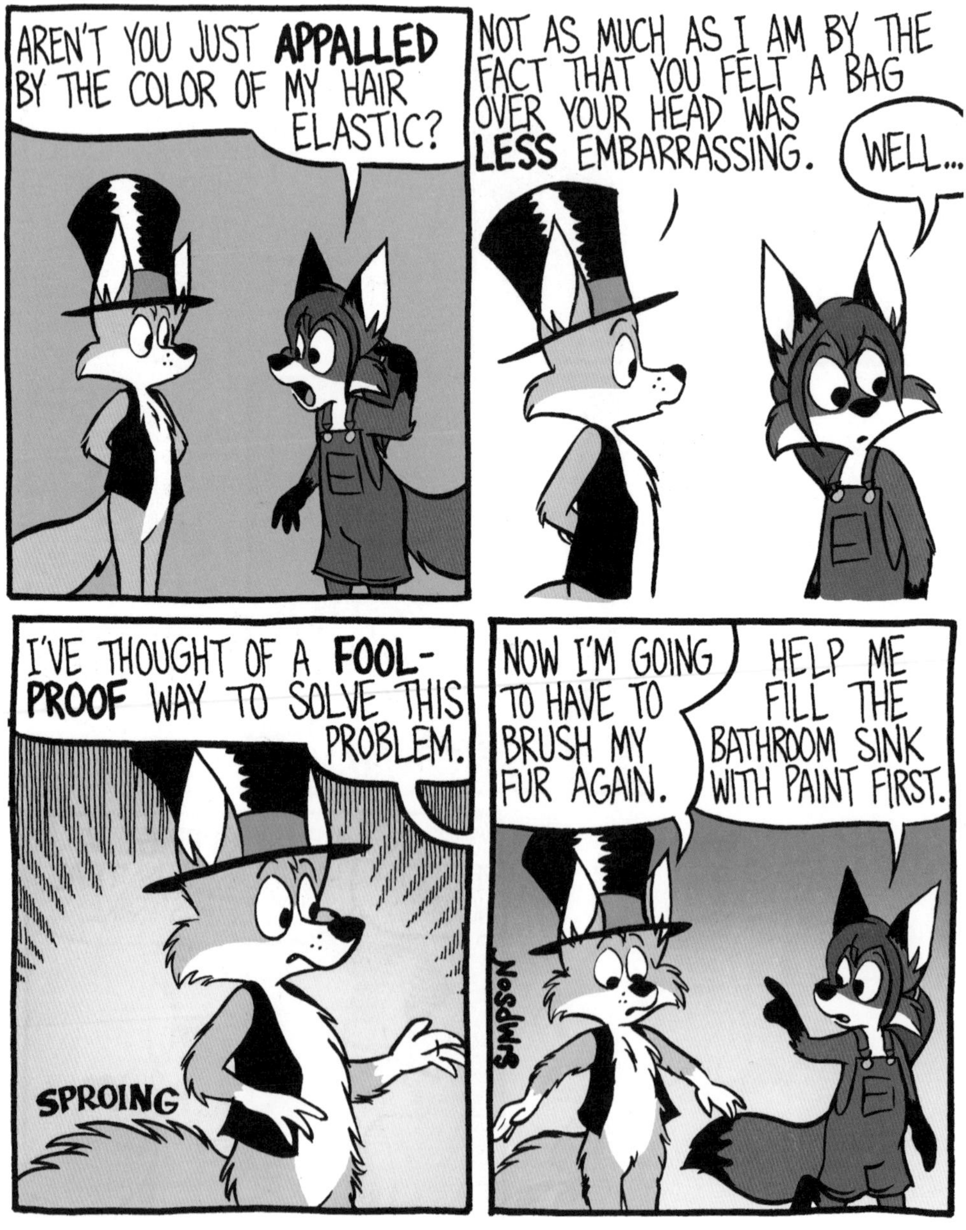

AREN'T YOU JUST **APPALLED** BY THE COLOR OF MY HAIR ELASTIC?
NOT AS MUCH AS I AM BY THE FACT THAT YOU FELT A BAG OVER YOUR HEAD WAS **LESS** EMBARRASSING.
WELL...
I'VE THOUGHT OF A **FOOL-PROOF** WAY TO SOLVE THIS PROBLEM.
SPROING
NOW I'M GOING TO HAVE TO BRUSH MY FUR AGAIN.
HELP ME FILL THE BATHROOM SINK WITH PAINT FIRST.
SIMPSON

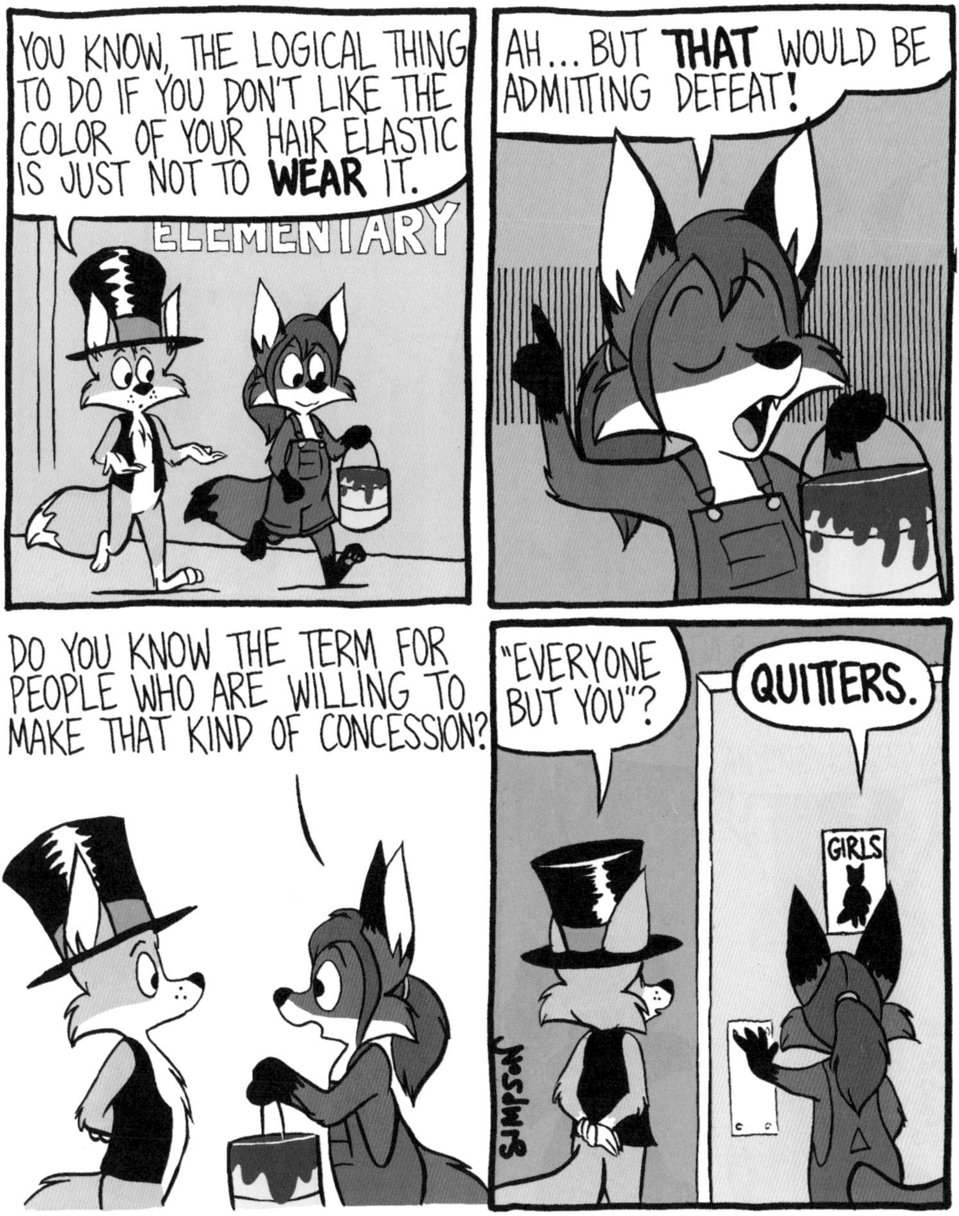
YOU KNOW, THE LOGICAL THING TO DO IF YOU DON'T LIKE THE COLOR OF YOUR HAIR ELASTIC IS JUST NOT TO **WEAR** IT.
ELEMENTARY
AH... BUT **THAT** WOULD BE ADMITTING DEFEAT!
DO YOU KNOW THE TERM FOR PEOPLE WHO ARE WILLING TO MAKE THAT KIND OF CONCESSION?
"EVERYONE BUT YOU"?
QUITTERS.
GIRLS
SJMPSON

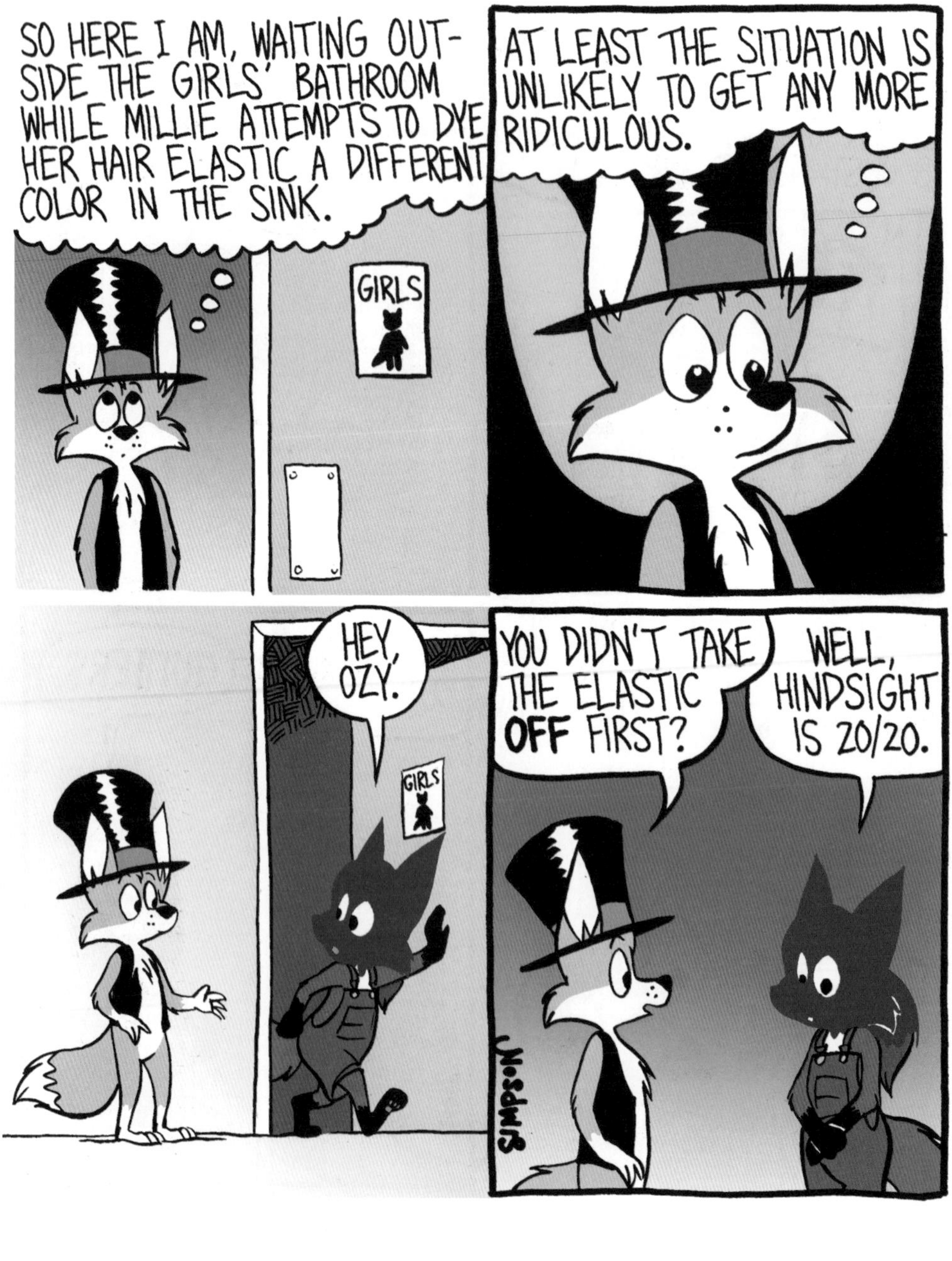
SO HERE I AM, WAITING OUTSIDE THE GIRLS' BATHROOM WHILE MILLIE ATTEMPTS TO DYE HER HAIR ELASTIC A DIFFERENT COLOR IN THE SINK.
GIRLS
AT LEAST THE SITUATION IS UNLIKELY TO GET ANY MORE RIDICULOUS.
HEY, OZY.
GIRLS
YOU DIDN'T TAKE THE ELASTIC **OFF** FIRST?
WELL, HINDSIGHT IS 20/20.
SIMPSON

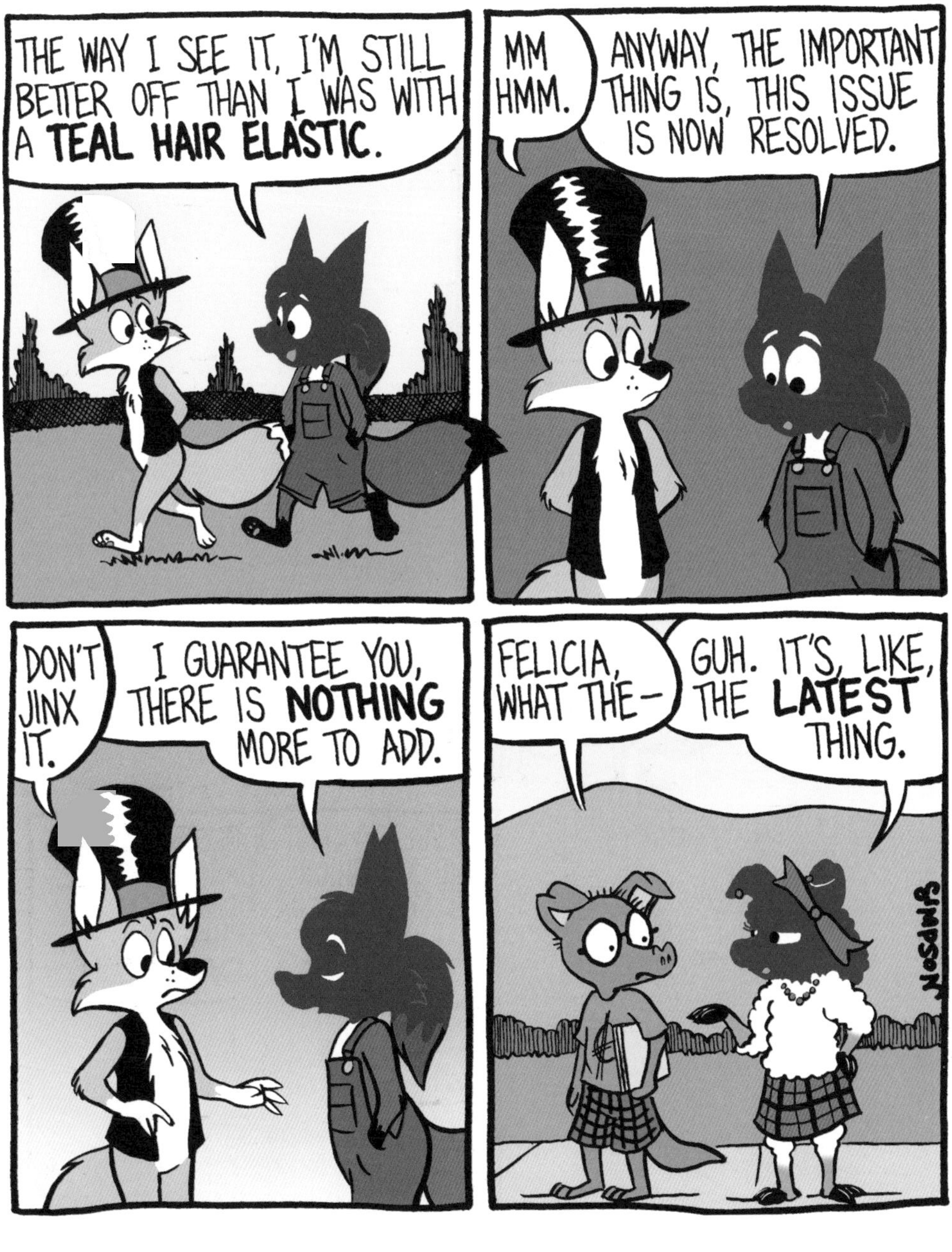
THE WAY I SEE IT, I'M STILL BETTER OFF THAN I WAS WITH A TEAL HAIR ELASTIC.
MM HMM.
ANYWAY, THE IMPORTANT THING IS, THIS ISSUE IS NOW RESOLVED.
DON'T JINX IT.
I GUARANTEE YOU, THERE IS NOTHING MORE TO ADD.
FELICIA, WHAT THE–
GUH. IT'S, LIKE, THE LATEST THING.
SIMPSON

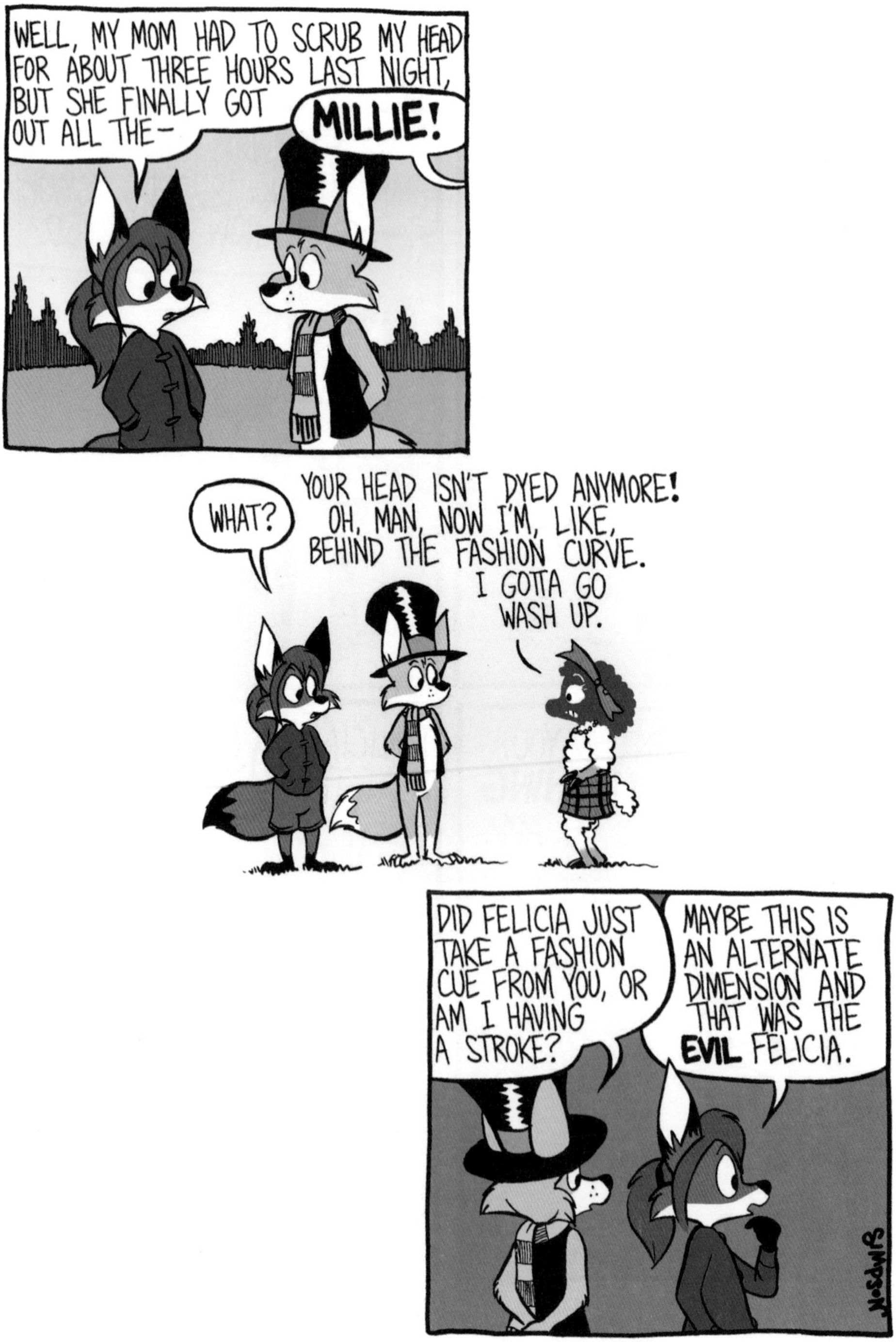
WELL, MY MOM HAD TO SCRUB MY HEAD FOR ABOUT THREE HOURS LAST NIGHT, BUT SHE FINALLY GOT OUT ALL THE—
MILLIE!
WHAT?
YOUR HEAD ISN'T DYED ANYMORE! OH, MAN, NOW I'M, LIKE, BEHIND THE FASHION CURVE.
I GOTTA GO WASH UP.
DID FELICIA JUST TAKE A FASHION CUE FROM YOU, OR AM I HAVING A STROKE?
MAYBE THIS IS AN ALTERNATE DIMENSION AND THAT WAS THE **EVIL** FELICIA.
SIMPSON

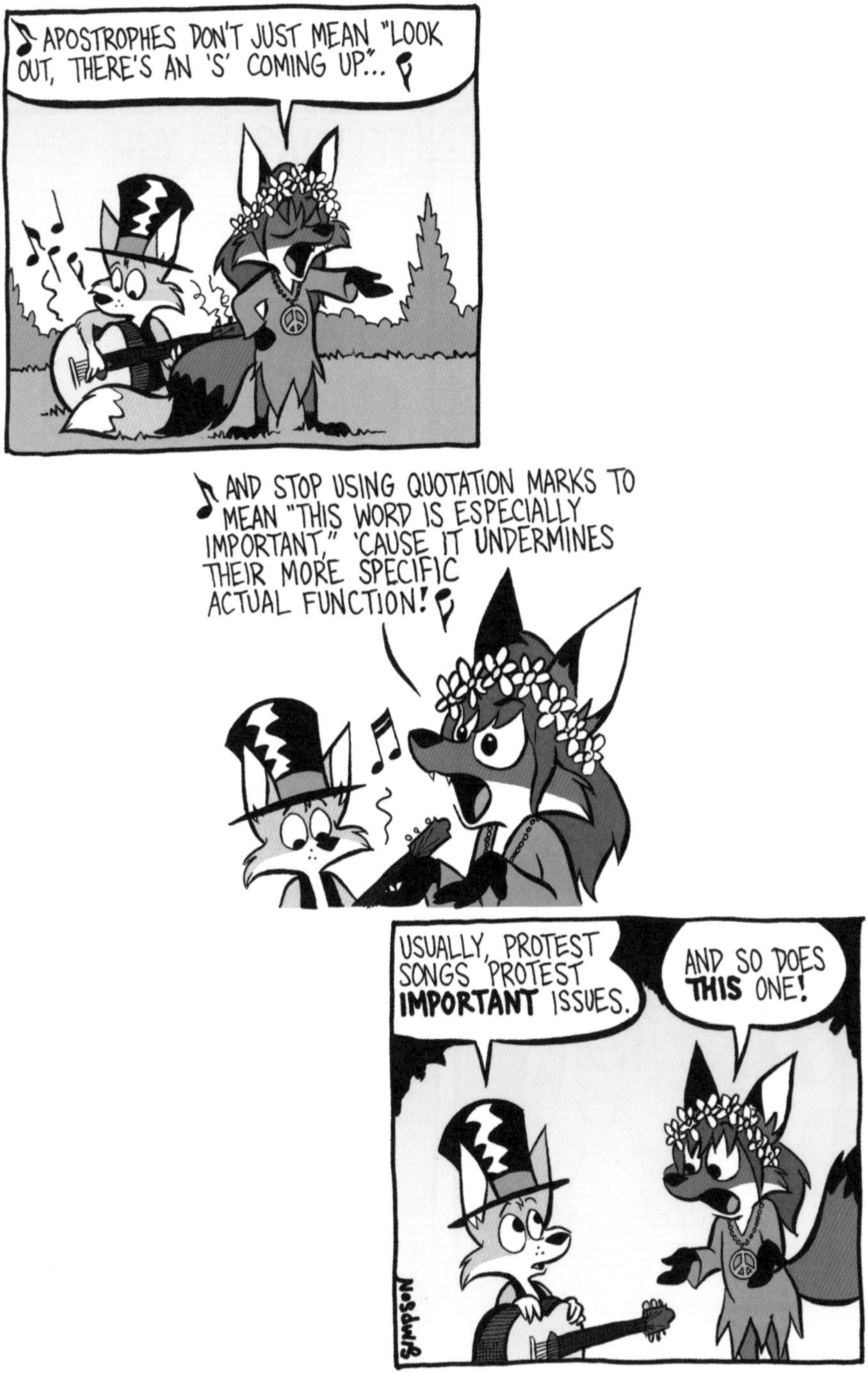
APOSTROPHES DON'T JUST MEAN "LOOK OUT, THERE'S AN 'S' COMING UP"...
AND STOP USING QUOTATION MARKS TO MEAN "THIS WORD IS ESPECIALLY IMPORTANT," 'CAUSE IT UNDERMINES THEIR MORE SPECIFIC ACTUAL FUNCTION!
USUALLY, PROTEST SONGS PROTEST **IMPORTANT** ISSUES.
AND SO DOES **THIS** ONE!

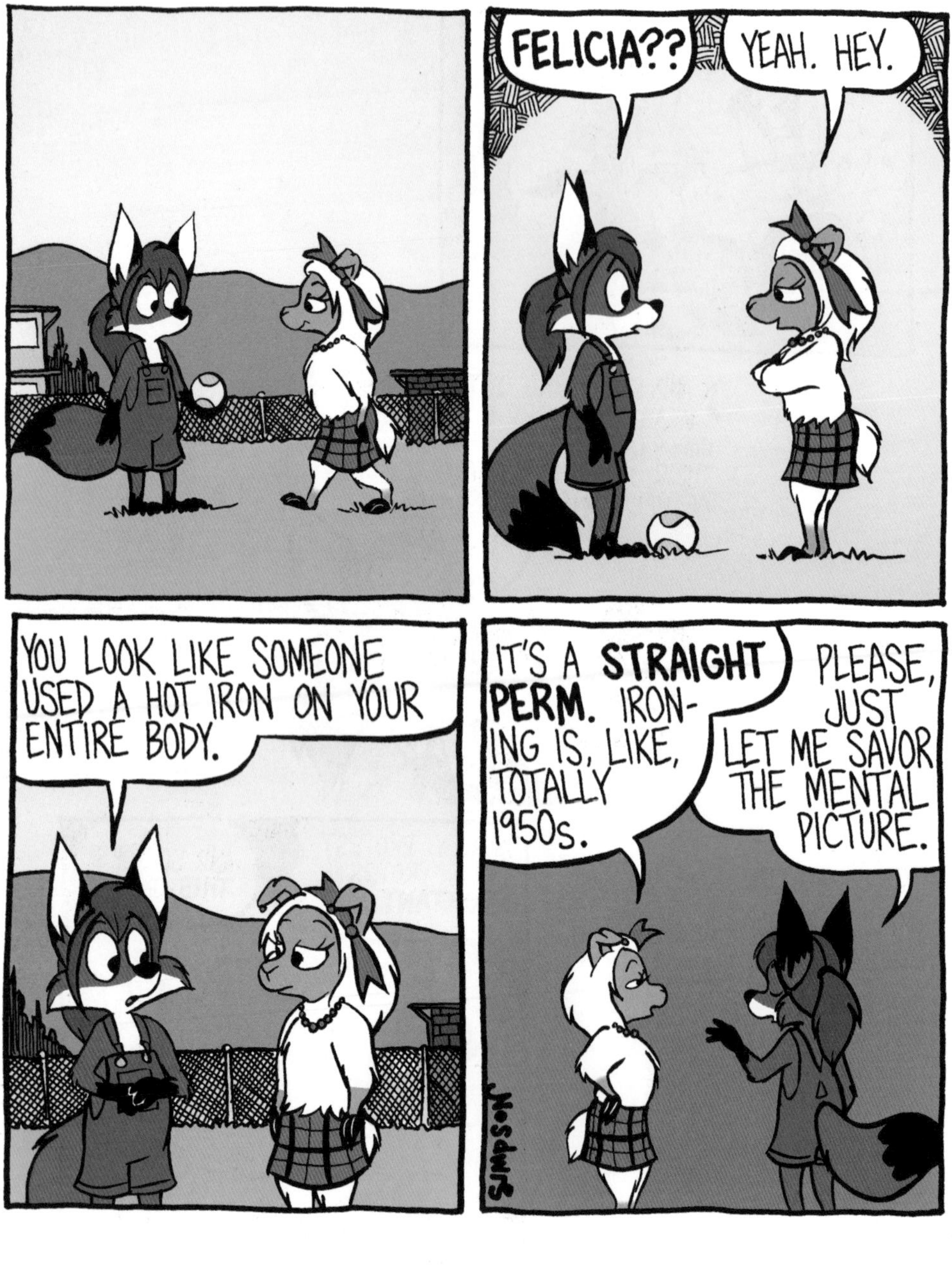
FELICIA??
YEAH. HEY.
YOU LOOK LIKE SOMEONE USED A HOT IRON ON YOUR ENTIRE BODY.
IT'S A **STRAIGHT PERM**. IRON-ING IS, LIKE, TOTALLY 1950s.
PLEASE, JUST LET ME SAVOR THE MENTAL PICTURE.
SIMPSON

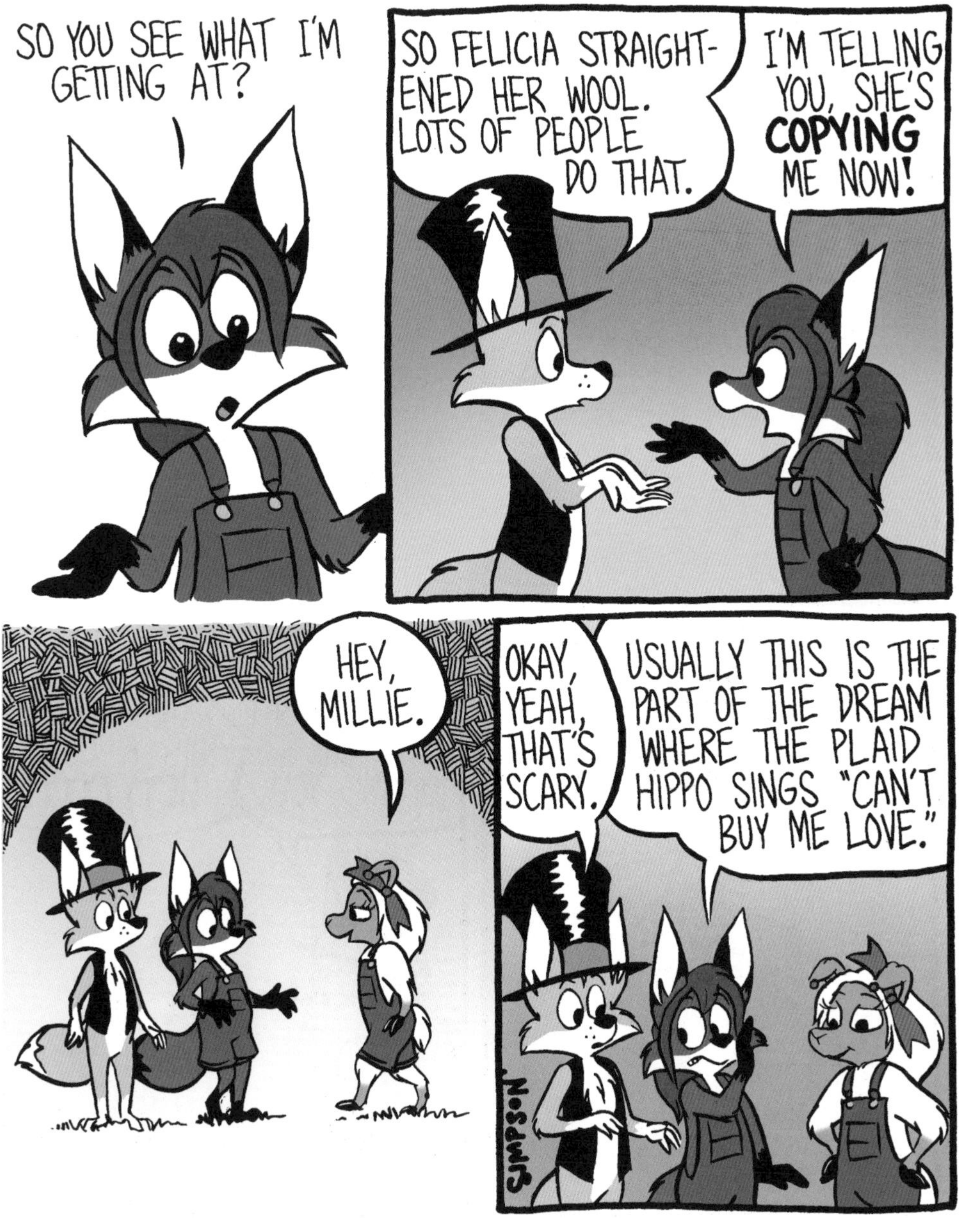
SO YOU SEE WHAT I'M GETTING AT?
SO FELICIA STRAIGHT-ENED HER WOOL. LOTS OF PEOPLE DO THAT.
I'M TELLING YOU, SHE'S **COPYING** ME NOW!
HEY, MILLIE.
OKAY, YEAH, THAT'S SCARY.
USUALLY THIS IS THE PART OF THE DREAM WHERE THE PLAID HIPPO SINGS "CAN'T BUY ME LOVE."
SIMPSON

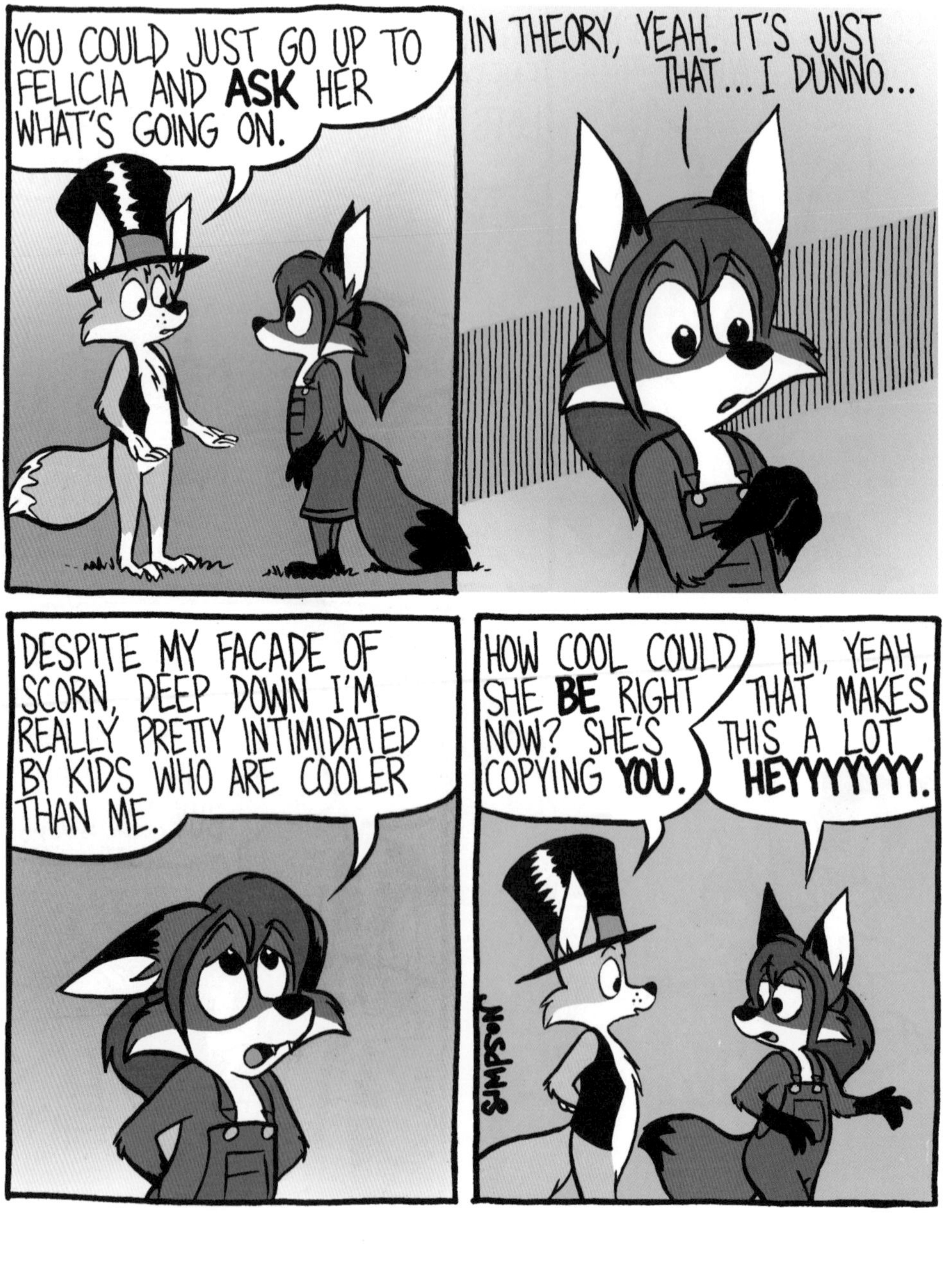

YOU COULD JUST GO UP TO FELICIA AND **ASK** HER WHAT'S GOING ON.
IN THEORY, YEAH. IT'S JUST THAT... I DUNNO...
DESPITE MY FACADE OF SCORN, DEEP DOWN I'M REALLY PRETTY INTIMIDATED BY KIDS WHO ARE COOLER THAN ME.
HOW COOL COULD SHE **BE** RIGHT NOW? SHE'S COPYING **YOU**.
HM, YEAH, THAT MAKES THIS A LOT **HEYYYYYYY**.
SIMPSON

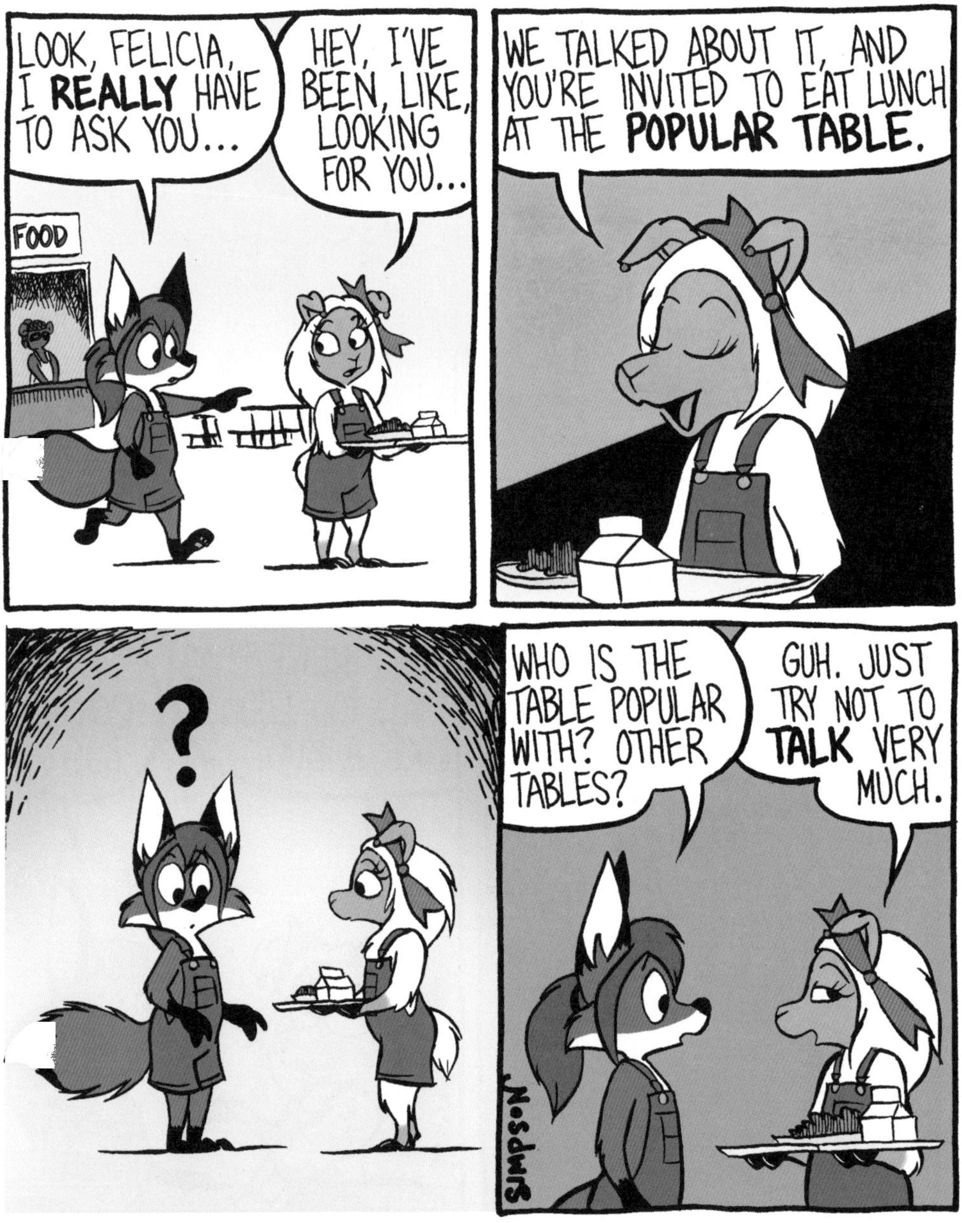
LOOK, FELICIA, I **REALLY** HAVE TO ASK YOU...
HEY, I'VE BEEN, LIKE, LOOKING FOR YOU...
FOOD
WE TALKED ABOUT IT, AND YOU'RE INVITED TO EAT LUNCH AT THE **POPULAR TABLE**.
?
WHO IS THE TABLE POPULAR WITH? OTHER TABLES?
GUH. JUST TRY NOT TO **TALK** VERY MUCH.
SIMPSON

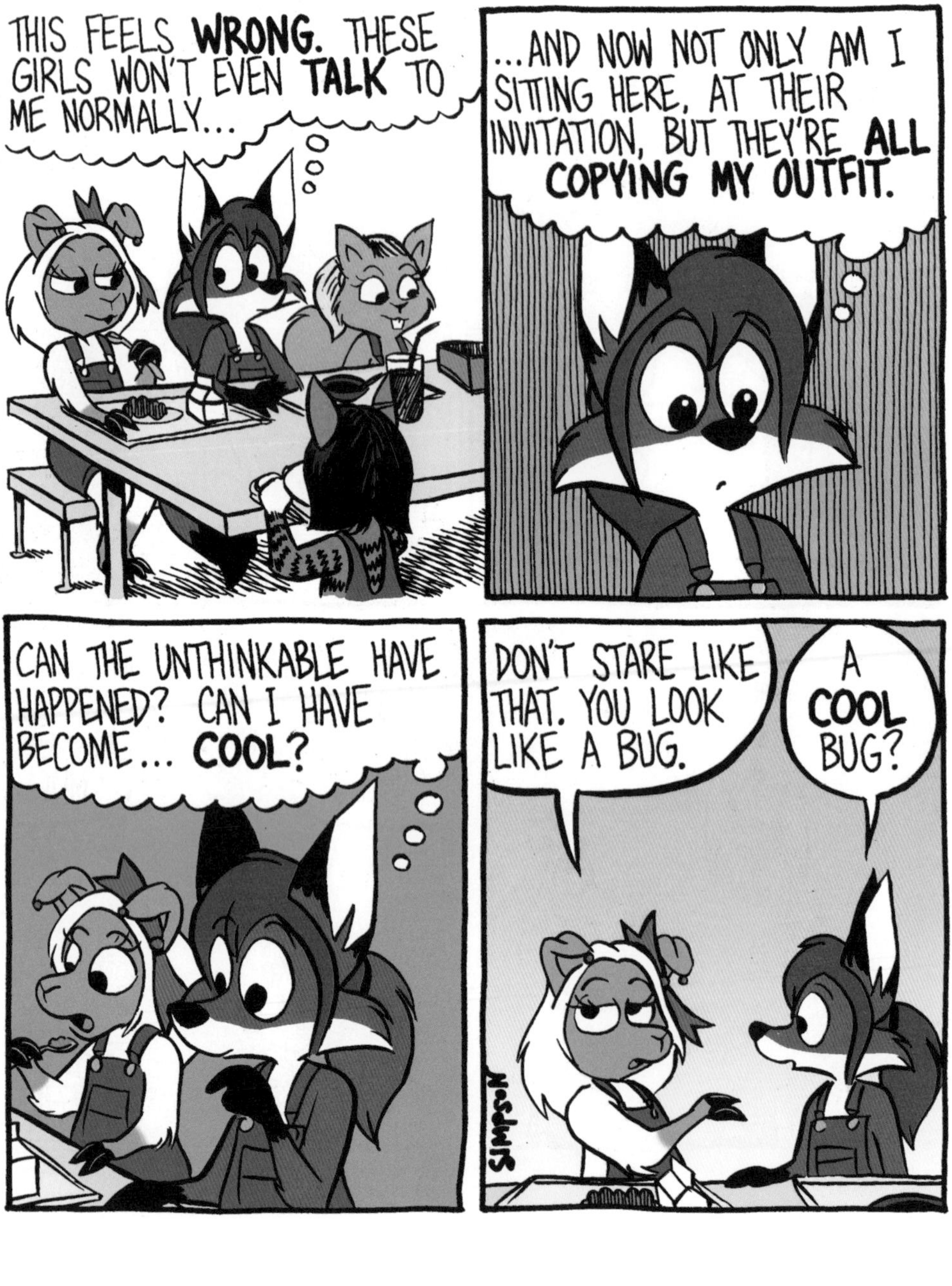
THIS FEELS **WRONG.** THESE GIRLS WON'T EVEN **TALK** TO ME NORMALLY...
...AND NOW NOT ONLY AM I SITTING HERE, AT THEIR INVITATION, BUT THEY'RE **ALL COPYING MY OUTFIT.**
CAN THE UNTHINKABLE HAVE HAPPENED? CAN I HAVE BECOME... **COOL?**
DON'T STARE LIKE THAT. YOU LOOK LIKE A BUG.
A **COOL** BUG?
SIMPSON

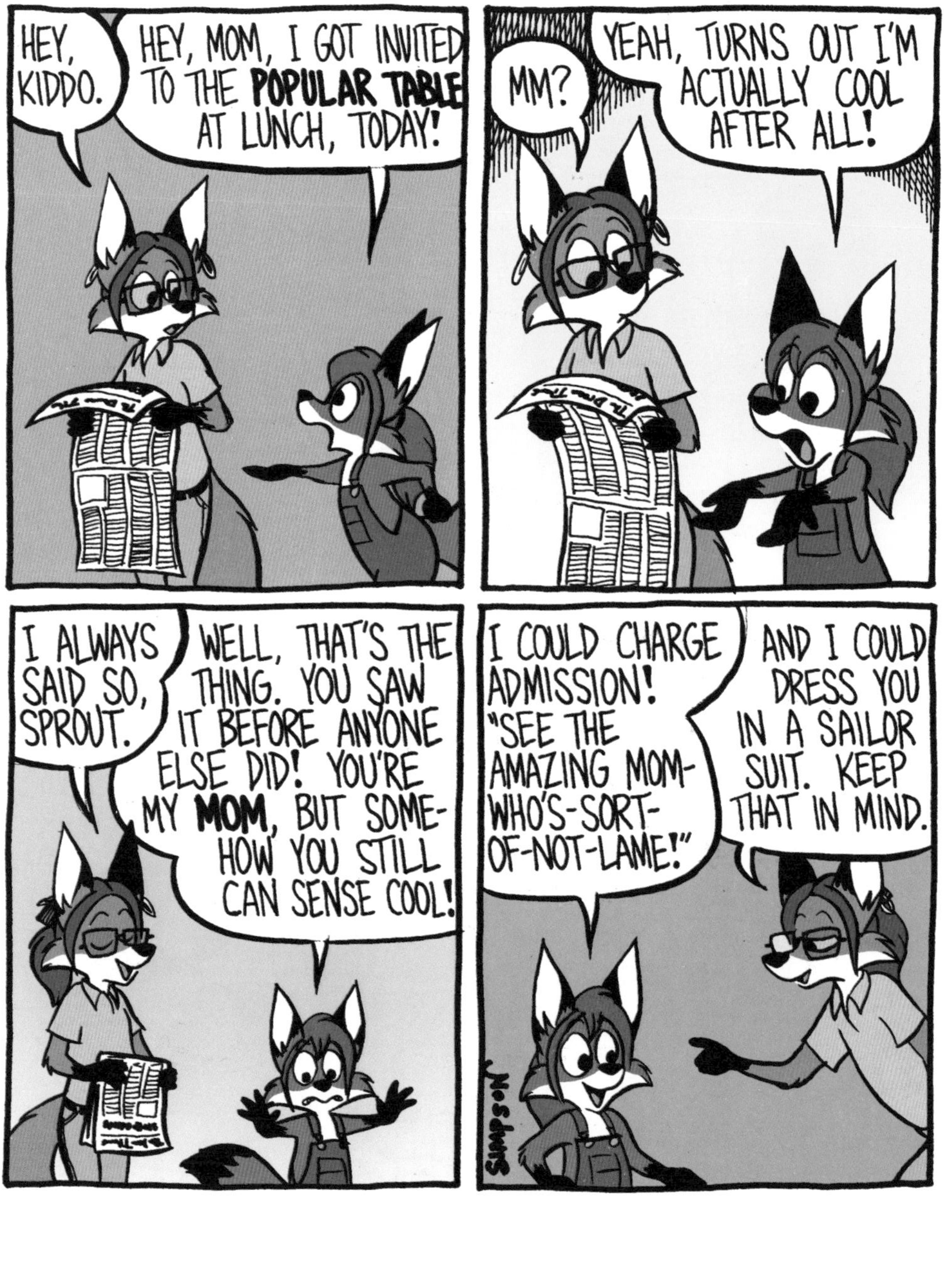

HEY, KIDDO.
HEY, MOM, I GOT INVITED TO THE POPULAR TABLE AT LUNCH, TODAY!
MM?
YEAH, TURNS OUT I'M ACTUALLY COOL AFTER ALL!
I ALWAYS SAID SO, SPROUT.
WELL, THAT'S THE THING. YOU SAW IT BEFORE ANYONE ELSE DID! YOU'RE MY MOM, BUT SOME-HOW YOU STILL CAN SENSE COOL!
I COULD CHARGE ADMISSION! "SEE THE AMAZING MOM-WHO'S-SORT-OF-NOT-LAME!"
AND I COULD DRESS YOU IN A SAILOR SUIT. KEEP THAT IN MIND.
SIMPSON

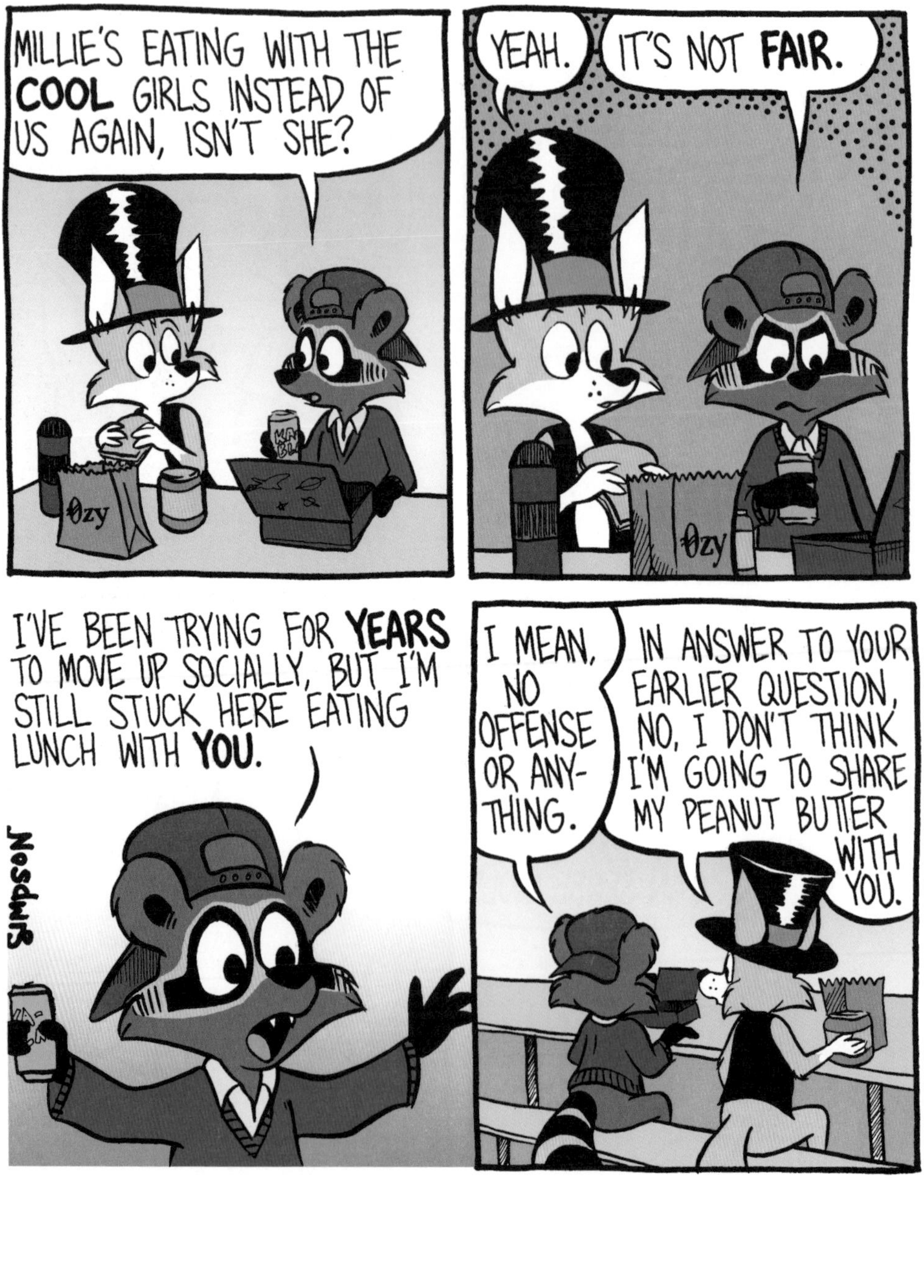
MILLIE'S EATING WITH THE **COOL** GIRLS INSTEAD OF US AGAIN, ISN'T SHE?
Ozy
YEAH.
IT'S NOT **FAIR.**
Ozy
I'VE BEEN TRYING FOR **YEARS** TO MOVE UP SOCIALLY, BUT I'M STILL STUCK HERE EATING LUNCH WITH **YOU**.
I MEAN, NO OFFENSE OR ANY-THING.
IN ANSWER TO YOUR EARLIER QUESTION, NO, I DON'T THINK I'M GOING TO SHARE MY PEANUT BUTTER WITH YOU.

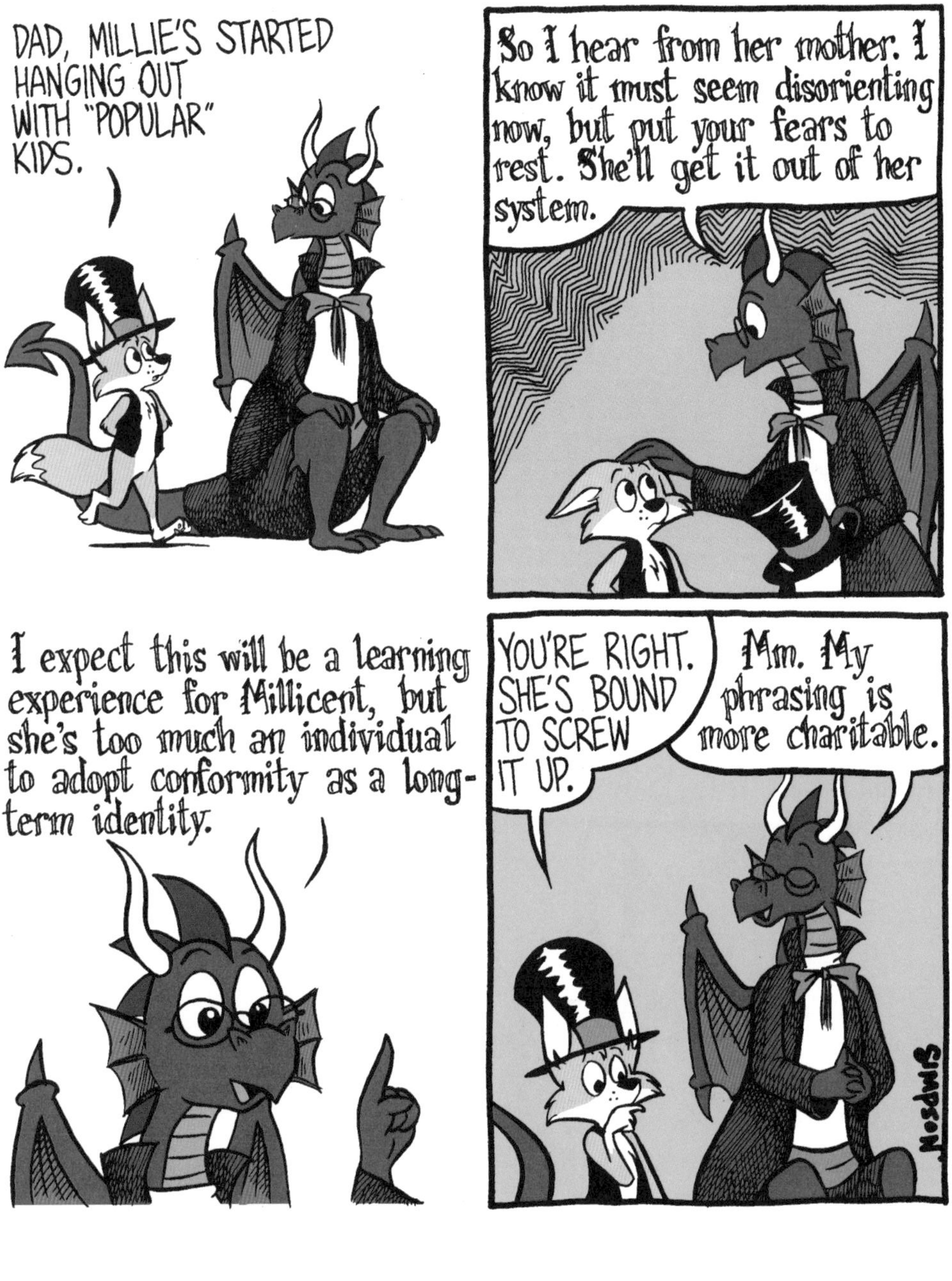
DAD, MILLIE'S STARTED HANGING OUT WITH "POPULAR" KIDS.
So I hear from her mother. I know it must seem disorienting now, but put your fears to rest. She'll get it out of her system.
I expect this will be a learning experience for Millicent, but she's too much an individual to adopt conformity as a long-term identity.
YOU'RE RIGHT. SHE'S BOUND TO SCREW IT UP.
Mm. My phrasing is more charitable.
SIMPSON

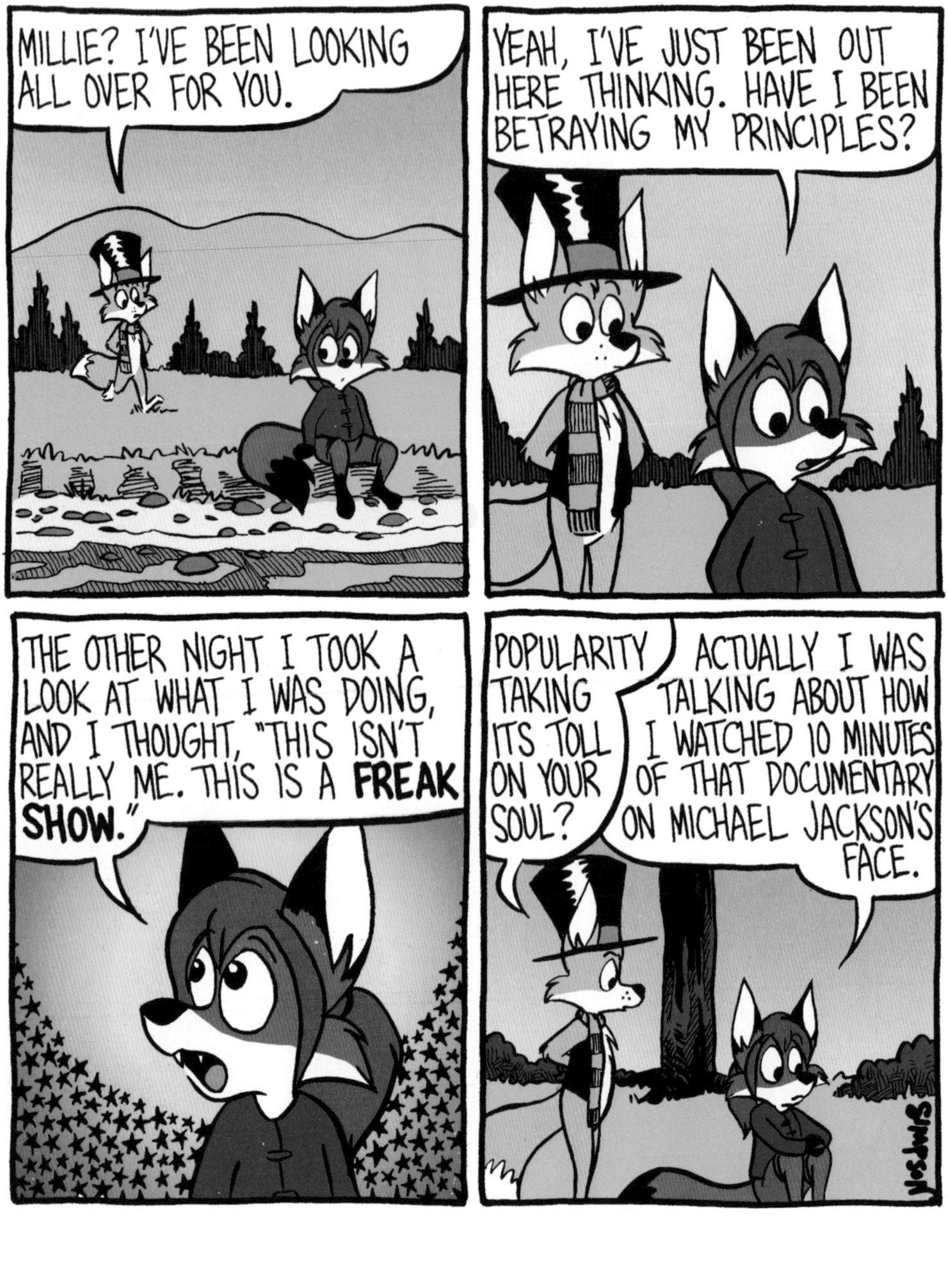
MILLIE? I'VE BEEN LOOKING ALL OVER FOR YOU.
YEAH, I'VE JUST BEEN OUT HERE THINKING. HAVE I BEEN BETRAYING MY PRINCIPLES?
THE OTHER NIGHT I TOOK A LOOK AT WHAT I WAS DOING, AND I THOUGHT, "THIS ISN'T REALLY ME. THIS IS A **FREAK SHOW.**"
POPULARITY TAKING ITS TOLL ON YOUR SOUL?
ACTUALLY I WAS TALKING ABOUT HOW I WATCHED 10 MINUTES OF THAT DOCUMENTARY ON MICHAEL JACKSON'S FACE.
SIMPSON

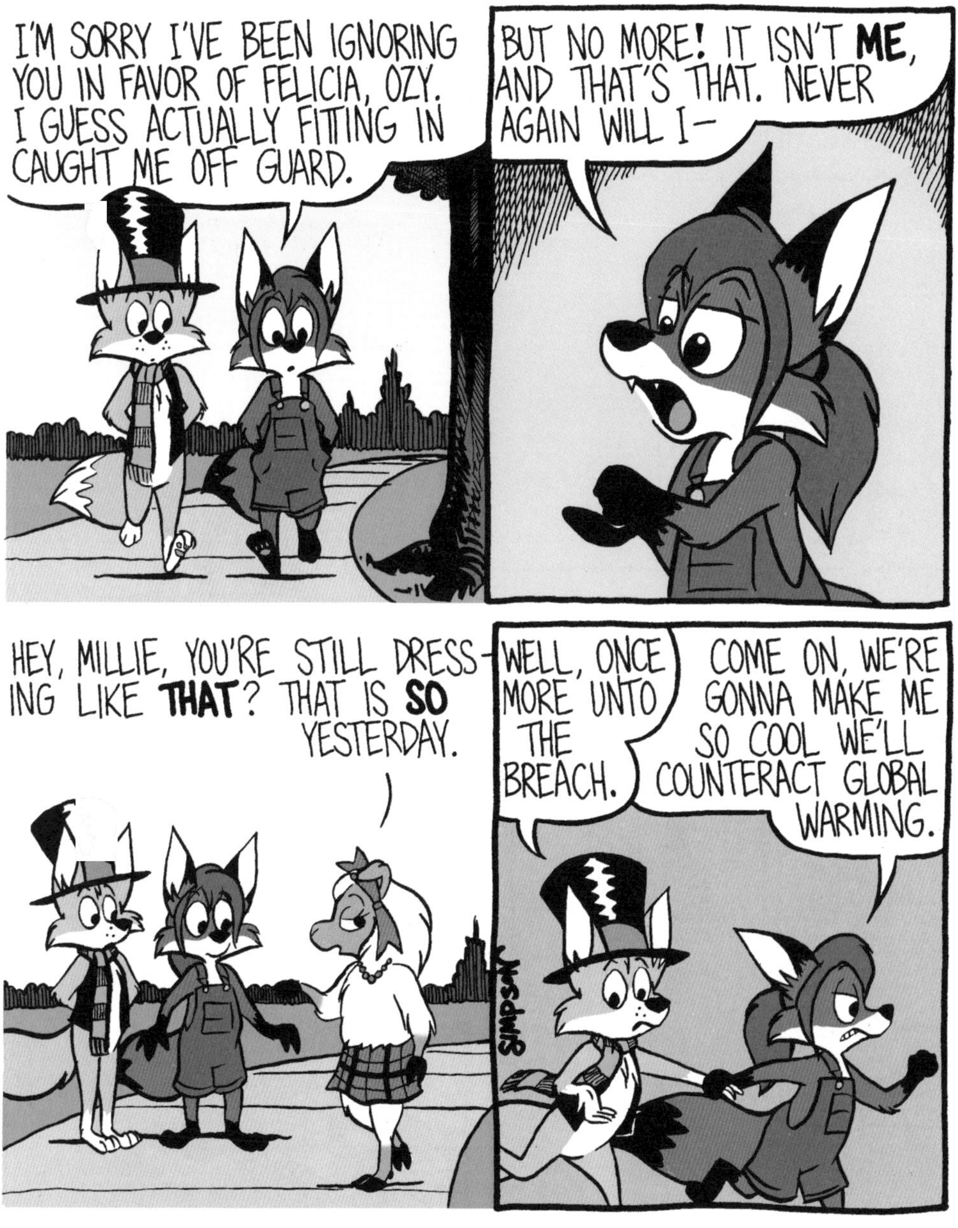
I'M SORRY I'VE BEEN IGNORING YOU IN FAVOR OF FELICIA, OZY. I GUESS ACTUALLY FITTING IN CAUGHT ME OFF GUARD.
BUT NO MORE! IT ISN'T **ME**, AND THAT'S THAT. NEVER AGAIN WILL I—
HEY, MILLIE, YOU'RE STILL DRESS-ING LIKE **THAT**? THAT IS **SO** YESTERDAY.
WELL, ONCE MORE UNTO THE BREACH.
COME ON, WE'RE GONNA MAKE ME SO COOL WE'LL COUNTERACT GLOBAL WARMING.
SIMPSON

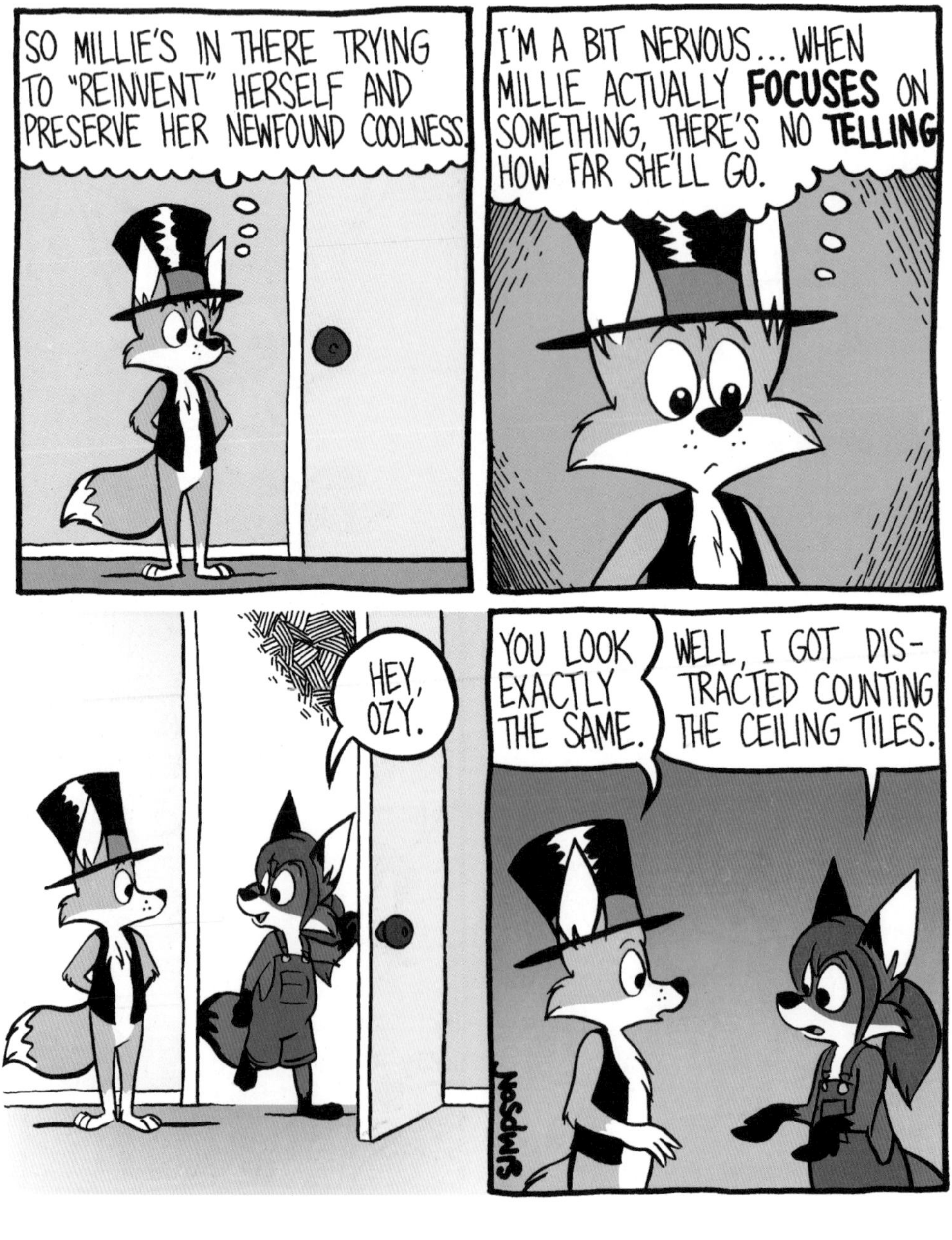
SO MILLIE'S IN THERE TRYING TO "REINVENT" HERSELF AND PRESERVE HER NEWFOUND COOLNESS.
I'M A BIT NERVOUS... WHEN MILLIE ACTUALLY **FOCUSES** ON SOMETHING, THERE'S NO **TELLING** HOW FAR SHE'LL GO.
HEY, OZY.
YOU LOOK EXACTLY THE SAME.
WELL, I GOT DISTRACTED COUNTING THE CEILING TILES.
SIMPSON

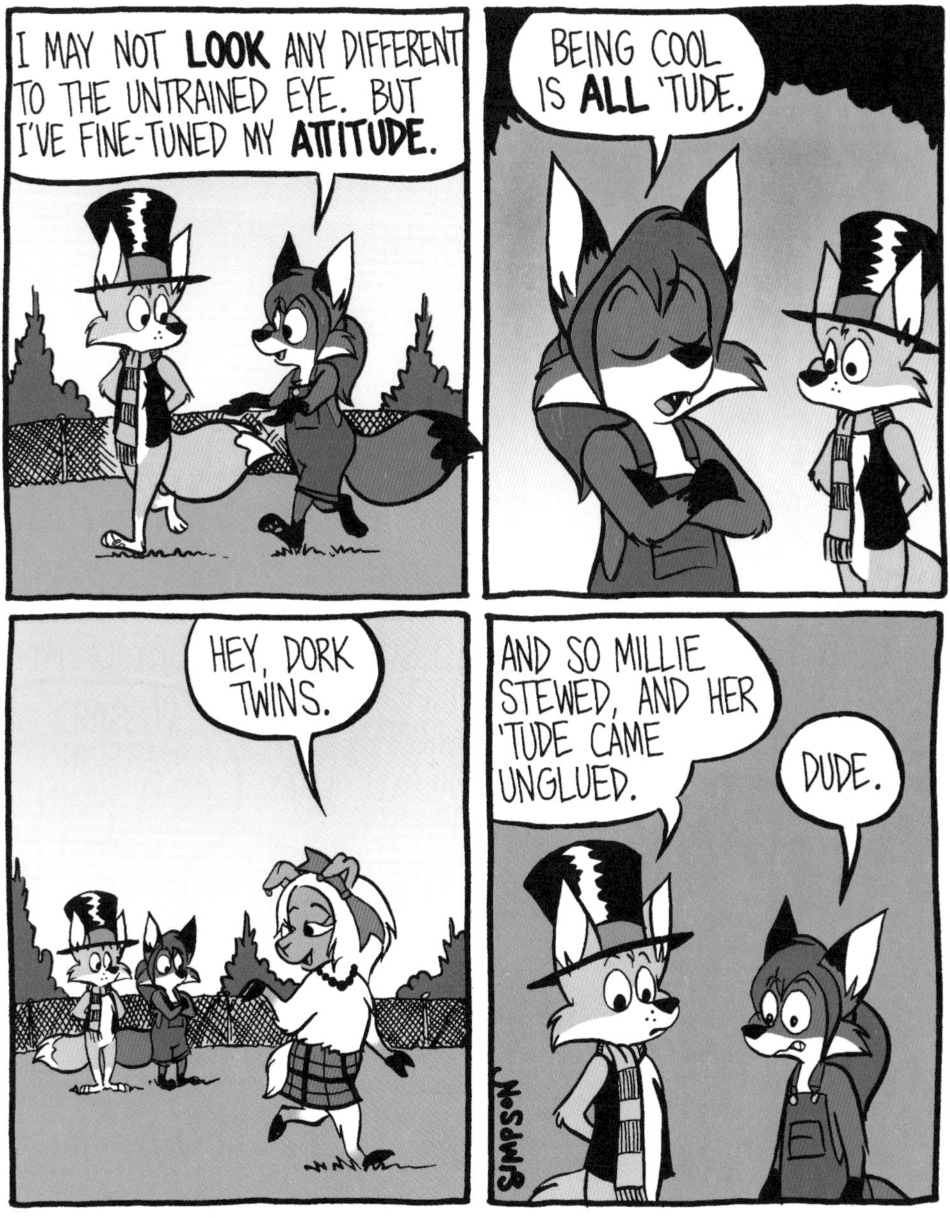
I MAY NOT **LOOK** ANY DIFFERENT TO THE UNTRAINED EYE. BUT I'VE FINE-TUNED MY **ATTITUDE**.
BEING COOL IS **ALL** 'TUDE.
HEY, DORK TWINS.
AND SO MILLIE STEWED, AND HER 'TUDE CAME UNGLUED.
DUDE.
SIMPSON

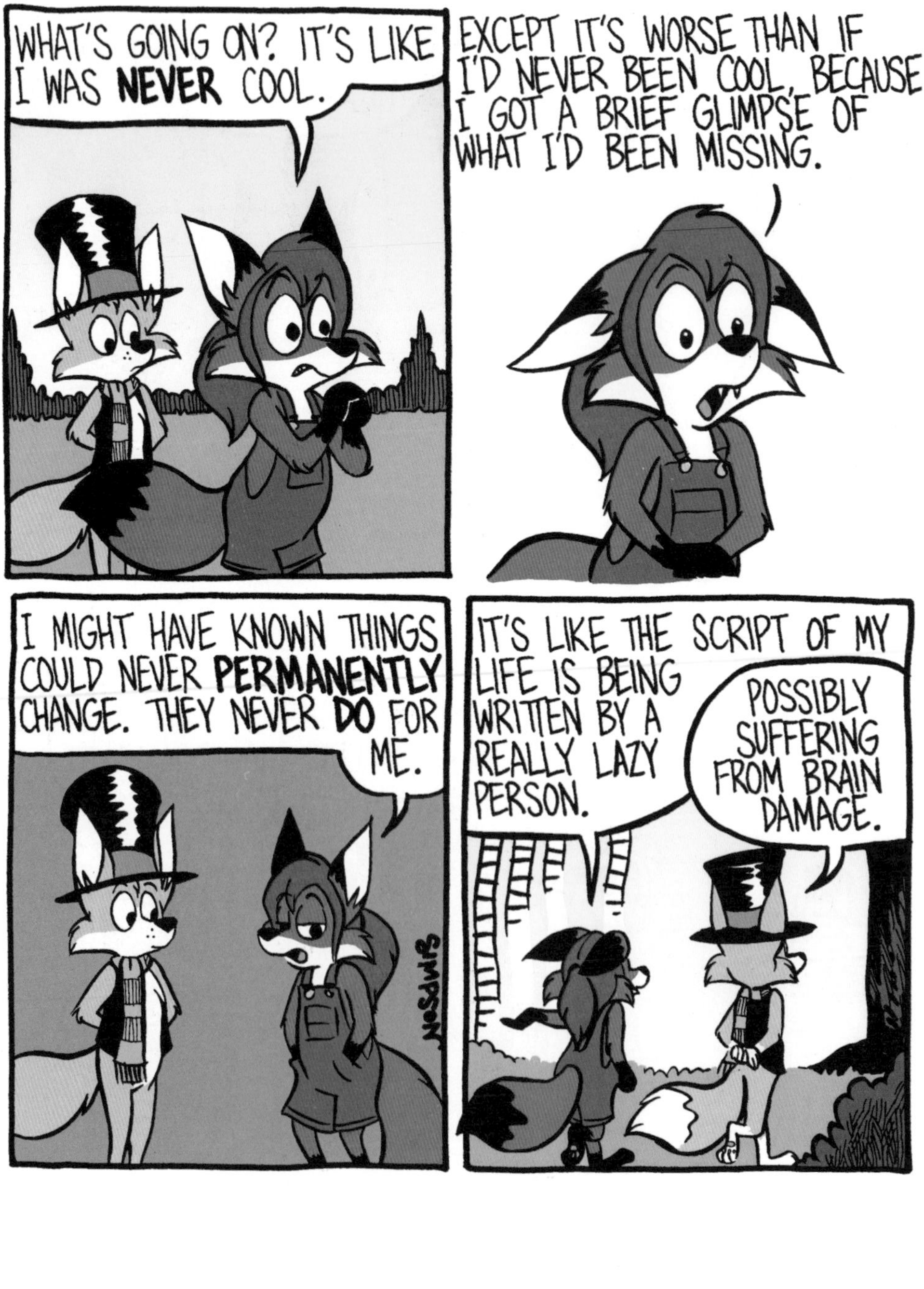
WHAT'S GOING ON? IT'S LIKE I WAS **NEVER** COOL.
EXCEPT IT'S WORSE THAN IF I'D NEVER BEEN COOL, BECAUSE I GOT A BRIEF GLIMPSE OF WHAT I'D BEEN MISSING.
I MIGHT HAVE KNOWN THINGS COULD NEVER **PERMANENTLY** CHANGE. THEY NEVER **DO** FOR ME.
SIMPSON
IT'S LIKE THE SCRIPT OF MY LIFE IS BEING WRITTEN BY A REALLY LAZY PERSON.
POSSIBLY SUFFERING FROM BRAIN DAMAGE.

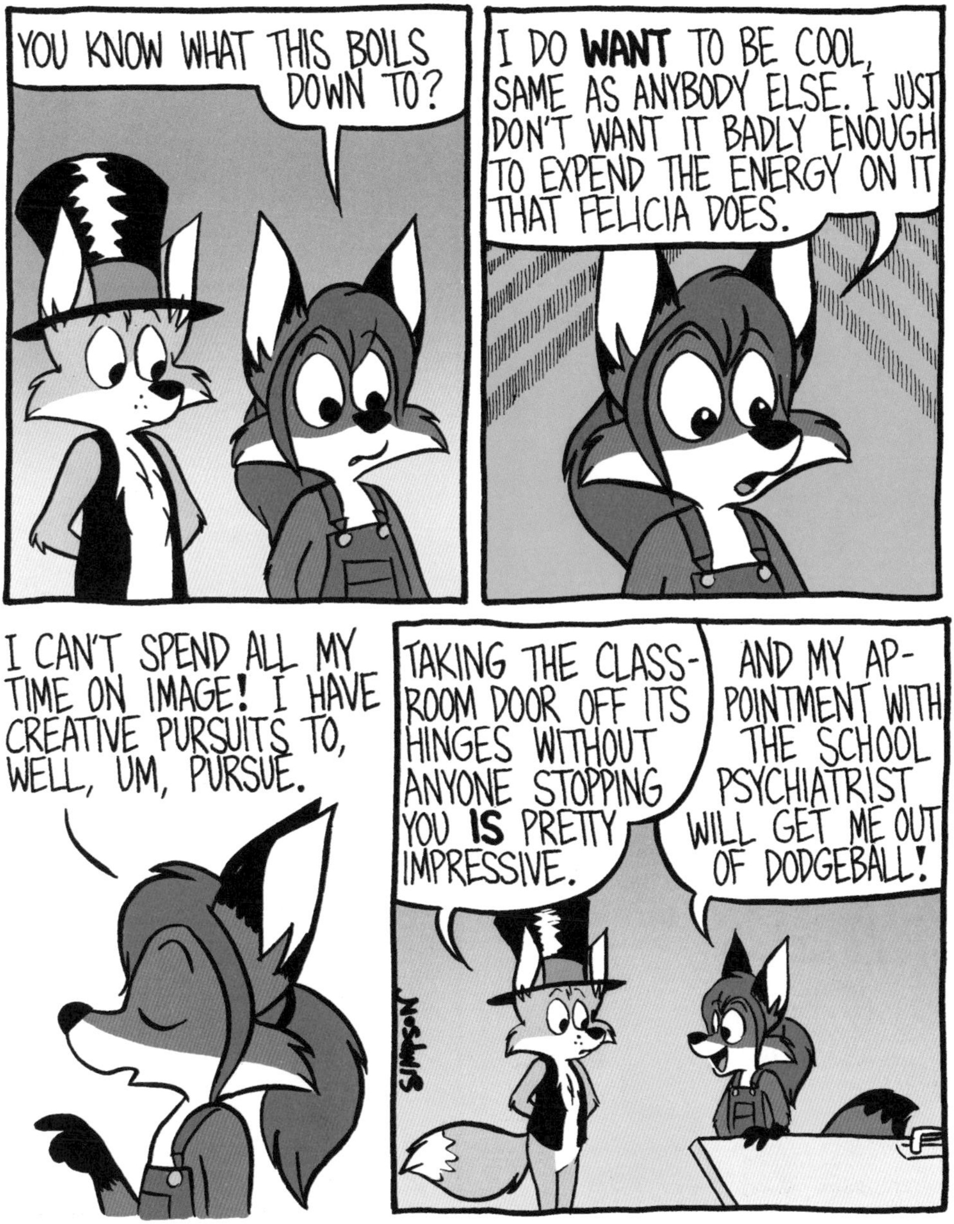
YOU KNOW WHAT THIS BOILS DOWN TO?
I DO WANT TO BE COOL, SAME AS ANYBODY ELSE. I JUST DON'T WANT IT BADLY ENOUGH TO EXPEND THE ENERGY ON IT THAT FELICIA DOES.
I CAN'T SPEND ALL MY TIME ON IMAGE! I HAVE CREATIVE PURSUITS TO, WELL, UM, PURSUE.
TAKING THE CLASS-ROOM DOOR OFF ITS HINGES WITHOUT ANYONE STOPPING YOU IS PRETTY IMPRESSIVE.
AND MY AP-POINTMENT WITH THE SCHOOL PSYCHIATRIST WILL GET ME OUT OF DODGEBALL!

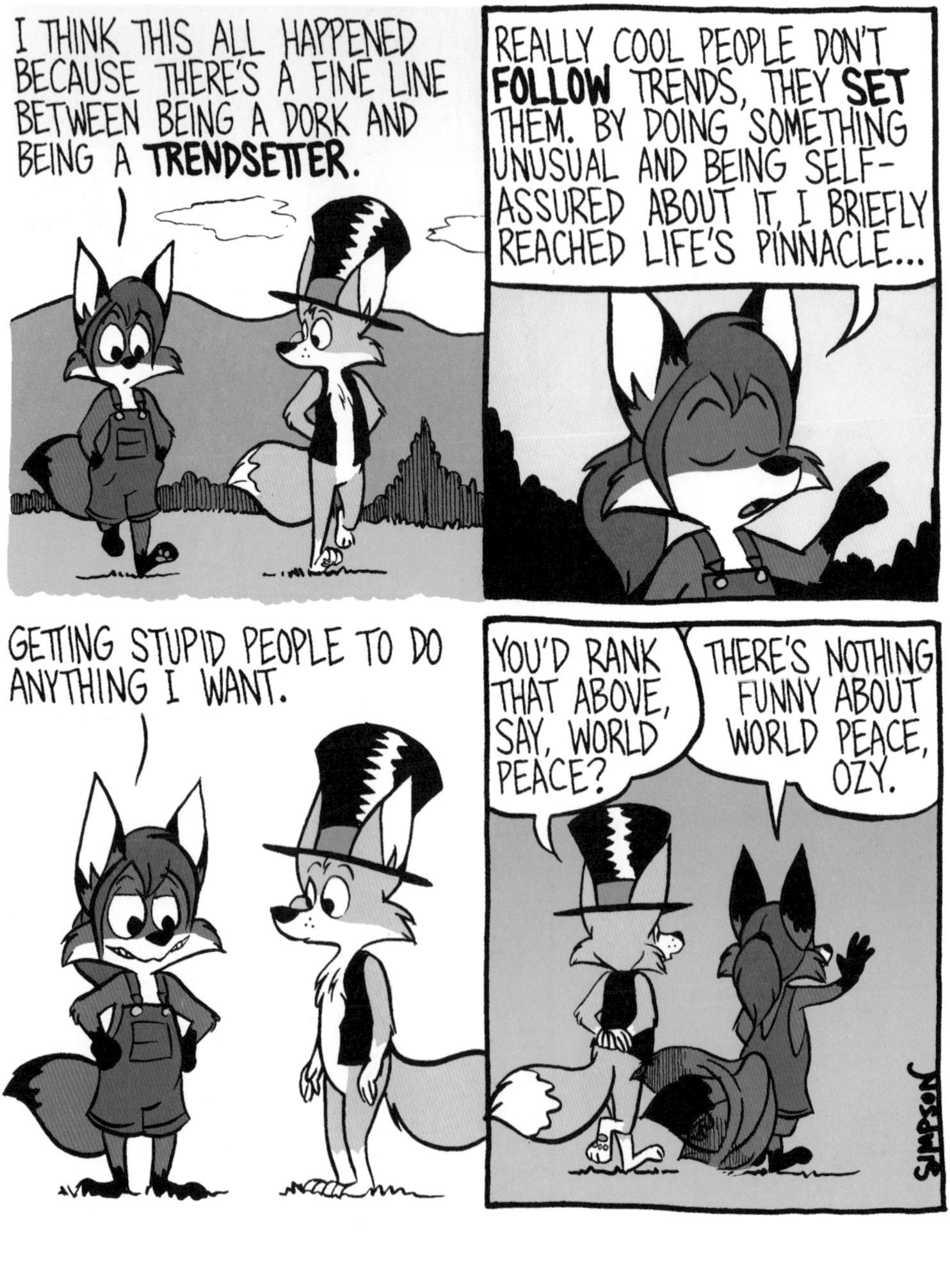
I THINK THIS ALL HAPPENED BECAUSE THERE'S A FINE LINE BETWEEN BEING A DORK AND BEING A **TRENDSETTER**.
REALLY COOL PEOPLE DON'T **FOLLOW** TRENDS, THEY **SET** THEM. BY DOING SOMETHING UNUSUAL AND BEING SELF-ASSURED ABOUT IT, I BRIEFLY REACHED LIFE'S PINNACLE...
GETTING STUPID PEOPLE TO DO ANYTHING I WANT.
YOU'D RANK THAT ABOVE, SAY, WORLD PEACE?
THERE'S NOTHING FUNNY ABOUT WORLD PEACE, OZY.
SIMPSON

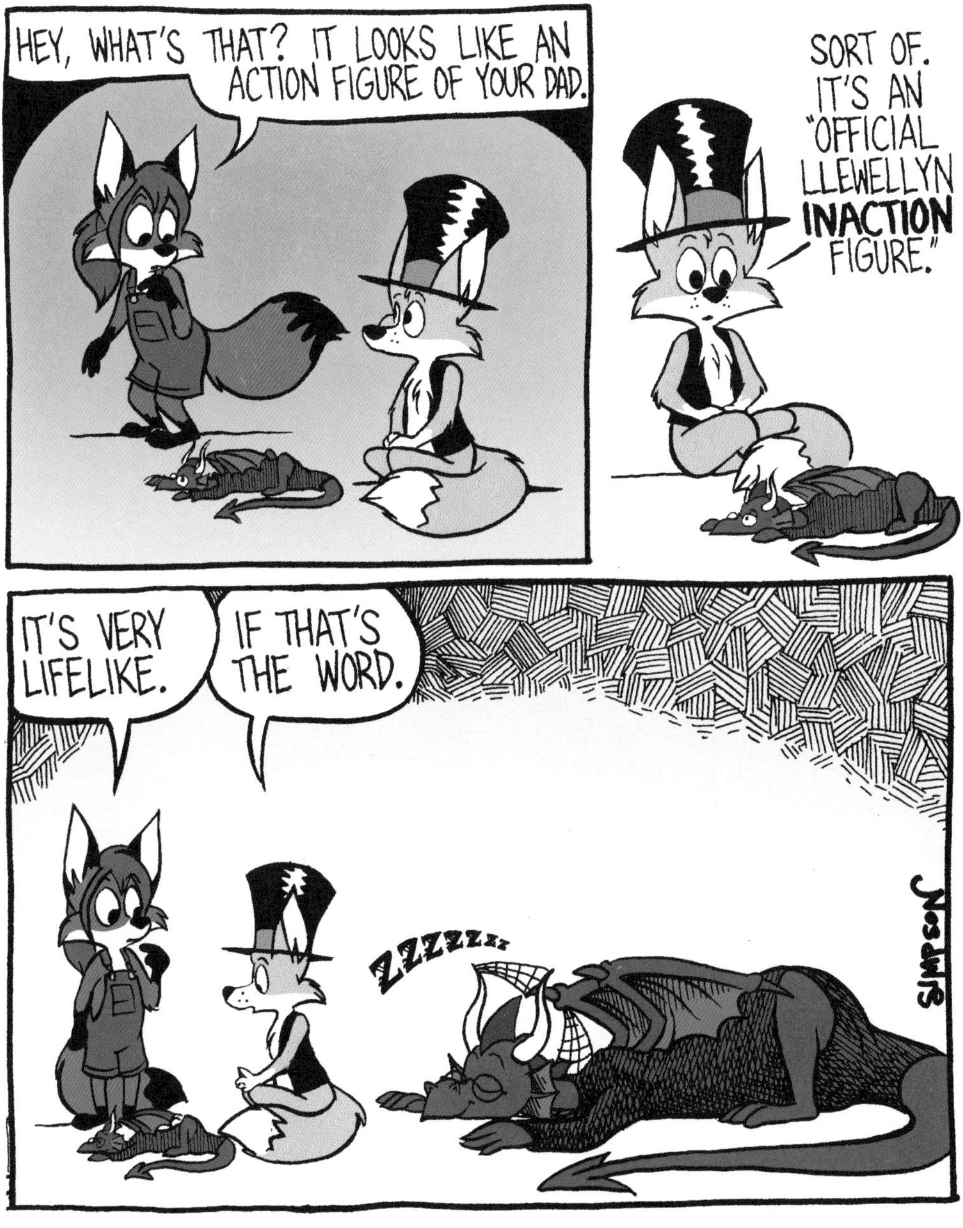
HEY, WHAT'S THAT? IT LOOKS LIKE AN ACTION FIGURE OF YOUR DAD.
SORT OF. IT'S AN "OFFICIAL LLEWELLYN **INACTION** FIGURE."
IT'S VERY LIFELIKE.
IF THAT'S THE WORD.
ZZZZZzz
SIMPSON

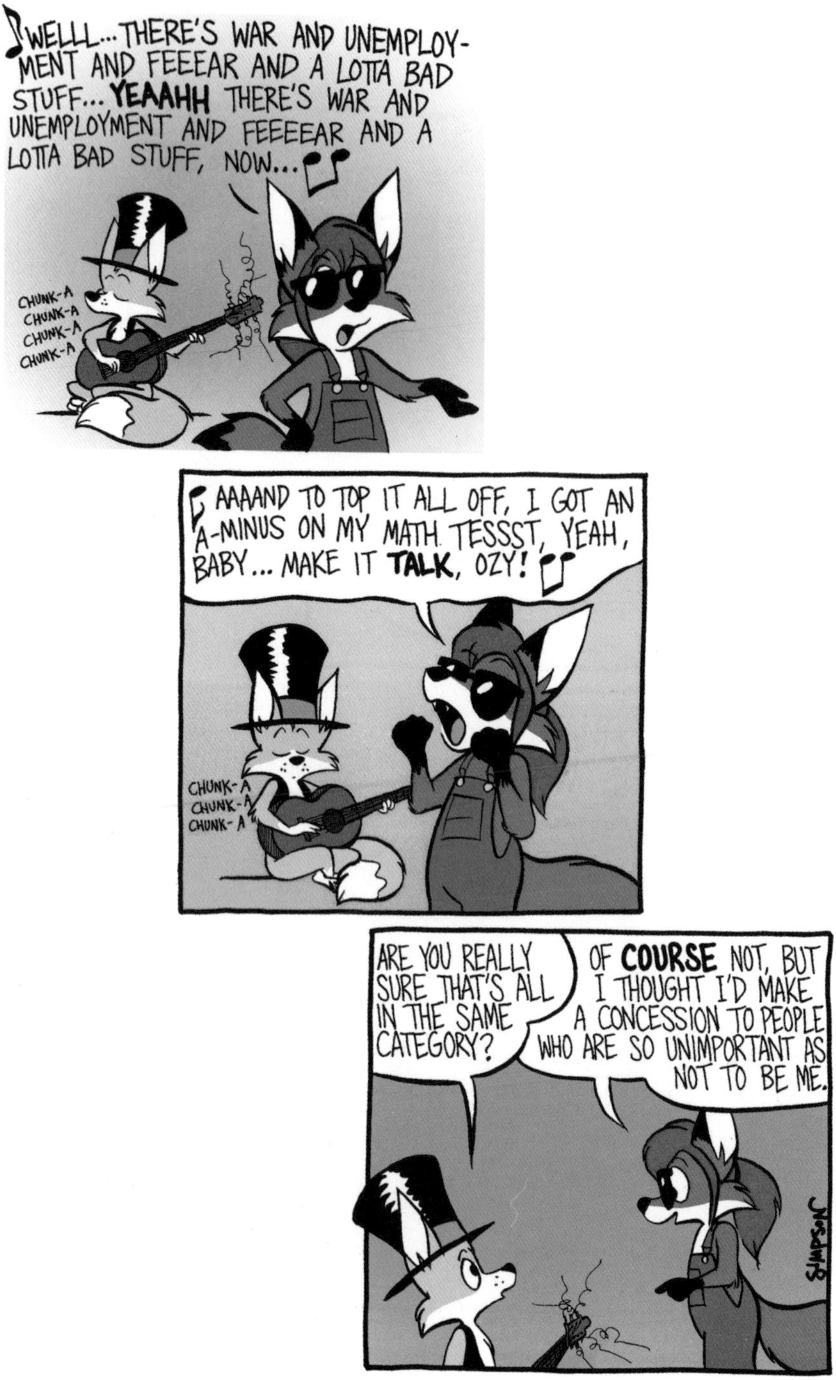
WELLL... THERE'S WAR AND UNEMPLOYMENT AND FEEEAR AND A LOTTA BAD STUFF... YEAAHH THERE'S WAR AND UNEMPLOYMENT AND FEEEEAR AND A LOTTA BAD STUFF, NOW...
CHUNK-A CHUNK-A CHUNK-A CHUNK-A
AAAAND TO TOP IT ALL OFF, I GOT AN A-MINUS ON MY MATH TESSST, YEAH, BABY... MAKE IT TALK, OZY!
CHUNK-A CHUNK-A CHUNK-A
ARE YOU REALLY SURE THAT'S ALL IN THE SAME CATEGORY?
OF COURSE NOT, BUT I THOUGHT I'D MAKE A CONCESSION TO PEOPLE WHO ARE SO UNIMPORTANT AS NOT TO BE ME.
SIMPSON

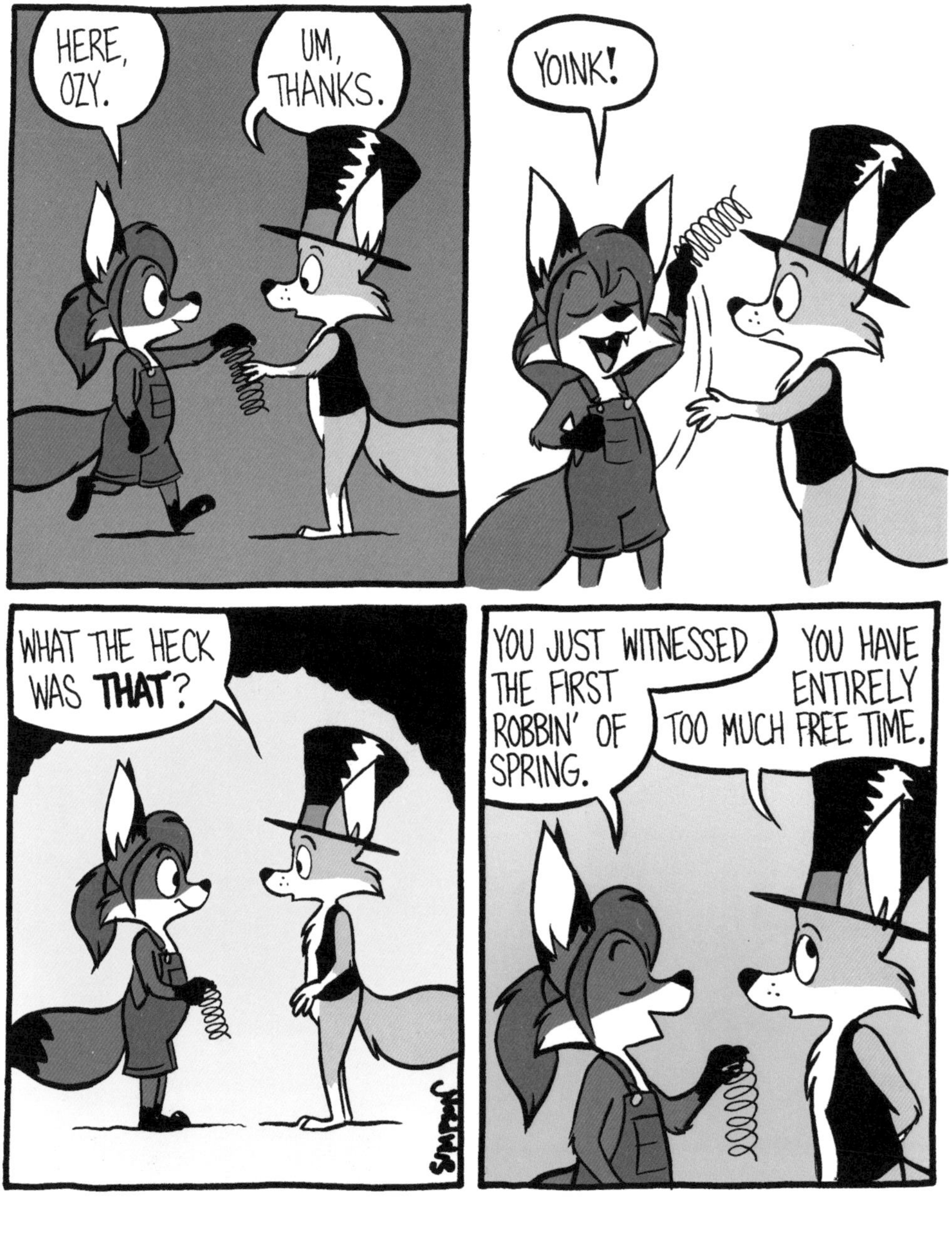
HERE, OZY.
UM, THANKS.
YOINK!
WHAT THE HECK WAS **THAT**?
YOU JUST WITNESSED THE FIRST ROBBIN' OF SPRING.
YOU HAVE ENTIRELY TOO MUCH FREE TIME.
SIMPSON

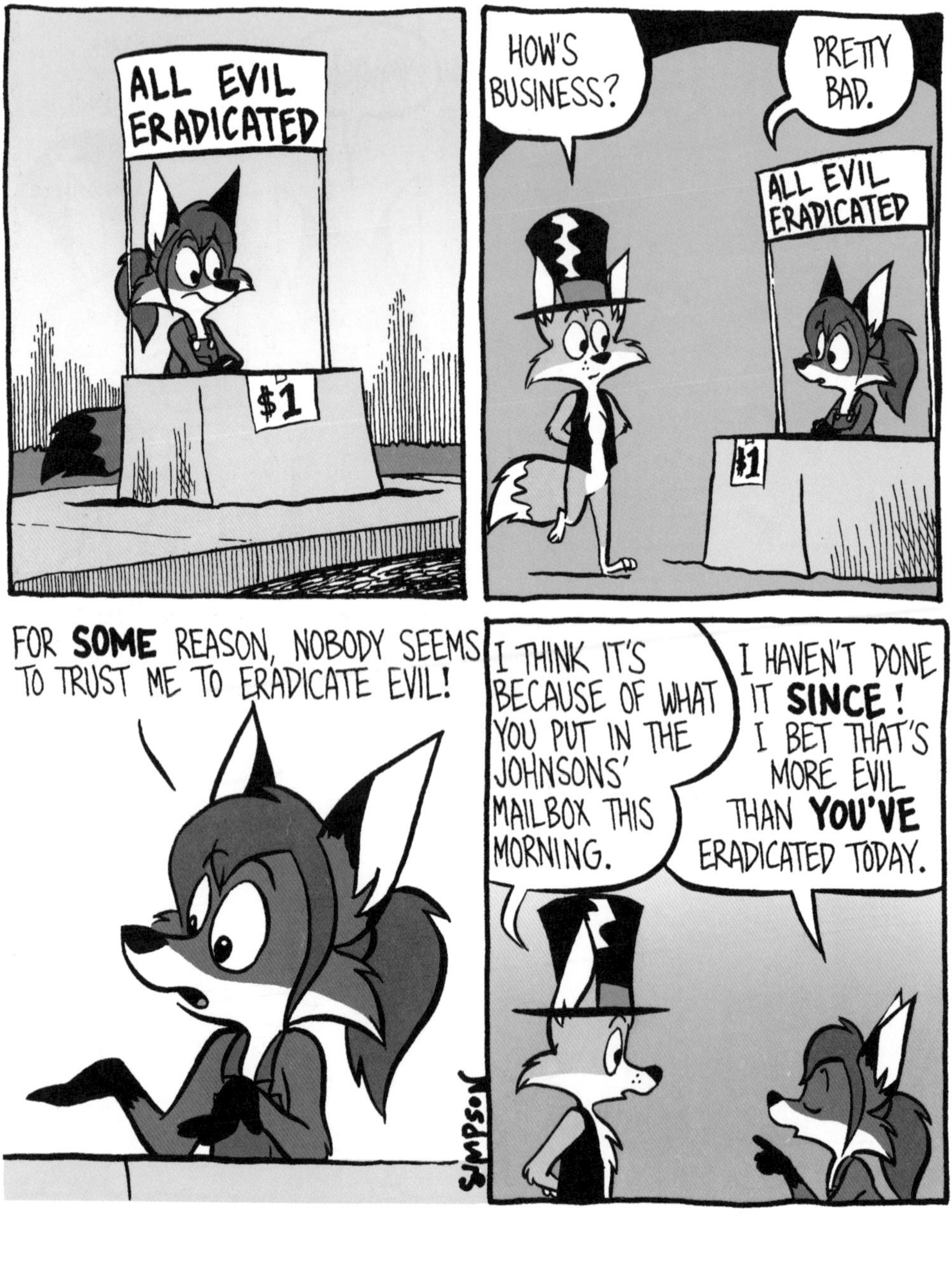
ALL EVIL ERADICATED
$1
HOW'S BUSINESS?
PRETTY BAD.
ALL EVIL ERADICATED
$1
FOR SOME REASON, NOBODY SEEMS TO TRUST ME TO ERADICATE EVIL!
I THINK IT'S BECAUSE OF WHAT YOU PUT IN THE JOHNSONS' MAILBOX THIS MORNING.
I HAVEN'T DONE IT SINCE! I BET THAT'S MORE EVIL THAN YOU'VE ERADICATED TODAY.
SIMPSON

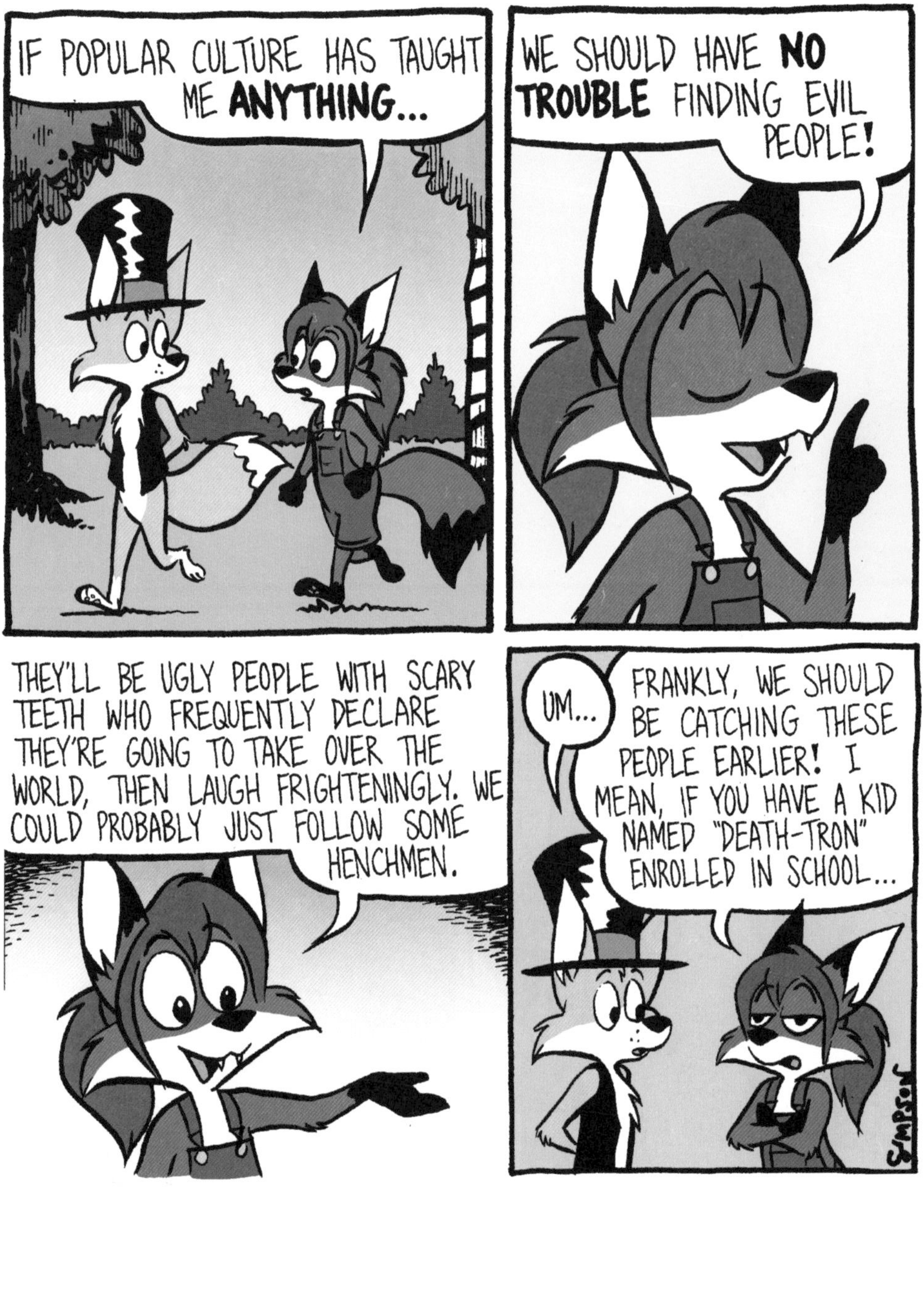
IF POPULAR CULTURE HAS TAUGHT ME **ANYTHING...**
WE SHOULD HAVE **NO TROUBLE** FINDING EVIL PEOPLE!
THEY'LL BE UGLY PEOPLE WITH SCARY TEETH WHO FREQUENTLY DECLARE THEY'RE GOING TO TAKE OVER THE WORLD, THEN LAUGH FRIGHTENINGLY. WE COULD PROBABLY JUST FOLLOW SOME HENCHMEN.
UM...
FRANKLY, WE SHOULD BE CATCHING THESE PEOPLE EARLIER! I MEAN, IF YOU HAVE A KID NAMED "DEATH-TRON" ENROLLED IN SCHOOL...
SIMPSON

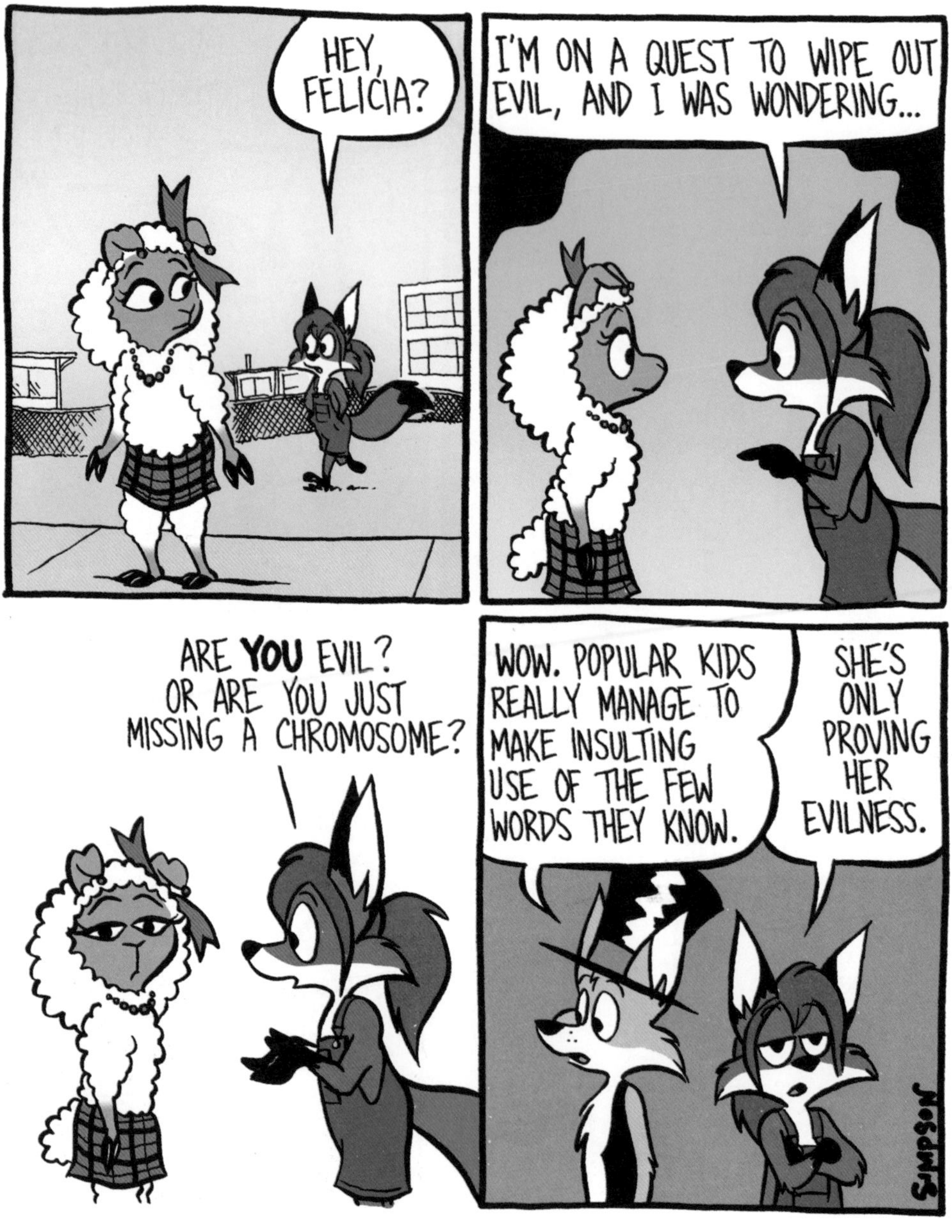
HEY, FELICIA?
I'M ON A QUEST TO WIPE OUT EVIL, AND I WAS WONDERING...
ARE **YOU** EVIL? OR ARE YOU JUST MISSING A CHROMOSOME?
WOW. POPULAR KIDS REALLY MANAGE TO MAKE INSULTING USE OF THE FEW WORDS THEY KNOW.
SHE'S ONLY PROVING HER EVILNESS.
SIMPSON

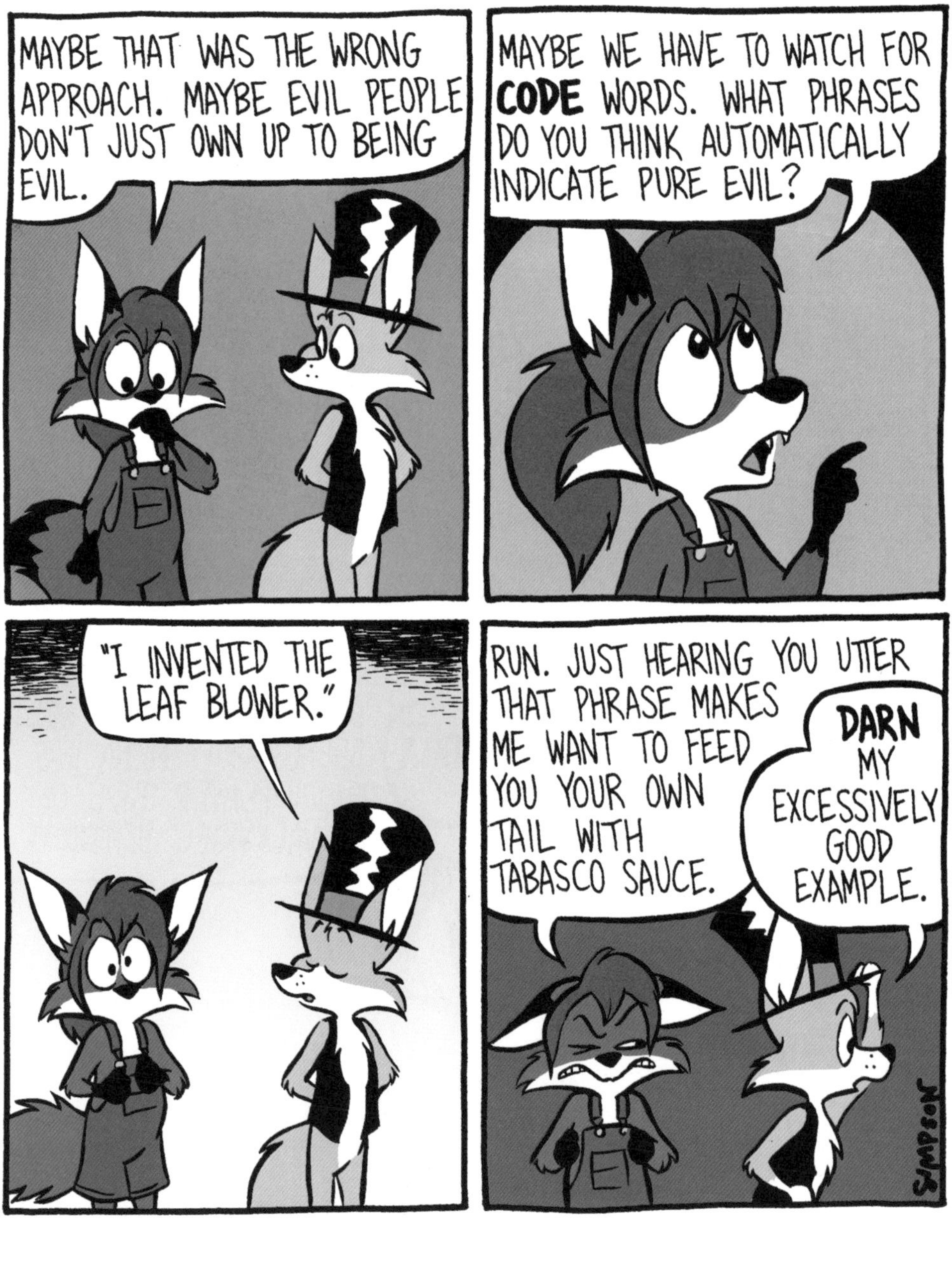

MAYBE THAT WAS THE WRONG APPROACH. MAYBE EVIL PEOPLE DON'T JUST OWN UP TO BEING EVIL.
MAYBE WE HAVE TO WATCH FOR **CODE** WORDS. WHAT PHRASES DO YOU THINK AUTOMATICALLY INDICATE PURE EVIL?
"I INVENTED THE LEAF BLOWER."
RUN. JUST HEARING YOU UTTER THAT PHRASE MAKES ME WANT TO FEED YOU YOUR OWN TAIL WITH TABASCO SAUCE.
DARN MY EXCESSIVELY GOOD EXAMPLE.
SIMPSON

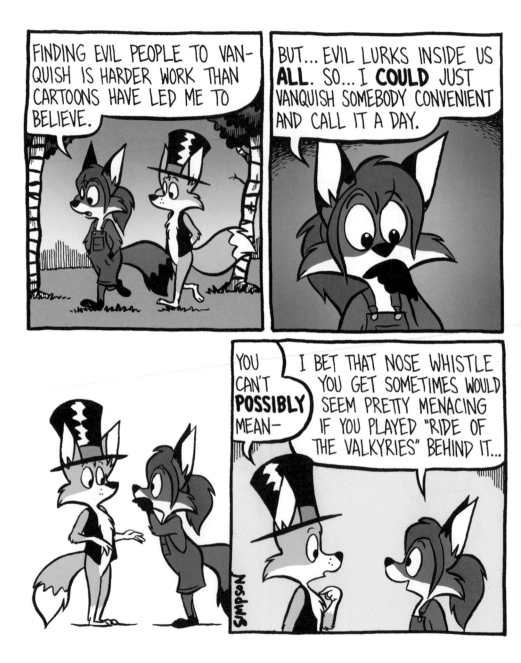

FINDING EVIL PEOPLE TO VAN-QUISH IS HARDER WORK THAN CARTOONS HAVE LED ME TO BELIEVE.

BUT... EVIL LURKS INSIDE US **ALL**. SO... I **COULD** JUST VANQUISH SOMEBODY CONVENIENT AND CALL IT A DAY.

YOU CAN'T **POSSIBLY** MEAN—

I BET THAT NOSE WHISTLE YOU GET SOMETIMES WOULD SEEM PRETTY MENACING IF YOU PLAYED "RIDE OF THE VALKYRIES" BEHIND IT...

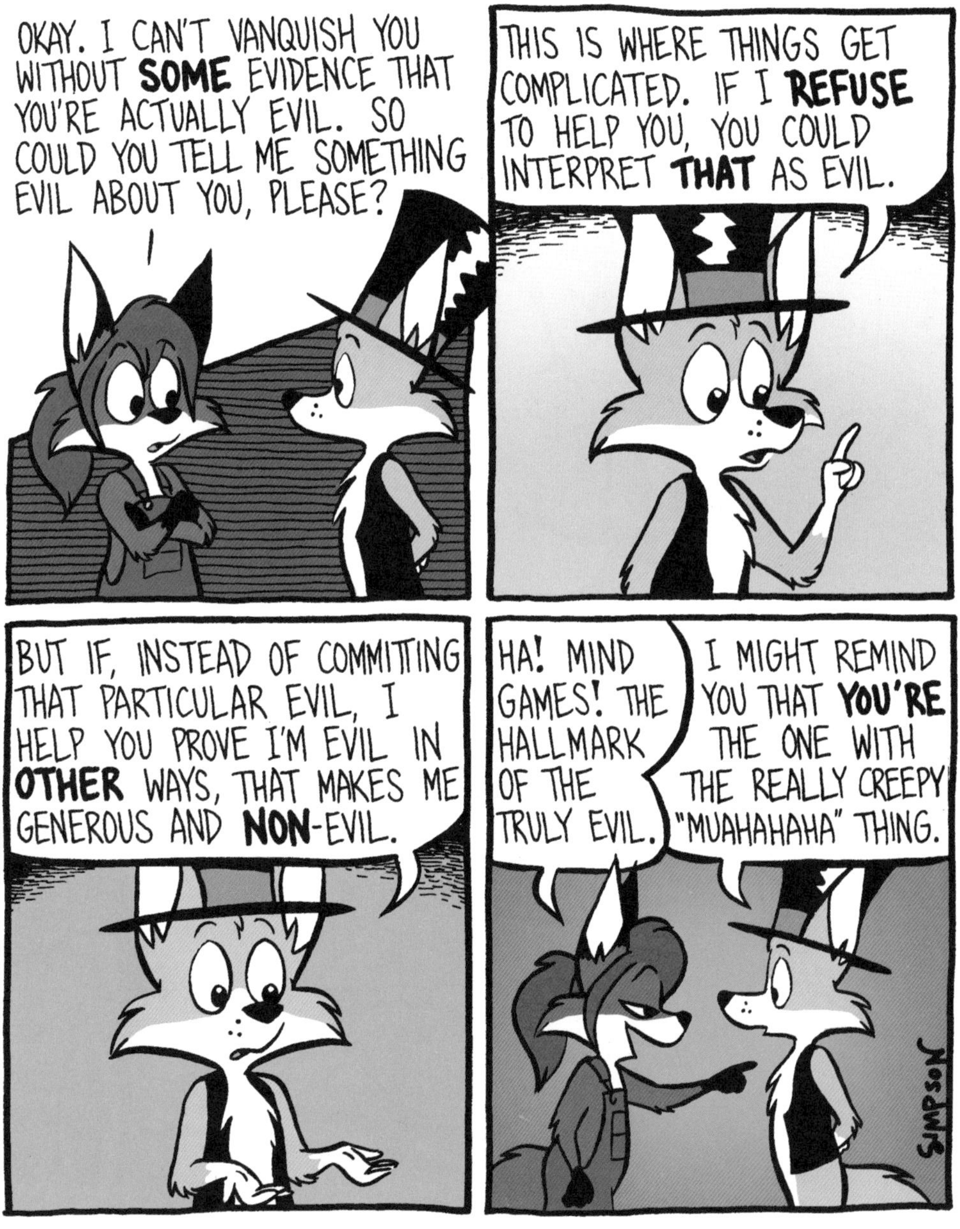
OKAY. I CAN'T VANQUISH YOU WITHOUT **SOME** EVIDENCE THAT YOU'RE ACTUALLY EVIL. SO COULD YOU TELL ME SOMETHING EVIL ABOUT YOU, PLEASE?
THIS IS WHERE THINGS GET COMPLICATED. IF I **REFUSE** TO HELP YOU, YOU COULD INTERPRET **THAT** AS EVIL.
BUT IF, INSTEAD OF COMMITTING THAT PARTICULAR EVIL, I HELP YOU PROVE I'M EVIL IN **OTHER** WAYS, THAT MAKES ME GENEROUS AND **NON**-EVIL.
HA! MIND GAMES! THE HALLMARK OF THE TRULY EVIL.
I MIGHT REMIND YOU THAT **YOU'RE** THE ONE WITH THE REALLY CREEPY "MUAHAHAHA" THING.
SIMPSON

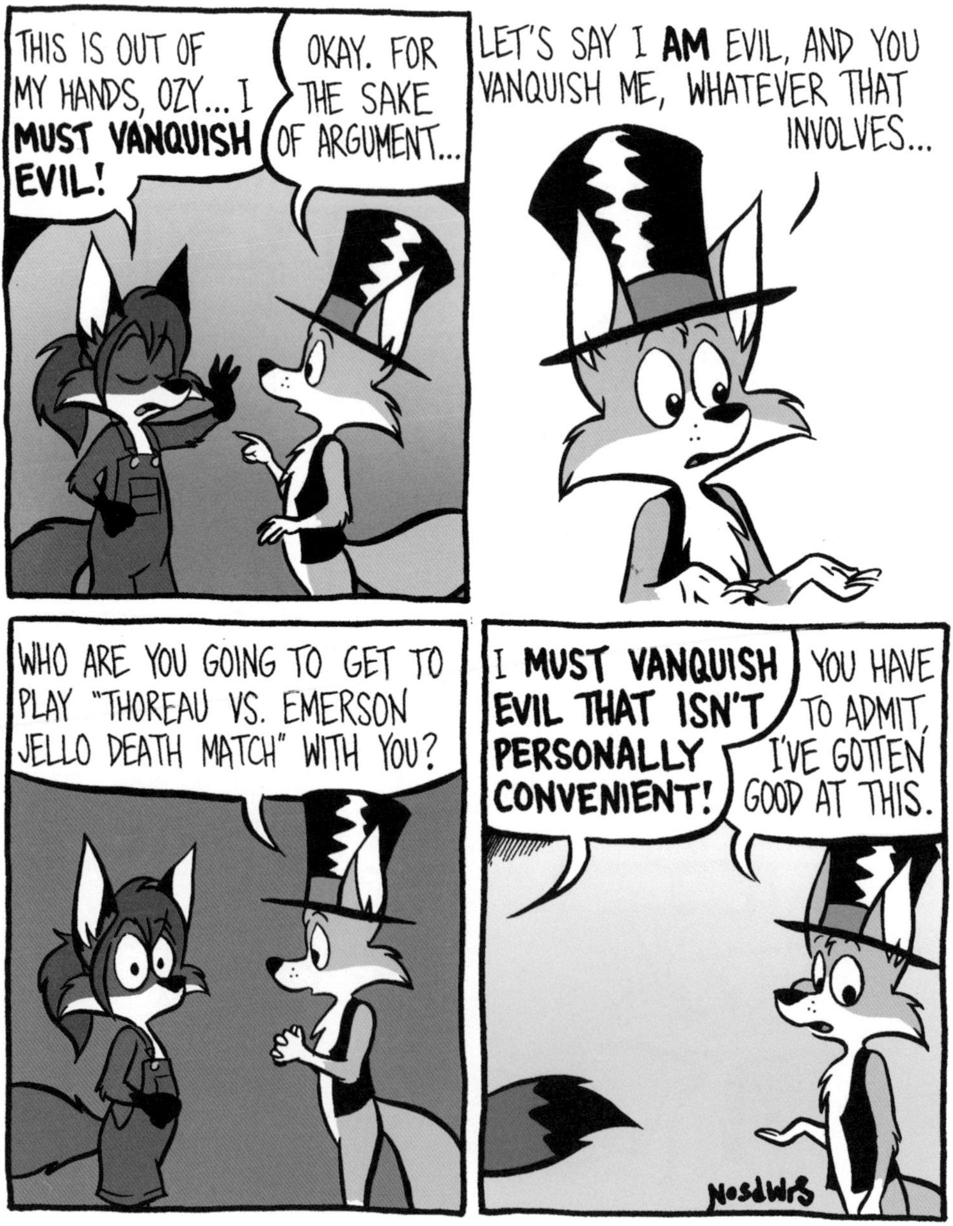
THIS IS OUT OF MY HANDS, OZY... I **MUST VANQUISH EVIL!**
OKAY. FOR THE SAKE OF ARGUMENT...
LET'S SAY I **AM** EVIL, AND YOU VANQUISH ME, WHATEVER THAT INVOLVES...
WHO ARE YOU GOING TO GET TO PLAY "THOREAU VS. EMERSON JELLO DEATH MATCH" WITH YOU?
I **MUST VANQUISH EVIL THAT ISN'T PERSONALLY CONVENIENT!**
YOU HAVE TO ADMIT, I'VE GOTTEN GOOD AT THIS.
NOSDWRS

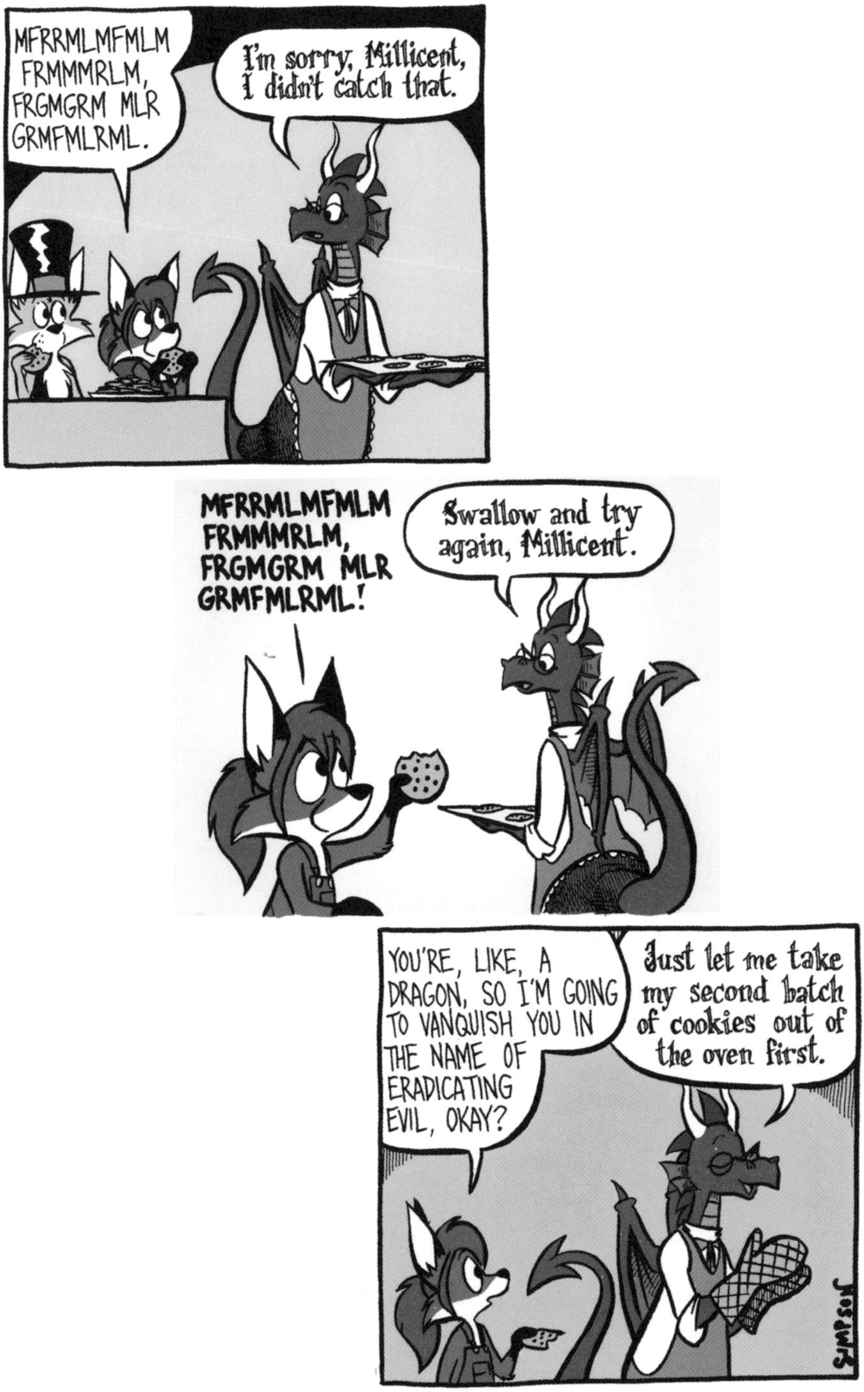
MFRRMLMFMLM FRMMMRLM, FRGMGRM MLR GRMFMLRML.
I'm sorry, Millicent, I didn't catch that.
MFRRMLMFMLM FRMMMRLM, FRGMGRM MLR GRMFMLRML!
Swallow and try again, Millicent.
YOU'RE, LIKE, A DRAGON, SO I'M GOING TO VANQUISH YOU IN THE NAME OF ERADICATING EVIL, OKAY?
Just let me take my second batch of cookies out of the oven first.
SIMPSON

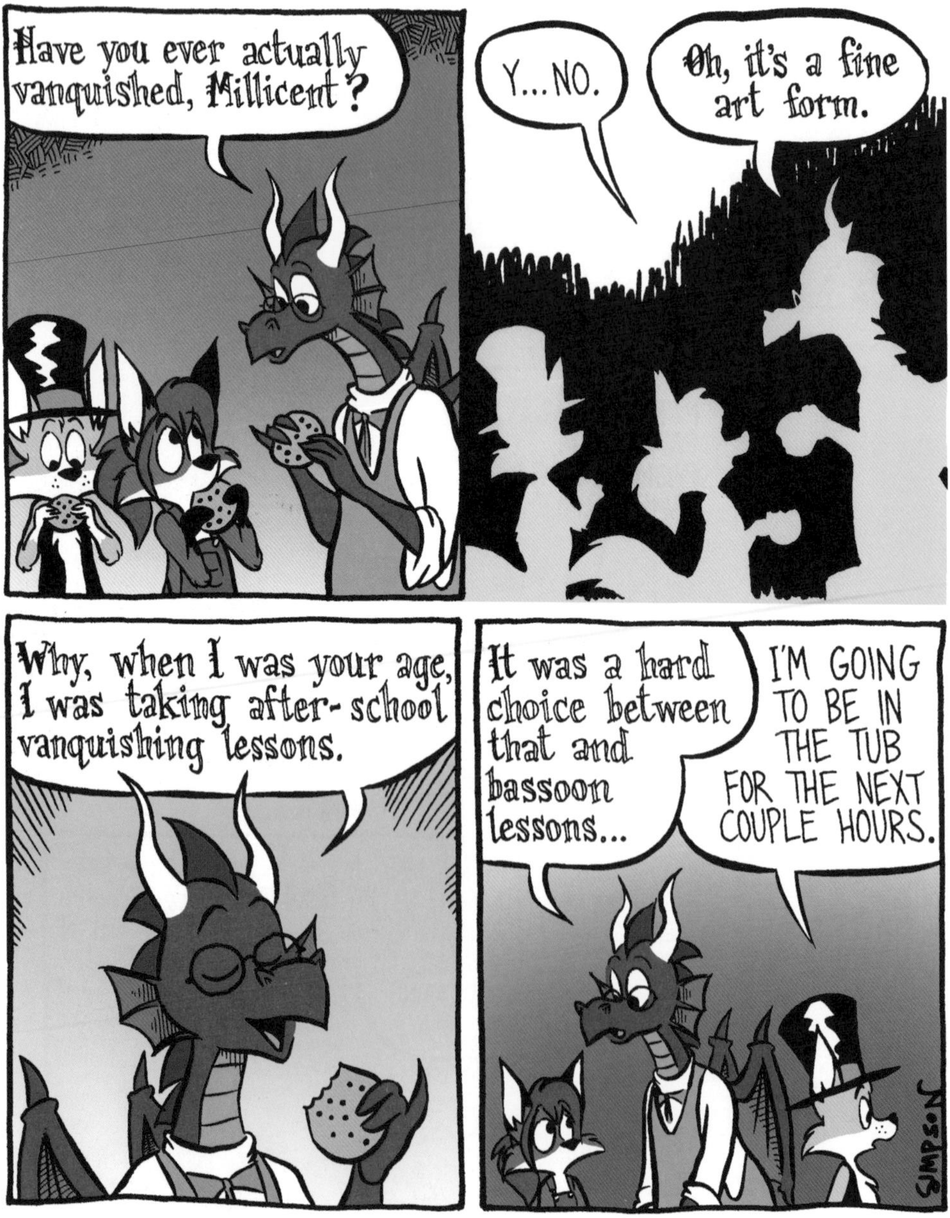
Have you ever actually vanquished, Millicent?
Y...NO.
Oh, it's a fine art form.
Why, when I was your age, I was taking after-school vanquishing lessons.
It was a hard choice between that and bassoon lessons...
I'M GOING TO BE IN THE TUB FOR THE NEXT COUPLE HOURS.
SIMPSON

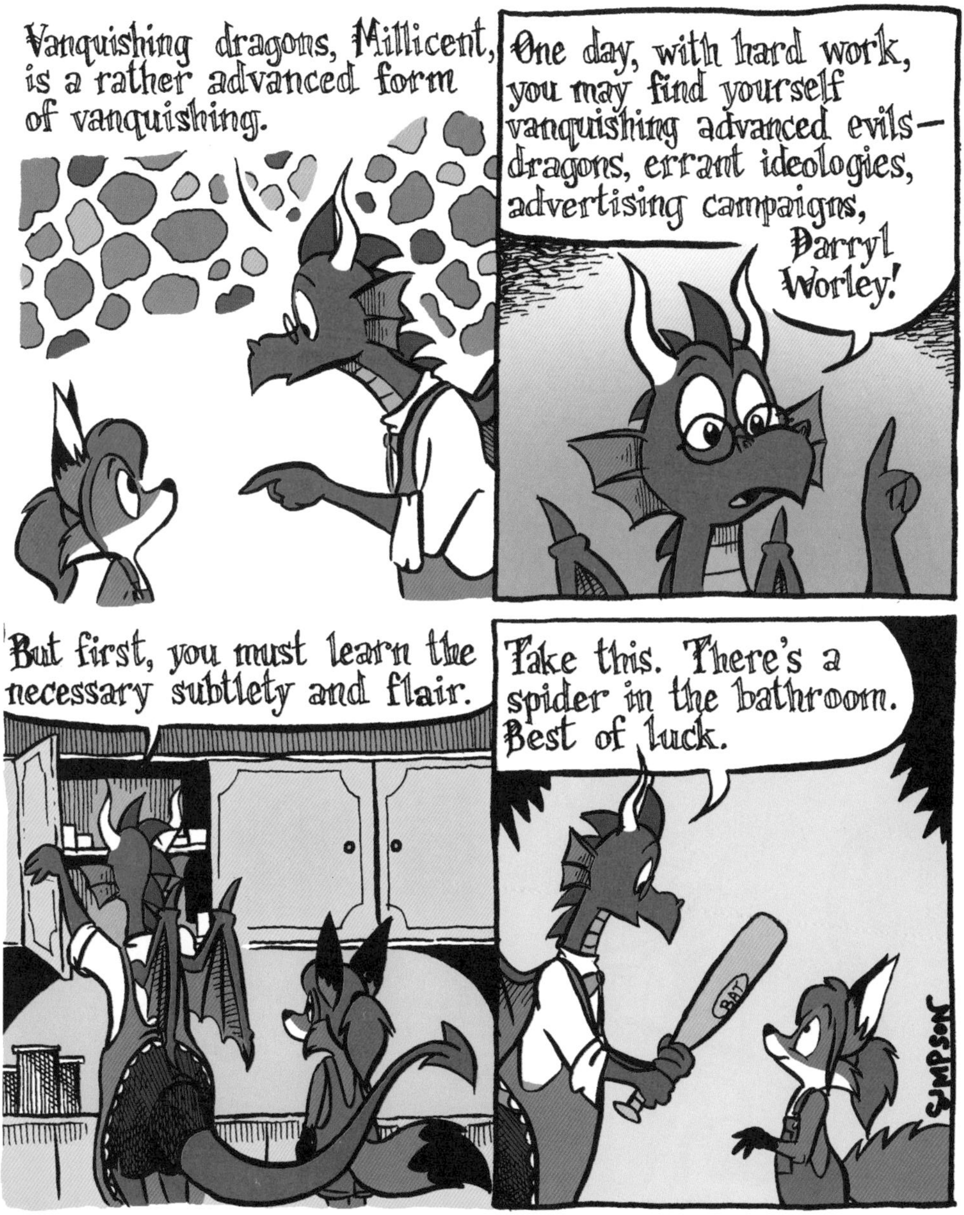
Vanquishing dragons, Millicent, is a rather advanced form of vanquishing.
One day, with hard work, you may find yourself vanquishing advanced evils— dragons, errant ideologies, advertising campaigns,
Darryl Worley!
But first, you must learn the necessary subtlety and flair.
Take this. There's a spider in the bathroom. Best of luck.
BAT
SIMPSON

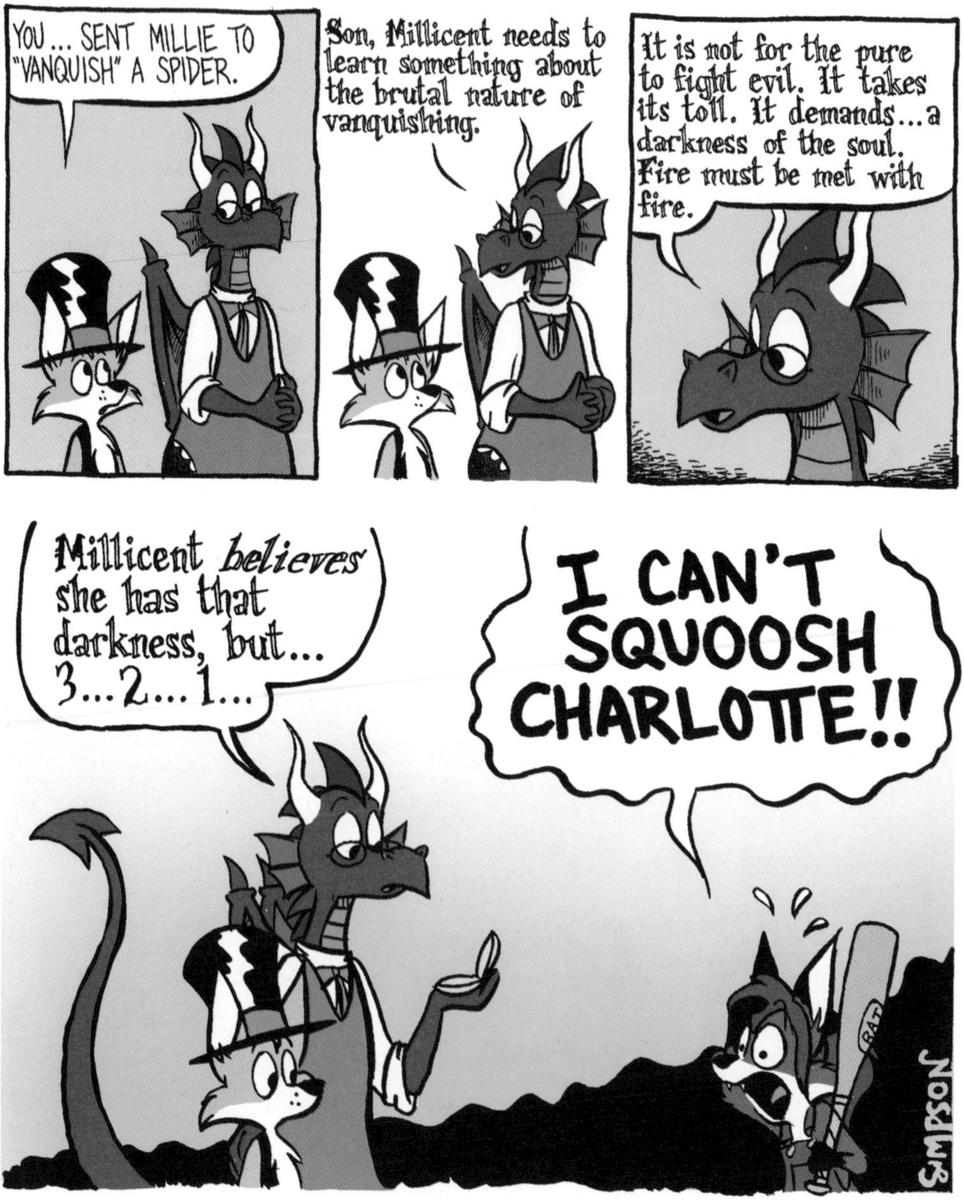
YOU ... SENT MILLIE TO "VANQUISH" A SPIDER.
Son, Millicent needs to learn something about the brutal nature of vanquishing.
It is not for the pure to fight evil. It takes its toll. It demands... a darkness of the soul. Fire must be met with fire.
Millicent *believes* she has that darkness, but... 3... 2... 1...
I CAN'T SQUOOSH CHARLOTTE!!
BAT
SIMPSON

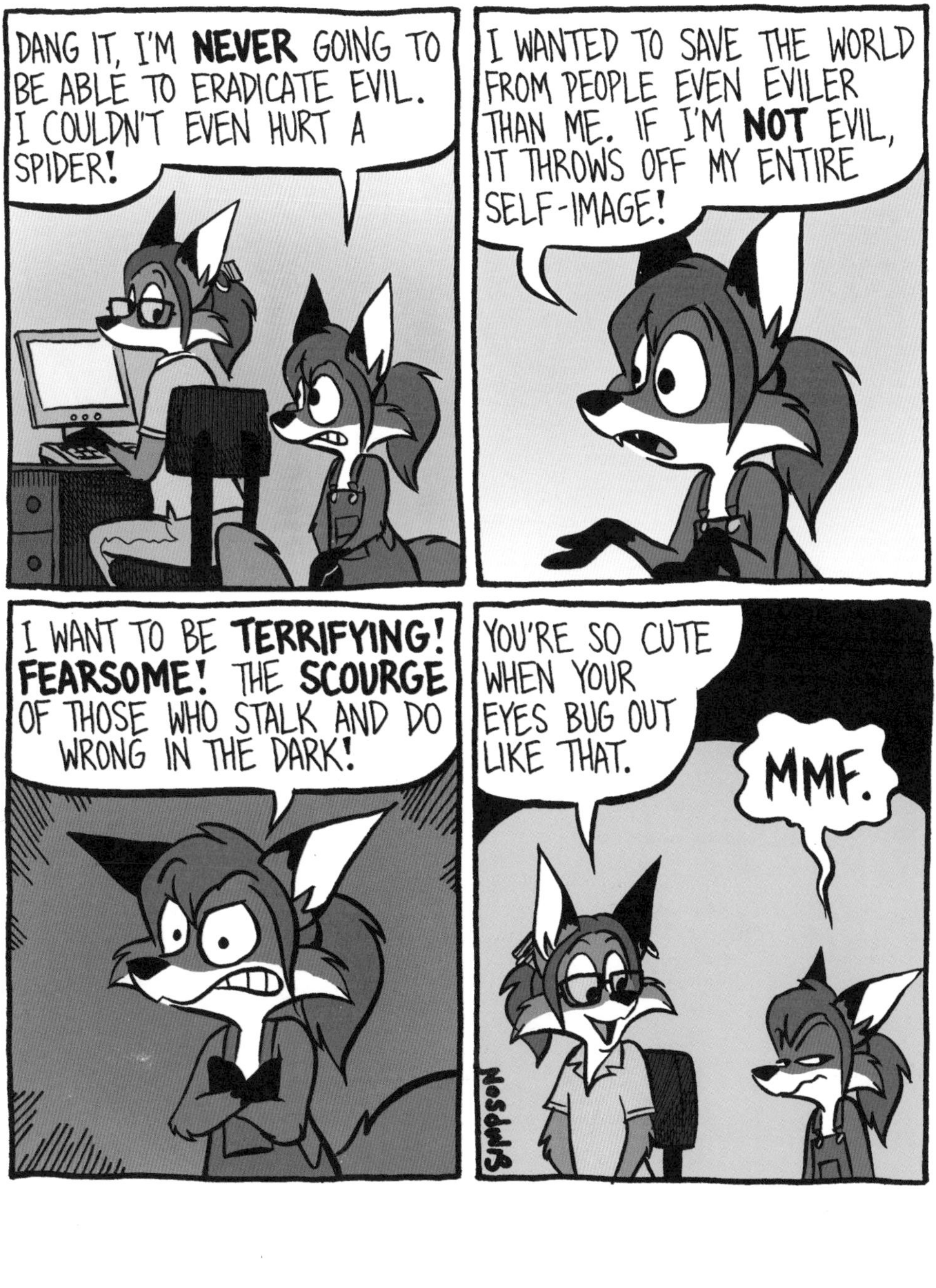
DANG IT, I'M **NEVER** GOING TO BE ABLE TO ERADICATE EVIL. I COULDN'T EVEN HURT A SPIDER!
I WANTED TO SAVE THE WORLD FROM PEOPLE EVEN EVILER THAN ME. IF I'M **NOT** EVIL, IT THROWS OFF MY ENTIRE SELF-IMAGE!
I WANT TO BE **TERRIFYING! FEARSOME!** THE **SCOURGE** OF THOSE WHO STALK AND DO WRONG IN THE DARK!
YOU'RE SO CUTE WHEN YOUR EYES BUG OUT LIKE THAT.
MMF.
Simpson

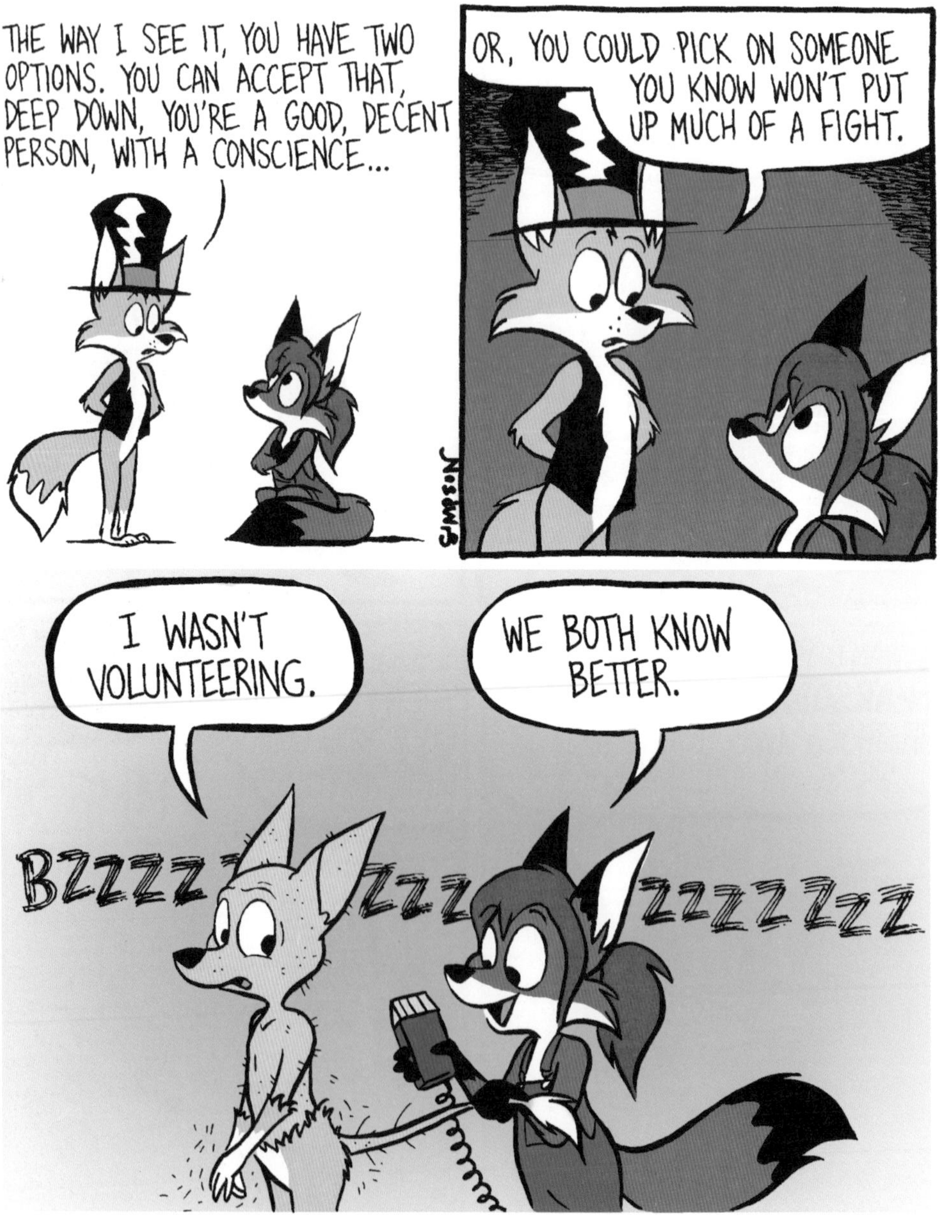
THE WAY I SEE IT, YOU HAVE TWO OPTIONS. YOU CAN ACCEPT THAT, DEEP DOWN, YOU'RE A GOOD, DECENT PERSON, WITH A CONSCIENCE...
SIMPSON
OR, YOU COULD PICK ON SOMEONE YOU KNOW WON'T PUT UP MUCH OF A FIGHT.
I WASN'T VOLUNTEERING.
WE BOTH KNOW BETTER.
BZZZZZZZZZZZZZZZZZZ

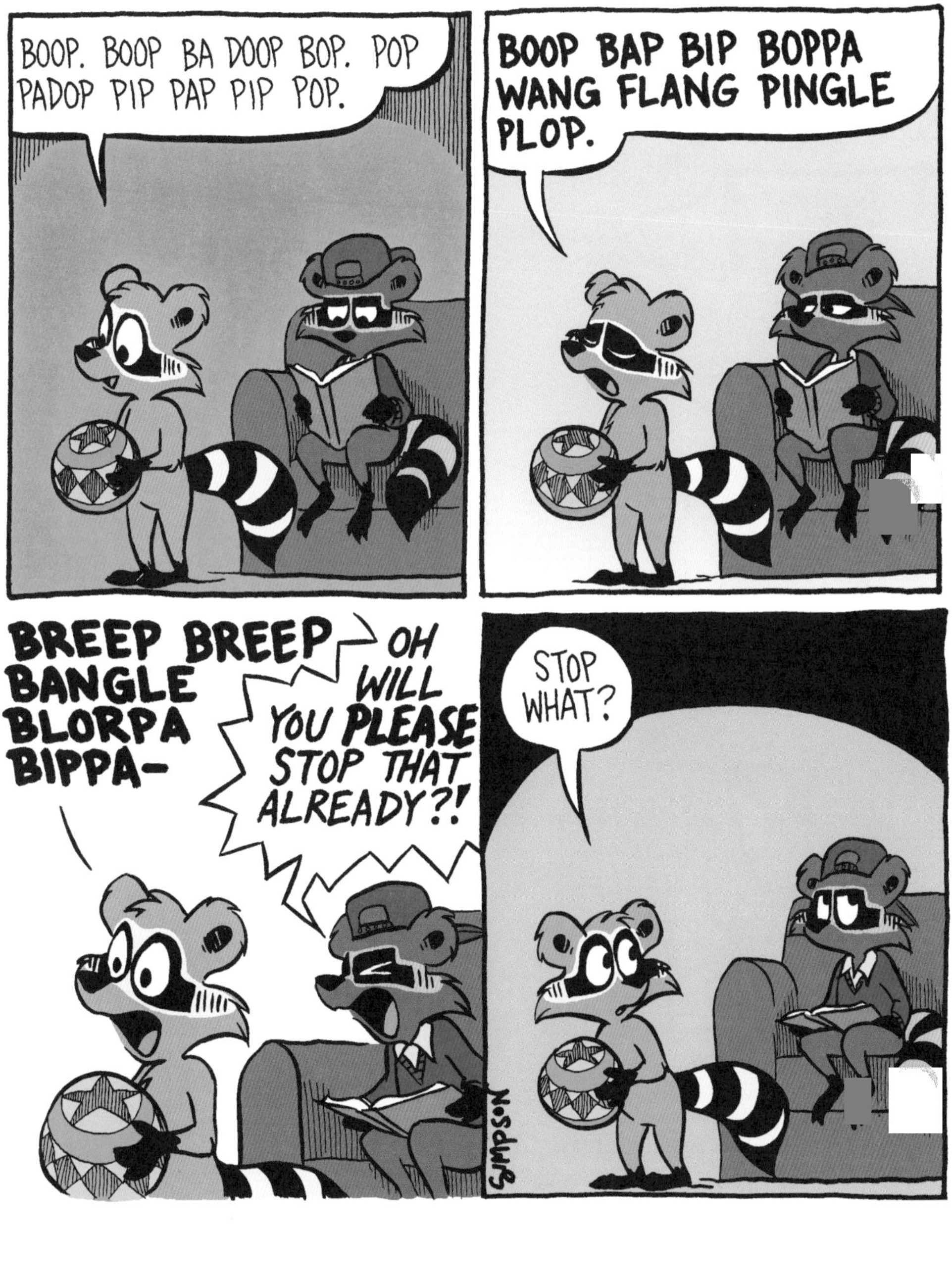
BOOP. BOOP BA DOOP BOP. POP PADOP PIP PAP PIP POP.
BOOP BAP BIP BOPPA WANG FLANG PINGLE PLOP.
BREEP BREEP BANGLE BLORPA BIPPA-
OH WILL YOU PLEASE STOP THAT ALREADY?!
STOP WHAT?
SIMPSON

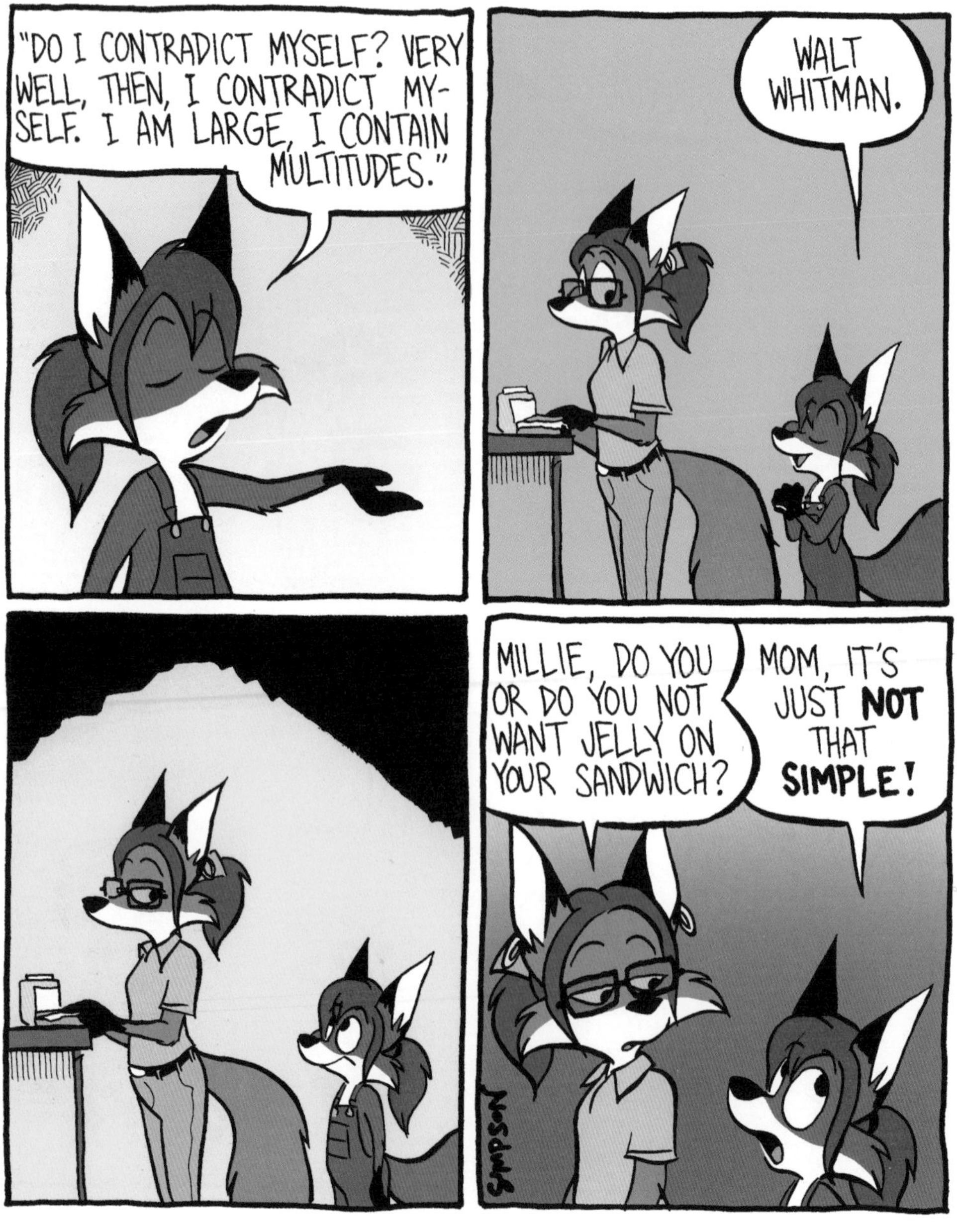
"DO I CONTRADICT MYSELF? VERY WELL, THEN, I CONTRADICT MY-SELF. I AM LARGE, I CONTAIN MULTITUDES."
WALT WHITMAN.
MILLIE, DO YOU OR DO YOU NOT WANT JELLY ON YOUR SANDWICH?
MOM, IT'S JUST **NOT** THAT **SIMPLE!**
SIMPSON

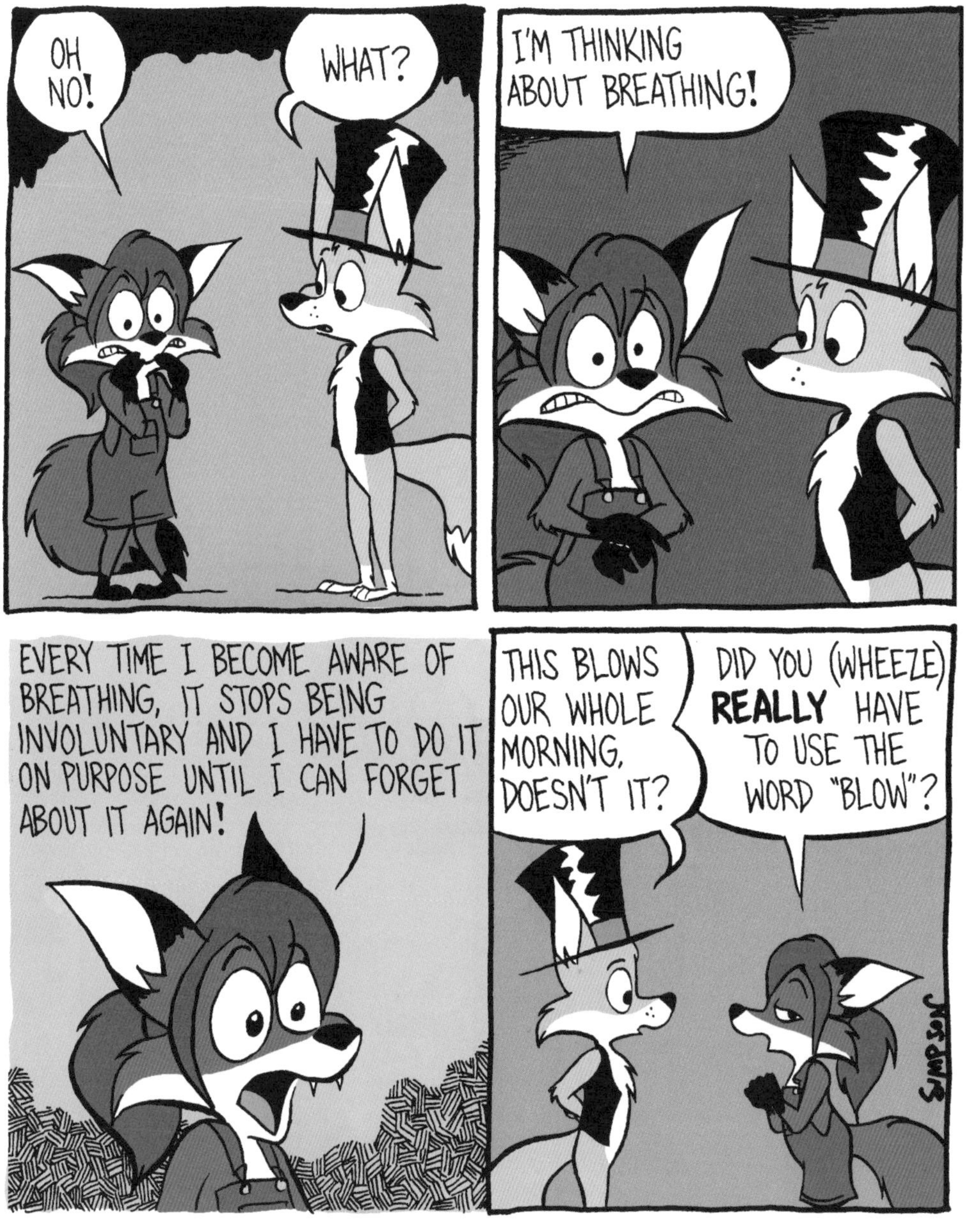
OH NO!
WHAT?
I'M THINKING ABOUT BREATHING!
EVERY TIME I BECOME AWARE OF BREATHING, IT STOPS BEING INVOLUNTARY AND I HAVE TO DO IT ON PURPOSE UNTIL I CAN FORGET ABOUT IT AGAIN!
THIS BLOWS OUR WHOLE MORNING, DOESN'T IT?
DID YOU (WHEEZE) REALLY HAVE TO USE THE WORD "BLOW"?
SIMPSON

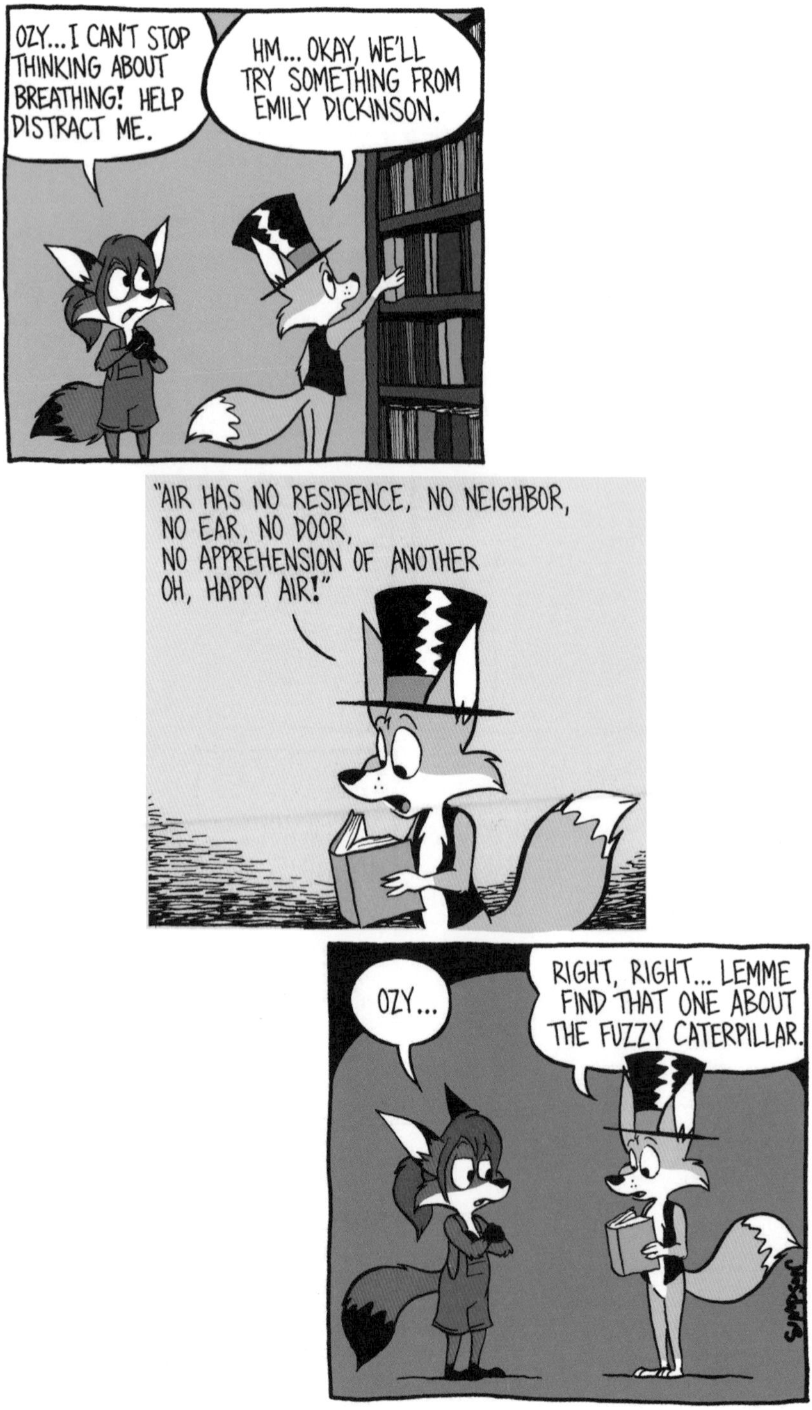
OZY... I CAN'T STOP THINKING ABOUT BREATHING! HELP DISTRACT ME.
HM... OKAY, WE'LL TRY SOMETHING FROM EMILY DICKINSON.
"AIR HAS NO RESIDENCE, NO NEIGHBOR, NO EAR, NO DOOR, NO APPREHENSION OF ANOTHER OH, HAPPY AIR!"
OZY...
RIGHT, RIGHT... LEMME FIND THAT ONE ABOUT THE FUZZY CATERPILLAR.
SIMPSON

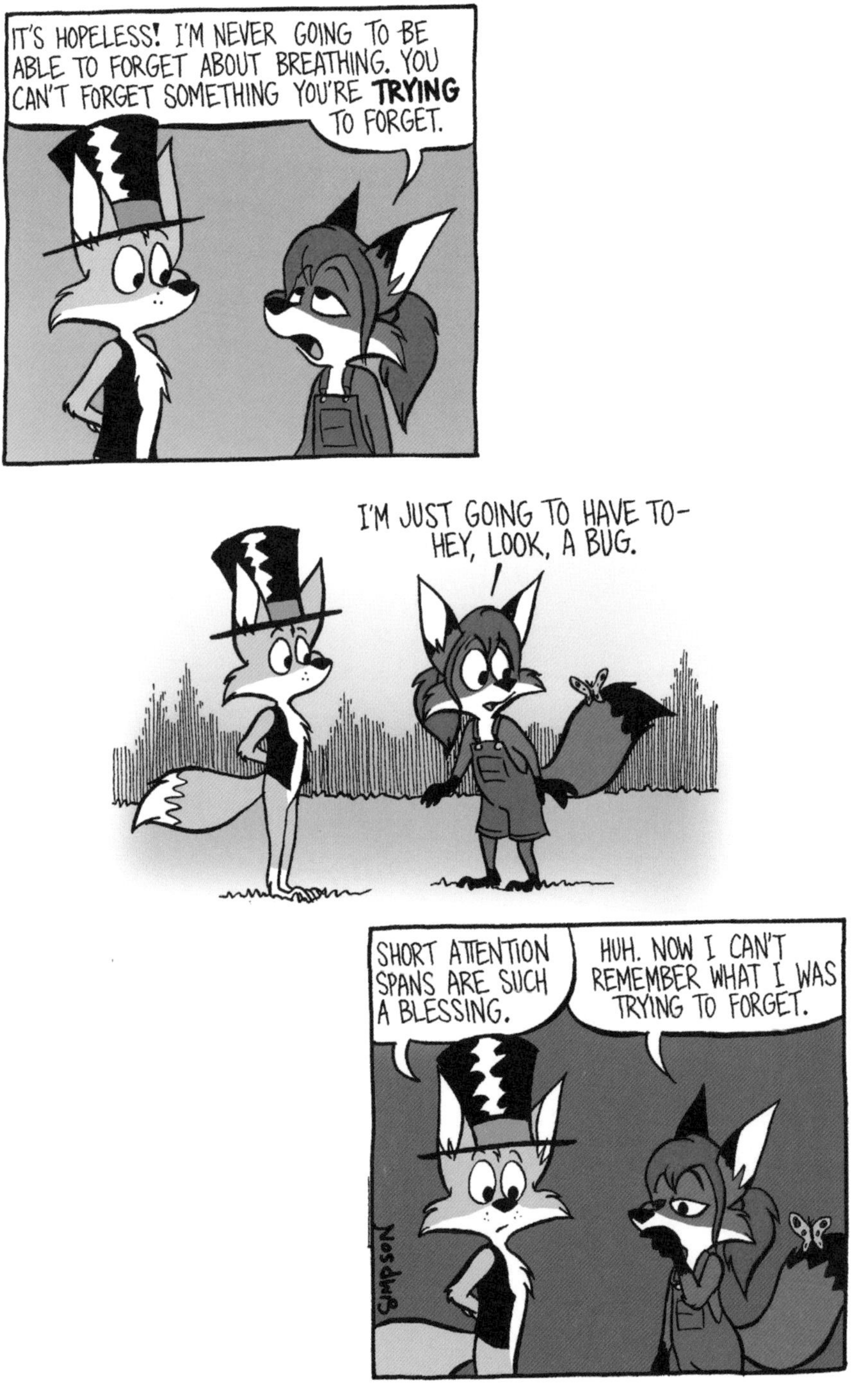
IT'S HOPELESS! I'M NEVER GOING TO BE ABLE TO FORGET ABOUT BREATHING. YOU CAN'T FORGET SOMETHING YOU'RE **TRYING** TO FORGET.
I'M JUST GOING TO HAVE TO- HEY, LOOK, A BUG.
SHORT ATTENTION SPANS ARE SUCH A BLESSING.
HUH. NOW I CAN'T REMEMBER WHAT I WAS TRYING TO FORGET.
SIMPSON

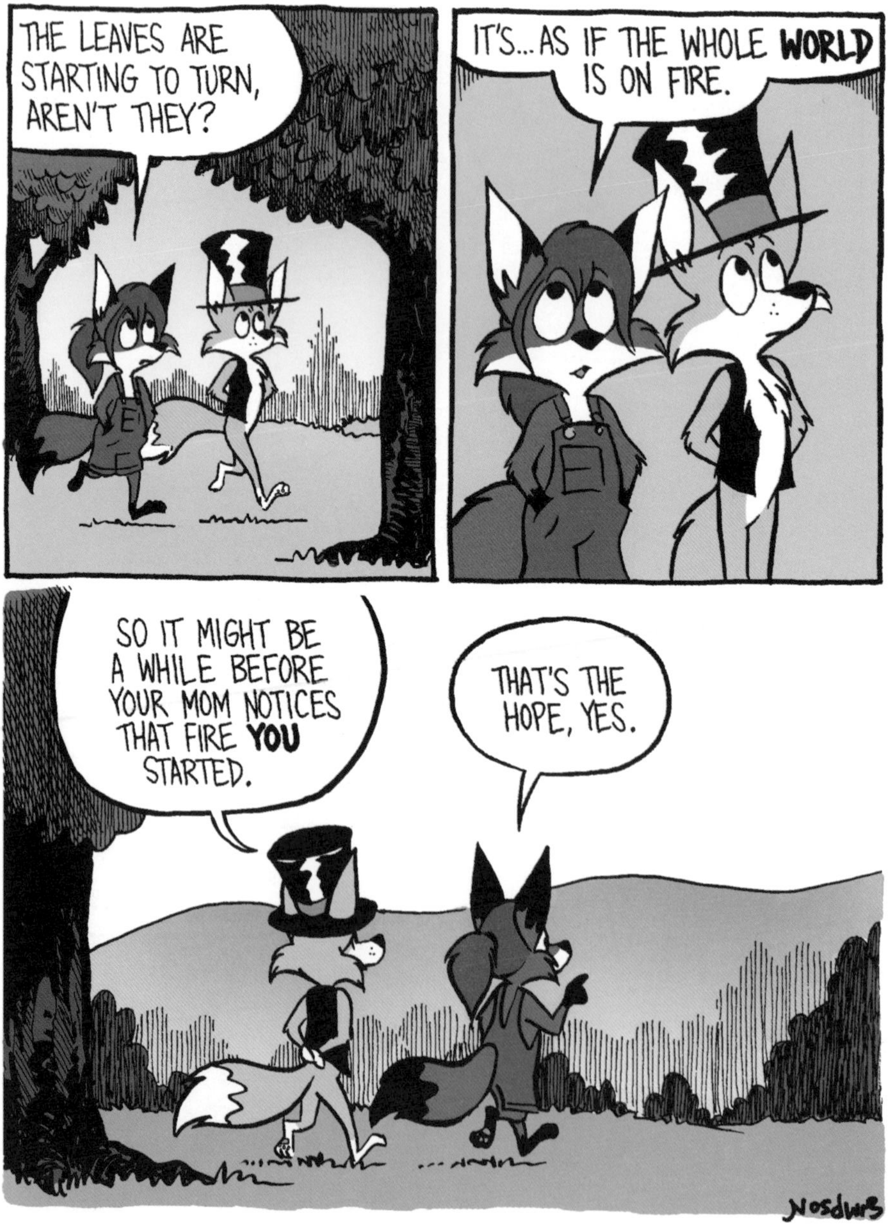
THE LEAVES ARE STARTING TO TURN, AREN'T THEY?
IT'S...AS IF THE WHOLE **WORLD** IS ON FIRE.
SO IT MIGHT BE A WHILE BEFORE YOUR MOM NOTICES THAT FIRE **YOU** STARTED.
THAT'S THE HOPE, YES.
Nosdurs

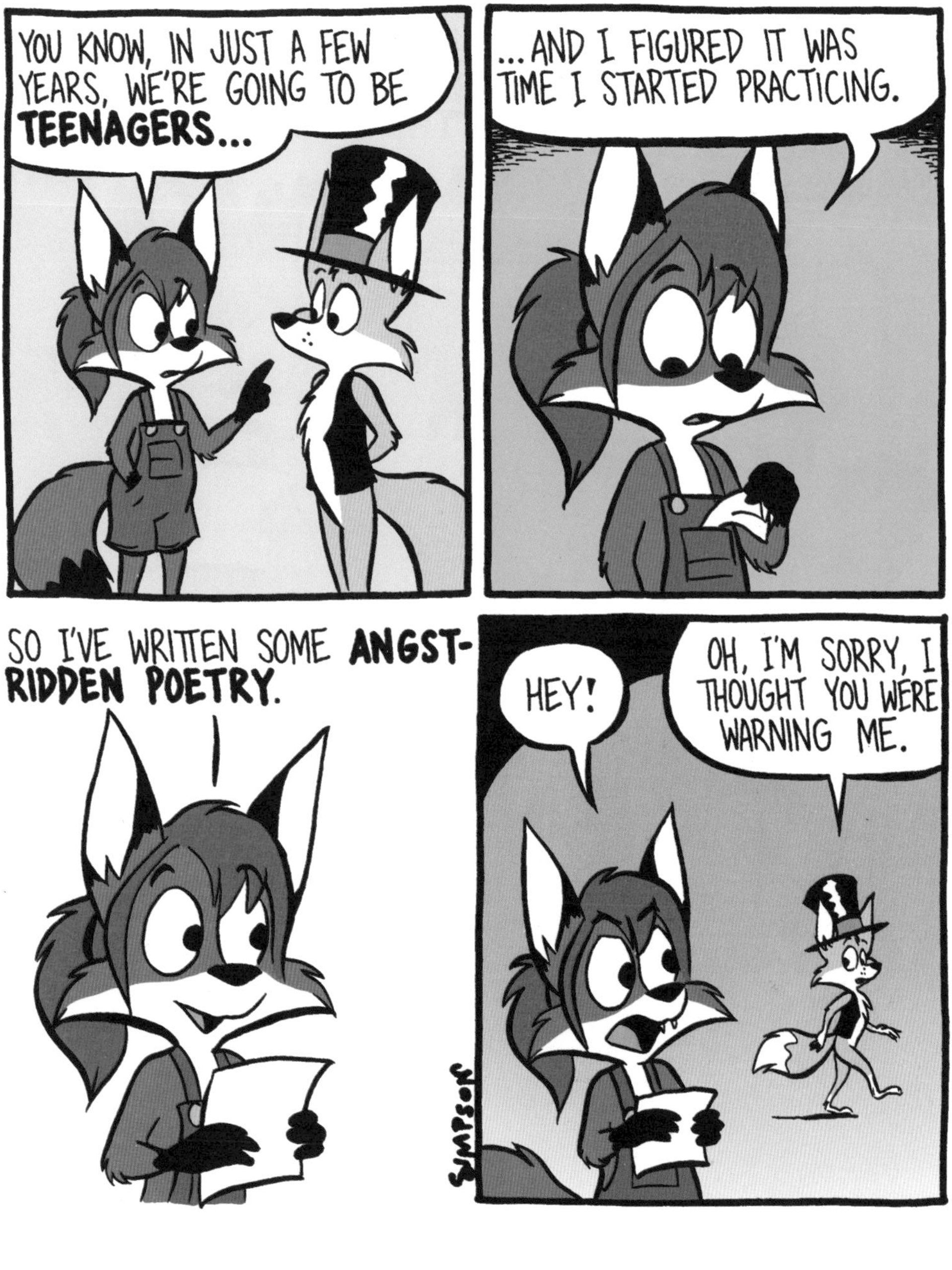
YOU KNOW, IN JUST A FEW YEARS, WE'RE GOING TO BE **TEENAGERS**...
...AND I FIGURED IT WAS TIME I STARTED PRACTICING.
SO I'VE WRITTEN SOME **ANGST-RIDDEN POETRY**.
HEY!
OH, I'M SORRY, I THOUGHT YOU WERE WARNING ME.
SIMPSON

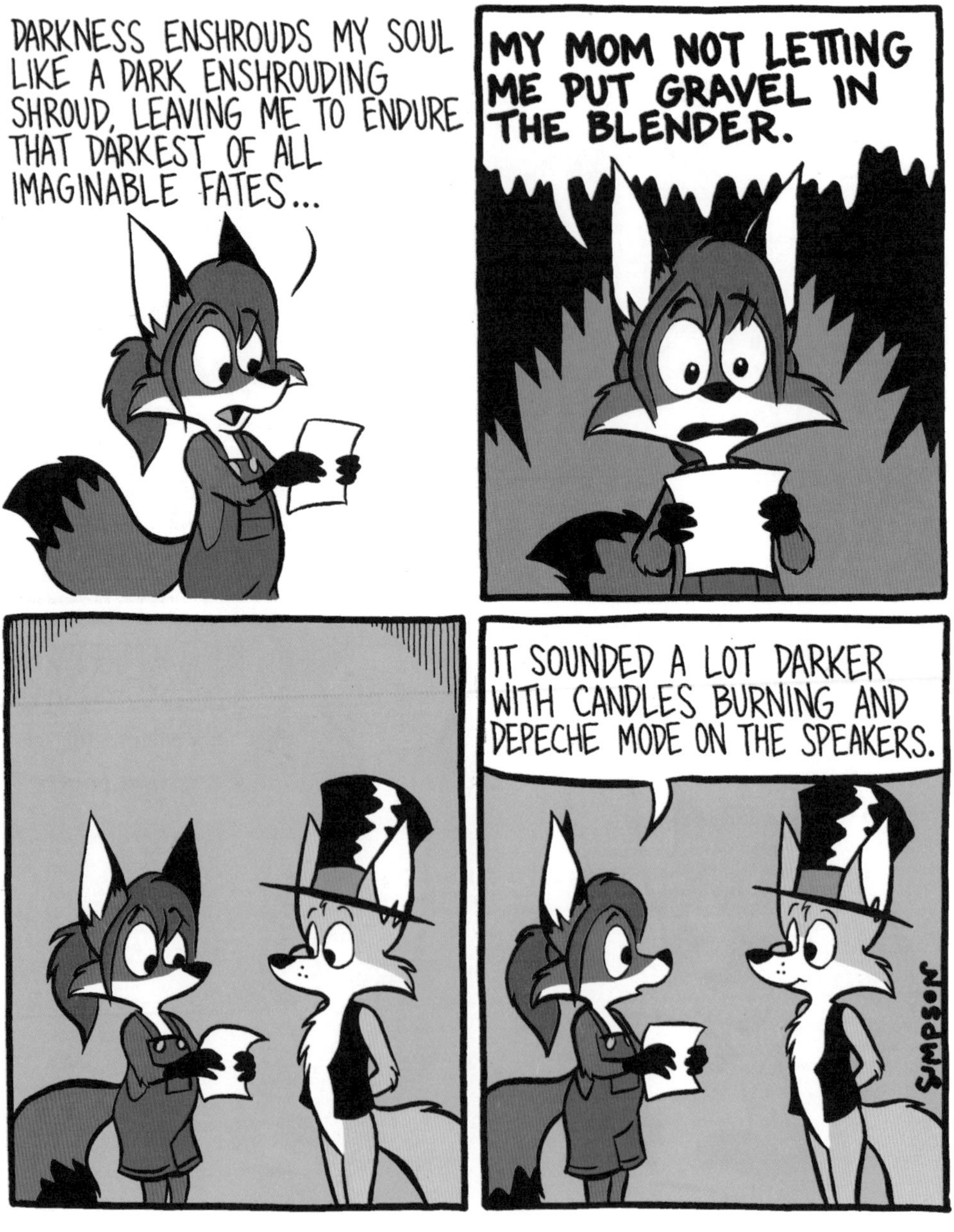
DARKNESS ENSHROUDS MY SOUL LIKE A DARK ENSHROUDING SHROUD, LEAVING ME TO ENDURE THAT DARKEST OF ALL IMAGINABLE FATES...
MY MOM NOT LETTING ME PUT GRAVEL IN THE BLENDER.
IT SOUNDED A LOT DARKER WITH CANDLES BURNING AND DEPECHE MODE ON THE SPEAKERS.
SIMPSON

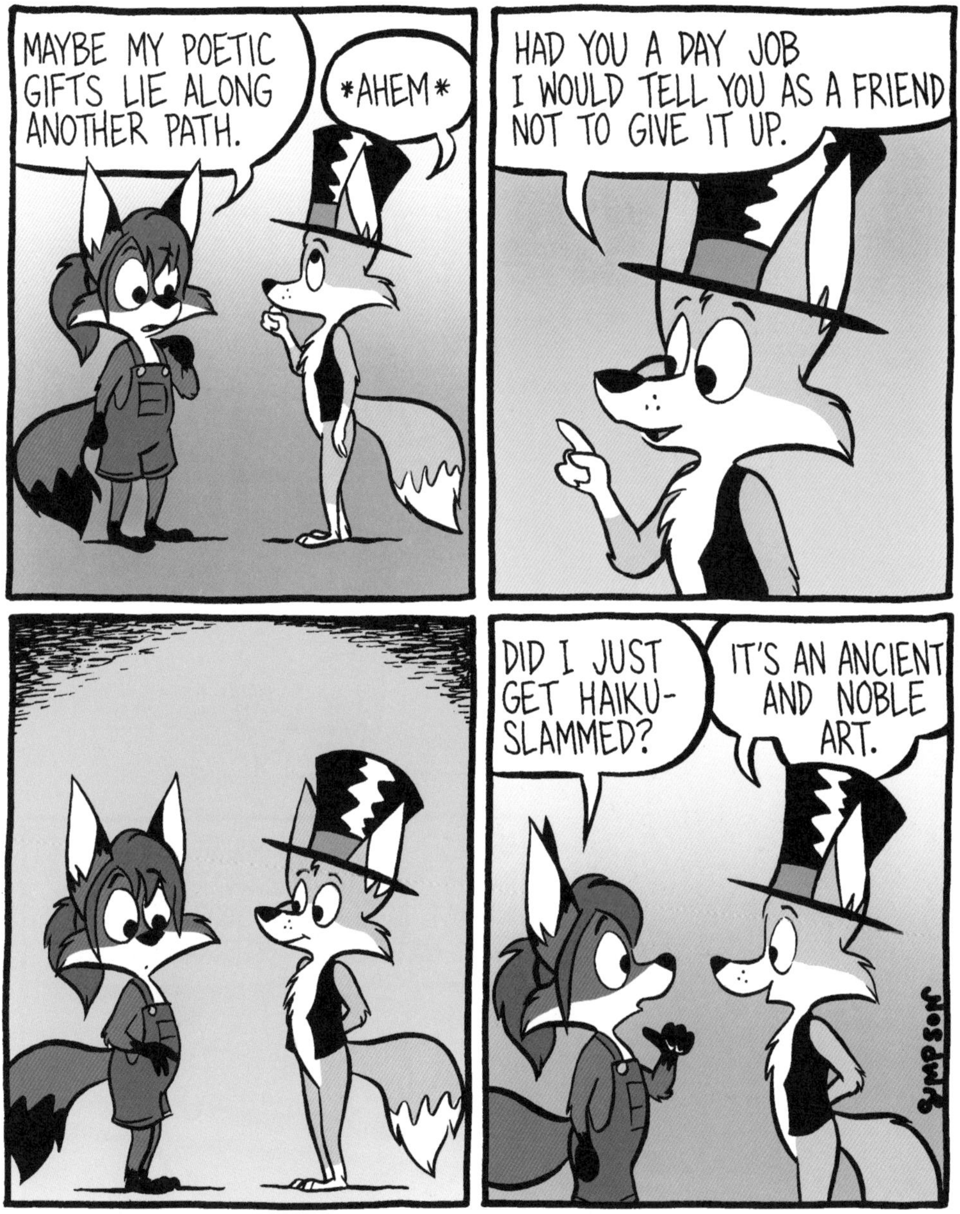
MAYBE MY POETIC GIFTS LIE ALONG ANOTHER PATH.
AHEM
HAD YOU A DAY JOB
I WOULD TELL YOU AS A FRIEND
NOT TO GIVE IT UP.
DID I JUST GET HAIKU-SLAMMED?
IT'S AN ANCIENT AND NOBLE ART.
SIMPSON

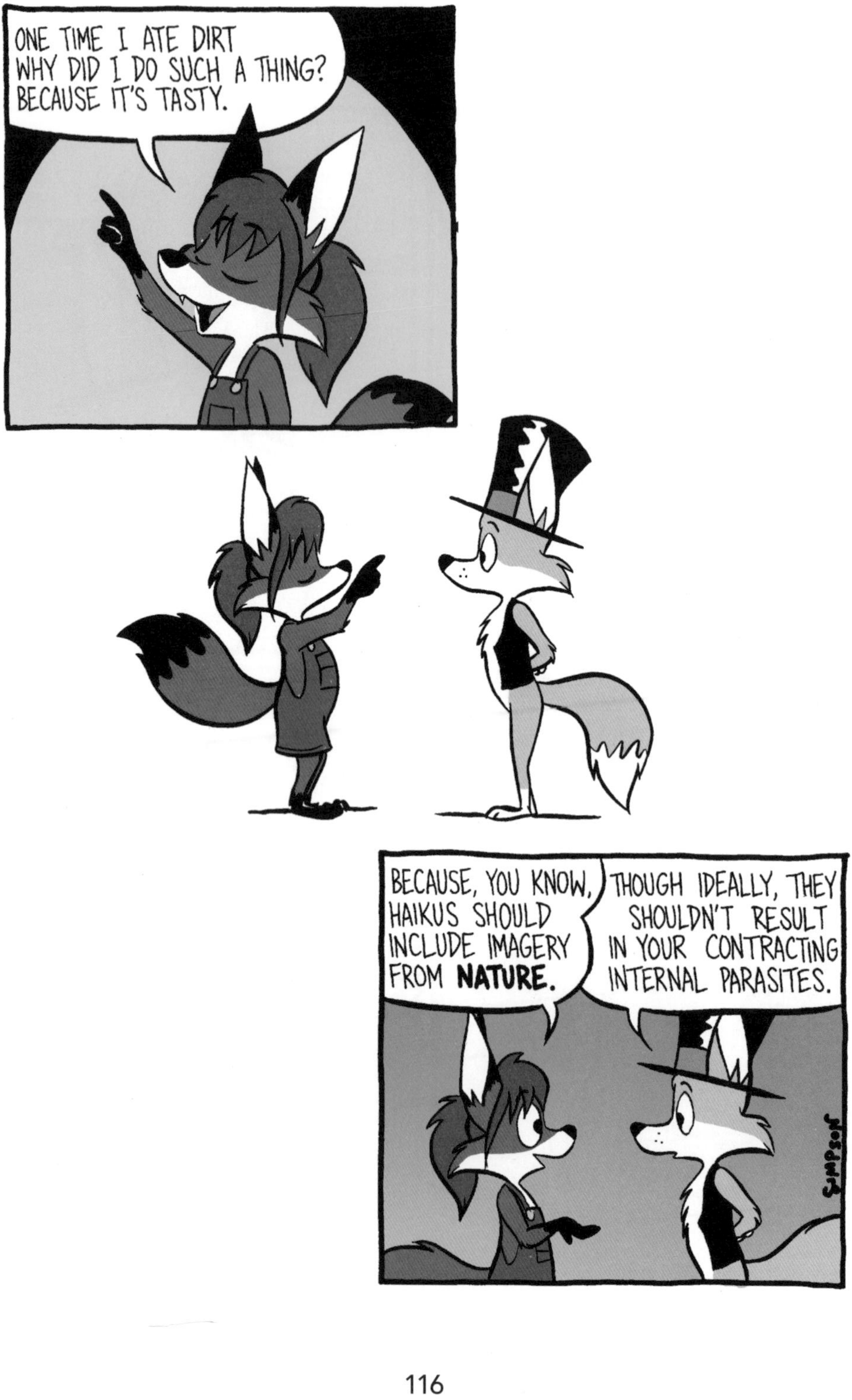
ONE TIME I ATE DIRT
WHY DID I DO SUCH A THING?
BECAUSE IT'S TASTY.
BECAUSE, YOU KNOW, HAIKUS SHOULD INCLUDE IMAGERY FROM **NATURE.**
THOUGH IDEALLY, THEY SHOULDN'T RESULT IN YOUR CONTRACTING INTERNAL PARASITES.
SIMPSON

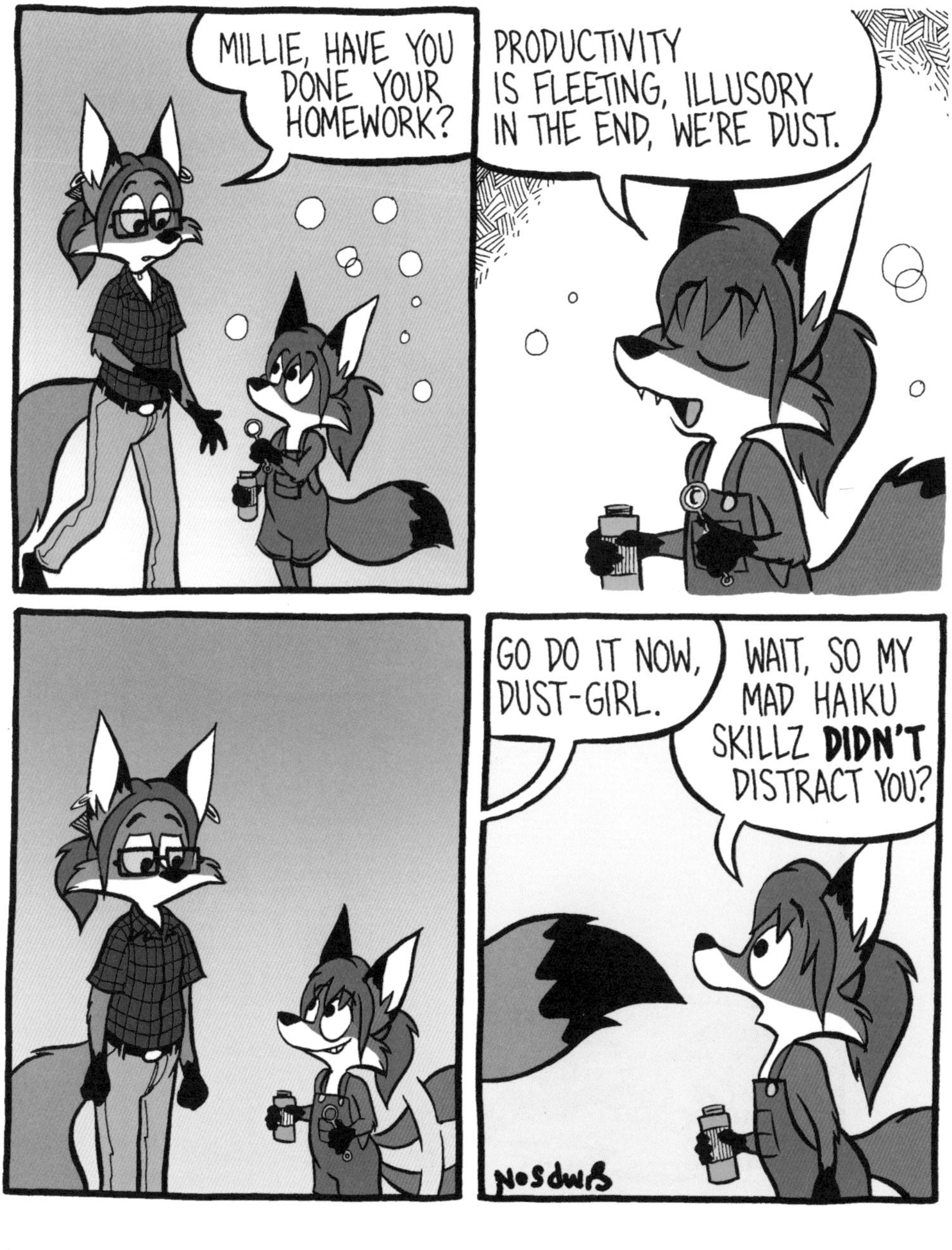
MILLIE, HAVE YOU DONE YOUR HOMEWORK?
PRODUCTIVITY IS FLEETING, ILLUSORY IN THE END, WE'RE DUST.
GO DO IT NOW, DUST-GIRL.
WAIT, SO MY MAD HAIKU SKILLZ **DIDN'T** DISTRACT YOU?
NOSDWIB

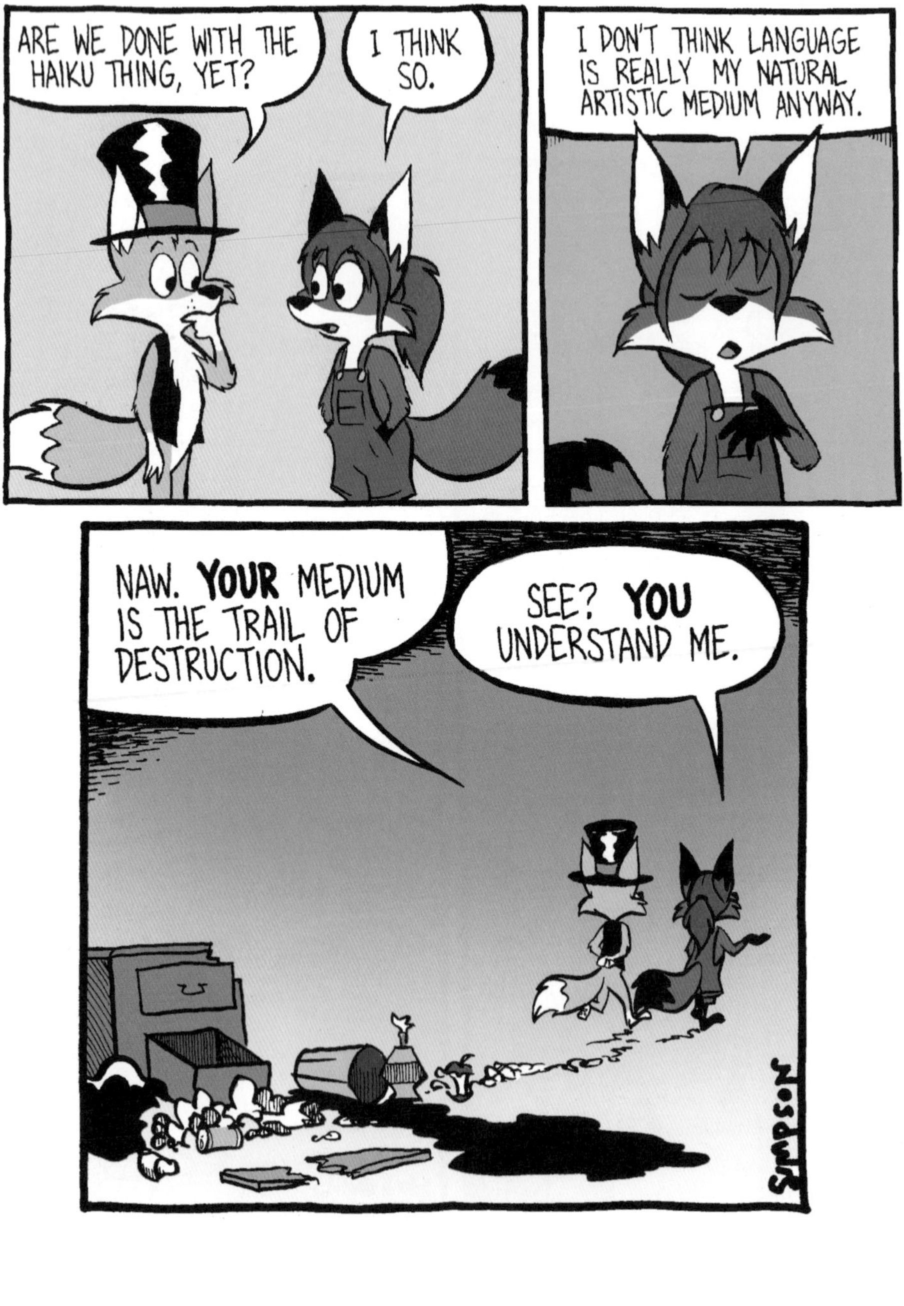
ARE WE DONE WITH THE HAIKU THING, YET?
I THINK SO.
I DON'T THINK LANGUAGE IS REALLY MY NATURAL ARTISTIC MEDIUM ANYWAY.
NAW. **YOUR** MEDIUM IS THE TRAIL OF DESTRUCTION.
SEE? **YOU** UNDERSTAND ME.
SIMPSON

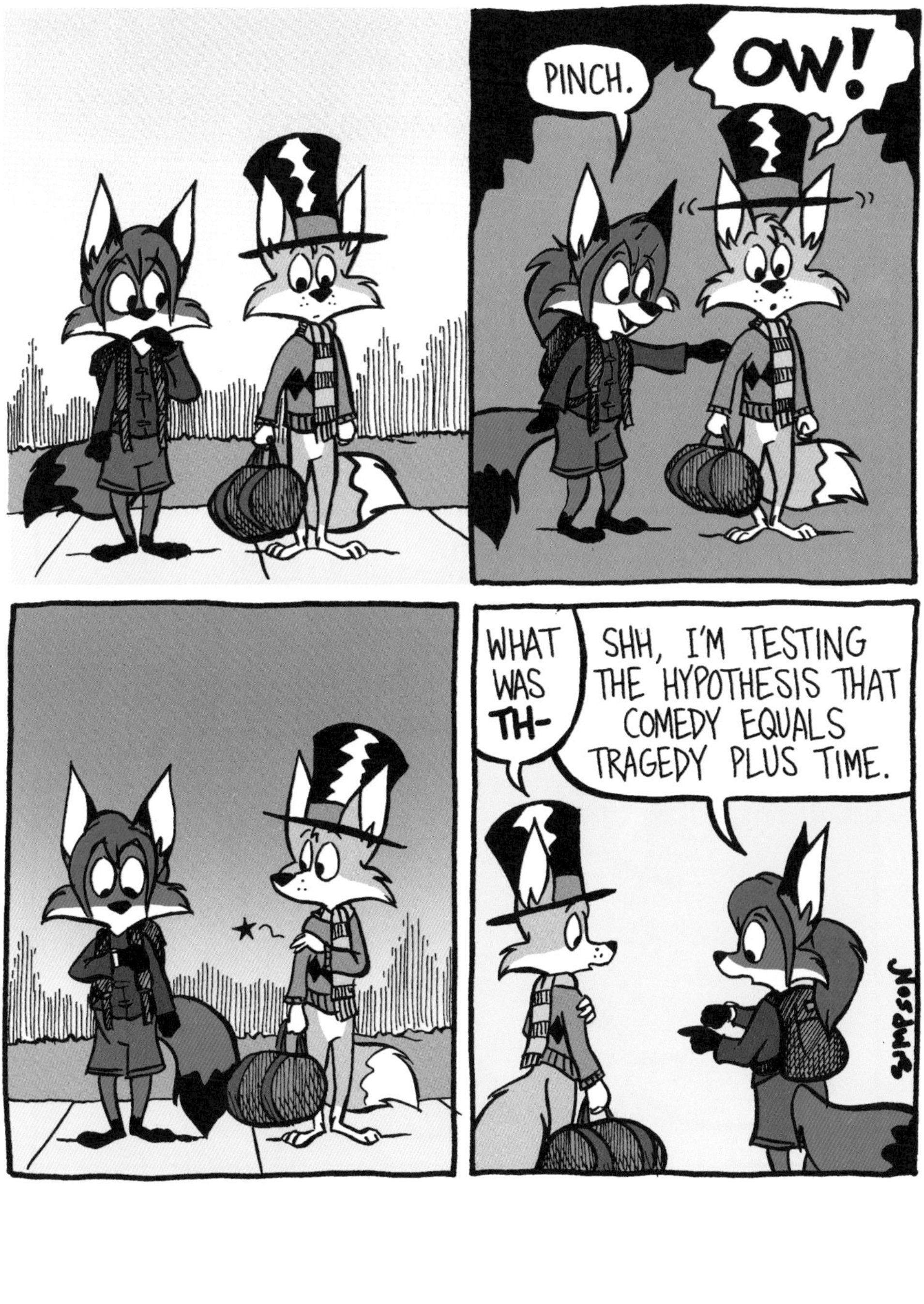
PINCH.
OW!
WHAT WAS TH-
SHH, I'M TESTING THE HYPOTHESIS THAT COMEDY EQUALS TRAGEDY PLUS TIME.
SIMPSON

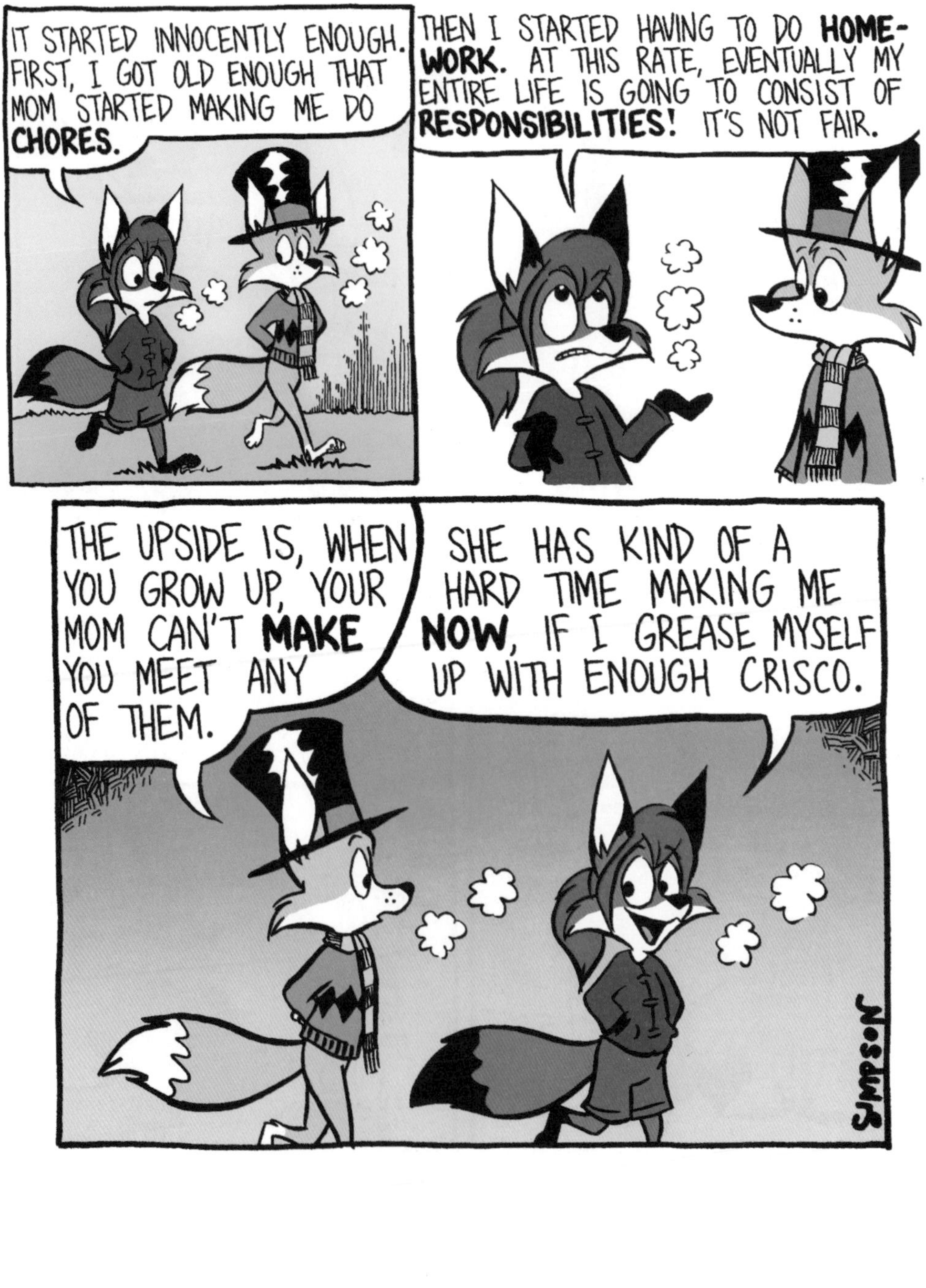
IT STARTED INNOCENTLY ENOUGH. FIRST, I GOT OLD ENOUGH THAT MOM STARTED MAKING ME DO **CHORES.**
THEN I STARTED HAVING TO DO **HOME-WORK.** AT THIS RATE, EVENTUALLY MY ENTIRE LIFE IS GOING TO CONSIST OF **RESPONSIBILITIES!** IT'S NOT FAIR.
THE UPSIDE IS, WHEN YOU GROW UP, YOUR MOM CAN'T **MAKE** YOU MEET ANY OF THEM.
SHE HAS KIND OF A HARD TIME MAKING ME **NOW**, IF I GREASE MYSELF UP WITH ENOUGH CRISCO.
SIMPSON

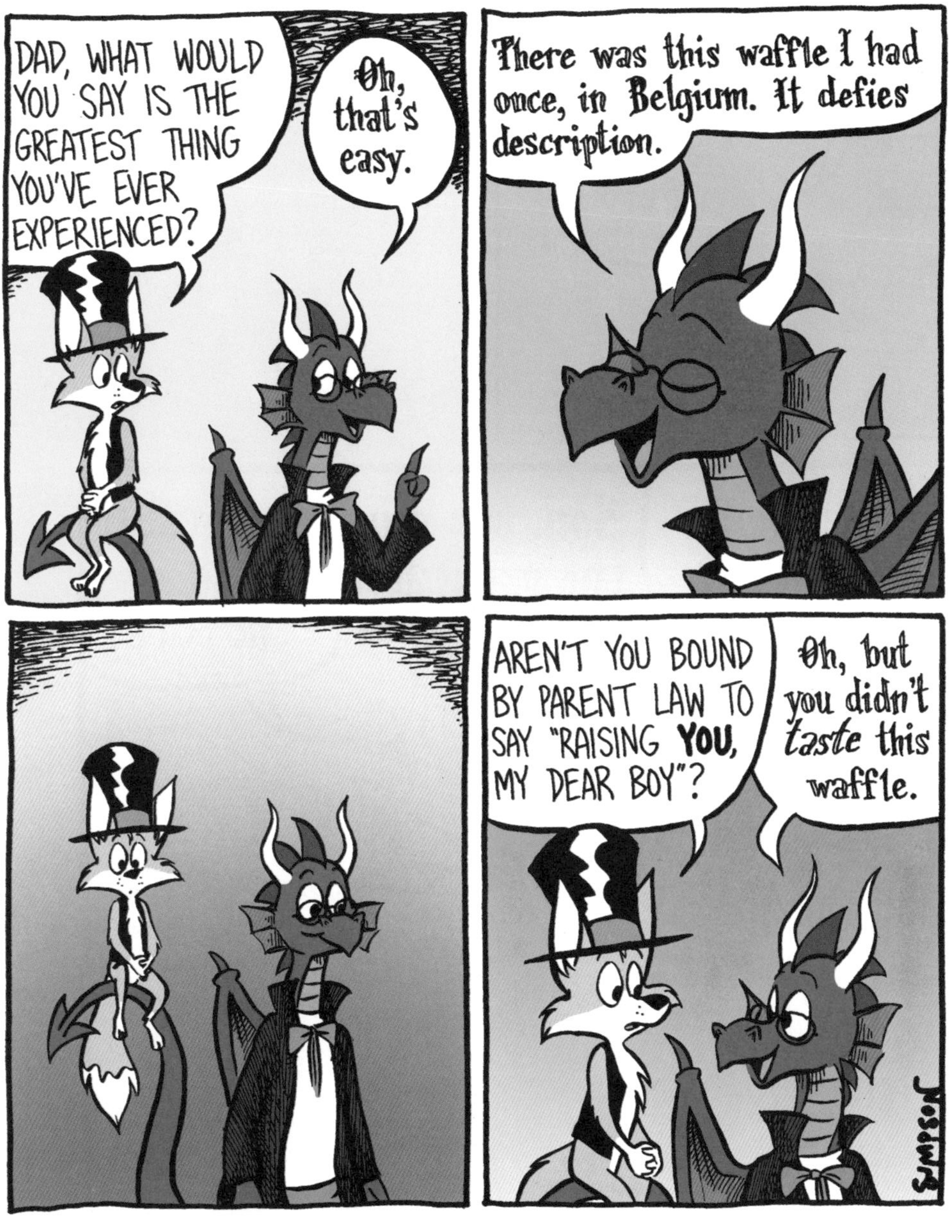
DAD, WHAT WOULD YOU SAY IS THE GREATEST THING YOU'VE EVER EXPERIENCED?
Oh, that's easy.
There was this waffle I had once, in Belgium. It defies description.
AREN'T YOU BOUND BY PARENT LAW TO SAY "RAISING **YOU**, MY DEAR BOY"?
Oh, but you didn't *taste* this waffle.
SIMPSON

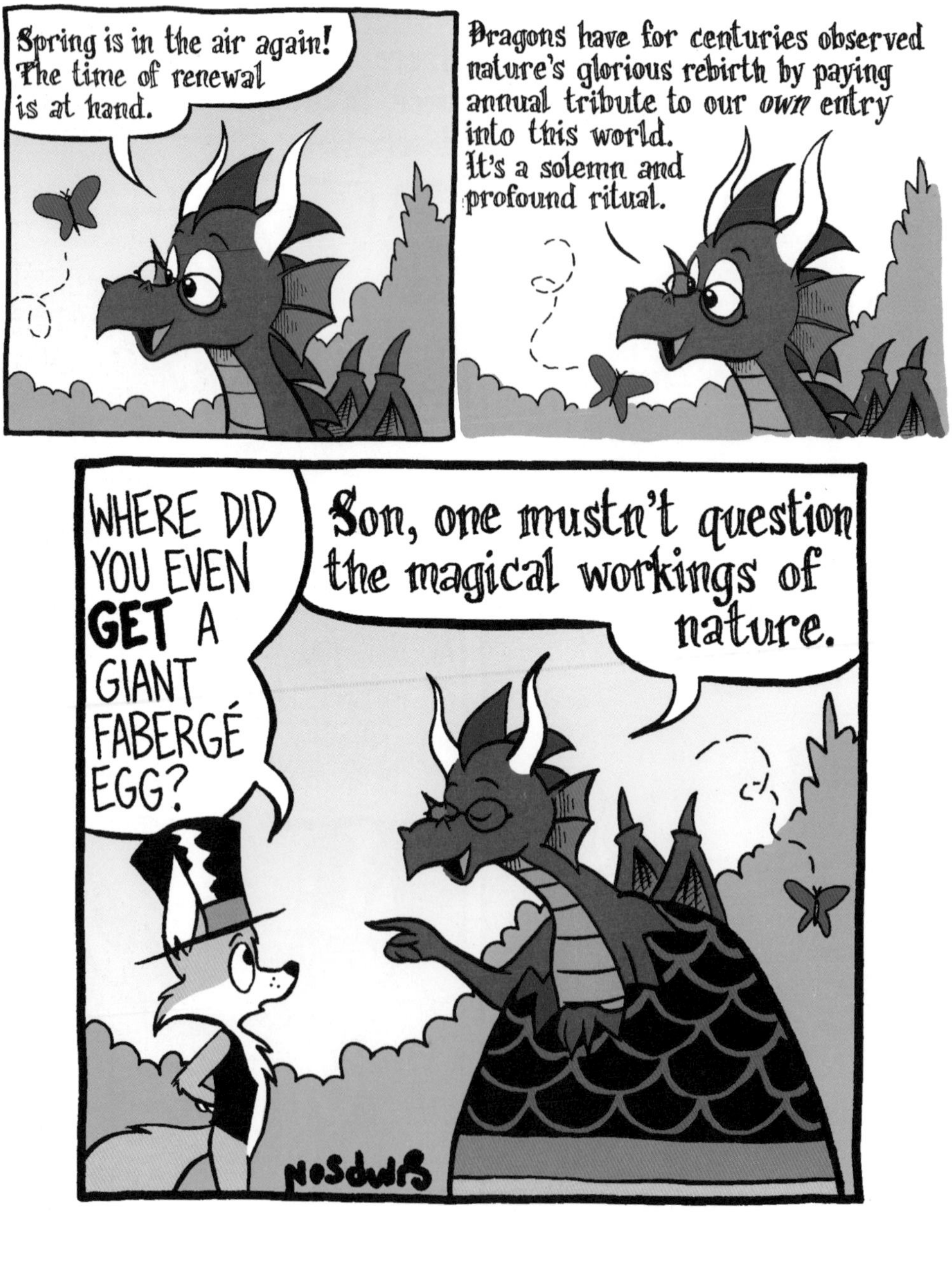
Spring is in the air again! The time of renewal is at hand.
Dragons have for centuries observed nature's glorious rebirth by paying annual tribute to our *own* entry into this world. It's a solemn and profound ritual.
WHERE DID YOU EVEN **GET** A GIANT FABERGÉ EGG?
Son, one mustn't question the magical workings of nature.

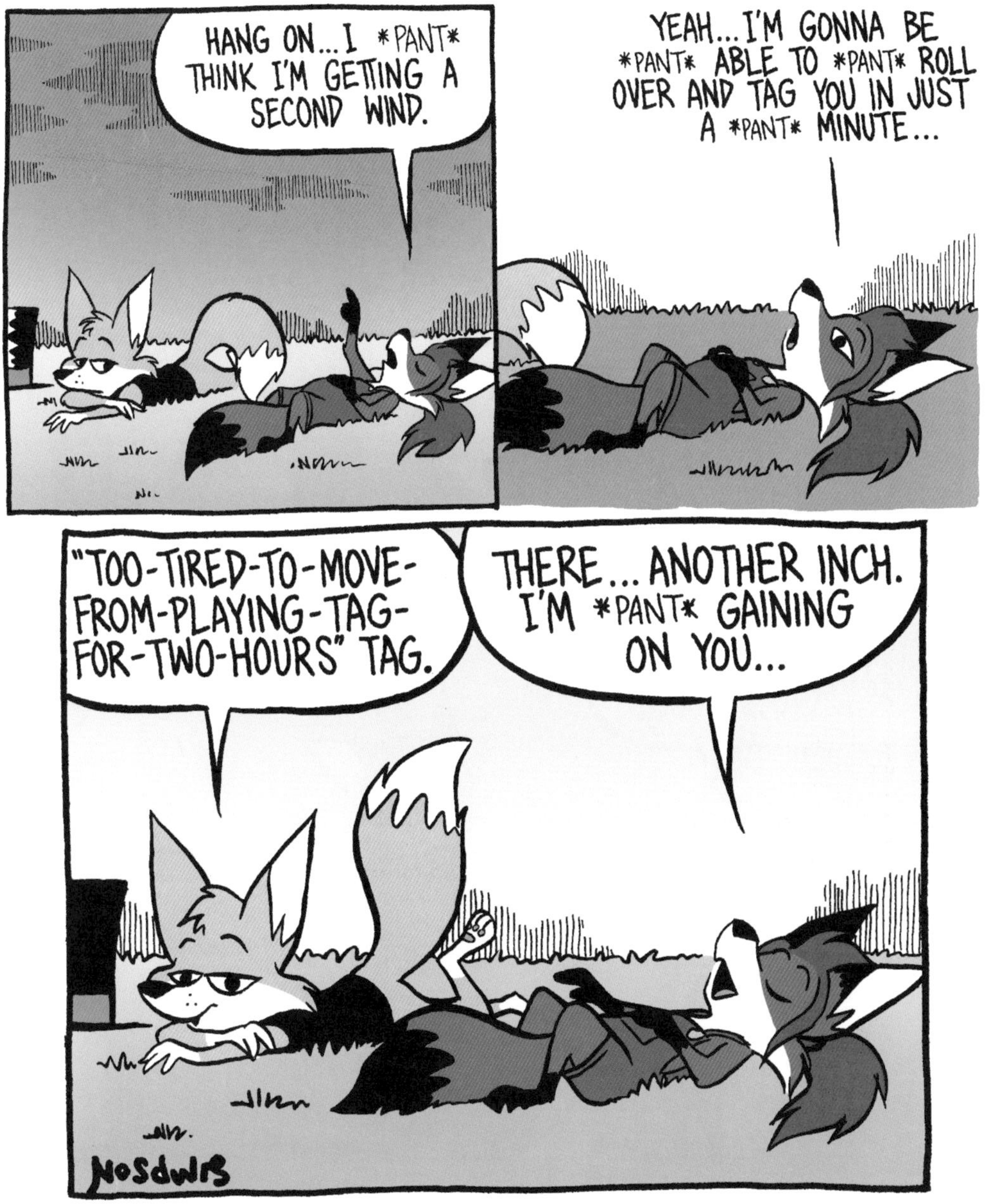
HANG ON... I *PANT* THINK I'M GETTING A SECOND WIND.
YEAH... I'M GONNA BE *PANT* ABLE TO *PANT* ROLL OVER AND TAG YOU IN JUST A *PANT* MINUTE...
"TOO-TIRED-TO-MOVE-FROM-PLAYING-TAG-FOR-TWO-HOURS" TAG.
THERE... ANOTHER INCH. I'M *PANT* GAINING ON YOU...
NOSDWIS

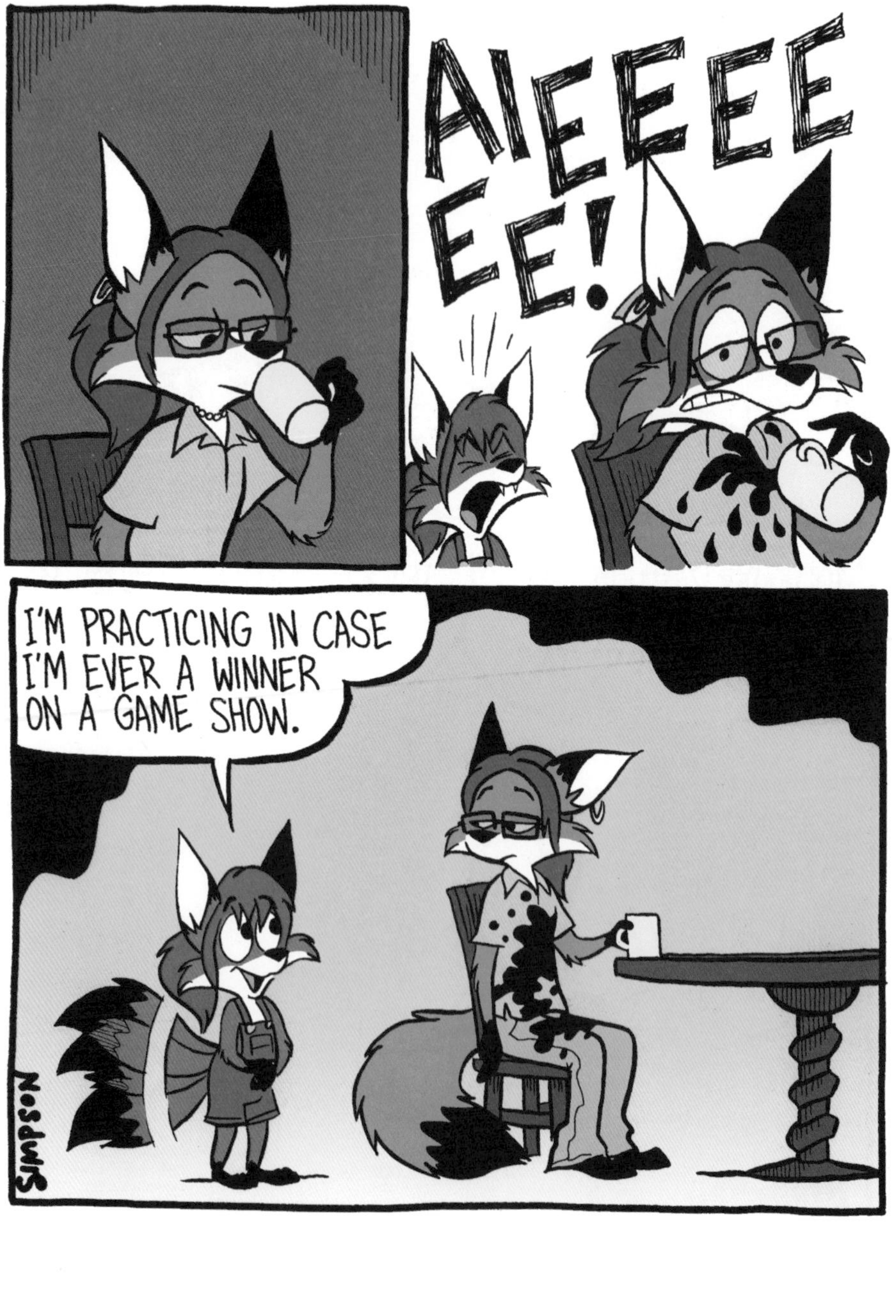
AIEEEEEE!
I'M PRACTICING IN CASE I'M EVER A WINNER ON A GAME SHOW.
SIMPSON

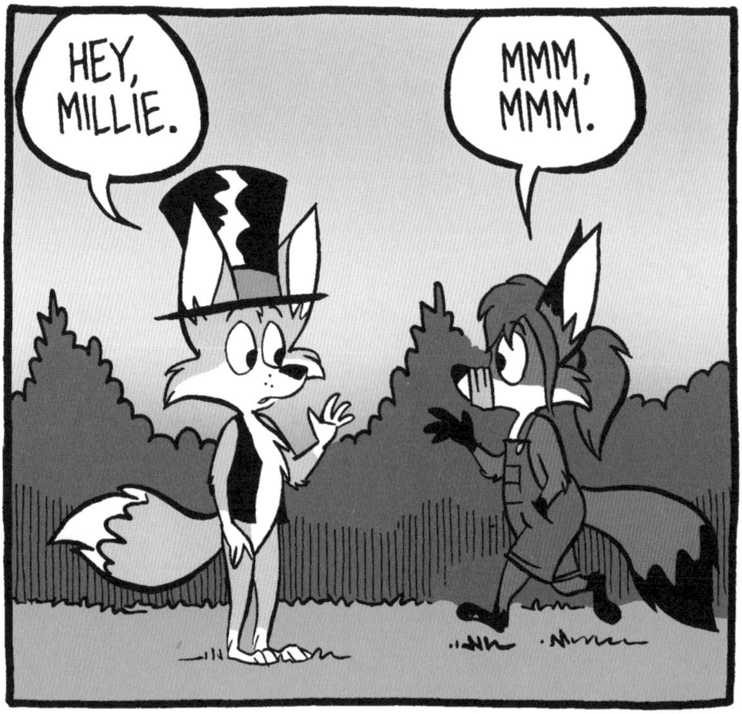
HEY, MILLIE.
MMM, MMM.

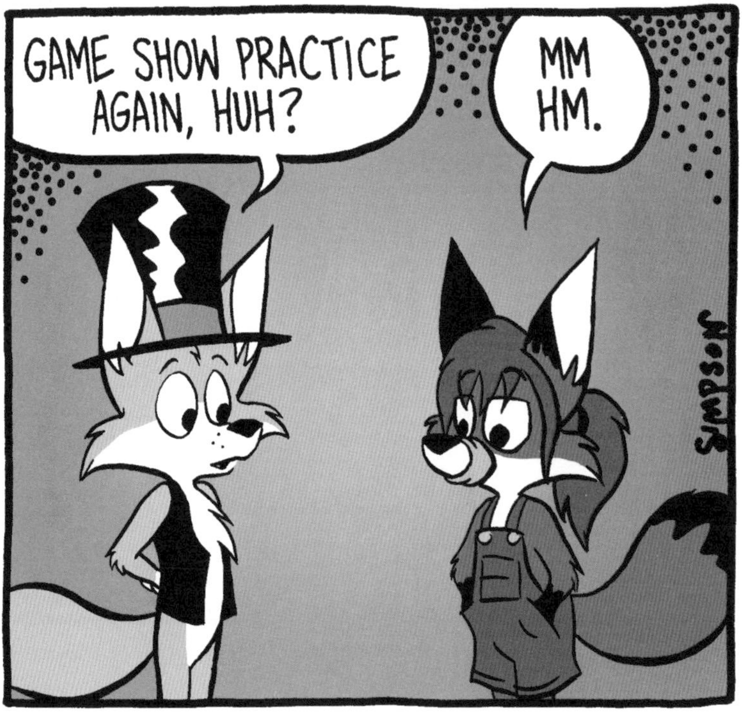
GAME SHOW PRACTICE AGAIN, HUH?
MM HM.
SIMPSON

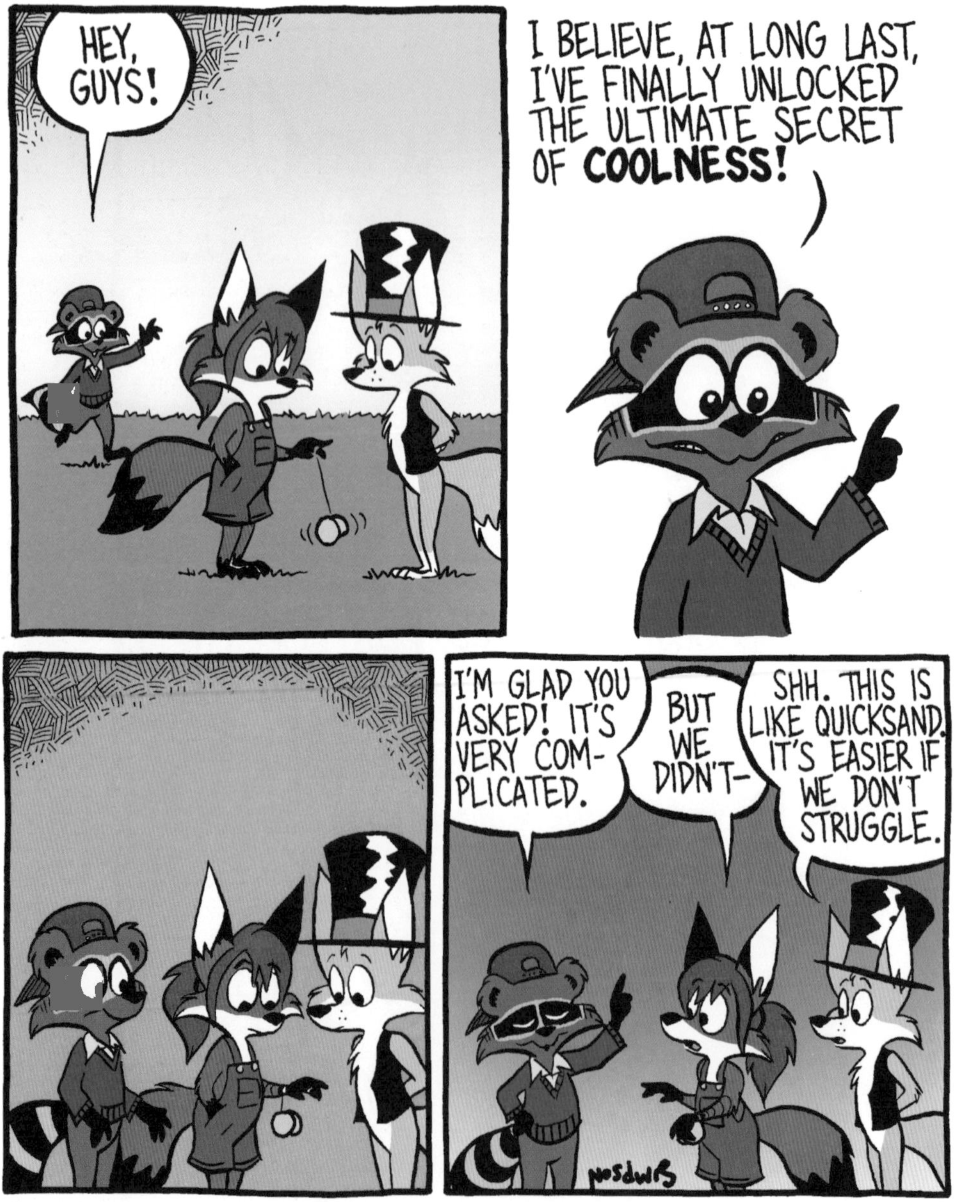
HEY, GUYS!
I BELIEVE, AT LONG LAST, I'VE FINALLY UNLOCKED THE ULTIMATE SECRET OF **COOLNESS**!
I'M GLAD YOU ASKED! IT'S VERY COM-PLICATED.
BUT WE DIDN'T-
SHH. THIS IS LIKE QUICKSAND. IT'S EASIER IF WE DON'T STRUGGLE.

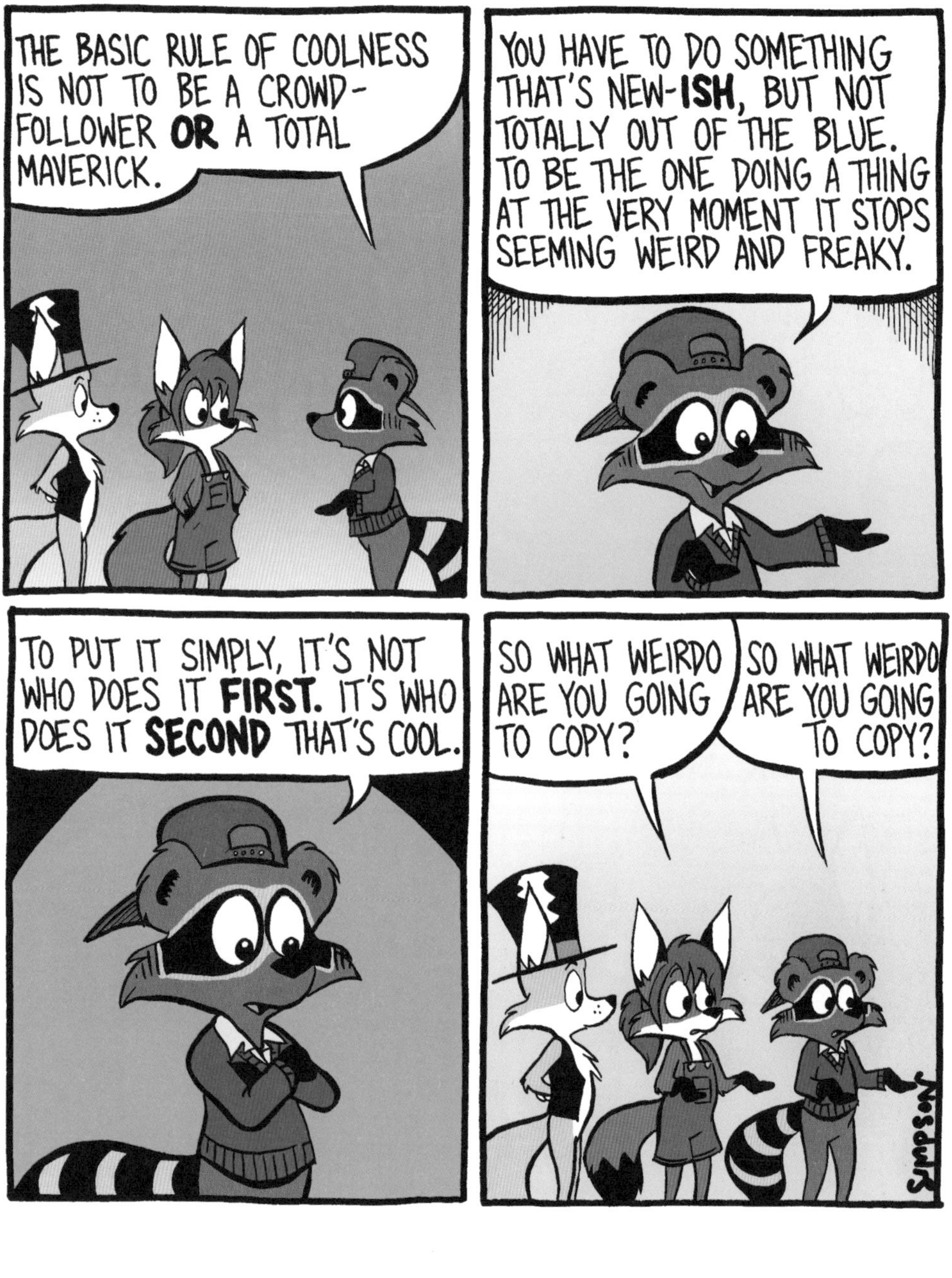
THE BASIC RULE OF COOLNESS IS NOT TO BE A CROWD-FOLLOWER **OR** A TOTAL MAVERICK.
YOU HAVE TO DO SOMETHING THAT'S NEW-**ISH**, BUT NOT TOTALLY OUT OF THE BLUE. TO BE THE ONE DOING A THING AT THE VERY MOMENT IT STOPS SEEMING WEIRD AND FREAKY.
TO PUT IT SIMPLY, IT'S NOT WHO DOES IT **FIRST.** IT'S WHO DOES IT **SECOND** THAT'S COOL.
SO WHAT WEIRDO ARE YOU GOING TO COPY?
SO WHAT WEIRDO ARE YOU GOING TO COPY?
SIMPSON

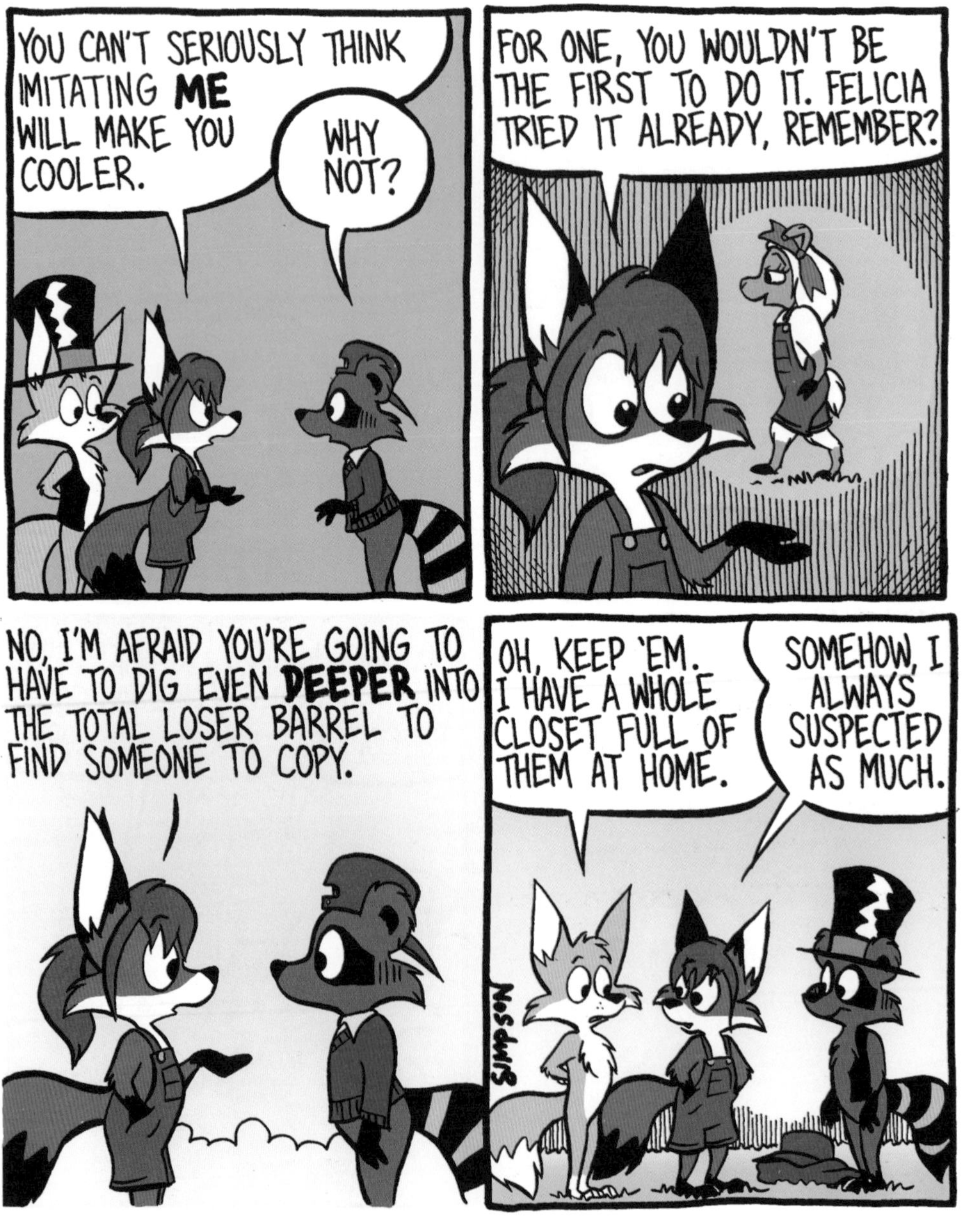
YOU CAN'T SERIOUSLY THINK IMITATING **ME** WILL MAKE YOU COOLER.
WHY NOT?
FOR ONE, YOU WOULDN'T BE THE FIRST TO DO IT. FELICIA TRIED IT ALREADY, REMEMBER?
NO, I'M AFRAID YOU'RE GOING TO HAVE TO DIG EVEN **DEEPER** INTO THE TOTAL LOSER BARREL TO FIND SOMEONE TO COPY.
OH, KEEP 'EM. I HAVE A WHOLE CLOSET FULL OF THEM AT HOME.
SOMEHOW, I ALWAYS SUSPECTED AS MUCH.
SIMPSON

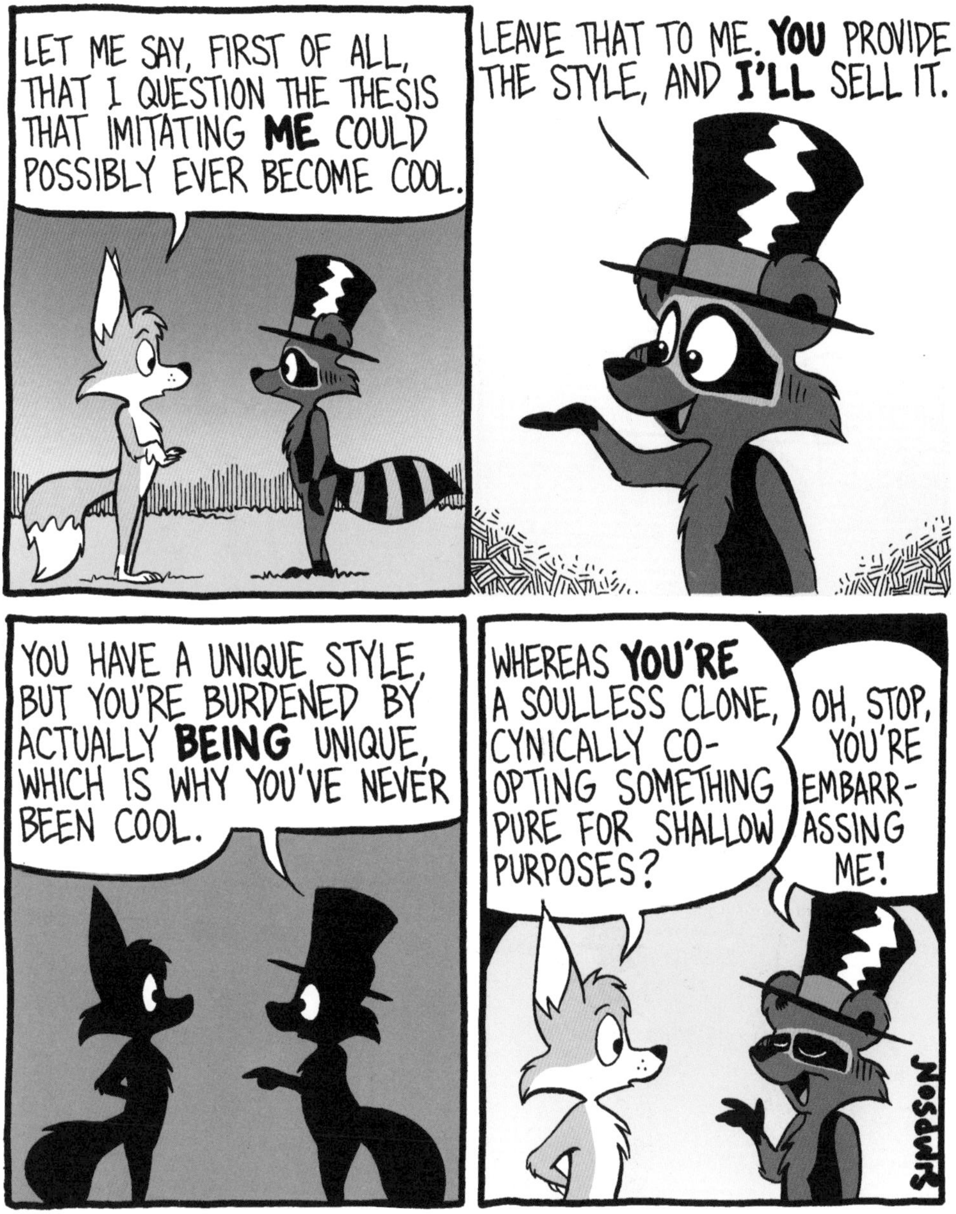
LET ME SAY, FIRST OF ALL, THAT I QUESTION THE THESIS THAT IMITATING ME COULD POSSIBLY EVER BECOME COOL.
LEAVE THAT TO ME. YOU PROVIDE THE STYLE, AND I'LL SELL IT.
YOU HAVE A UNIQUE STYLE, BUT YOU'RE BURDENED BY ACTUALLY BEING UNIQUE, WHICH IS WHY YOU'VE NEVER BEEN COOL.
WHEREAS YOU'RE A SOULLESS CLONE, CYNICALLY CO-OPTING SOMETHING PURE FOR SHALLOW PURPOSES?
OH, STOP, YOU'RE EMBARR-ASSING ME!
SIMPSON

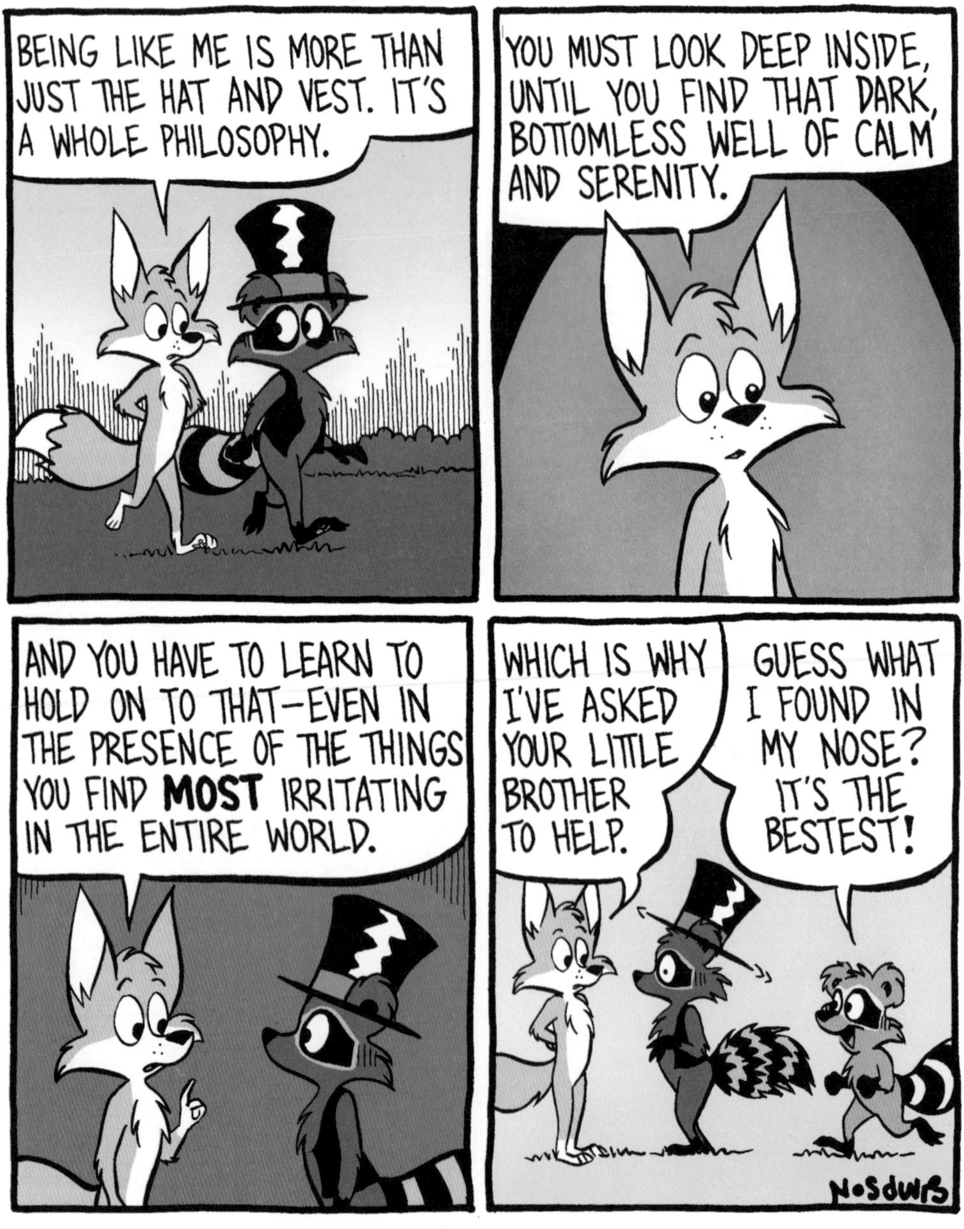
BEING LIKE ME IS MORE THAN JUST THE HAT AND VEST. IT'S A WHOLE PHILOSOPHY.
YOU MUST LOOK DEEP INSIDE, UNTIL YOU FIND THAT DARK, BOTTOMLESS WELL OF CALM AND SERENITY.
AND YOU HAVE TO LEARN TO HOLD ON TO THAT—EVEN IN THE PRESENCE OF THE THINGS YOU FIND **MOST** IRRITATING IN THE ENTIRE WORLD.
WHICH IS WHY I'VE ASKED YOUR LITTLE BROTHER TO HELP.
GUESS WHAT I FOUND IN MY NOSE? IT'S THE BESTEST!
NOSDUWB

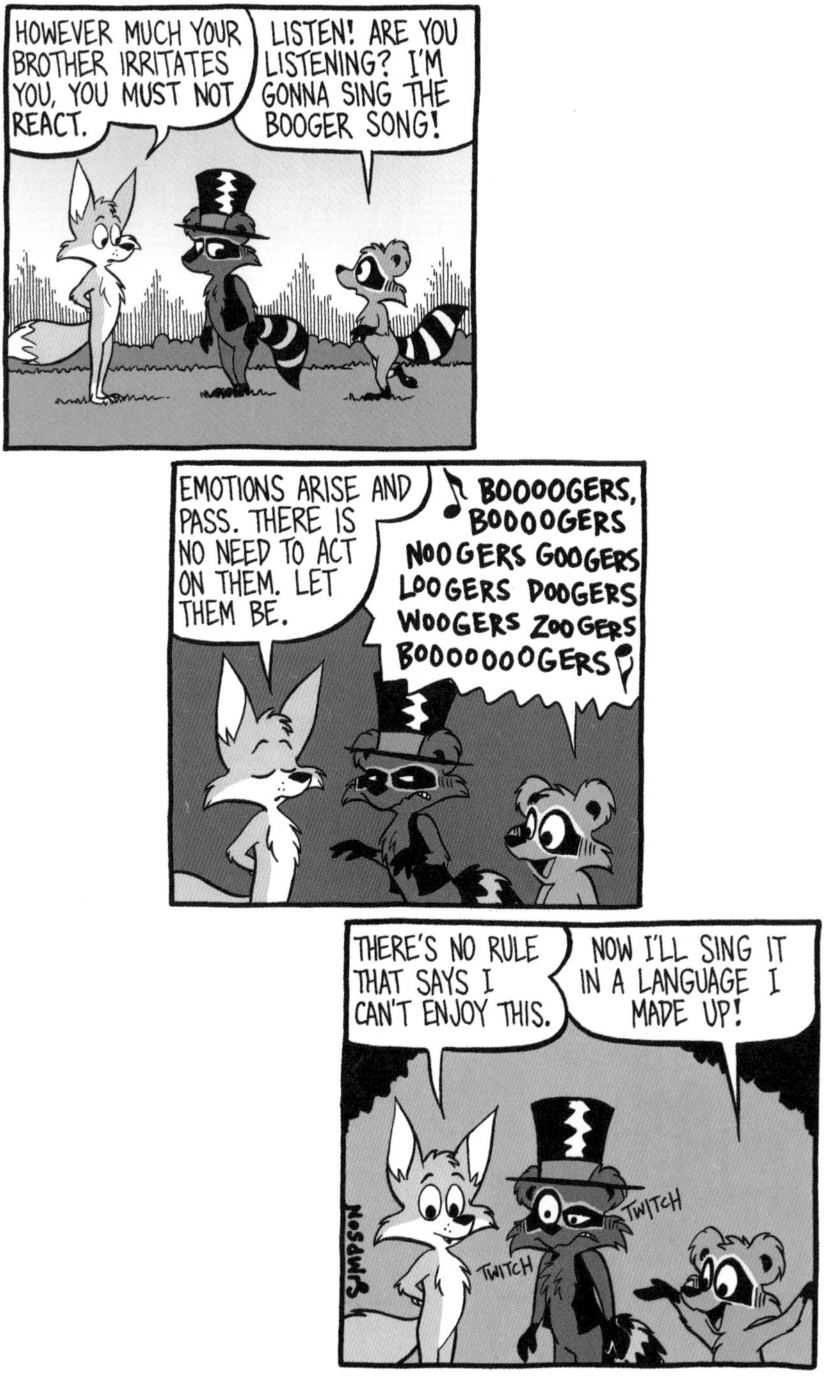
HOWEVER MUCH YOUR BROTHER IRRITATES YOU, YOU MUST NOT REACT.
LISTEN! ARE YOU LISTENING? I'M GONNA SING THE BOOGER SONG!
EMOTIONS ARISE AND PASS. THERE IS NO NEED TO ACT ON THEM. LET THEM BE.
BOOOOGERS, BOOOOGERS NOOGERS GOOGERS LOOGERS DOOGERS WOOGERS ZOOGERS BOOOOOOOGERS
THERE'S NO RULE THAT SAYS I CAN'T ENJOY THIS.
NOW I'LL SING IT IN A LANGUAGE I MADE UP!
TWITCH
TWITCH
SIMPSON

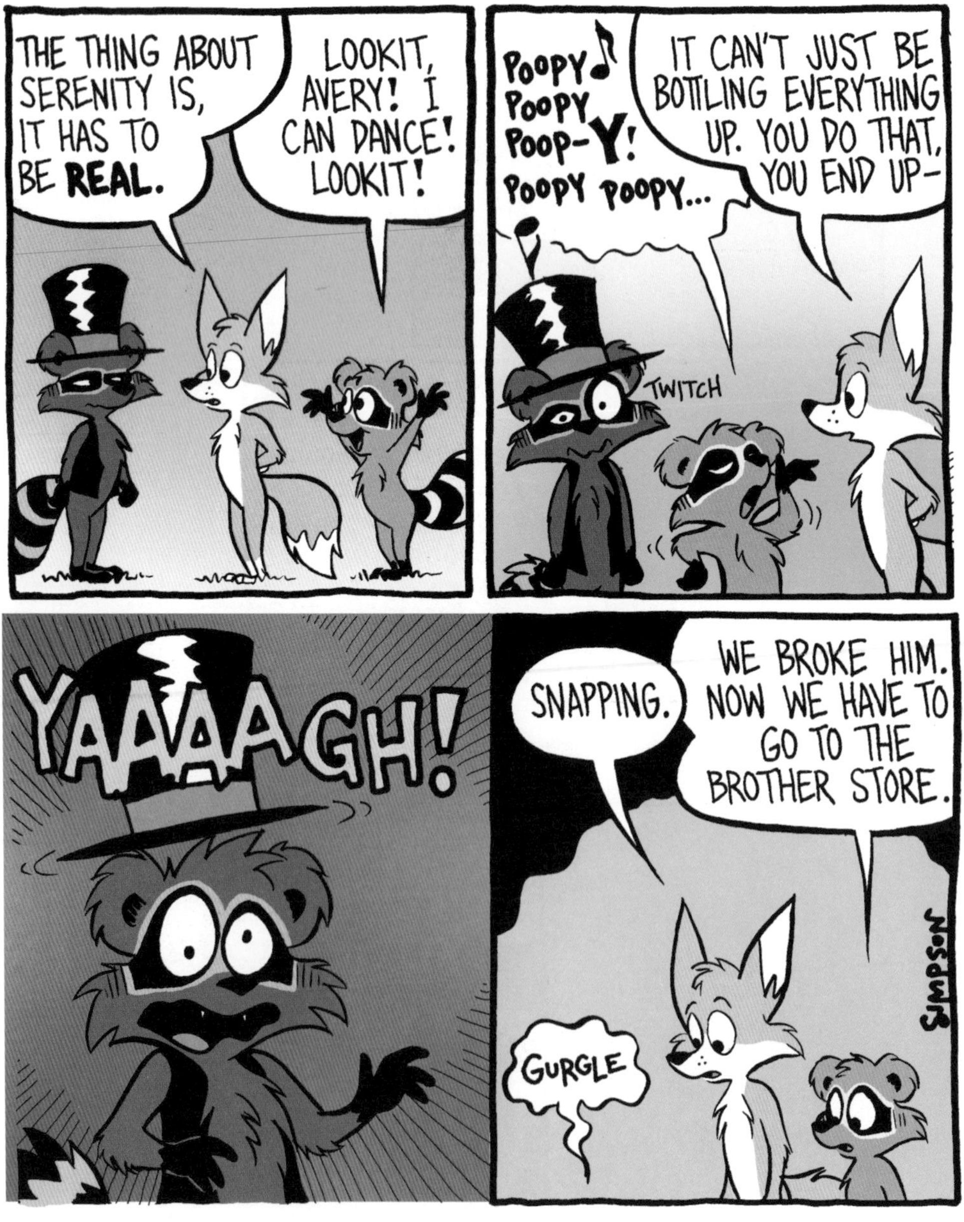
THE THING ABOUT SERENITY IS, IT HAS TO BE **REAL.**
LOOKIT, AVERY! I CAN DANCE! LOOKIT!
POOPY POOPY POOP-Y! POOPY POOPY...
IT CAN'T JUST BE BOTTLING EVERYTHING UP. YOU DO THAT, YOU END UP-
TWITCH
YAAAAGH!
SNAPPING.
WE BROKE HIM. NOW WE HAVE TO GO TO THE BROTHER STORE.
GURGLE
SIMPSON

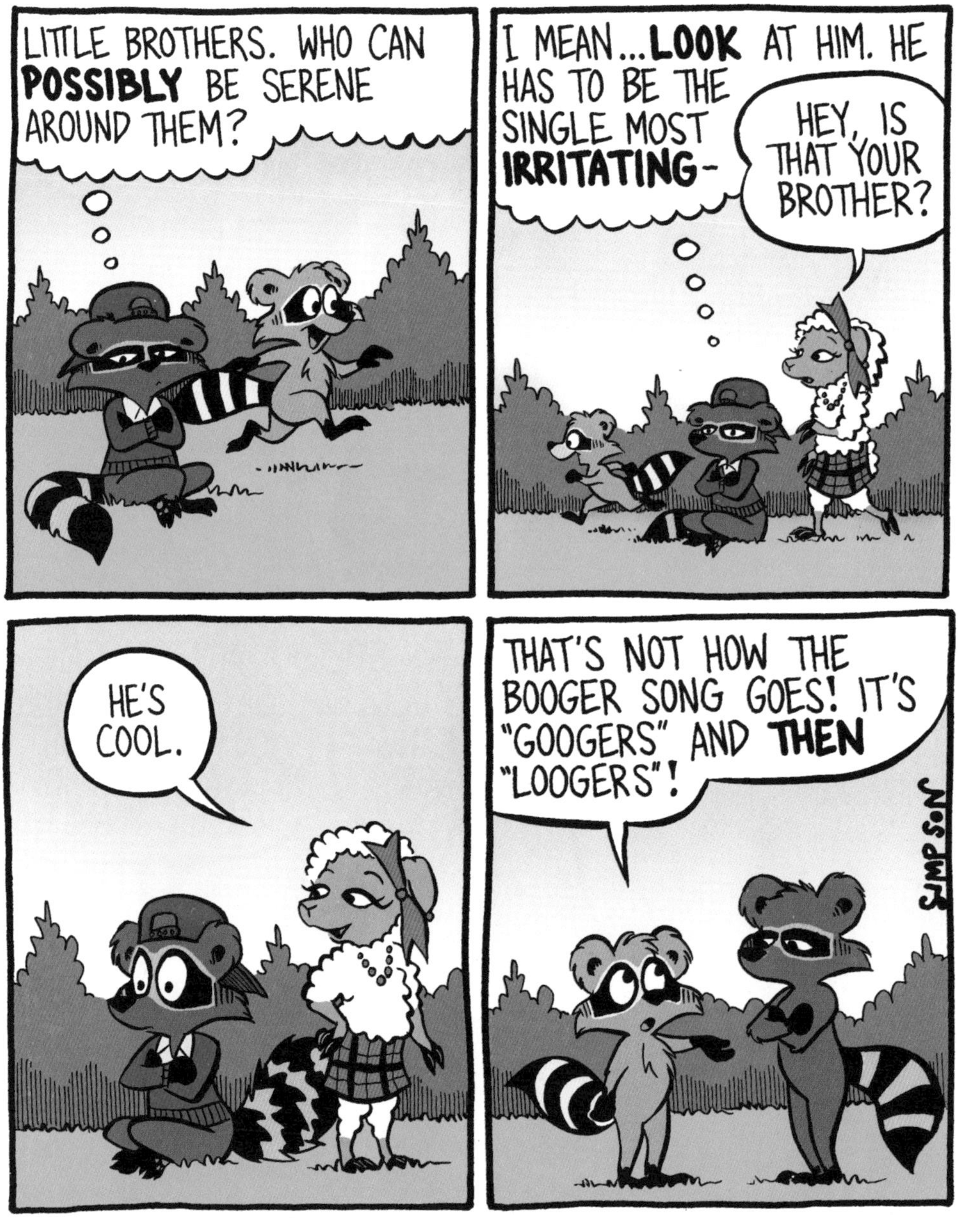
LITTLE BROTHERS. WHO CAN **POSSIBLY** BE SERENE AROUND THEM?
I MEAN...**LOOK** AT HIM. HE HAS TO BE THE SINGLE MOST **IRRITATING**-
HEY, IS THAT YOUR BROTHER?
HE'S COOL.
THAT'S NOT HOW THE BOOGER SONG GOES! IT'S "GOOGERS" AND **THEN** "LOOGERS"!
SIMPSON

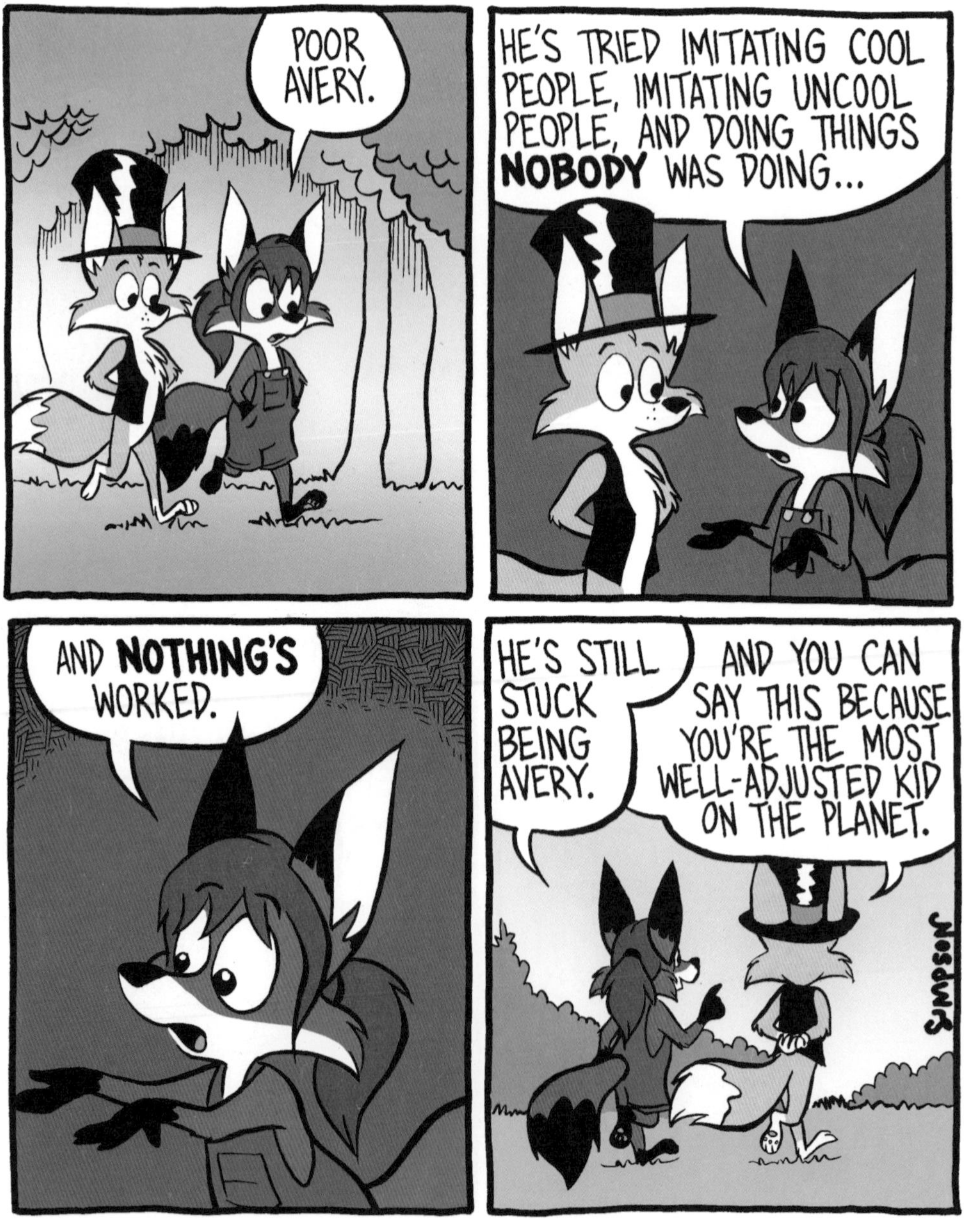
POOR AVERY.
HE'S TRIED IMITATING COOL PEOPLE, IMITATING UNCOOL PEOPLE, AND DOING THINGS **NOBODY** WAS DOING...
AND **NOTHING'S** WORKED.
HE'S STILL STUCK BEING AVERY.
AND YOU CAN SAY THIS BECAUSE YOU'RE THE MOST WELL-ADJUSTED KID ON THE PLANET.
SIMPSON

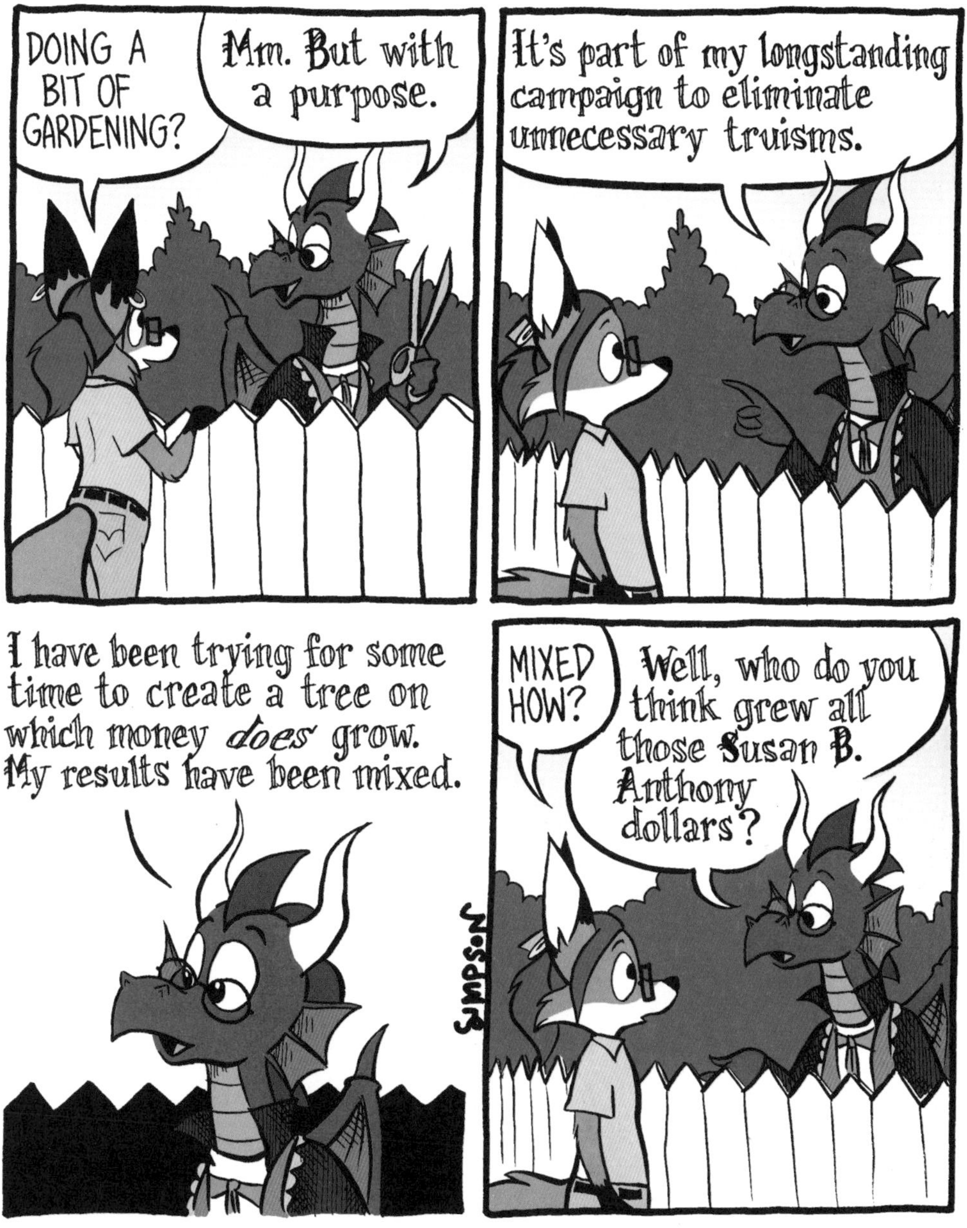
DOING A BIT OF GARDENING?
Mm. But with a purpose.
It's part of my longstanding campaign to eliminate unnecessary truisms.
I have been trying for some time to create a tree on which money *does* grow. My results have been mixed.
SIMPSON
MIXED HOW?
Well, who do you think grew all those Susan B. Anthony dollars?

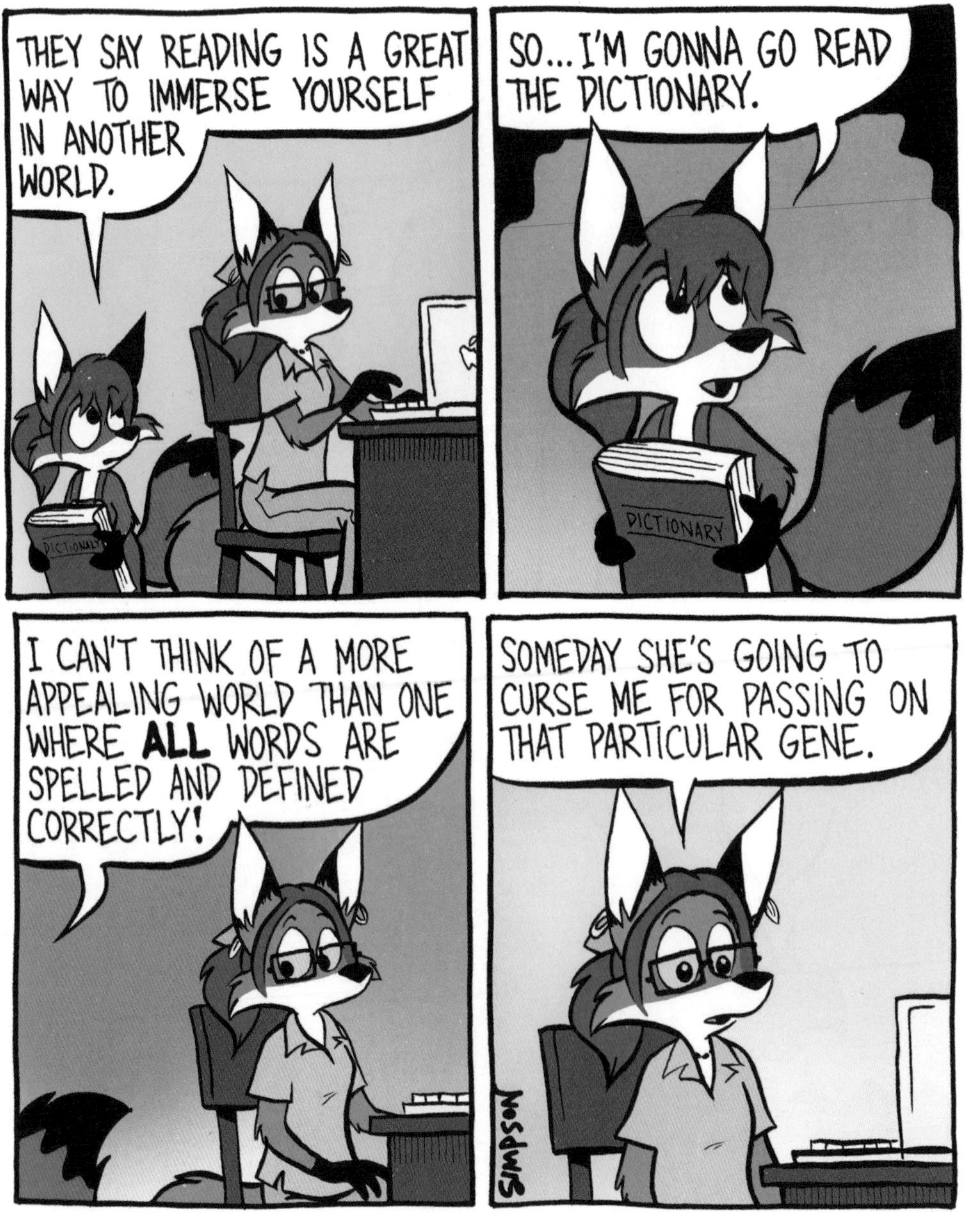
THEY SAY READING IS A GREAT WAY TO IMMERSE YOURSELF IN ANOTHER WORLD.
SO... I'M GONNA GO READ THE DICTIONARY.
DICTIONARY
I CAN'T THINK OF A MORE APPEALING WORLD THAN ONE WHERE **ALL** WORDS ARE SPELLED AND DEFINED CORRECTLY!
SOMEDAY SHE'S GOING TO CURSE ME FOR PASSING ON THAT PARTICULAR GENE.
SIMPSON

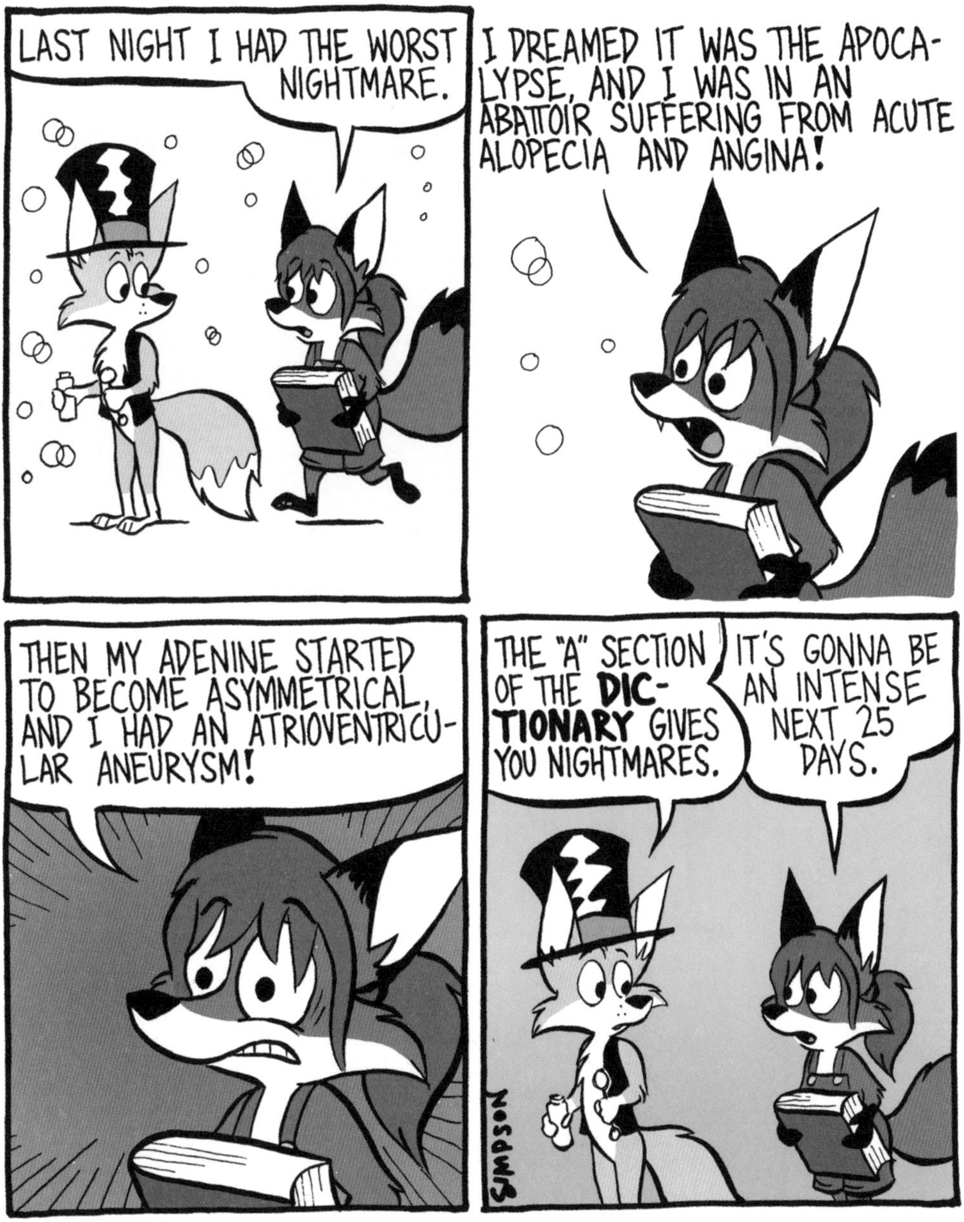
LAST NIGHT I HAD THE WORST NIGHTMARE.
I DREAMED IT WAS THE APOCALYPSE, AND I WAS IN AN ABATTOIR SUFFERING FROM ACUTE ALOPECIA AND ANGINA!
THEN MY ADENINE STARTED TO BECOME ASYMMETRICAL, AND I HAD AN ATRIOVENTRICULAR ANEURYSM!
THE "A" SECTION OF THE **DICTIONARY** GIVES YOU NIGHTMARES.
IT'S GONNA BE AN INTENSE NEXT 25 DAYS.
SIMPSON

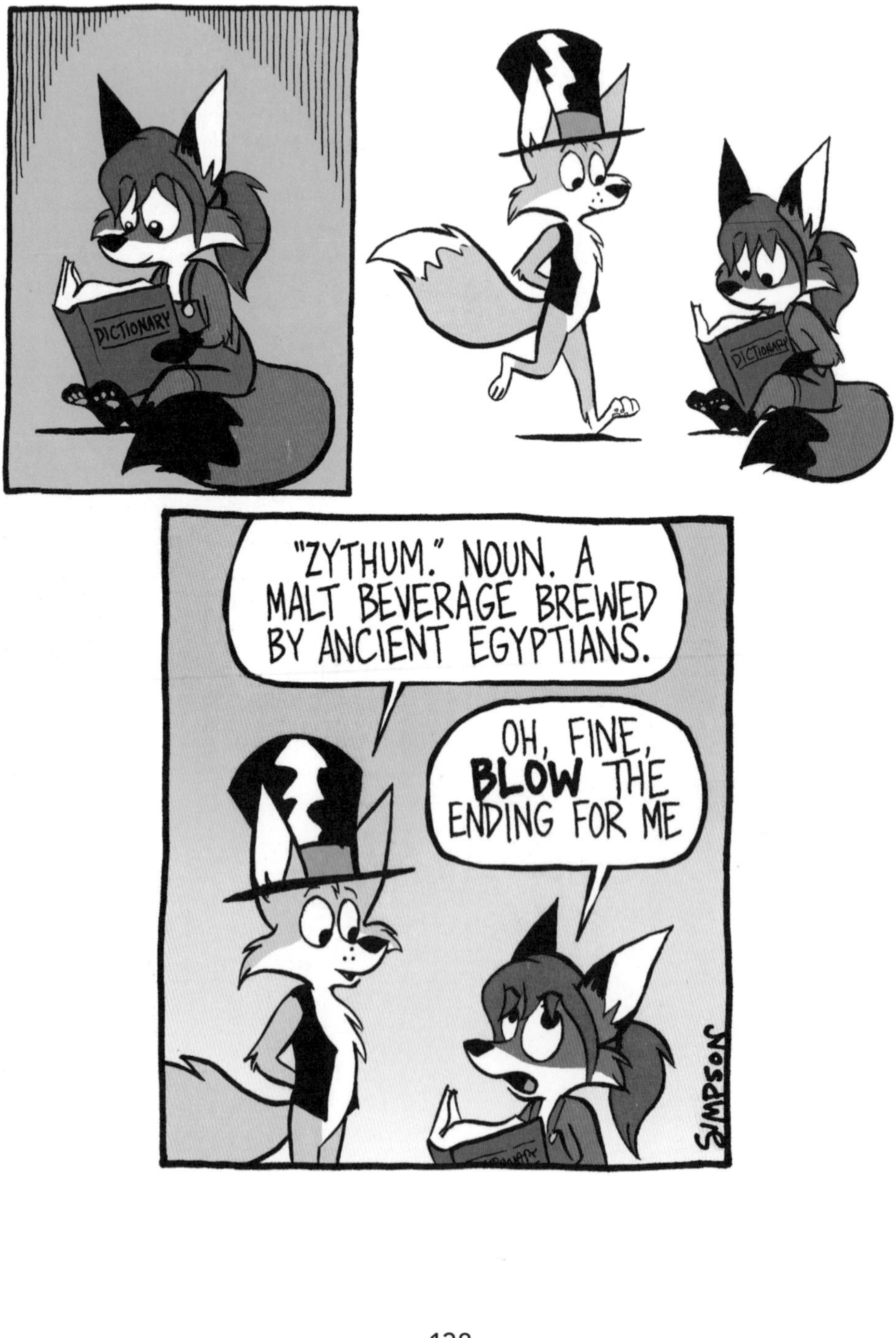
DICTIONARY
DICTIONARY
"ZYTHUM." NOUN. A MALT BEVERAGE BREWED BY ANCIENT EGYPTIANS.
OH, FINE, **BLOW** THE ENDING FOR ME
SIMPSON

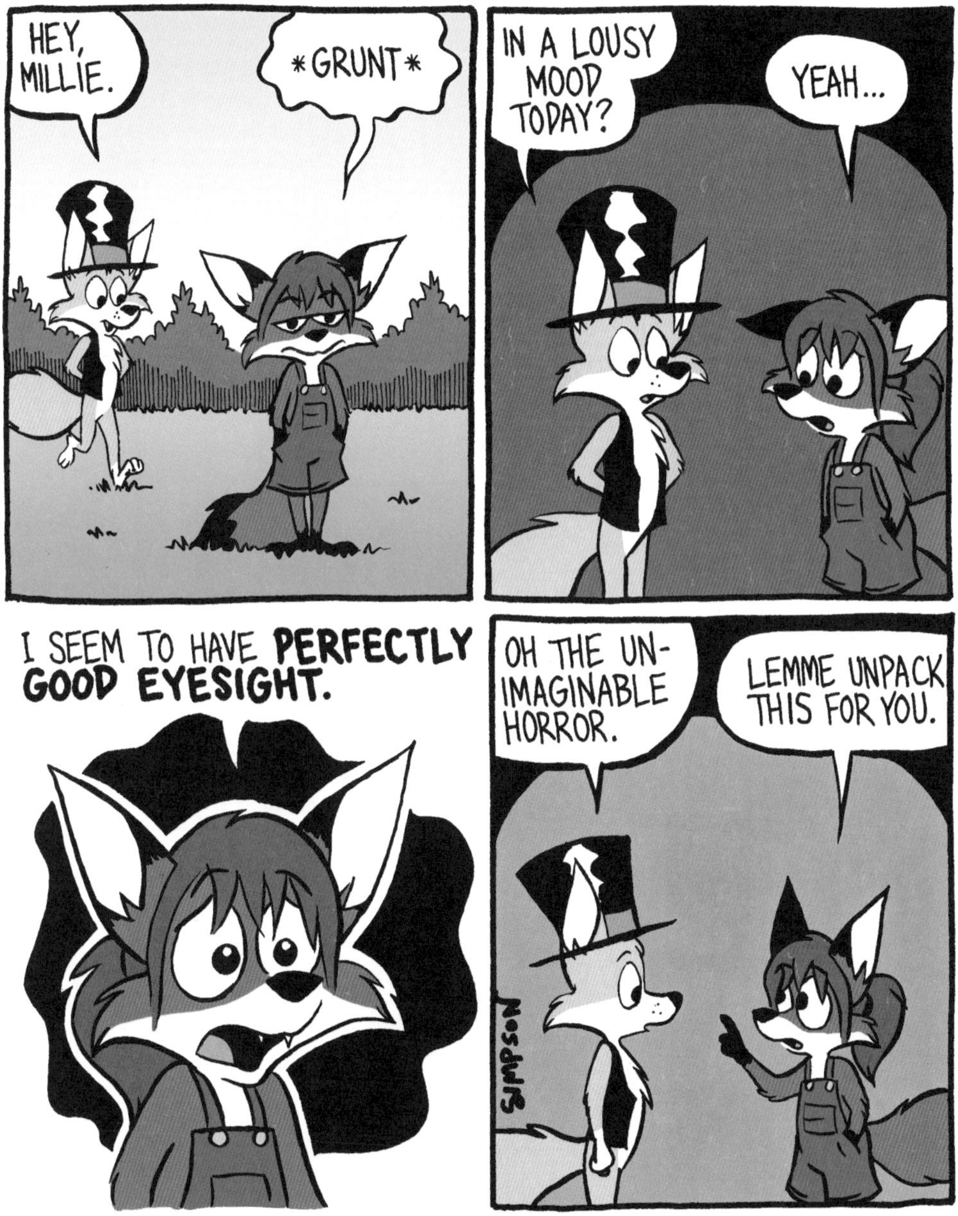
HEY, MILLIE.
GRUNT
IN A LOUSY MOOD TODAY?
YEAH...
I SEEM TO HAVE PERFECTLY GOOD EYESIGHT.
OH THE UN-IMAGINABLE HORROR.
LEMME UNPACK THIS FOR YOU.
SIMPSON

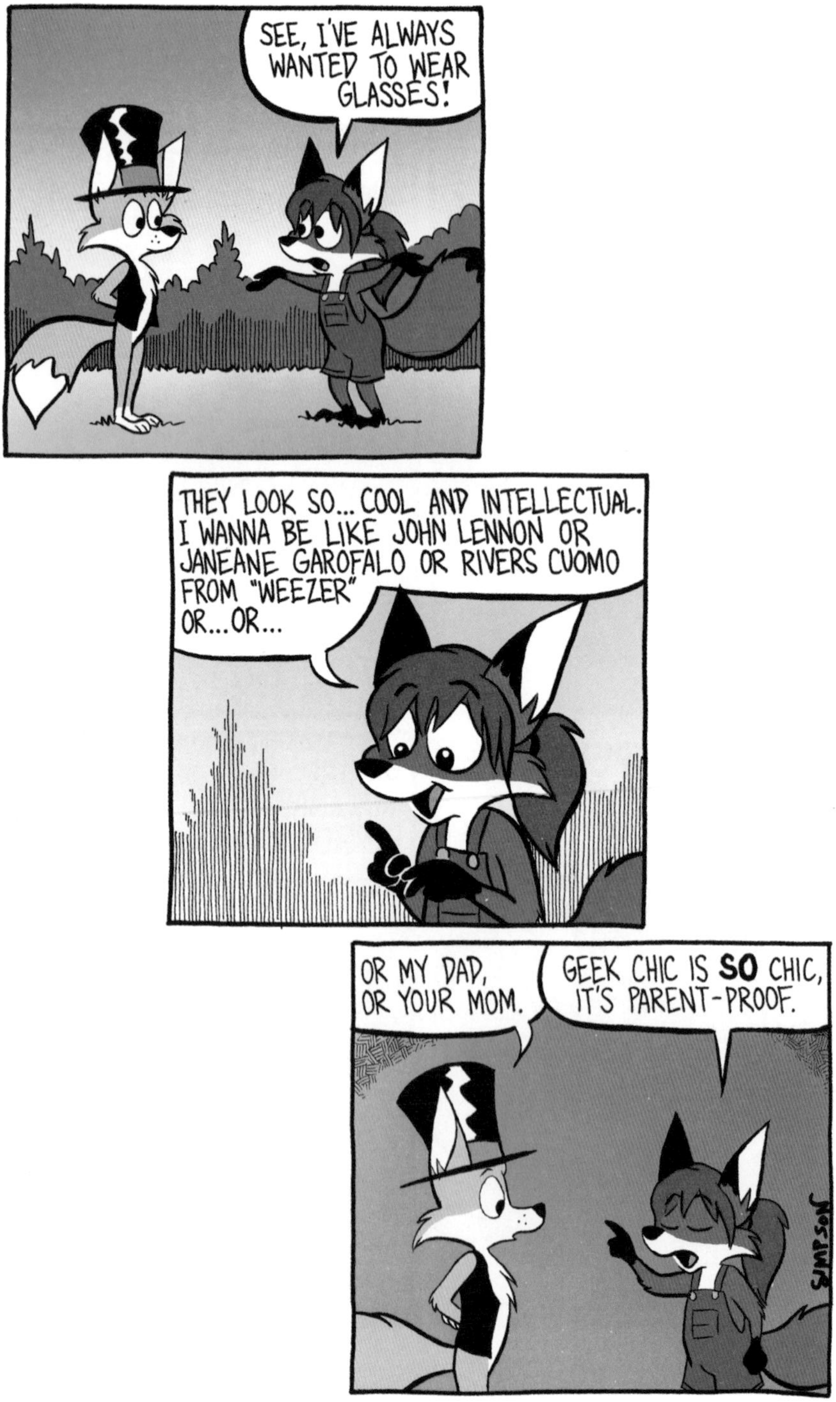
SEE, I'VE ALWAYS WANTED TO WEAR GLASSES!
THEY LOOK SO... COOL AND INTELLECTUAL. I WANNA BE LIKE JOHN LENNON OR JANEANE GAROFALO OR RIVERS CUOMO FROM "WEEZER" OR... OR...
OR MY DAD, OR YOUR MOM.
GEEK CHIC IS **SO** CHIC, IT'S PARENT-PROOF.
SIMPSON

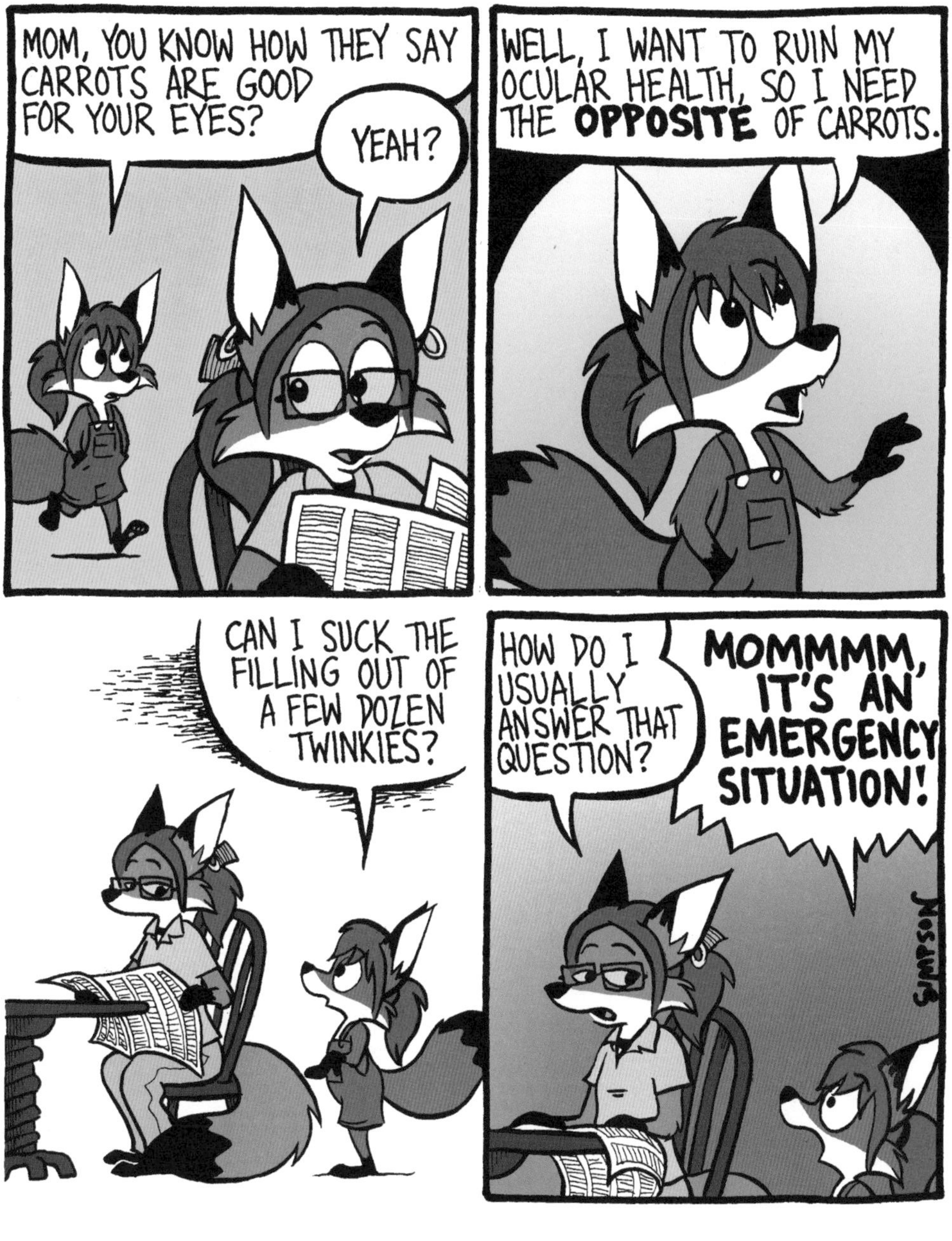
MOM, YOU KNOW HOW THEY SAY CARROTS ARE GOOD FOR YOUR EYES?
YEAH?
WELL, I WANT TO RUIN MY OCULAR HEALTH, SO I NEED THE **OPPOSITE** OF CARROTS.
CAN I SUCK THE FILLING OUT OF A FEW DOZEN TWINKIES?
HOW DO I USUALLY ANSWER THAT QUESTION?
MOMMMM, IT'S AN EMERGENCY SITUATION!
SIMPSON

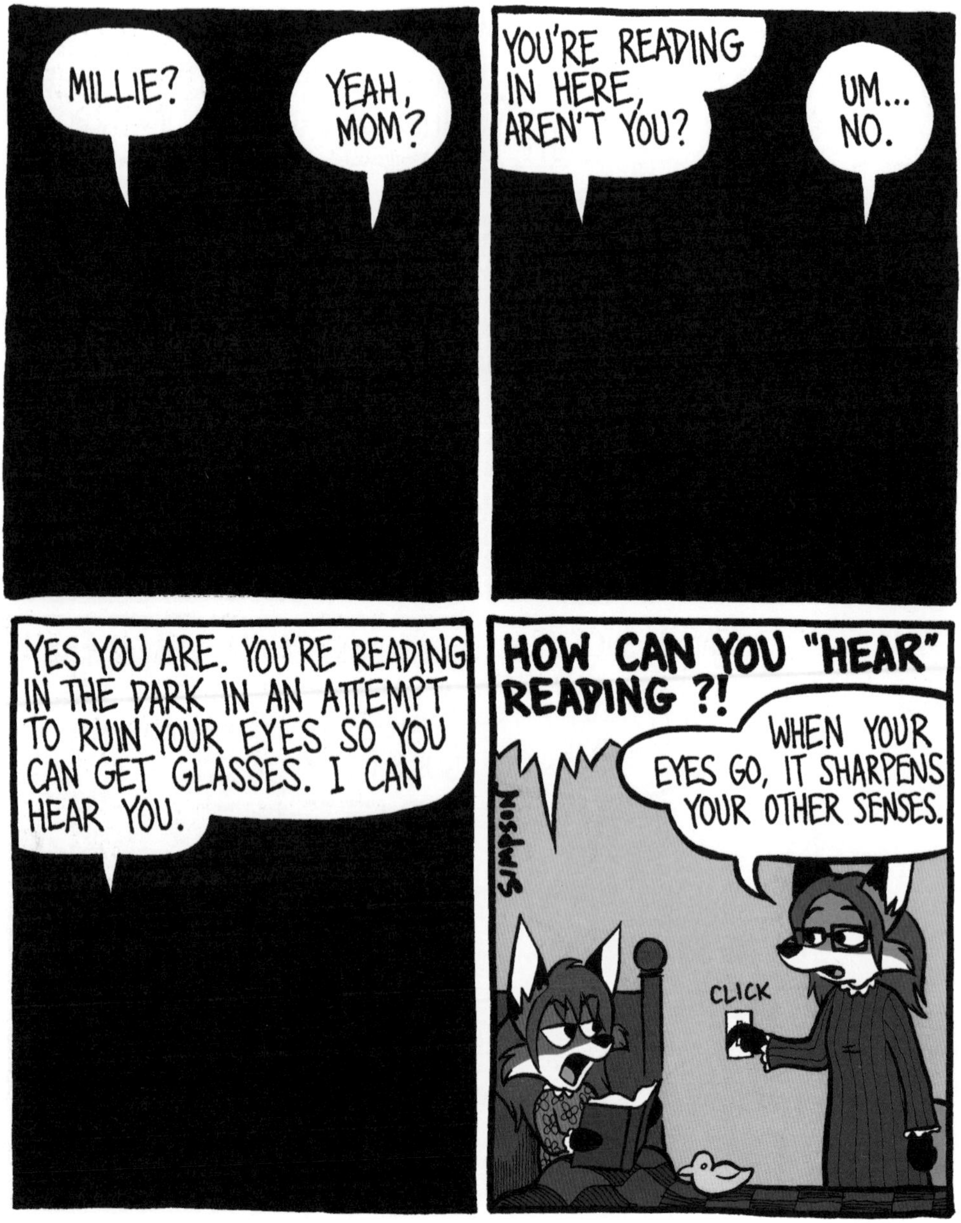

MILLIE?
YEAH, MOM?
YOU'RE READING IN HERE, AREN'T YOU?
UM... NO.
YES YOU ARE. YOU'RE READING IN THE DARK IN AN ATTEMPT TO RUIN YOUR EYES SO YOU CAN GET GLASSES. I CAN HEAR YOU.
HOW CAN YOU "HEAR" READING?!
WHEN YOUR EYES GO, IT SHARPENS YOUR OTHER SENSES.
SIMPSON
CLICK

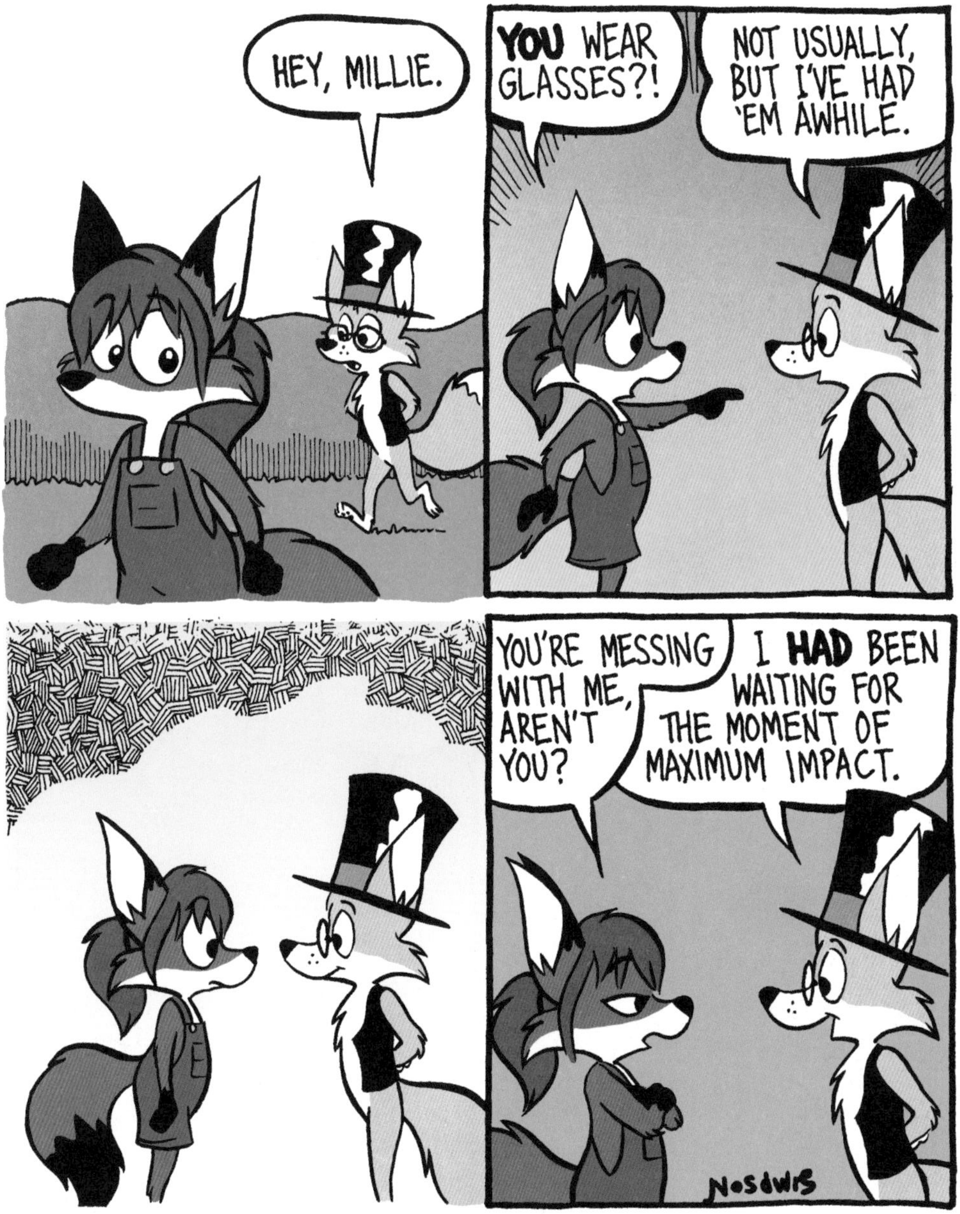
HEY, MILLIE.
YOU WEAR GLASSES?!
NOT USUALLY, BUT I'VE HAD 'EM AWHILE.
YOU'RE MESSING WITH ME, AREN'T YOU?
I HAD BEEN WAITING FOR THE MOMENT OF MAXIMUM IMPACT.
NOSDWIS

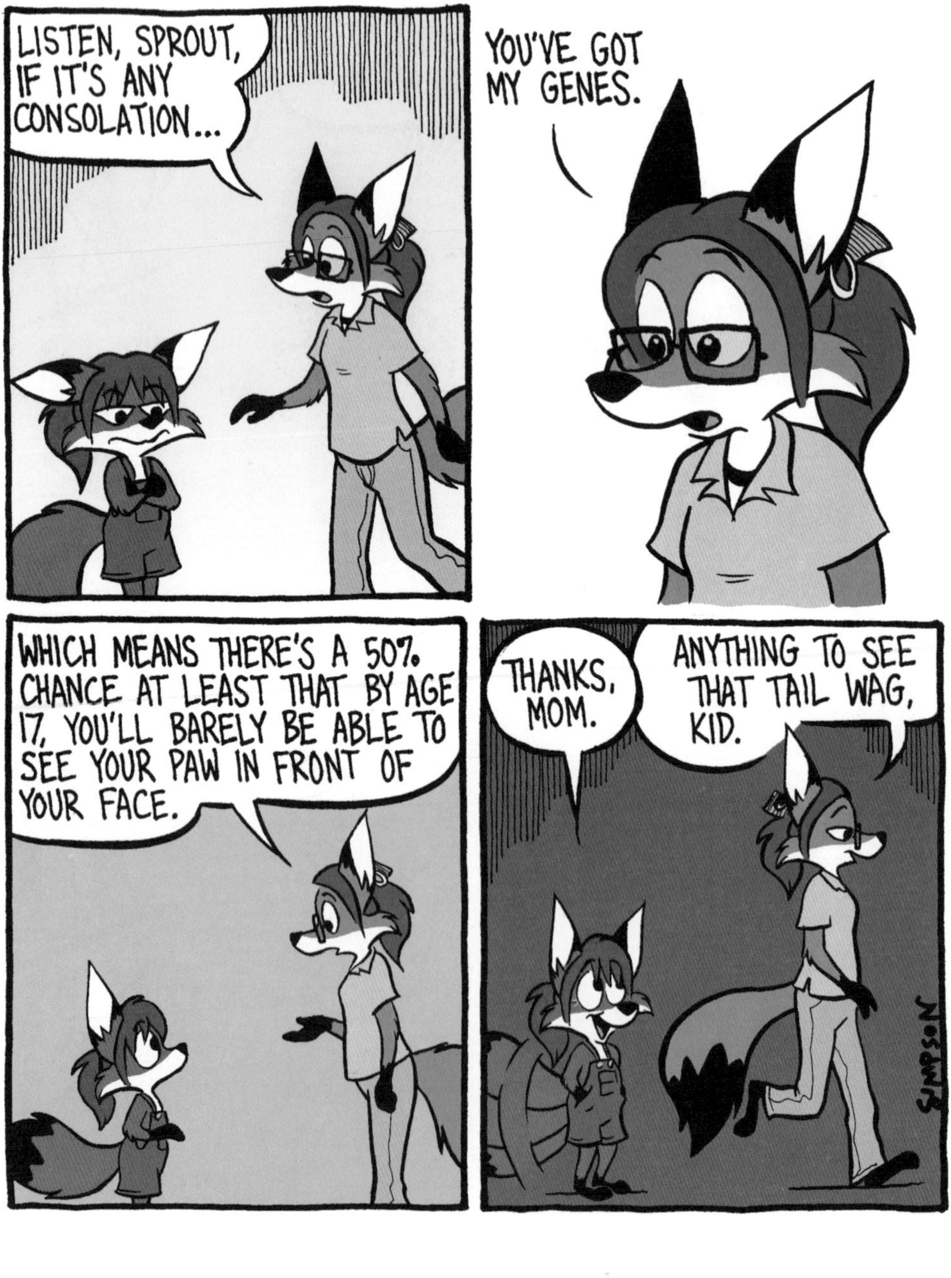
LISTEN, SPROUT, IF IT'S ANY CONSOLATION...
YOU'VE GOT MY GENES.
WHICH MEANS THERE'S A 50% CHANCE AT LEAST THAT BY AGE 17, YOU'LL BARELY BE ABLE TO SEE YOUR PAW IN FRONT OF YOUR FACE.
THANKS, MOM.
ANYTHING TO SEE THAT TAIL WAG, KID.
SIMPSON

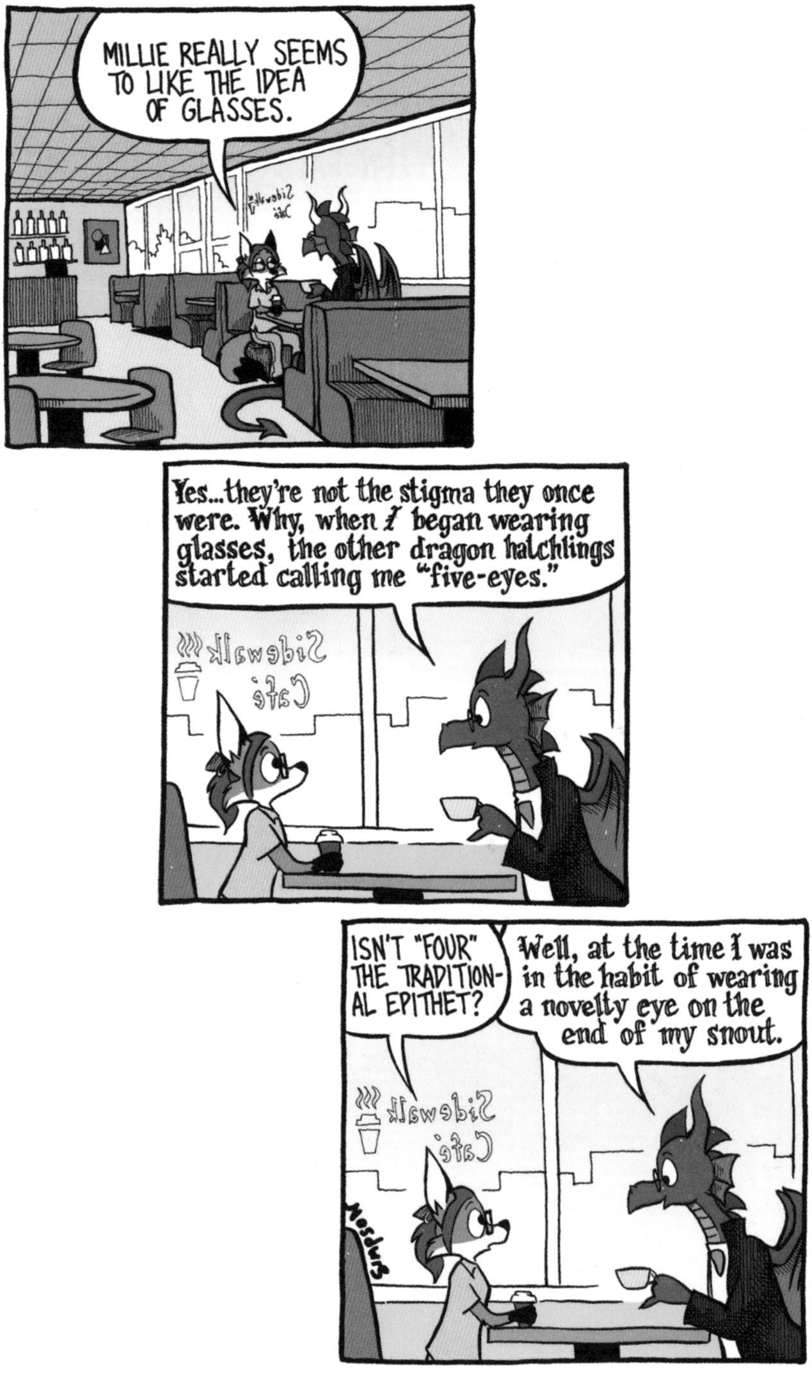
MILLIE REALLY SEEMS TO LIKE THE IDEA OF GLASSES.
Sidewalk Café
Yes...they're not the stigma they once were. Why, when I began wearing glasses, the other dragon hatchlings started calling me "five-eyes."
Sidewalk Café
ISN'T "FOUR" THE TRADITION-AL EPITHET?
Well, at the time I was in the habit of wearing a novelty eye on the end of my snout.
Sidewalk Café
Simpson

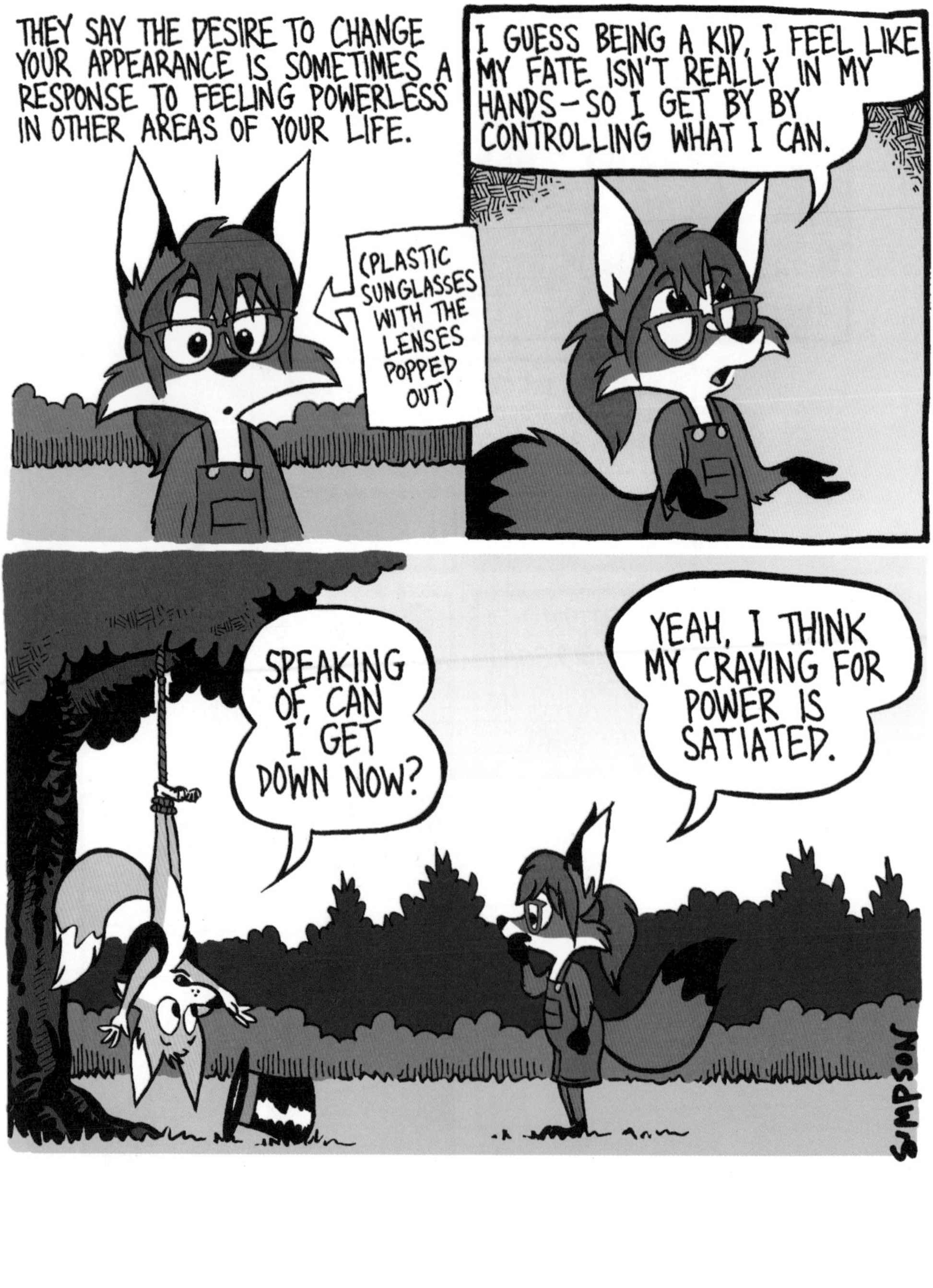
THEY SAY THE DESIRE TO CHANGE YOUR APPEARANCE IS SOMETIMES A RESPONSE TO FEELING POWERLESS IN OTHER AREAS OF YOUR LIFE.
(PLASTIC SUNGLASSES WITH THE LENSES POPPED OUT)
I GUESS BEING A KID, I FEEL LIKE MY FATE ISN'T REALLY IN MY HANDS—SO I GET BY BY CONTROLLING WHAT I CAN.
SPEAKING OF, CAN I GET DOWN NOW?
YEAH, I THINK MY CRAVING FOR POWER IS SATIATED.
SIMPSON

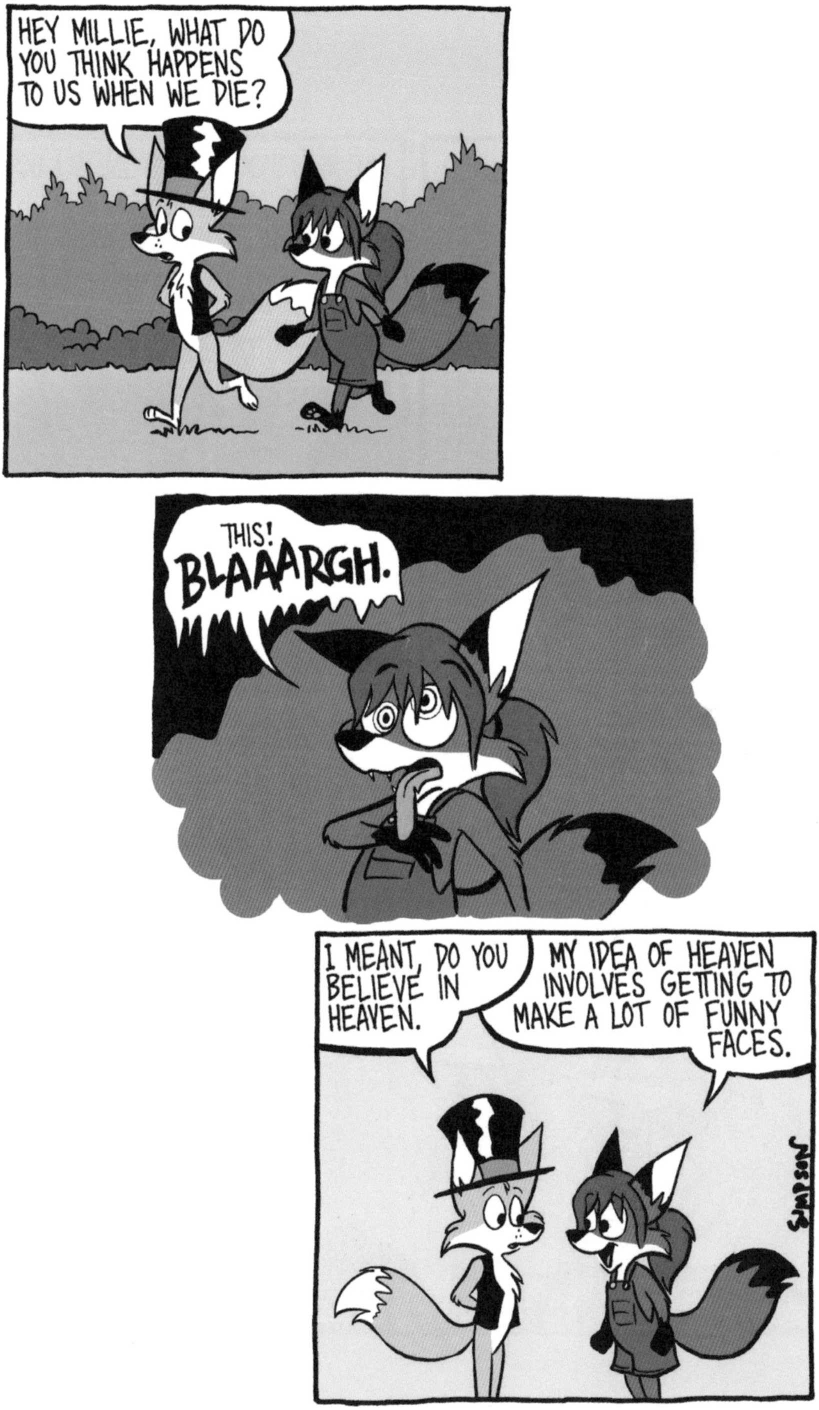
HEY MILLIE, WHAT DO YOU THINK HAPPENS TO US WHEN WE DIE?
THIS! BLAAARGH.
I MEANT, DO YOU BELIEVE IN HEAVEN.
MY IDEA OF HEAVEN INVOLVES GETTING TO MAKE A LOT OF FUNNY FACES.
SIMPSON

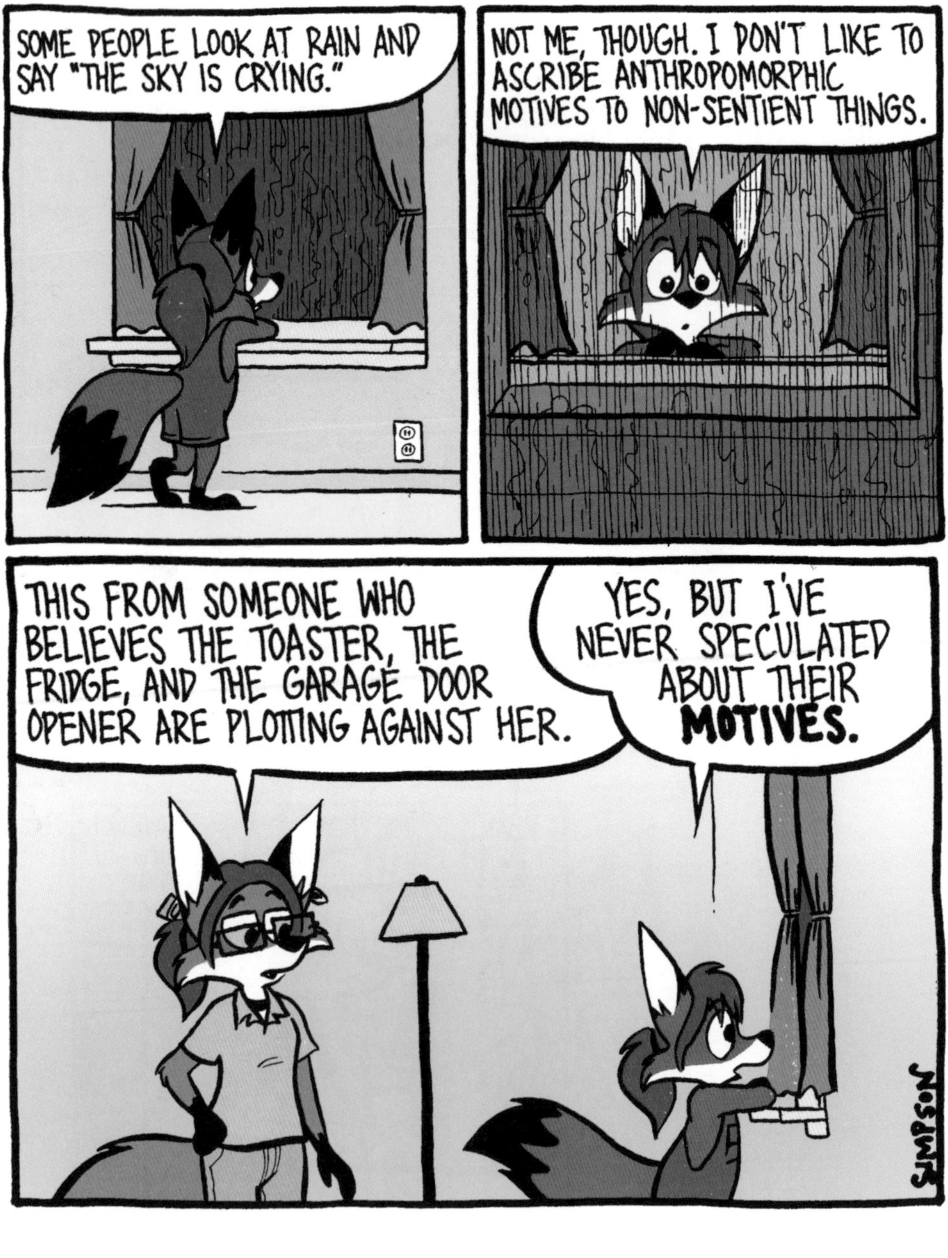
SOME PEOPLE LOOK AT RAIN AND SAY "THE SKY IS CRYING."
NOT ME, THOUGH. I DON'T LIKE TO ASCRIBE ANTHROPOMORPHIC MOTIVES TO NON-SENTIENT THINGS.
THIS FROM SOMEONE WHO BELIEVES THE TOASTER, THE FRIDGE, AND THE GARAGE DOOR OPENER ARE PLOTTING AGAINST HER.
YES, BUT I'VE NEVER SPECULATED ABOUT THEIR **MOTIVES.**
SIMPSON

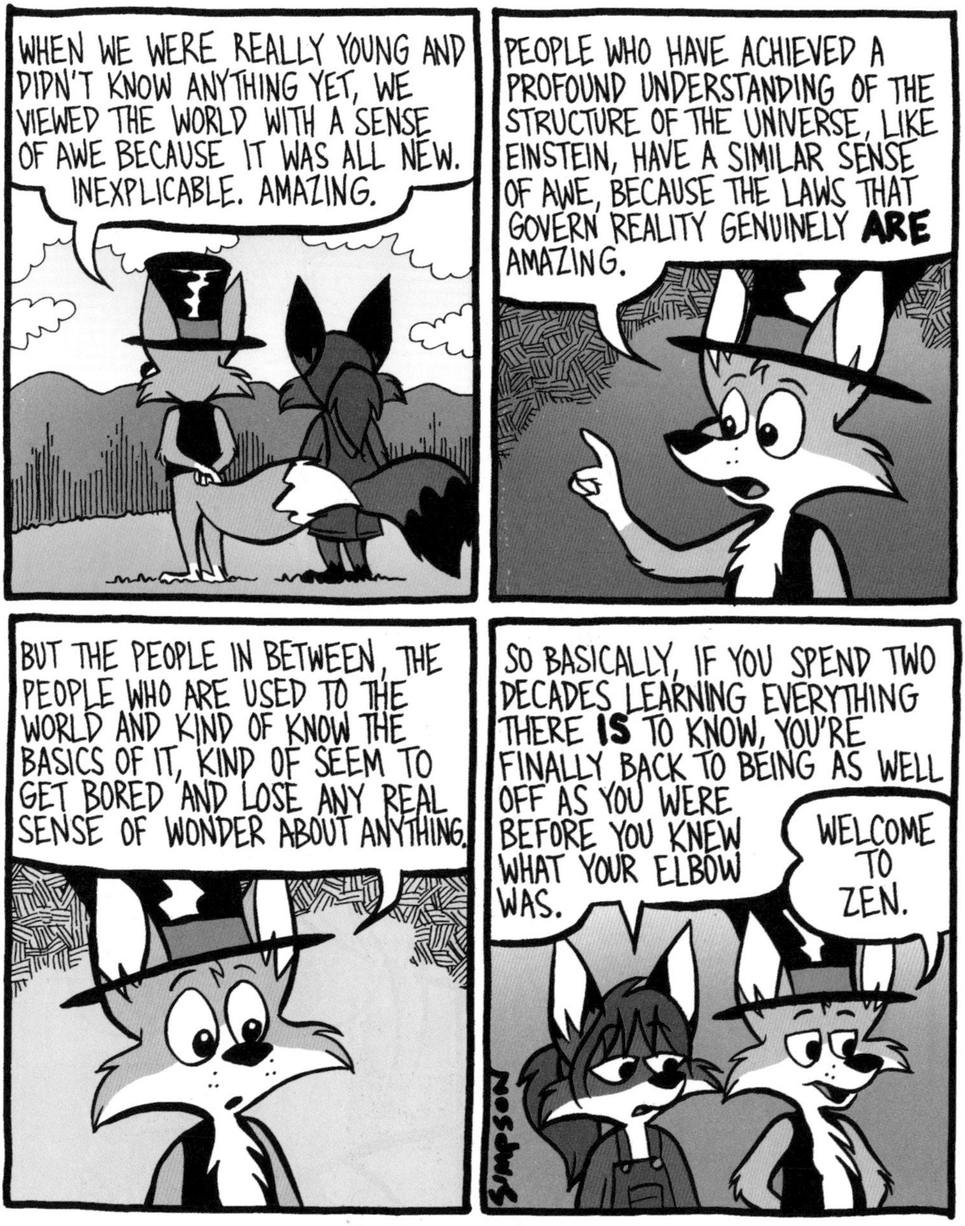
WHEN WE WERE REALLY YOUNG AND DIDN'T KNOW ANYTHING YET, WE VIEWED THE WORLD WITH A SENSE OF AWE BECAUSE IT WAS ALL NEW. INEXPLICABLE. AMAZING.
PEOPLE WHO HAVE ACHIEVED A PROFOUND UNDERSTANDING OF THE STRUCTURE OF THE UNIVERSE, LIKE EINSTEIN, HAVE A SIMILAR SENSE OF AWE, BECAUSE THE LAWS THAT GOVERN REALITY GENUINELY **ARE** AMAZING.
BUT THE PEOPLE IN BETWEEN, THE PEOPLE WHO ARE USED TO THE WORLD AND KIND OF KNOW THE BASICS OF IT, KIND OF SEEM TO GET BORED AND LOSE ANY REAL SENSE OF WONDER ABOUT ANYTHING.
SO BASICALLY, IF YOU SPEND TWO DECADES LEARNING EVERYTHING THERE **IS** TO KNOW, YOU'RE FINALLY BACK TO BEING AS WELL OFF AS YOU WERE BEFORE YOU KNEW WHAT YOUR ELBOW WAS.
WELCOME TO ZEN.
SIMPSON

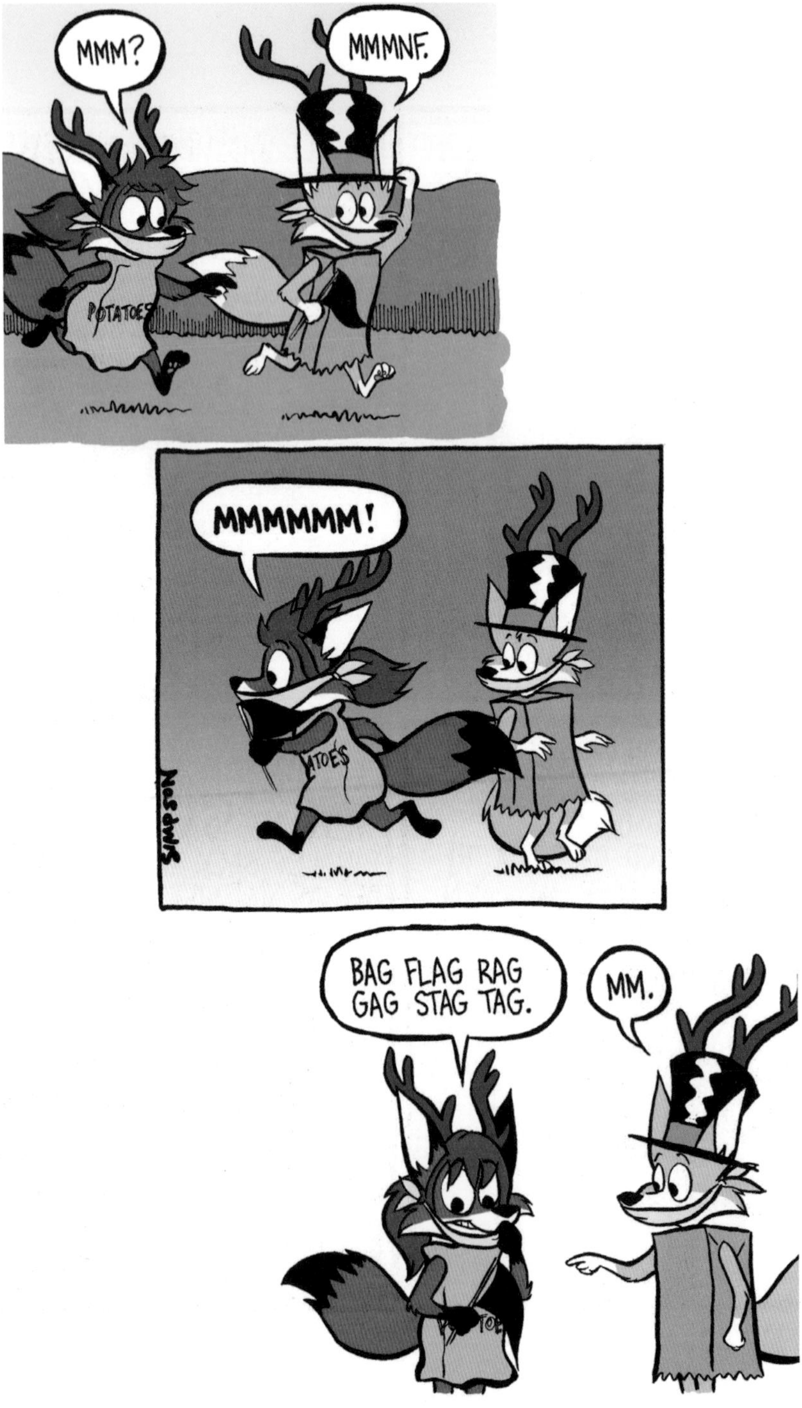
MMM?
MMMNF.
POTATOES
MMMMMM!
BAG FLAG RAG
GAG STAG TAG.
MM.

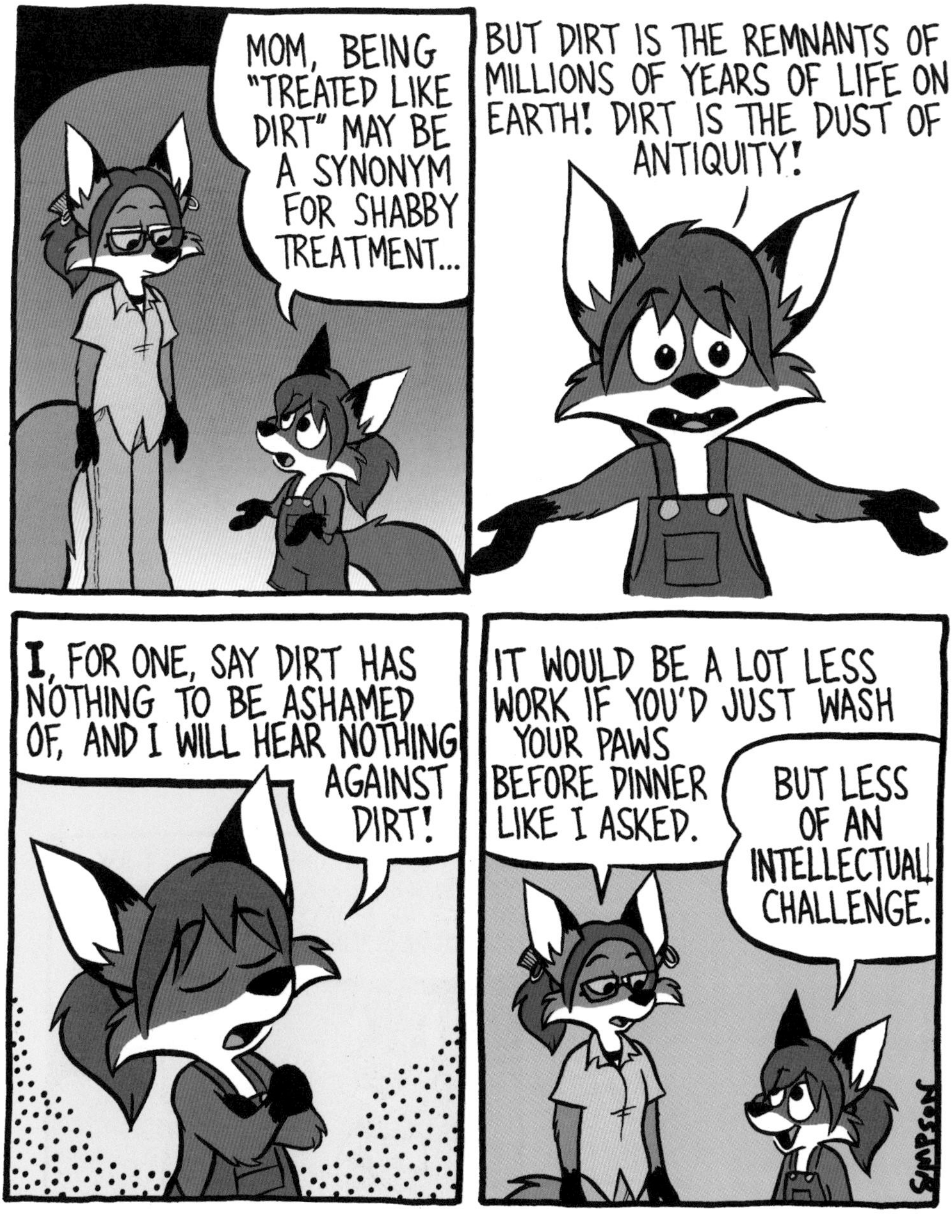
MOM, BEING "TREATED LIKE DIRT" MAY BE A SYNONYM FOR SHABBY TREATMENT...
BUT DIRT IS THE REMNANTS OF MILLIONS OF YEARS OF LIFE ON EARTH! DIRT IS THE DUST OF ANTIQUITY!
I, FOR ONE, SAY DIRT HAS NOTHING TO BE ASHAMED OF, AND I WILL HEAR NOTHING AGAINST DIRT!
IT WOULD BE A LOT LESS WORK IF YOU'D JUST WASH YOUR PAWS BEFORE DINNER LIKE I ASKED.
BUT LESS OF AN INTELLECTUAL CHALLENGE.
SIMPSON

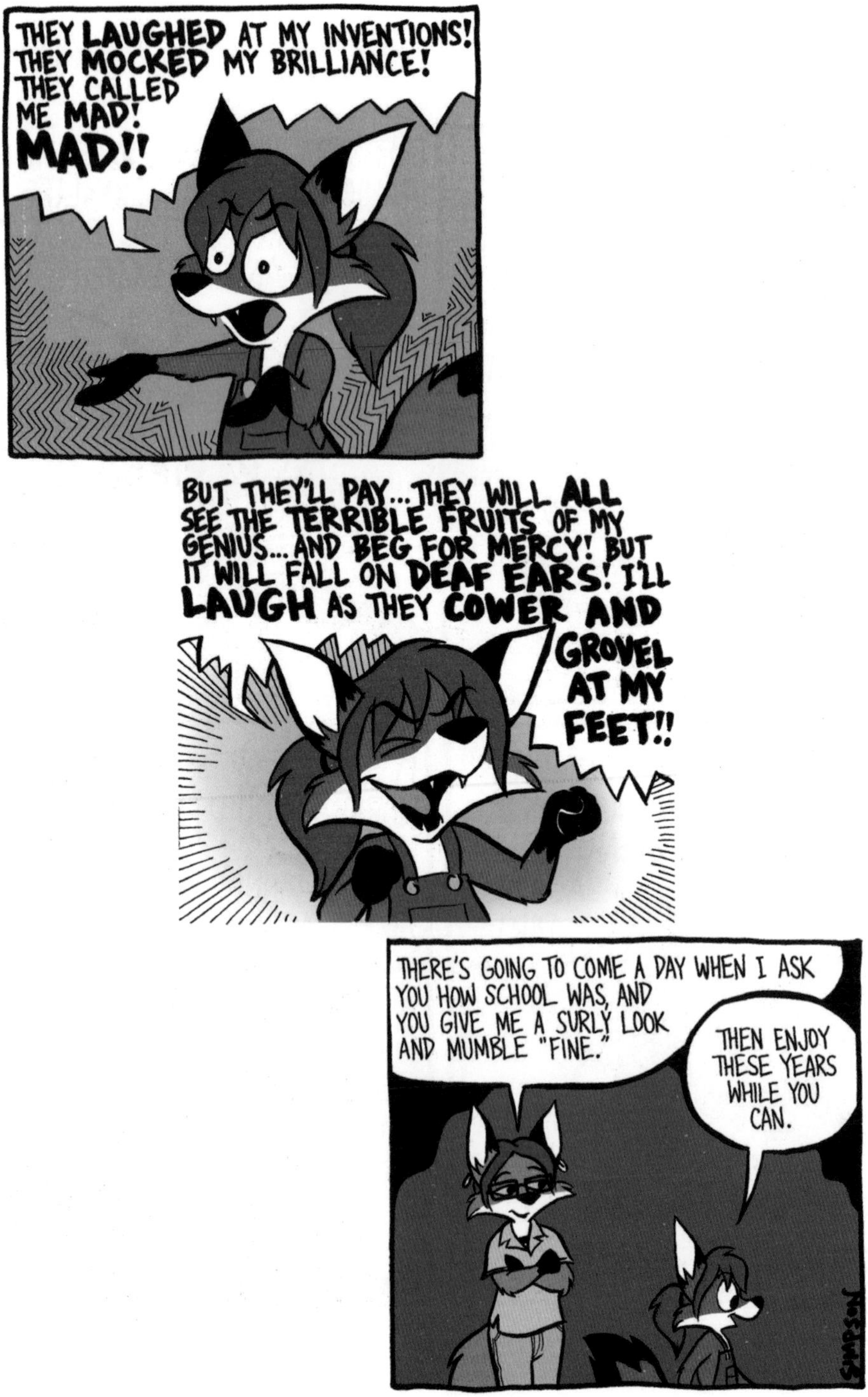
THEY LAUGHED AT MY INVENTIONS! THEY MOCKED MY BRILLIANCE! THEY CALLED ME MAD! MAD!!
BUT THEY'LL PAY...THEY WILL ALL SEE THE TERRIBLE FRUITS OF MY GENIUS... AND BEG FOR MERCY! BUT IT WILL FALL ON DEAF EARS! I'LL LAUGH AS THEY COWER AND GROVEL AT MY FEET!!
THERE'S GOING TO COME A DAY WHEN I ASK YOU HOW SCHOOL WAS, AND YOU GIVE ME A SURLY LOOK AND MUMBLE "FINE."
THEN ENJOY THESE YEARS WHILE YOU CAN.
SIMPSON

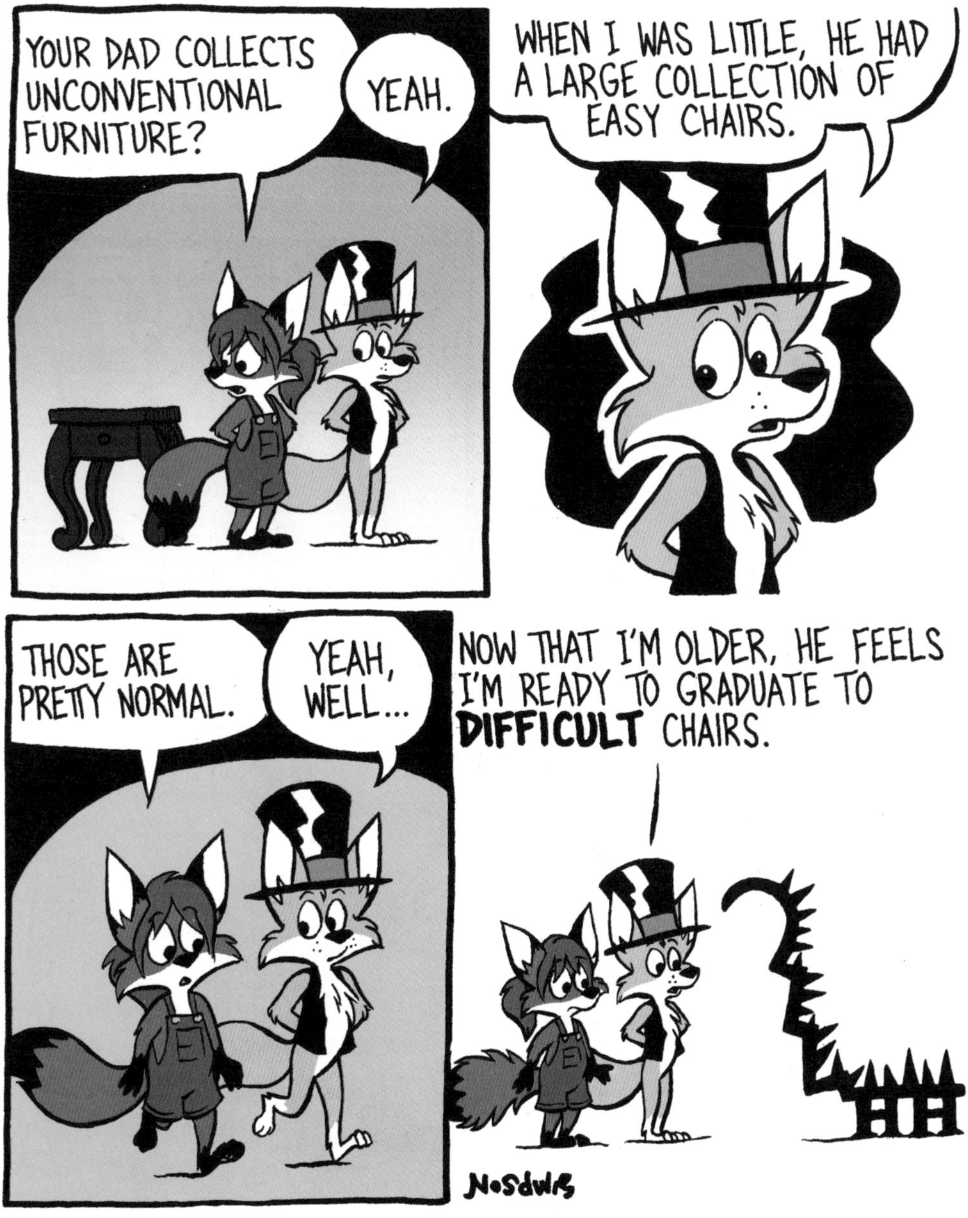
YOUR DAD COLLECTS UNCONVENTIONAL FURNITURE?
YEAH.
WHEN I WAS LITTLE, HE HAD A LARGE COLLECTION OF EASY CHAIRS.
THOSE ARE PRETTY NORMAL.
YEAH, WELL...
NOW THAT I'M OLDER, HE FEELS I'M READY TO GRADUATE TO **DIFFICULT** CHAIRS.
NOSDWIB

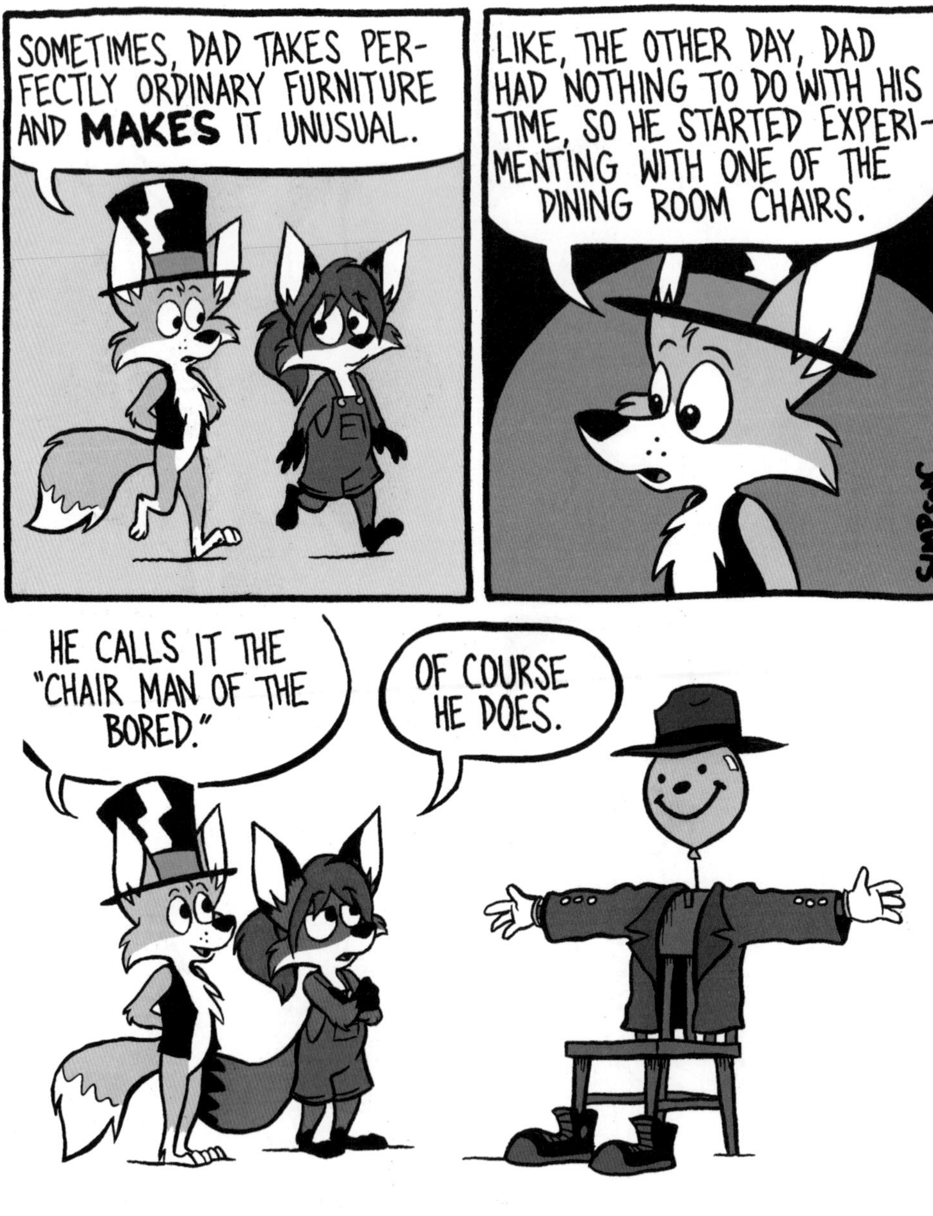
SOMETIMES, DAD TAKES PERFECTLY ORDINARY FURNITURE AND **MAKES** IT UNUSUAL.
LIKE, THE OTHER DAY, DAD HAD NOTHING TO DO WITH HIS TIME, SO HE STARTED EXPERIMENTING WITH ONE OF THE DINING ROOM CHAIRS.
SIMPSON
HE CALLS IT THE "CHAIR MAN OF THE BORED."
OF COURSE HE DOES.

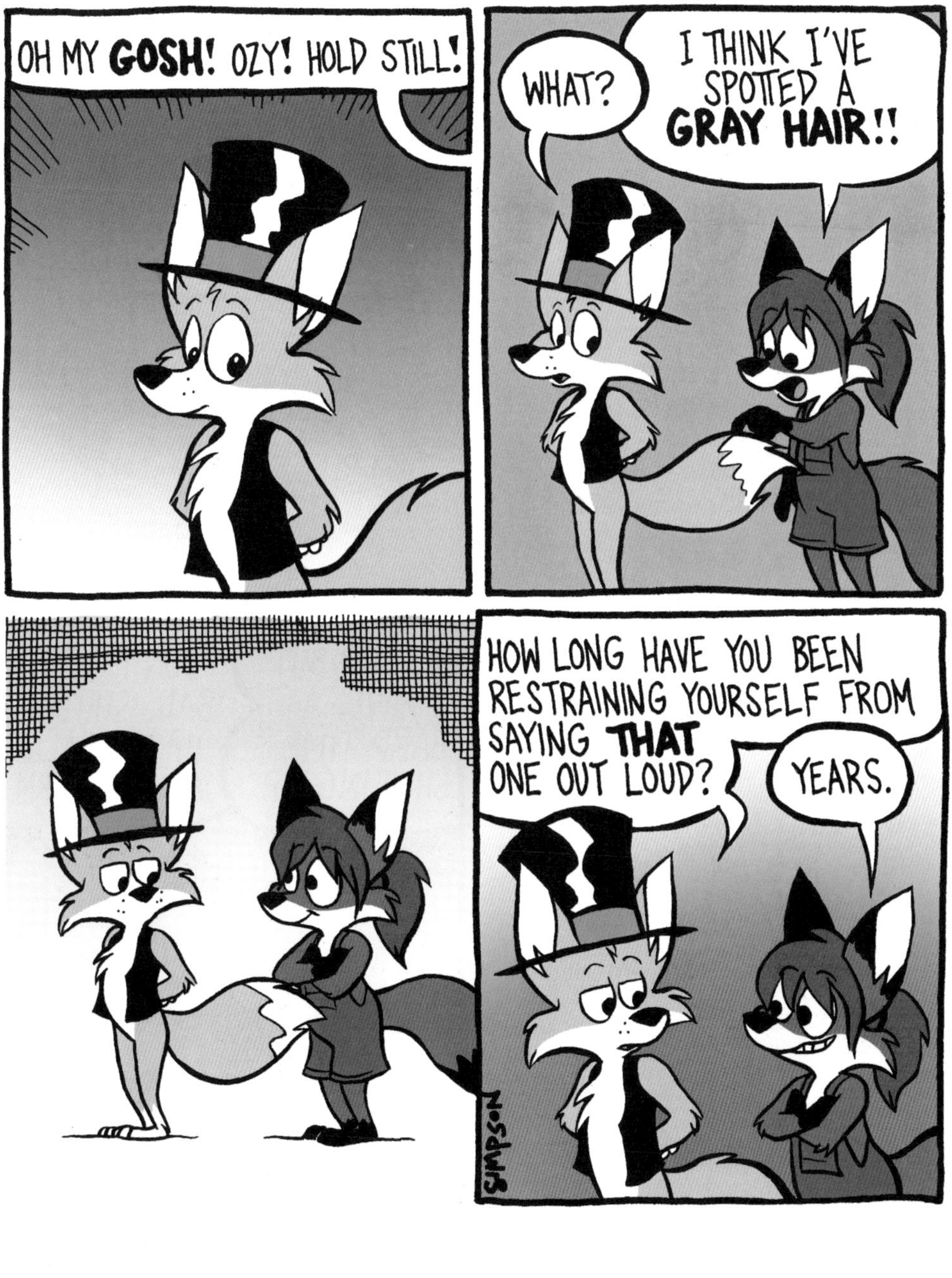
OH MY GOSH! OZY! HOLD STILL!
WHAT?
I THINK I'VE SPOTTED A GRAY HAIR!!
HOW LONG HAVE YOU BEEN RESTRAINING YOURSELF FROM SAYING THAT ONE OUT LOUD?
YEARS.
SIMPSON

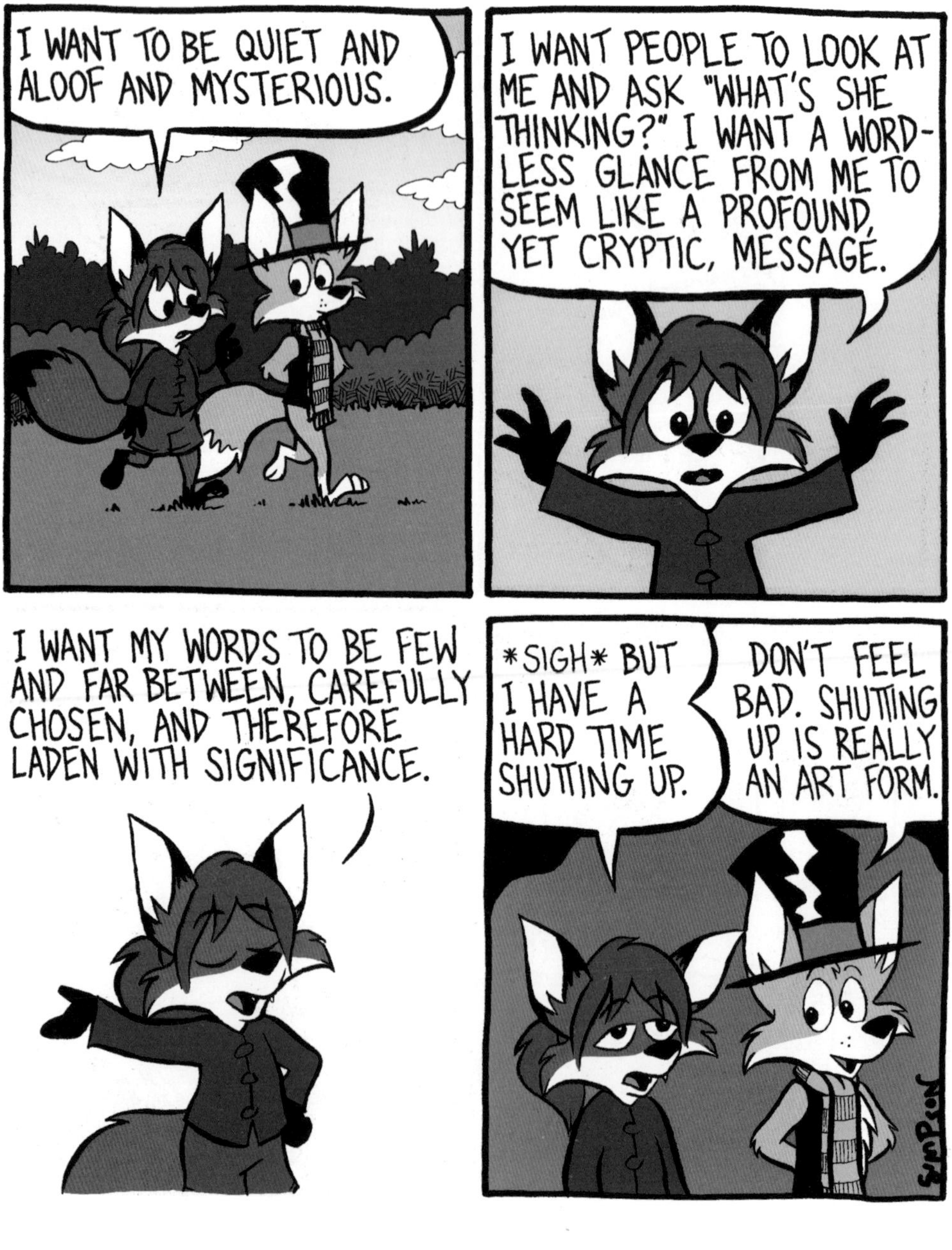
I WANT TO BE QUIET AND ALOOF AND MYSTERIOUS.
I WANT PEOPLE TO LOOK AT ME AND ASK "WHAT'S SHE THINKING?" I WANT A WORDLESS GLANCE FROM ME TO SEEM LIKE A PROFOUND, YET CRYPTIC, MESSAGE.
I WANT MY WORDS TO BE FEW AND FAR BETWEEN, CAREFULLY CHOSEN, AND THEREFORE LADEN WITH SIGNIFICANCE.
SIGH BUT I HAVE A HARD TIME SHUTTING UP.
DON'T FEEL BAD. SHUTTING UP IS REALLY AN ART FORM.
SIMPSON

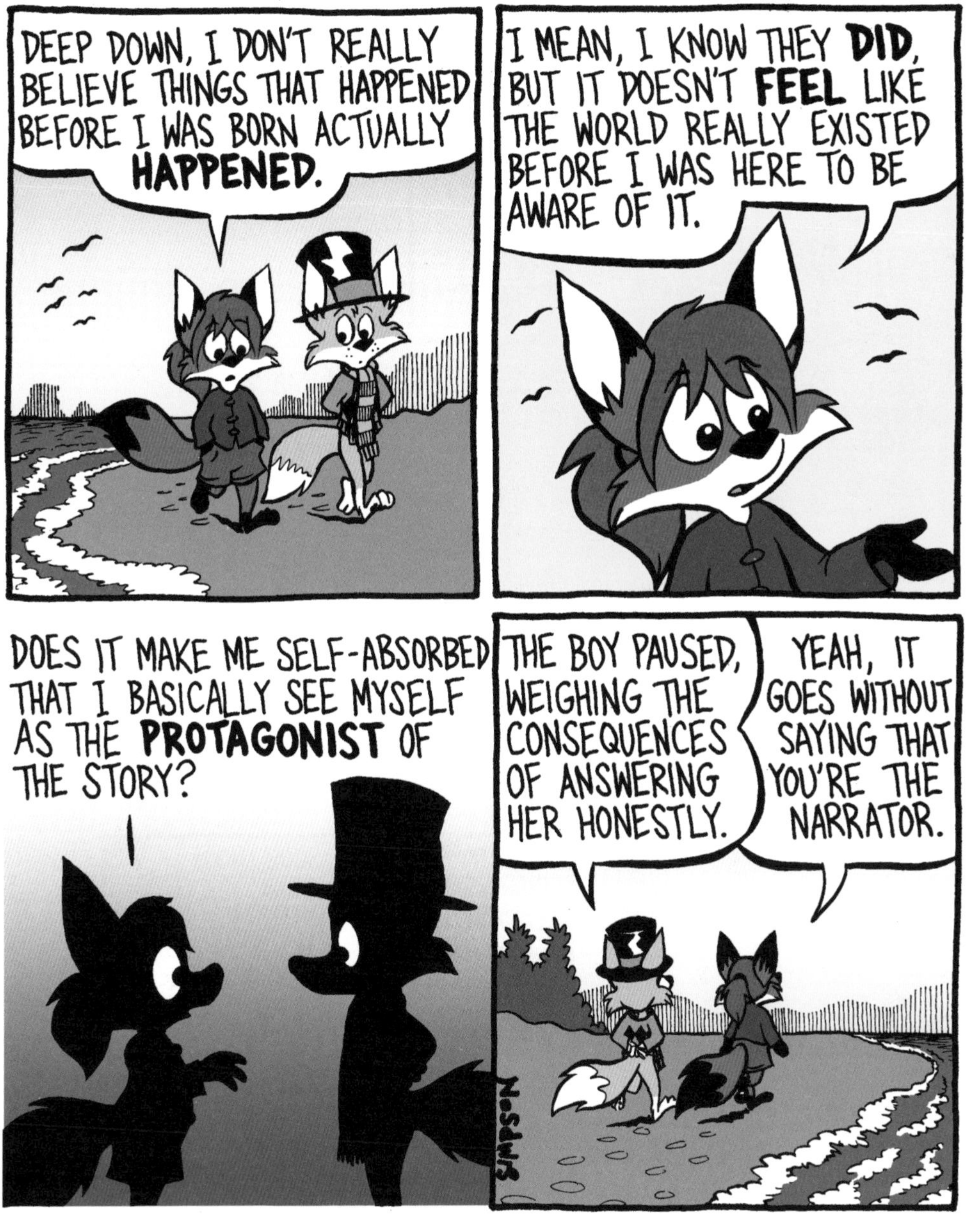
DEEP DOWN, I DON'T REALLY BELIEVE THINGS THAT HAPPENED BEFORE I WAS BORN ACTUALLY **HAPPENED.**
I MEAN, I KNOW THEY **DID**, BUT IT DOESN'T **FEEL** LIKE THE WORLD REALLY EXISTED BEFORE I WAS HERE TO BE AWARE OF IT.
DOES IT MAKE ME SELF-ABSORBED THAT I BASICALLY SEE MYSELF AS THE **PROTAGONIST** OF THE STORY?
THE BOY PAUSED, WEIGHING THE CONSEQUENCES OF ANSWERING HER HONESTLY.
YEAH, IT GOES WITHOUT SAYING THAT YOU'RE THE NARRATOR.
SIMPSON

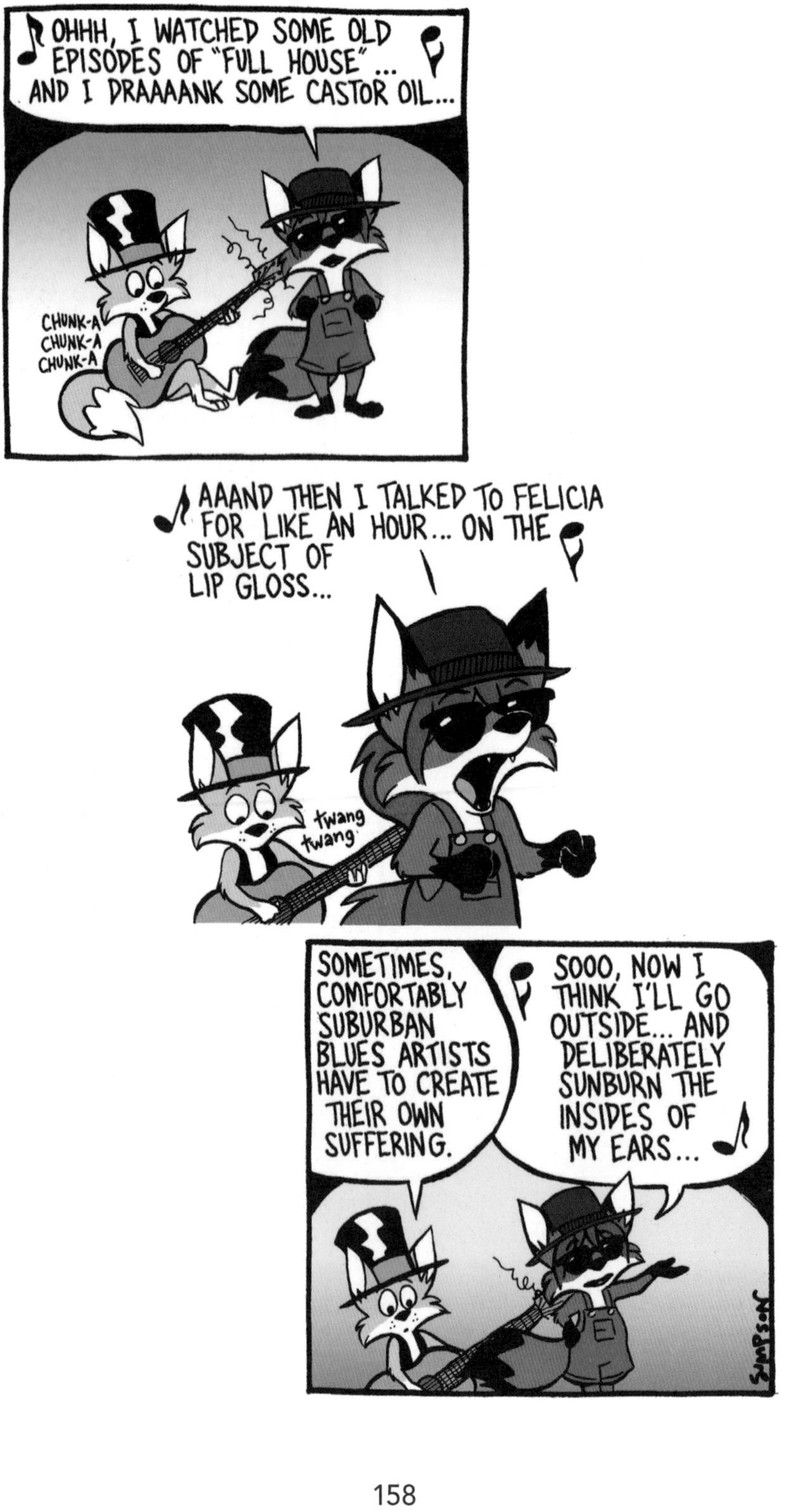
OHHH, I WATCHED SOME OLD EPISODES OF "FULL HOUSE"... AND I DRAAAANK SOME CASTOR OIL...
CHUNK-A CHUNK-A CHUNK-A
AAAND THEN I TALKED TO FELICIA FOR LIKE AN HOUR... ON THE SUBJECT OF LIP GLOSS...
twang twang
SOMETIMES, COMFORTABLY SUBURBAN BLUES ARTISTS HAVE TO CREATE THEIR OWN SUFFERING.
SOOO, NOW I THINK I'LL GO OUTSIDE... AND DELIBERATELY SUNBURN THE INSIDES OF MY EARS...
SIMPSON

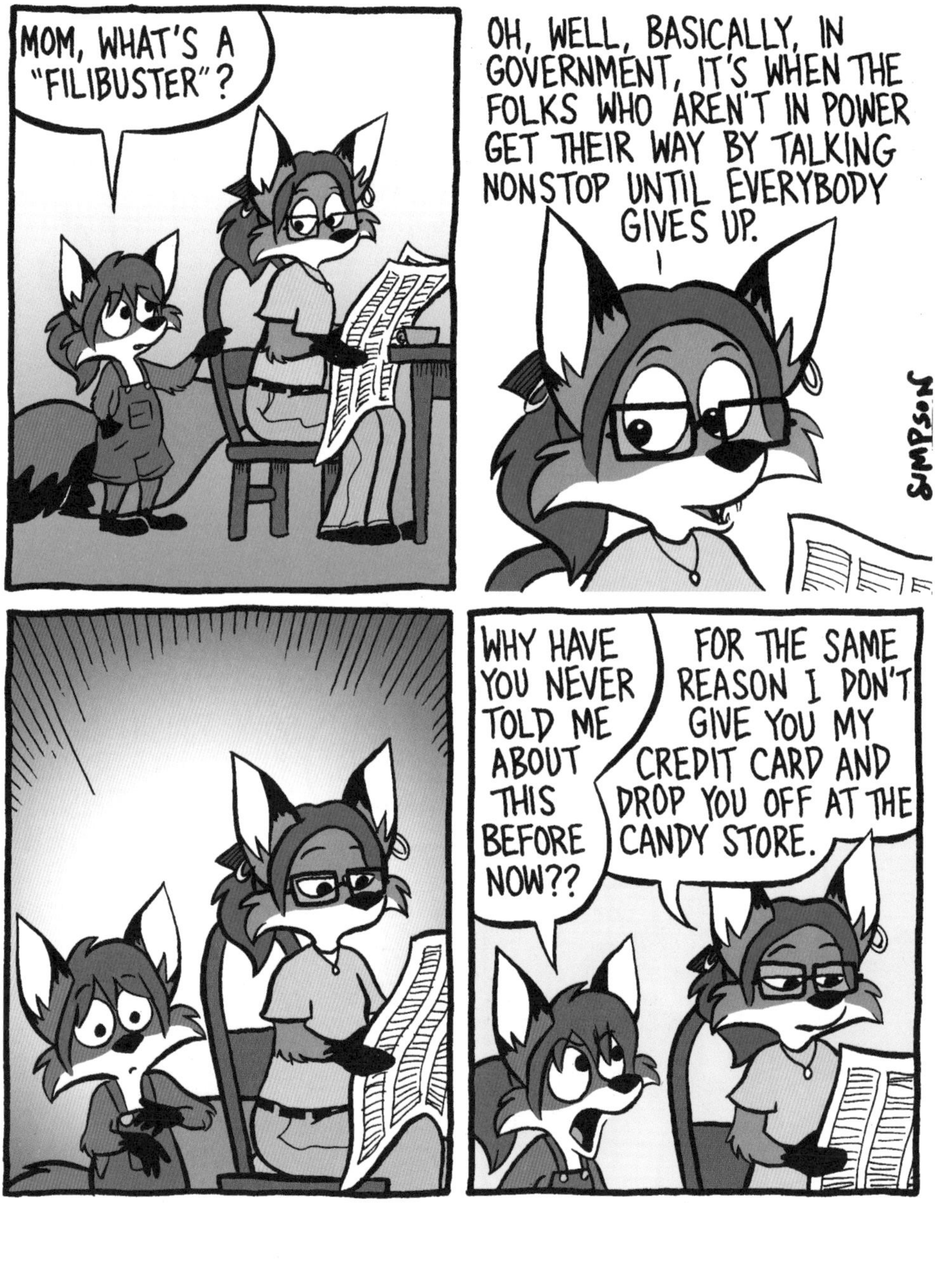
MOM, WHAT'S A "FILIBUSTER"?
OH, WELL, BASICALLY, IN GOVERNMENT, IT'S WHEN THE FOLKS WHO AREN'T IN POWER GET THEIR WAY BY TALKING NONSTOP UNTIL EVERYBODY GIVES UP.
SIMPSON
WHY HAVE YOU NEVER TOLD ME ABOUT THIS BEFORE NOW??
FOR THE SAME REASON I DON'T GIVE YOU MY CREDIT CARD AND DROP YOU OFF AT THE CANDY STORE.

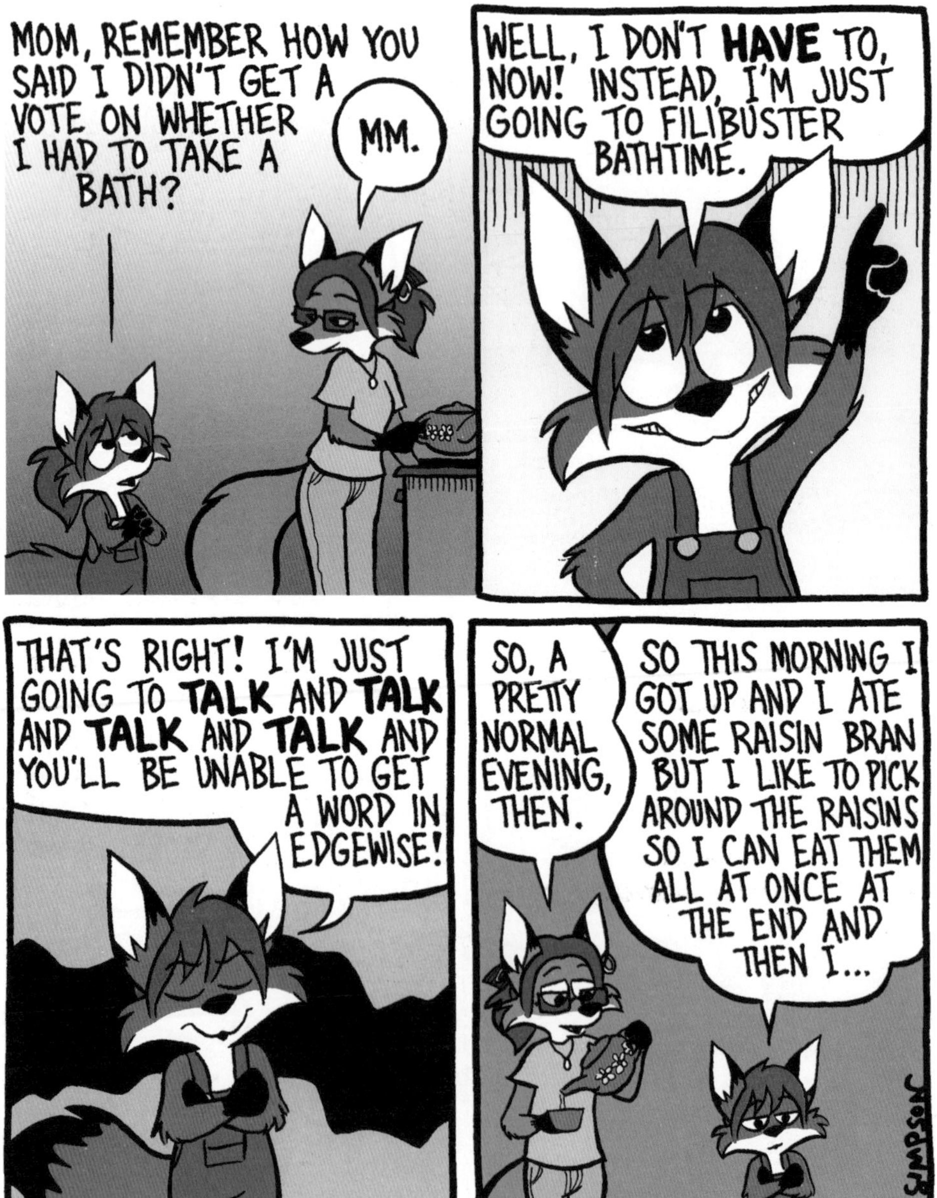

MOM, REMEMBER HOW YOU SAID I DIDN'T GET A VOTE ON WHETHER I HAD TO TAKE A BATH?
MM.
WELL, I DON'T **HAVE** TO, NOW! INSTEAD, I'M JUST GOING TO FILIBUSTER BATHTIME.
THAT'S RIGHT! I'M JUST GOING TO **TALK** AND **TALK** AND **TALK** AND **TALK** AND YOU'LL BE UNABLE TO GET A WORD IN EDGEWISE!
SO THIS MORNING I GOT UP AND I ATE SOME RAISIN BRAN BUT I LIKE TO PICK AROUND THE RAISINS SO I CAN EAT THEM ALL AT ONCE AT THE END AND THEN I...
SO, A PRETTY NORMAL EVENING, THEN.
SIMPSON

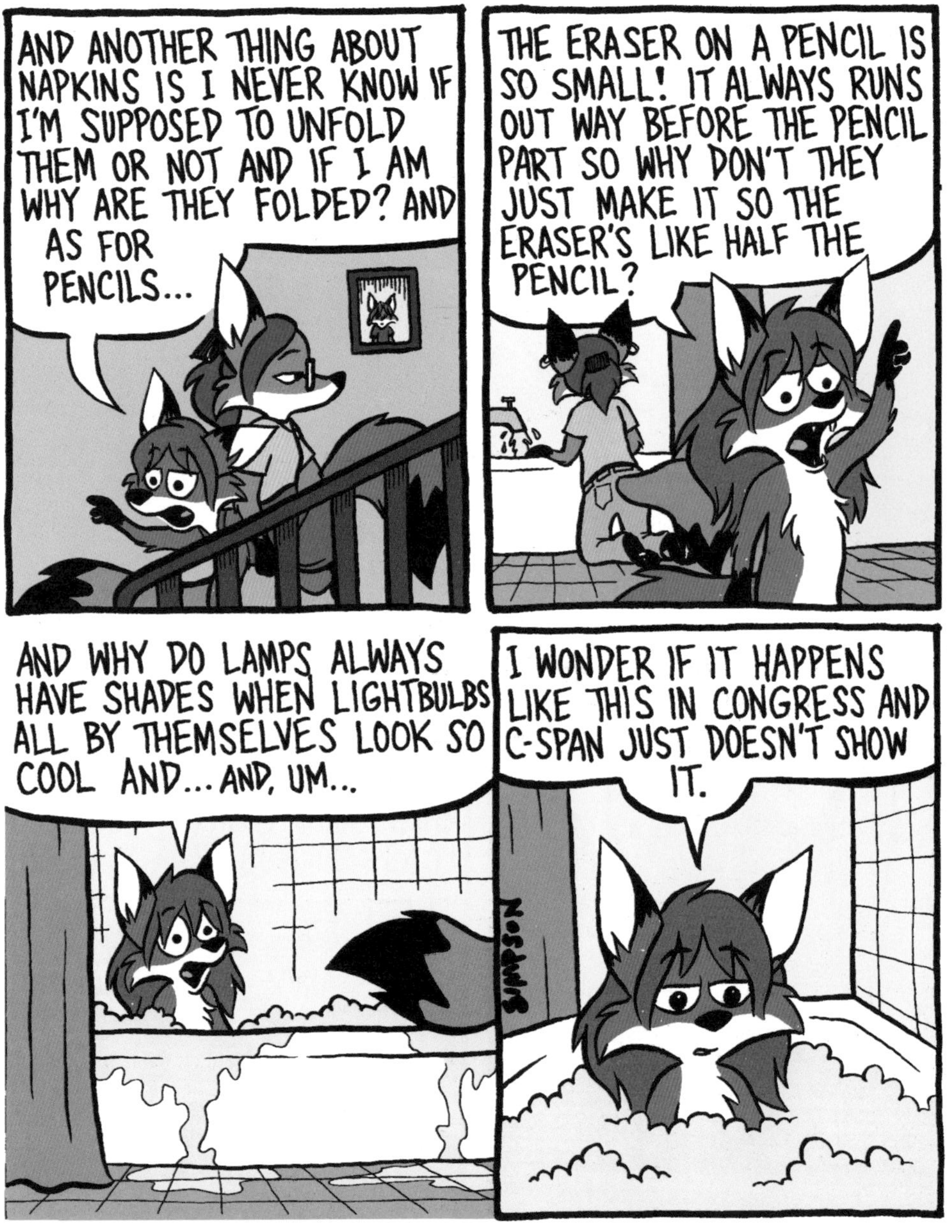
AND ANOTHER THING ABOUT NAPKINS IS I NEVER KNOW IF I'M SUPPOSED TO UNFOLD THEM OR NOT AND IF I AM WHY ARE THEY FOLDED? AND AS FOR PENCILS...
THE ERASER ON A PENCIL IS SO SMALL! IT ALWAYS RUNS OUT WAY BEFORE THE PENCIL PART SO WHY DON'T THEY JUST MAKE IT SO THE ERASER'S LIKE HALF THE PENCIL?
AND WHY DO LAMPS ALWAYS HAVE SHADES WHEN LIGHTBULBS ALL BY THEMSELVES LOOK SO COOL AND... AND, UM...
SIMPSON
I WONDER IF IT HAPPENS LIKE THIS IN CONGRESS AND C-SPAN JUST DOESN'T SHOW IT.

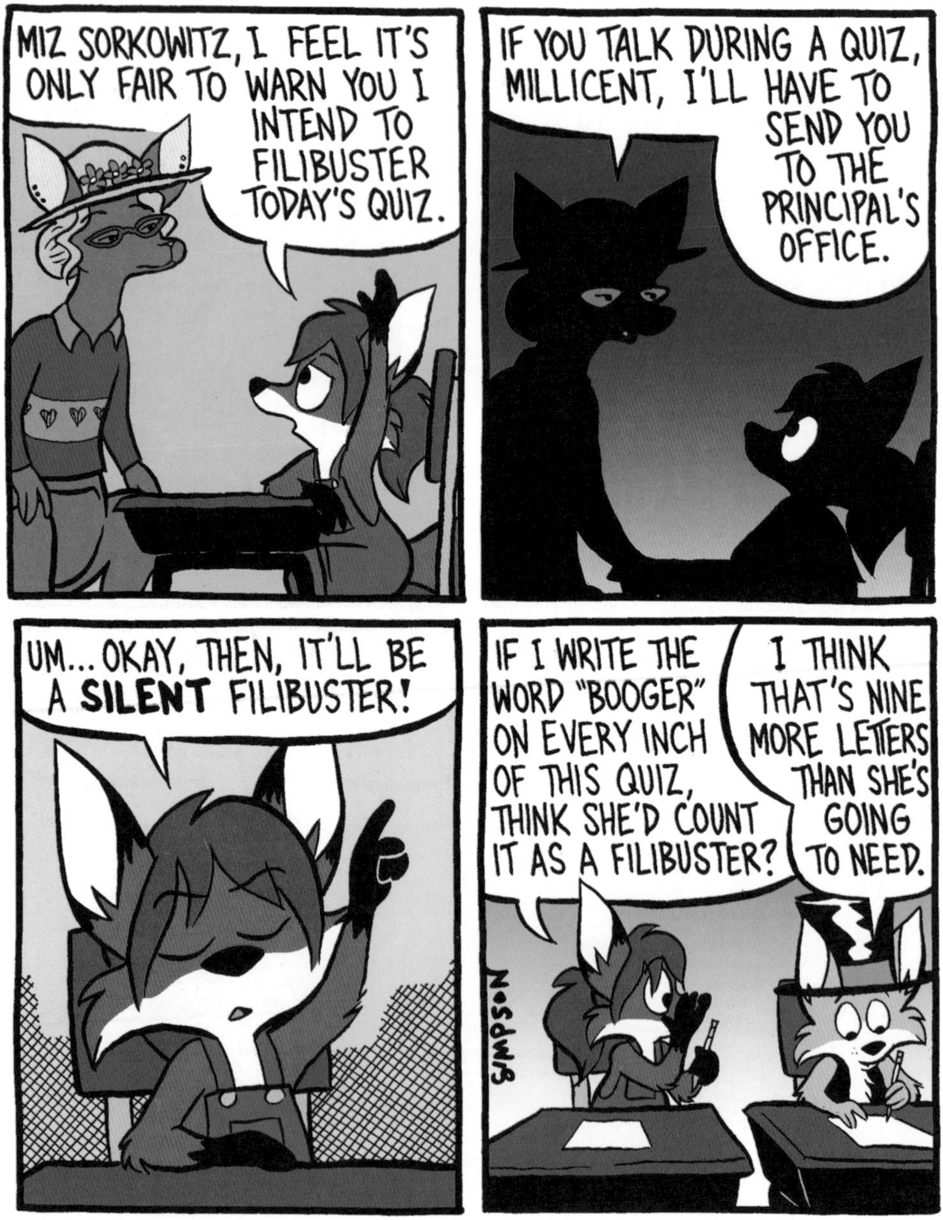
MIZ SORKOWITZ, I FEEL IT'S ONLY FAIR TO WARN YOU I INTEND TO FILIBUSTER TODAY'S QUIZ.
IF YOU TALK DURING A QUIZ, MILLICENT, I'LL HAVE TO SEND YOU TO THE PRINCIPAL'S OFFICE.
UM... OKAY, THEN, IT'LL BE A **SILENT** FILIBUSTER!
IF I WRITE THE WORD "BOOGER" ON EVERY INCH OF THIS QUIZ, THINK SHE'D COUNT IT AS A FILIBUSTER?
I THINK THAT'S NINE MORE LETTERS THAN SHE'S GOING TO NEED.
SIMPSON

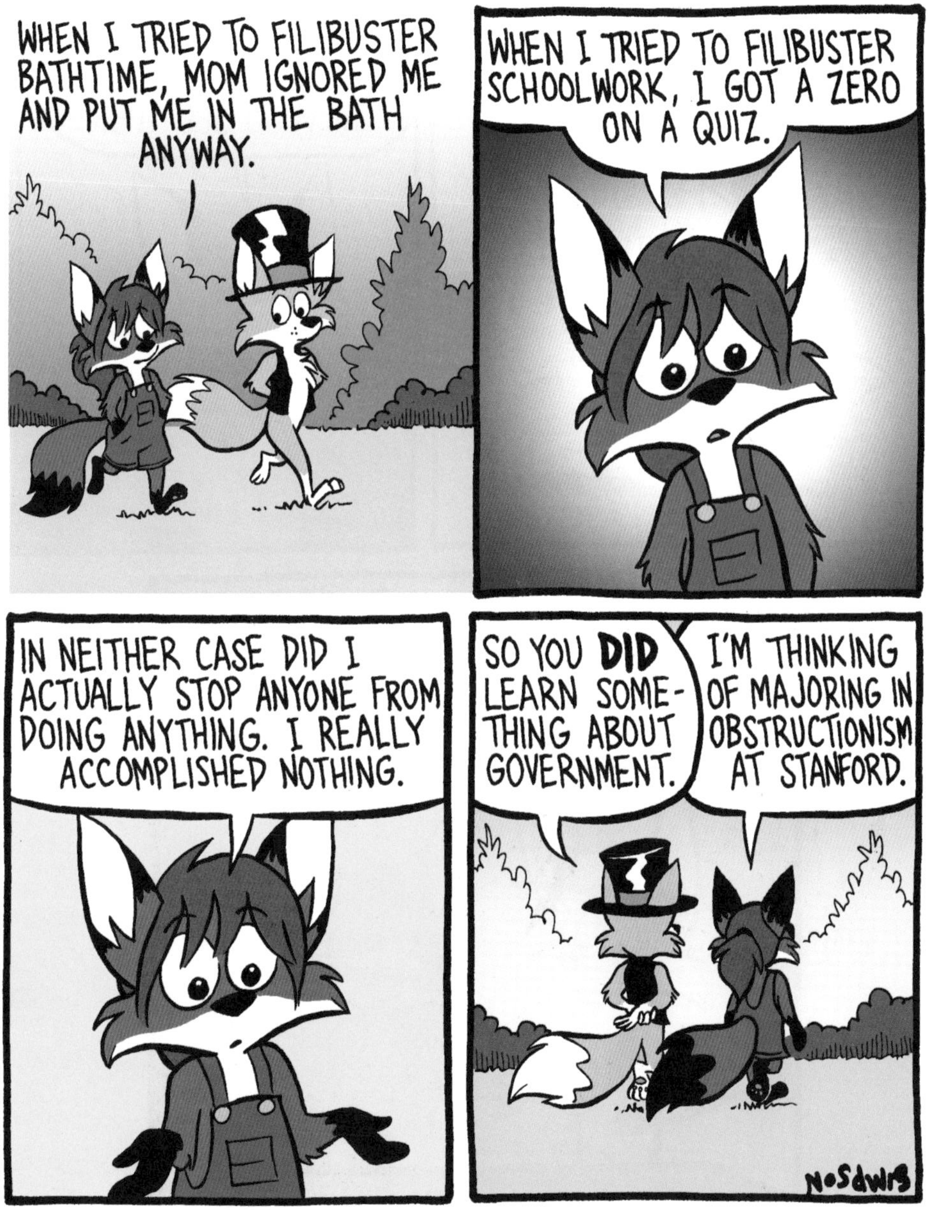
WHEN I TRIED TO FILIBUSTER BATHTIME, MOM IGNORED ME AND PUT ME IN THE BATH ANYWAY.
WHEN I TRIED TO FILIBUSTER SCHOOLWORK, I GOT A ZERO ON A QUIZ.
IN NEITHER CASE DID I ACTUALLY STOP ANYONE FROM DOING ANYTHING. I REALLY ACCOMPLISHED NOTHING.
SO YOU **DID** LEARN SOME-THING ABOUT GOVERNMENT.
I'M THINKING OF MAJORING IN OBSTRUCTIONISM AT STANFORD.
NoSdwrs

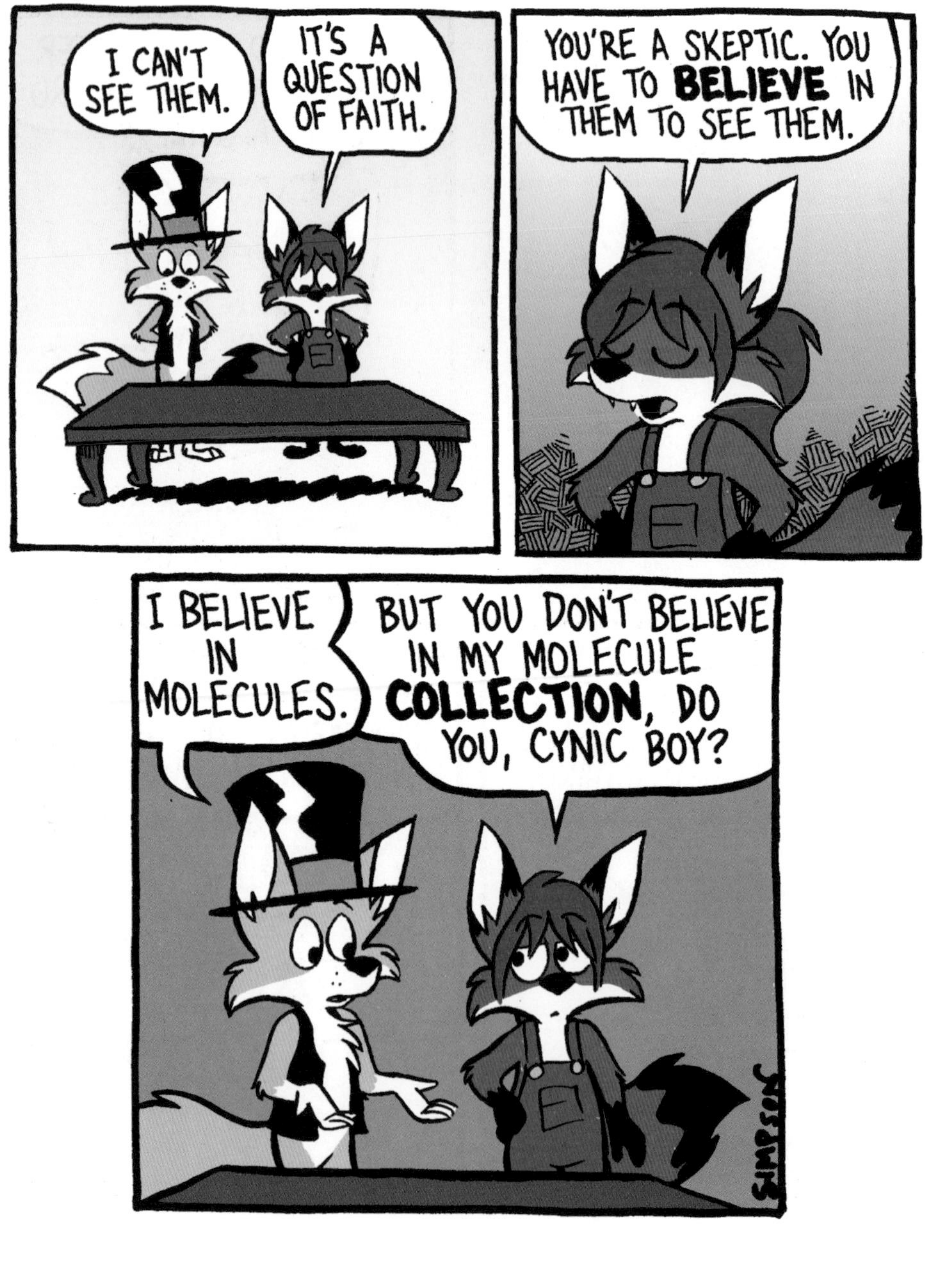
I CAN'T SEE THEM.
IT'S A QUESTION OF FAITH.
YOU'RE A SKEPTIC. YOU HAVE TO **BELIEVE** IN THEM TO SEE THEM.
I BELIEVE IN MOLECULES.
BUT YOU DON'T BELIEVE IN MY MOLECULE **COLLECTION**, DO YOU, CYNIC BOY?
SIMPSON

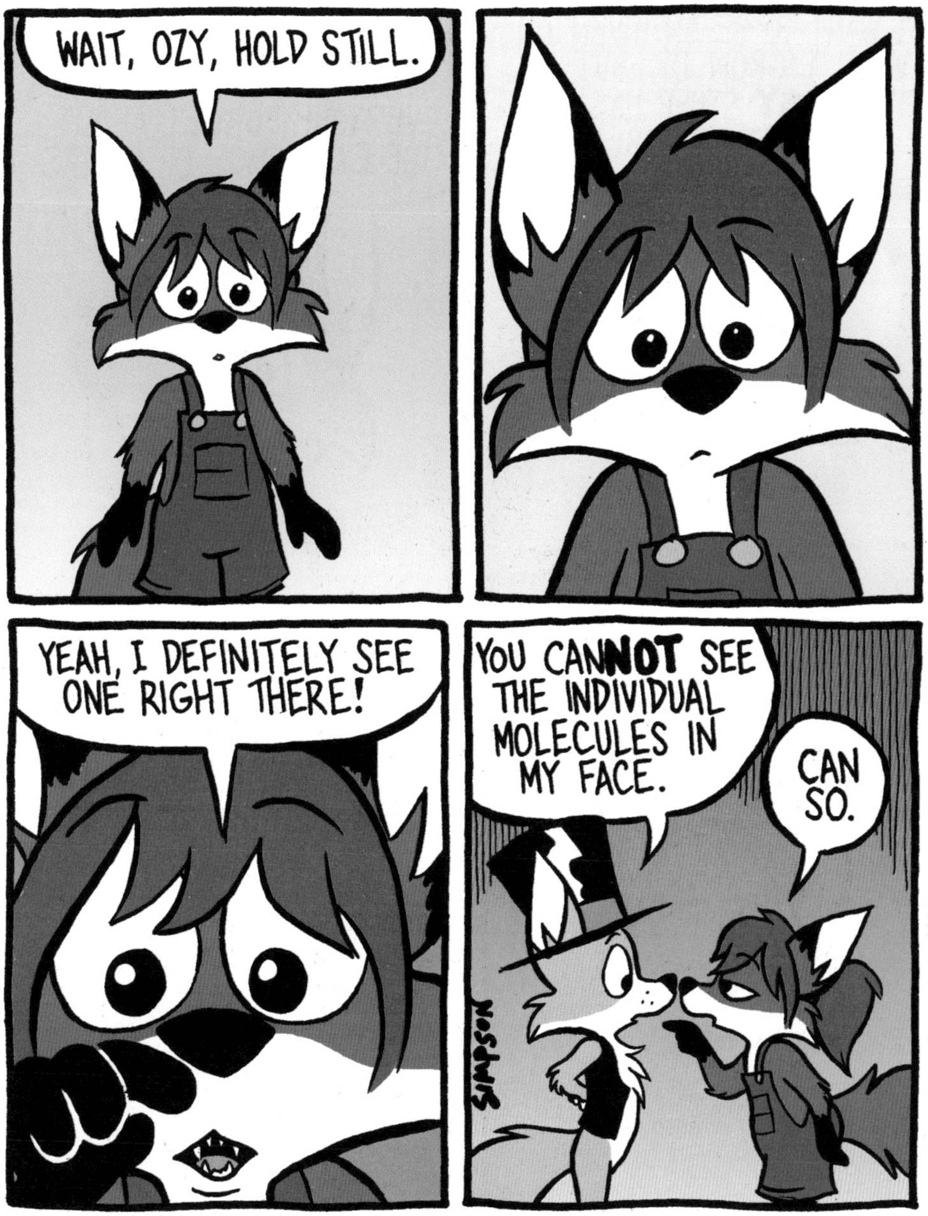
WAIT, OZY, HOLD STILL.
YEAH, I DEFINITELY SEE ONE RIGHT THERE!
YOU CANNOT SEE THE INDIVIDUAL MOLECULES IN MY FACE.
CAN SO.
SIMPSON

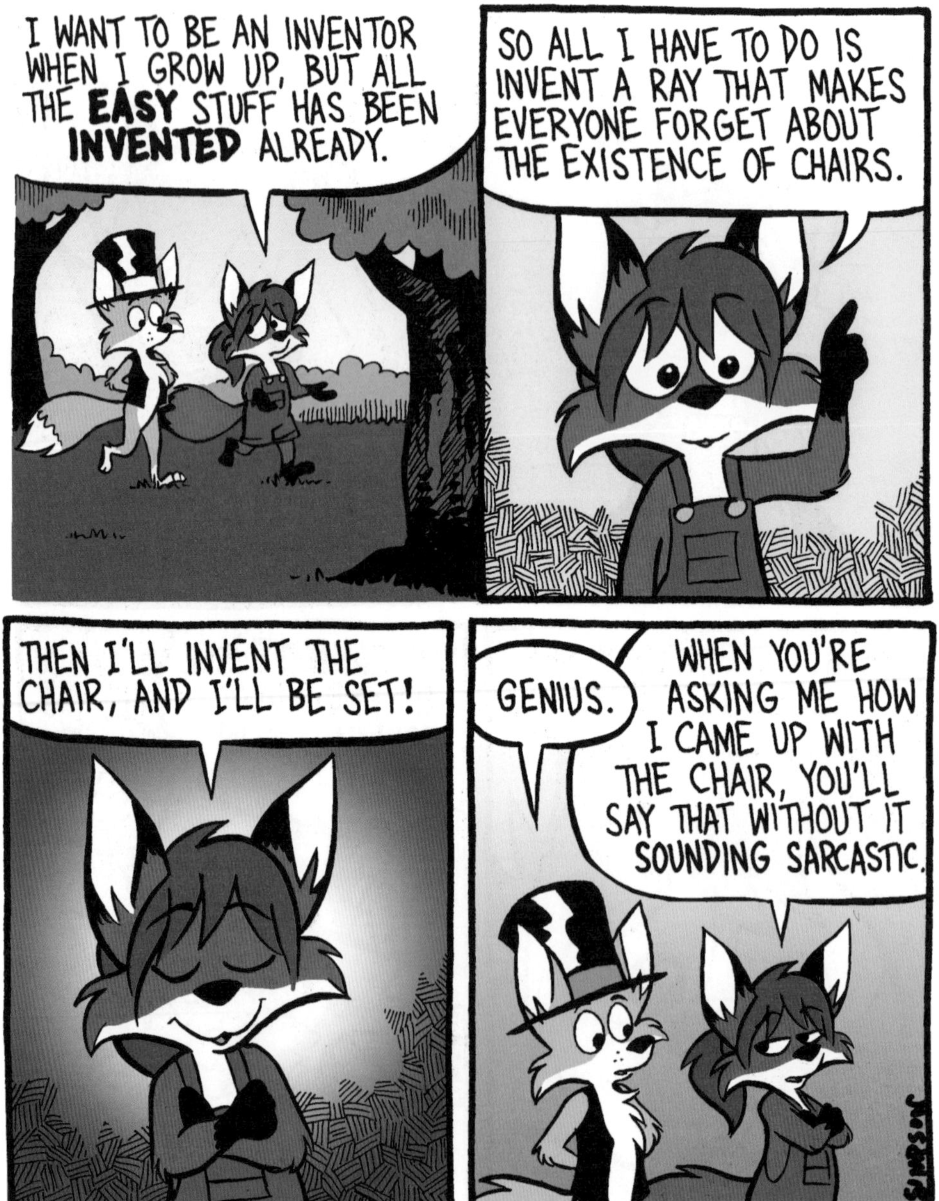
I WANT TO BE AN INVENTOR WHEN I GROW UP, BUT ALL THE **EASY** STUFF HAS BEEN **INVENTED** ALREADY.
SO ALL I HAVE TO DO IS INVENT A RAY THAT MAKES EVERYONE FORGET ABOUT THE EXISTENCE OF CHAIRS.
THEN I'LL INVENT THE CHAIR, AND I'LL BE SET!
GENIUS.
WHEN YOU'RE ASKING ME HOW I CAME UP WITH THE CHAIR, YOU'LL SAY THAT WITHOUT IT SOUNDING SARCASTIC.
SIMPSON

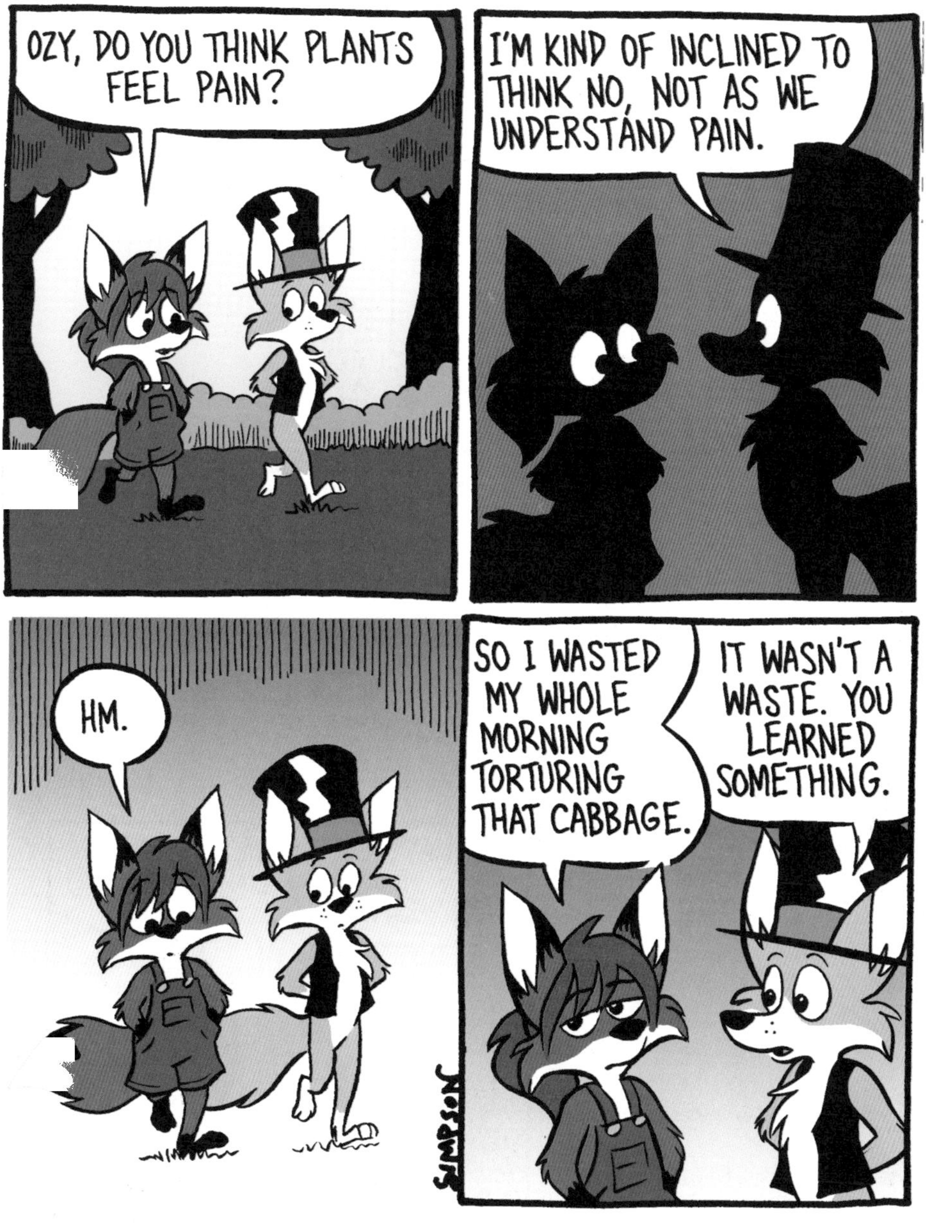
OZY, DO YOU THINK PLANTS FEEL PAIN?
I'M KIND OF INCLINED TO THINK NO, NOT AS WE UNDERSTAND PAIN.
HM.
SO I WASTED MY WHOLE MORNING TORTURING THAT CABBAGE.
IT WASN'T A WASTE. YOU LEARNED SOMETHING.
SIMPSON

IF YOU'RE "IT," THEN WE'RE PLAYING TAG. WE **ARE** PLAYING TAG. THEREFORE, YOU'RE "IT."
MOST PEOPLE IN A GAME OF TAG ARE NOT "IT." I'M PLAYING TAG, THEREFORE I'M NOT "IT," SO THEREFORE **YOU'RE** "IT."
OH, **SNAP!** GOOD USE OF INDUCTIVE ARGUMENT.
WE'RE PLAYING "LOGICAL FALLACY TAG."
SIMPSON

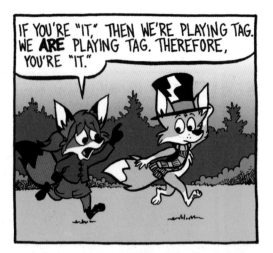

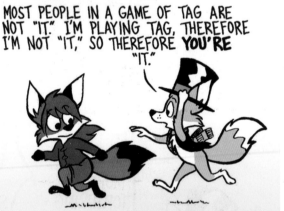

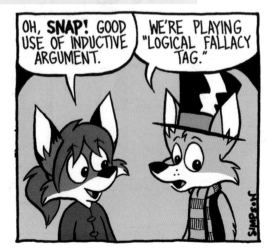

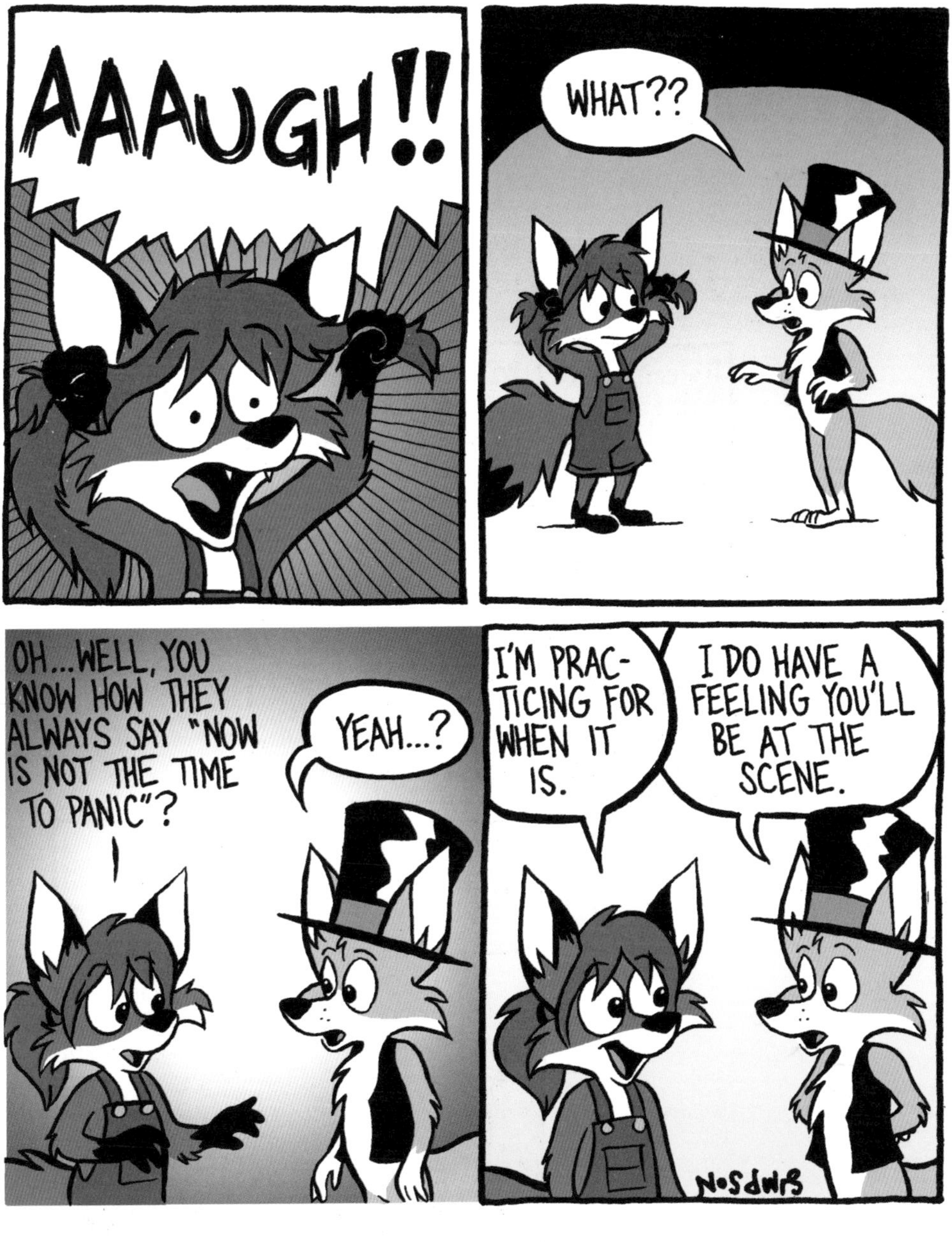
AAAUGH!!
WHAT??
OH...WELL, YOU KNOW HOW THEY ALWAYS SAY "NOW IS NOT THE TIME TO PANIC"?
YEAH...?
I'M PRAC-TICING FOR WHEN IT IS.
I DO HAVE A FEELING YOU'LL BE AT THE SCENE.
SIMPSON

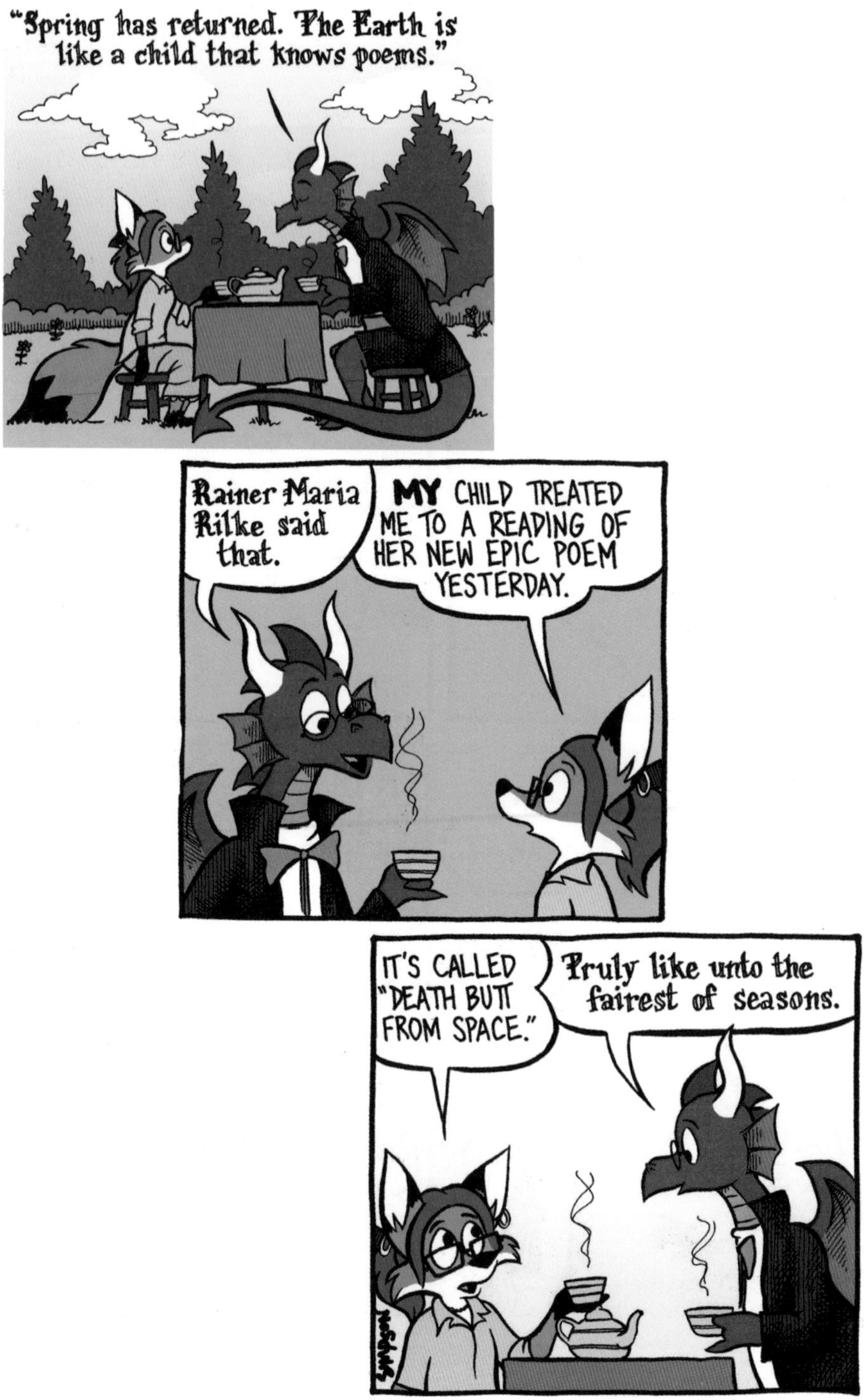
"Spring has returned. The Earth is like a child that knows poems."
Rainer Maria Rilke said that.
MY CHILD TREATED ME TO A READING OF HER NEW EPIC POEM YESTERDAY.
IT'S CALLED "DEATH BUTT FROM SPACE."
Truly like unto the fairest of seasons.

GLOSSARY

AESTHETICALLY (ES-THE-TIK-LEE): pg. 20 – adverb / in a way that is visually appealing and provides enjoyment and satisfaction through beauty

ALOOF (UH-LOOF): pg. 156 – adjective / distant and uninterested, not friendly

ANTHROPOMORPHIC (AN-THROH-POH-MOR-FICK): pg. 148 – adjective / having characteristics of a human, even for something that is not human

CACOPHONY (KA-KOF-UH-NEE): pg. 48 – noun / an incredibly loud noise or series of sounds

CHROMOSOME (CROW-MUH-SOHM): pg. 96 – noun / small bundles of DNA found in living cells containing information about a living organism's genetic material

COMPLICIT (COME-PLI-SIT): pg. 52 – adjective / being involved in or knowing about a crime or something that is wrong

CRYOGENICS (KRY-I-JE-NICKS): pg. 16 – noun / branch of physics studying the production, behavior, and effects of materials at a very low temperature

CRYPTIC (KRIP-TICK): pg. 156 – adjective / mysterious or hard to understand

DISORIENTING (DIS-OR-EE-ENT-ING): pg. 83 – adjective / causing someone to be confused or lose their sense of direction

DISPEL (DI-SPELL): pg. 47 – verb / to cast out or drive away something

ENNUI (AHN-WEE): pg. 22 – noun / a French word to describe a feeling of restlessness or boredom

ENSHROUD (IN-SHROWD): pg. 114 – verb / to conceal or cover up (as with a cloth, or "shroud")

EPHEMERALITY (I-FEH-MUH-RA-LUH-TEE): pg. 33 – noun / the quality of being "ephemeral" or fleeting, not long-lasting

EPITHET (E-PUH-THET): pg. 145 – noun / a descriptive phrase or nickname for someone that can either be friendly or cruel

ERADICATE (I-RA-DUH-KAYT): pg. 94 – verb / to get rid of

FACADE (FUH-SOD): pg. 78 – noun / a false appearance that hides what someone is really feeling

FALLACY (FA-LUH-SEE): pg. 168 – noun / a mistaken belief or an argument that uses faulty reasoning

HYPOTHESIS (HI-PAH-THUH-SIS): pg. 119 – noun / an idea or theory that is a starting point for further investigation

IGNORANCE (IG-NOR-INTS): pg. 9 – noun / a lack of awareness or knowledge about something

ILLUSION (I-LOO-ZHEN): pg. 21 – noun / a false idea or deceptive appearance

IMPENETRABLE (IM-PE-NUH-TRUH-BUHL): pg. 32, 44 – adjective / unable to be entered or conquered

INEVITABILITY (I-NE-VUH-TUH-BI-LUH-TEE): pg. 49 – noun / something that is certain to happen

INNOVATIVE (I-NUH-VAY-TIV): pg. 16 – adjective / inventive and original in a creative way

IRRELEVANCE (I-RE-LUH-VINTS): pg. 14 – noun / the condition of being not connected or related to something

LADEN (LAY-DIN): pg. 156 – adjective / heavy with

LIABILITY (LIE-UH-BI-LUH-TEE): pg. 9 – noun / the state of being responsible for something, often a person or thing that could cause harm or embarrassment

LIBERATED (LI-BUH-RAY-TED): pg. 49 – adjective / set free from something

MEDIOCRE (MEE-DEE-OH-KER): pg. 44 – adjective / of a not very good quality; ordinary

METICULOUSLY (MUH-TICK-YOU-LUS-LEE): pg. 68 – adverb / carefully and with great attention to detail

NAIVE (NIGH-EEV): pg. 48 – adjective / showing a lack of experience or wisdom

NUANCED (NOO-AHNST): pg. 43 – adjective / containing very small or subtle shades of meaning; often characterized by complex qualities or distinctions

PINNACLE (PI-NI-KUHL): pg. 90 – noun / the highest point of development or achievement; the culmination

SATIATED (SAY-SHE-A-TED): pg. 146 – verb / satisfied

SCOURGE (SKURJ): pg. 105 – noun / something or someone that causes suffering

SENTIENT (SENT-SHE-INT): pg. 148 – adjective / having awareness and the ability to think and feel

SERENITY (SUH-RE-NUH-TEE): pg. 29 – noun / peace and calm

STIGMA (STIG-MUH): pg. 145 – noun / a mark of negative attitudes, shame, or disgrace

SUBTLE (SUH-TUHL): pg. 43 – adjective / very precise, delicate, or indirect; difficult to analyze

TRITE (TRIGHT): pg. 34 – adjective / not very original or fresh; hackneyed

TRUISM (TROO-I-ZUM): pg. 47, 135 – noun / something that is true but also very obvious and unoriginal

Important People, Places, and Things

ALBERT EINSTEIN (1879–1955): pg. 149 / a German-born physicist who is known as one of the most brilliant scientific thinkers and is famous for his theory of relativity; he won the Nobel Prize in Physics in 1921

EMILY DICKINSON (1830–1886): pg. 110 / an American poet who wrote highly original poetry that was not widely published until after she died

HENRY DAVID THOREAU (1817–1862) and **RALPH WALDO EMERSON** (1803–1882): pg. 100 / two famous American writers, thinkers, and philosophers of the nineteenth century who wrote about "transcendentalism," a belief in the importance of humankind's interaction with nature

MING (1368–1644): pg. 11 / the ruling dynasty of China from 1368 to 1644 in which China had immense cultural and political influence on Asia

RAINER MARIA RILKE (1875–1926): pg. 170 / a Bohemian-Austrian poet and novelist who wrote mystical and lyrical lines of verse

SUSAN B. ANTHONY (1820–1906): pg. 135 / an American social reformer and women's rights activist who fought against slavery and helped earn women the right to vote with the Nineteenth Amendment in 1920

WALT WHITMAN (1819–1892): pg. 108 / an American poet and author who wrote the famous collection of poetry *Leaves of Grass* in 1855

WILLIAM HOWARD TAFT (1857–1930): pg. 26 / the twenty-seventh president of the United States and the nation's fattest president

WINSTON CHURCHILL (1874–1965): pg. 14 / A British statesman, army officer, and writer who served as Prime Minister of the United Kingdom during World War II

Andrews McMeel Publishing
a division of Andrews McMeel Universal
1130 Walnut Street, Kansas City, Missouri 64106

www.andrewsmcmeel.com

21 22 23 24 25 SDB 10 9 8 7 6 5 4 3 2 1

ISBN: 978-1-5248-6509-2

Library of Congress Control Number: 2020944330

Made by:
King Yip (Dongguan) Printing & Packaging Factory Ltd.
Address and location of manufacturer:
Daning Administrative District, Humen Town
Dongguan Guangdong, China 523930
1st Printing—11/23/20

ATTENTION: SCHOOLS AND BUSINESSES

Andrews McMeel books are available at quantity discounts with bulk purchase for educational, business, or sales promotional use. For information, please e-mail the Andrews McMeel Publishing Special Sales Department: specialsales@amuniversal.com.

Look for these books!

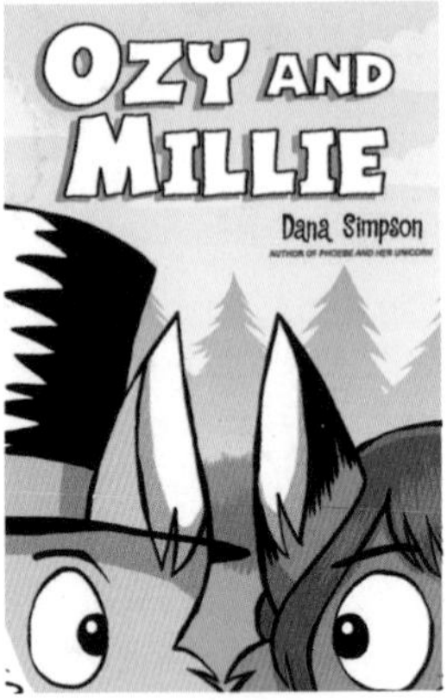
OZY AND MILLIE
Dana Simpson

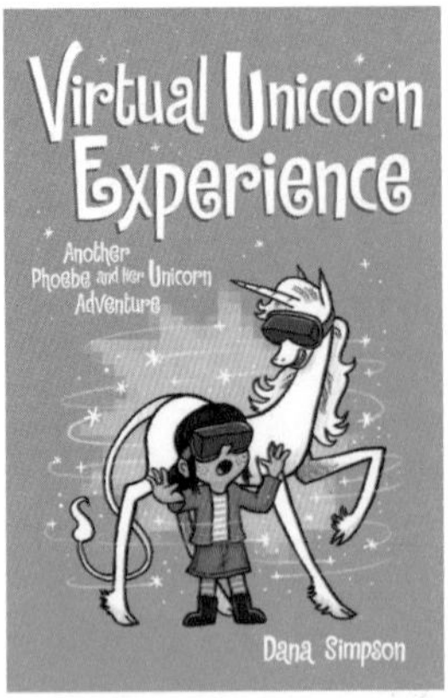
Virtual Unicorn Experience
Another Phoebe and her Unicorn Adventure
Dana Simpson

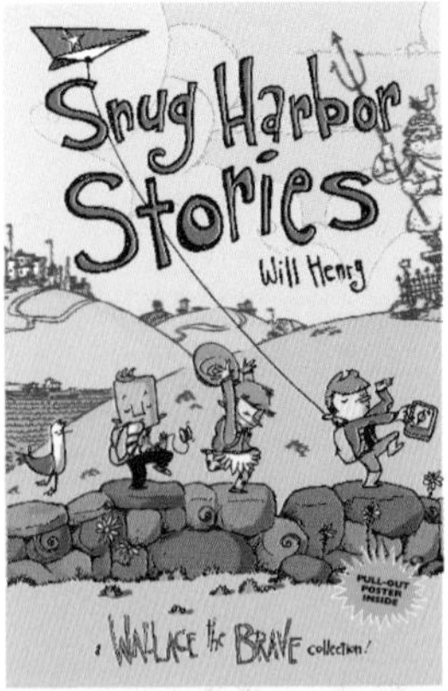
Snug Harbor Stories
Will Henry
PULL-OUT POSTER INSIDE
a WALLACE the BRAVE collection!

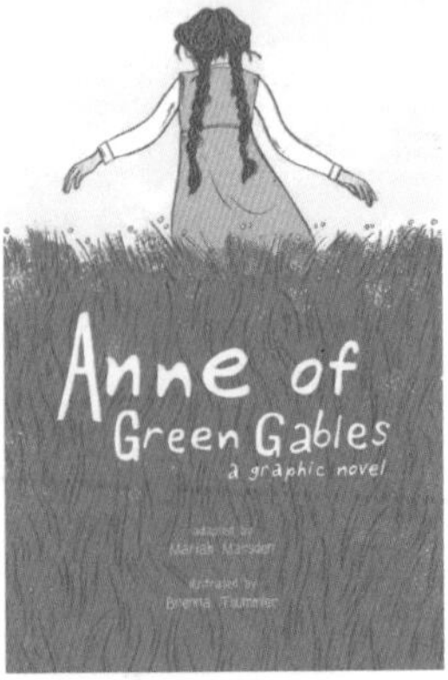
Anne of Green Gables
a graphic novel

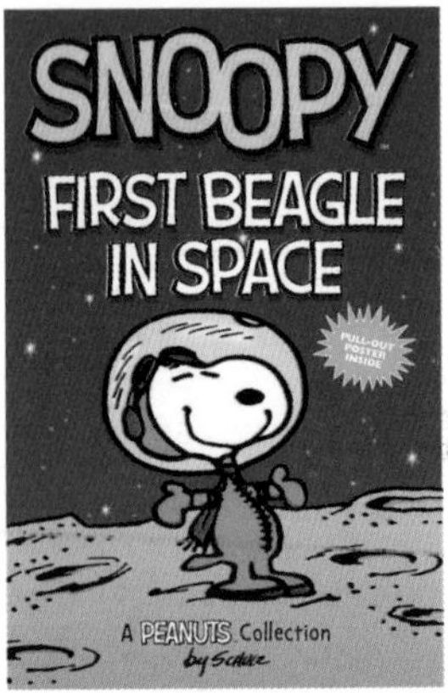
SNOOPY
FIRST BEAGLE IN SPACE
PULL-OUT POSTER INSIDE
A PEANUTS Collection
by Schulz

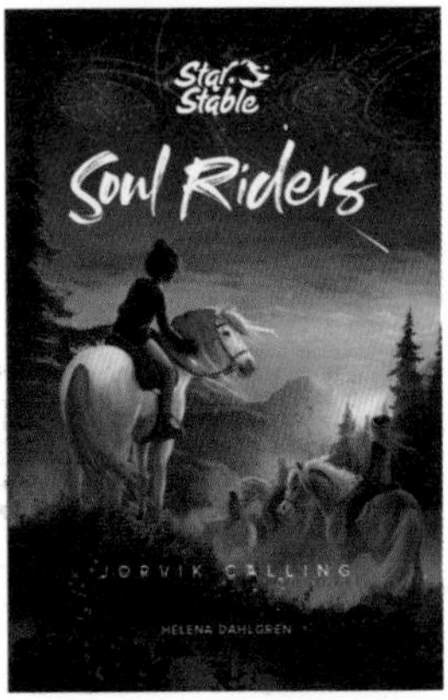
Star Stable
Soul Riders
JORVIK CALLING
HELENA DAHLGREN

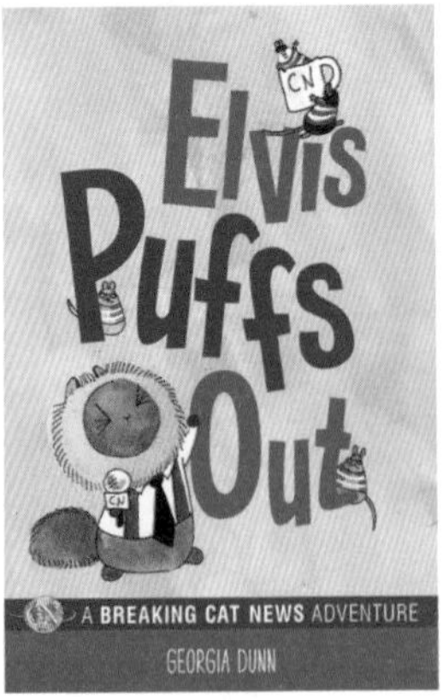
Elvis Puffs Out
A BREAKING CAT NEWS ADVENTURE
GEORGIA DUNN

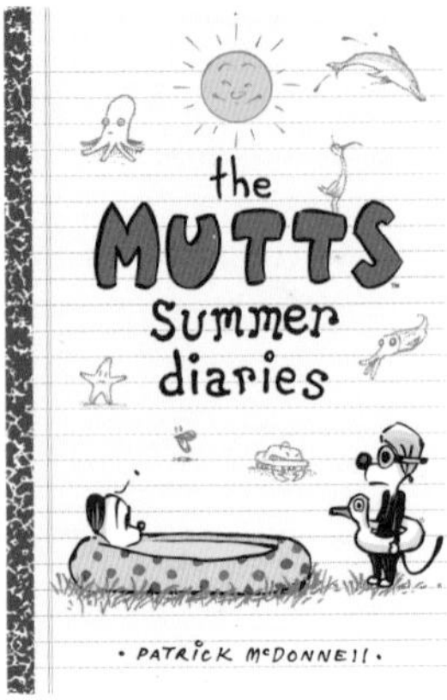
the MUTTS Summer diaries
PATRICK McDONNELL

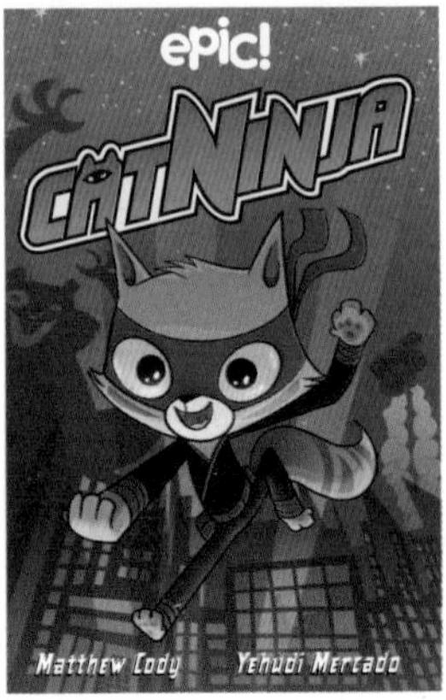
epic!
CATNINJA
Matthew Cody
Yehudi Mercado